OJ's KNIFE

"No one alive knows the O   better than John Gibson.   er all his formidable knowle ⌣   iis book is a raw, bare knuckled, gritty, nail biting page turner that will keep you breathless and awake long into the night. I loved it so much I read it twice."
>   Judge Andrew P. Napolitano,
>   Senior Judicial Analyst, *Fox News*

"In *OJ'S Knife*, John Gibson deftly weaves fact and fiction in this cunningly written novel. Where is the missing murder weapon mentioned in the OJ Simpson trial? Gibson's protagonist, Mickey Judge, local NBC reporter with eyes on prime time, thinks he knows. Gibson, who covered the trial, takes us on an action-driven search as Mickey encounters drug dealers, murderers, lawyers, Armenian bosses and two guys who just want OJ's autograph. It's a hell of an entertaining ride."
>   Melodie Johnson Howe,
>   author of the Diana Poole novels

"From the bizarre white Bronco slow speed chase on the 405 Freeway to the bloody crime scene outside Nicole's home to the Trial of the Century, John and I worked to report what really happened that awful night Simpson killed Goldman and nearly decapitated the mother of his children. In this rollicking, vividly entertaining book, John expands the world we knew and the one we suspected, to bring us this thriller."
>   Geraldo Rivera

OJ's Knife

A MICKEY JUDGE MYSTERY

by John Gibson

Stark House Press • Eureka California

OJ'S KNIFE

Published by Stark House Press
1315 H Street
Eureka, CA 95501, USA
griffinskye3@sbcglobal.net
www.starkhousepress.com

ISBN: 978-1-951473-43-3

Book design by Mark Shepard, shepgraphics.com
Proofreading by Bill Kelly

First Stark House Press Edition: September 2021

PROLOGUE

The OJ Simpson trial was bookended—start to finish—with courtroom intrigue about a small backpack belonging to Simpson, which the prosecutors believed hid the murder weapon, the bloody knife.

Early in the trial, on March 29, 1995, Prosecutor Marcia Clark put limo driver Allan Park on the witness stand. She focused on that particular small piece of luggage.

When Park was loading Simpson's garment bag and golf bag into the limo at Simpson's Rockingham estate for the ride to LAX, where Simpson was to catch a flight to Chicago, Park testified that he saw a small dark backpack-type bag near a duffel bag on the curb. Both Kato Kaelin and Park offered to load them in the car, but Simpson would not let either man touch them. Simpson insisted on handling both bags himself.

Prosecutor Clark focused on what happened at the American Airlines terminal at LAX. "When Mr. Simpson was over by the Skycap, sir, did you see—other than the garment bag and the golf bag, did you see where the other bags were?" Marcia Clark asked.

Park answered: "I remember there was the one over his shoulder and there was another one sitting on top of a trash can next to the Skycap stand."

"So there was a bag sitting on top of the trashcan next to the Skycap stand?"

"Yes," Park answered.

Six months later in closing arguments, Marcia Clark brought up the small bag again.

Addressing the jury, she said "Now, back to loading up the car. You may recall that there was testimony about a small dark bag that was on the edge of the driveway by the Bentley. And Kato, as they were loading up the bags, offered to go and get that bag for him. The Defendant said 'No, no, no, no, no. I'll get it.' And the testimony was that all of the bags were loaded by either Kato or Allan Park except for that one. And after the Defendant walked towards it, after saying 'No, I'll get it,' no one ever saw that little black, dark bag again."

(Not quite. As noted above, Allan Park testified that he observed that bag again at the airport, on top of the trash can where OJ was standing at the Skycap podium).

Marcia Clark continued, zeroing in on the importance of the "small dark bag," long missing: "Nor have we ever found the knife the Defendant used."

She paced the length of the jury box, demeaning defendant OJ Simpson: "And it's so typical. It's so common. They get rid of the murder weapon, they think 'that's it, can't get me, home free.' But you see, as you've seen, it's not that easy. Evidence was left behind. So we don't need the murder weapon, because we have much, much more proof than that."

That small backpack-style bag was never recovered by police.

The murder weapon, likewise, was never found by police.

But as the world knows, it turned out that the jury found the prosecutors' other "proof" unpersuasive.

1

June 12, 1994. The 11 p.m. hour.

Allan Park was at the wheel of a stretch Lincoln limousine, driving as fast as he could sensibly and safely.

OJ Simpson was in the back seat.

OJ had a flight to Chicago at 11:45 p.m. on American Airlines, from Terminal 4 at LAX. In Allan Park's opinion, OJ was irresponsibly late at the pickup on Rockingham. He claimed he'd taken a nap and overslept. Now the pressure was on Allan Park to get him to the plane.

Park brought the limo to a stop at the curb at Terminal 4 at 11:25 p.m. The flight was scheduled to push back at 11:45.

Normally not the anxious type, tonight Park was worried what he would tell his boss if OJ missed the flight. A handsome twenty-five-year-old, Park wore a limo driver's black suit, white shirt, and black tie. Tonight, Park's hair was matted to his forehead, sweating this job. His eyes fixed on the Skycap, he leapt from the driver's side, urgently signaling for help.

Nearby, Skycap James Williams, a young black man, told him to hold on. "When I finish with a customer," he said.

Seeming considerably less concerned, OJ slid across the back seat and pushed open the passenger door at curbside. Yes, he was late, but he was OJ Simpson. He expected that the Skycaps would call the gate to hold the plane.

Park scurried inside, looking for a baggage cart, his eyes searching the sidewalk for another Skycap.

As he stood at the Skycap podium, OJ dropped a black duffel bag off his shoulder. A small black backpack sat atop an adjacent trash can at his elbow. He gave the skycap his flight number. He then walked to the rear of the limo to retrieve his golf bag and garment bag.

He passed an airport courier van idling at the curb. In the driver's seat, Michael Norris caught his eye and said "What's happening, OJ?" Simpson smiled and returned the greeting. Norris's partner in the passenger seat leaned across Norris. "Hey, Juice, got time for an autograph?"

OJ said sure. "Let me take care of my bags first."

By this time, Park was back with a luggage cart. OJ brought over the golf bag. Park grabbed the garment bag. He loaded OJ's gear and turned it all over to Skycap Williams.

Williams was at the podium. He entered Simpson's information in the computer, pulled the baggage tags off the printer.

Simpson stopped to give the courier an autograph.

He searched his pockets for cash to give Skycap Williams for handling his bags. Simpson gave Williams a twenty and asked for ten back. Williams gave him two fives.

Williams took the garment bag and the golf bag in hand, leaving the cart behind. Williams and Park headed inside.

OJ slung the duffel bag over his shoulder.

At that moment, two off-duty ramp workers walked out of the terminal, hoping to spot the famous football player, television and movie star.

Gordon Grove, nicknamed "Garden" after the nearby city, and Luther "Lummie" Malcolm had been in the kitchen of the American Airlines first-class lounge sneaking a couple of drinks from their friend, the woman who ran the American lounge. Garden was a ramp supervisor, Lummie one of his baggage handlers. The African American woman running the lounge bar was a friend. She brought them drinks as long as they made sure they were standing in the kitchen, out of sight of the travelers in the lounge.

She mentioned that OJ Simpson was on the Chicago flight, but he was late. Hadn't checked in yet. Garden and Lummie looked at each other and realized they might be able to bump into the famous OJ Simpson if they hustled. They slugged down their drinks and headed to the Skycap stand, hoping to encounter him.

Garden had to duck into the men's room on the way. When he caught up with his friend, Lummie pointed. "There he is."

"Garden" Grove approached Simpson immediately. "Hey, OJ, you need that bag checked?"

"Nah, I'm taking that with me," Simpson said, his voice in the low rumble familiar to television viewers and moviegoers.

Limo driver Allan Park escorted the luggage inside as far as the baggage conveyor, then turned around and came back out. He asked Simpson if everything seemed good, and OJ said "Add twenty percent." Park thanked him and returned to the limo. He waited until he saw Simpson headed to the gate with his duffel bag. He waited a little longer until he saw Skycap Williams return to the Skycap stand. Only then did he pull the limo away from the curb, relieved to be done with the celebrity.

Garden and Lummie watched Simpson walk away toward airport security. They stood at the curb, a little unsteady from those drinks and the excitement of seeing the celebrity. Garden laughed. "That's OJ fucking Simpson," he said to his friend. "I talked to OJ Simpson."

"And he talked to you." Lummie marveled at his friend's easy way with the famous celebrity. "OJ talked to you, man. Like you and him was friends." He grinned.

"Sure did," Garden said. "Fucking guy is great."

"Sure is," Lummie agreed.

"I watched him at SC," Garden said, remembering with pride OJ's years at the University of Southern California, "and of course at the Bills. The guy was amazing." Garden was a few inches shorter than Luther. His belly swelled against his light jacket. He was balding, looking all of his fifty years, but he had a quick smile and alert eyes.

Luther Malcolm nodded in agreement. "No doubt." Lummie was more of a background guy. Taller and younger than Garden, he tended to stand back, say little, and watch.

An LA Sanitation truck pulled to a stop in the lane outside the curb, a spurt of black diesel smoke burped out the stack. A muscled black man was at the wheel. Armen Shabaglian swung out the passenger side. A swarthy Armenian in his twenties dressed in dirty overalls, he crossed over to the Skycap trash can. He nodded hello to Garden and Luther. "Hey, guys." He flipped the lid off the container and pulled out the plastic bag. "How's it hangin'?" he asked, not expecting an answer. He put a new bag in the can. It was clear plastic.

"We just saw OJ," Garden said.

"No shit?" Shabaglian wrapped up the trash bag. "Cool." He gave them a thumbs-up, crossed back over to his truck, and flipped the trash bag in the back.

With a roar of the big diesel engine, the black man at the wheel jumped the garbage truck forward, headed down toward Terminal 5.

Lummie watched the truck go. But a thought popped into his head: the small backpack he'd seen on the trash can where OJ was waiting for his bag checks. "Hey, man, while I was waiting for you to come out of the pisser, I noticed something."

"What?" Garden asked absently.

"When OJ walked to the plane, did you see him carrying a little backpack?"

Garden looked up at his partner, alarm crossing his face. "He had a duffel over his shoulder. Why?"

"Yeah, but I saw a small backpack. He was at the Skycap, standing next to the trash can, the backpack on top. Did you see OJ walk away with it?"

"No, I definitely did not," Garden said, his brow furrowed in concern. "He just had the duffel."

"There was a backpack on the trash can," Lummie said. "Seemed like it was his. He was waiting on his bag checks."

Garden frowned, his brow wrinkled, his eyes on Lummie but his focus on the memory of OJ Simpson walking away. "I saw him with a duffel over his shoulder. Didn't see no backpack at all."

"Think the truck might have hauled it off?" Lummie asked.

"For Chrissakes," Garden said. "Maybe OJ left his backpack. I gotta chase down that truck."

Garden Grove ran toward Terminal 5. Maybe he could catch the trash truck. Maybe if he were fast enough, he could save OJ's small backpack.

He was absolutely certain OJ would appreciate it.

2

Lummie Malcolm had long legs, but he wasn't in the best shape. He hustled to keep up with Garden, but somehow the older man was faster. Lummie fell behind.

But it didn't really matter. By the time he got to Terminal 5, Garden was already going through the back of the truck, Armen Shabaglian at his side, pissed off.

"You're hanging me up," Shabaglian said to Garden, who didn't respond. "A supervisor or a cop comes along, sees you in the back, I'm fucked."

Marcus Blake, the big black driver, stood behind Shabaglian, giving Garden a skeptical side-eye. Marcus was twenty four, six foot three inches, two hundred fifty pounds. He briefly played football at USC, but got kicked off the team for suspected gang involvement. He knew who OJ Simpson was. The only reason he stopped the truck was that Garden had thrown out Simpson's name. "His bag is in the back!" Garden shouted, in the command voice of a boss.

Garden heard Shabaglian, but he didn't answer. He was out of breath, his heart pounding against his chest. He stood on the bumper, bent at the waist, half in and half out of the compactor. "Here it is!" he grunted. "Gimme a hand."

Lummie and Shabaglian held on to Garden as he pulled on a trash bag that had already been crushed into other bags. The compactor compartment smelled of rotting animals. "You throw dead dogs in here, or what?" Garden complained.

"It happens," Shabaglian said, annoyed. "It's a fucking garbage truck."

The trash bags were clear plastic. Garden pulled it to the edge of the compactor compartment. "There it is. Right on top. OJ's bag," he announced triumphantly.

"What you gonna do with it?" Shabaglian asked, now wary of this situation. "We find something that belongs to a passenger, we gotta turn it in."

Garden pulled the small black knapsack from the trash bag. "I'm gonna return it to him personally. The fuckin' guy stopped and we had a conversation, like we always do." As long as Garden was exaggerating, might as well go farther. "He invited me to drop by his mansion and hang," said Garden, making himself sound like a friend. "It's the least I can do."

Garden bent over, hands on his knees, trying to catch his breath. He briefly wondered if he should sit down. His heart was fluttering and racing.

"I don't know, man," Shabaglian said through pursed lips.

Lummie spoke up to vouch for his friend. "Cut him some slack," he said to the Sani driver and his partner. "Him and OJ real close. He'll return it."

"You fuckin' guys," Shabaglian shook his head. "My ass better not end up in a sling."

Garden stood up straight, took a couple of deep breaths. "Thanks, man," he said, effectively ending the discussion.

He and Lummie headed for the stop for the employee bus.

When they were out of earshot of the truck, Lummie leaned down and whispered to Garden. "You gonna look inside?"

"Hell, no," Garden said indignantly. "It's OJ's shit. I'm gonna bring it back to him unmolested by me or you." Garden seemed insulted.

Lummie made a face that said he wasn't satisfied. "Hey, man, what if it's money? We could split the money, toss the bag. He'll just figure his money went to the landfill."

Garden scowled at his friend. "Yeah, we could," he said, drawing out the word "could." But Garden was insulted. "But I ain't stealing from OJ. Fuck that."

Lummie felt scolded. "It ain't really stealing," he objected. "Matter of fact, you don't even know for sure that bag is OJ's. Could be anybody's."

"You the one said it was his."

Easily chastised, Lummie backed down. "Yeah, you're right."

Standing with others waiting for the employee bus, the conversation was put on hold. The bus arrived; they got onboard. By the time they took seats at the back, Garden was fuming. "I take it personal you would think I'd steal from a guy like OJ," he whispered in a hiss. "He's a hero to black people. White people and Mexicans don't understand. This guy is an idol. Great football career. All them movies. You ever see *Airplane*? The Hertz commercials? OJ Simpson give black people a public face that everybody likes. He raises black people up. I ain't fucking with him."

Now Lummie was put out. "Don't lump me in with white people and Mexicans," he whispered back.

Garden didn't respond. He let it drop and held the bag tightly.

They rode in silence. Lummie changed the subject. "Doesn't seem like there's anything in it."

Garden looked over at his partner, wrinkling his nose. "There's something. I can feel it. But I ain't squeezing it. Might be a box of cookies. I ain't bringing busted cookies back to Orenthal James Simpson. Whatever it is, it belongs to OJ Simpson and neither of us is going to fuck with his stuff. Conversation closed."

Lummie shrugged. "Fine by me."

Garden sniffed. "Damn right."

At the employee parking lot, Garden put the bag in the trunk of his '89 Camry. "If you get over being a prick," he said, scolding Lummie again, "when OJ invites me to his mansion to return his property, I'll bring you along."

"You think you get him on the phone?"

"Hell, yes."

"How?"

"I know people. I'll figure it out." Garden seemed annoyed.

Lummie waved him off. "Okay, okay, sorry I brought it up. See you tomorrow."

Lummie was fairly certain Garden didn't have a way to call OJ Simpson. He figured Garden would just drive up to Simpson's place in Brentwood and hope the star would notice him at the gate.

In any case, he figured Garden would calm down by tomorrow. The both of them had the day off. He'd drop by, bring some beers.

3

The morning of June 13, Lummie Malcolm parked his '72 Monte Carlo on the street in front of Garden Grove's house on Manchester Terrace in Inglewood, not far from Hollywood Park. Beach fog hung over Inglewood, the gray day matching Lummie's glum mood.

Malcolm was carrying a six-pack of Colt 45's in a brown bag. He hurried to the door, pressed the doorbell hard, letting it ring longer than he should.

A petite black woman answered the door, her brow wrinkled in annoyance.

"Morning, Louise, I got to see Garden. Is he home?"

Mrs. Grove was slim, dressed in a fashion-aware outfit: bright yellow pants and a cobalt blue short-sleeve silk shirt. Her hair was in a cropped wave, the style of the day. She had bright eyes, sharp and penetrating. She gave Lummie a peeved look. "Gordon is here," she said, drawing out her husband's first name. She didn't like him called "Garden." She thought it disrespectful. "But I'm not sure I like the way you pushed on that bell. Seemed insistent. Like you was important and needed someone at the door right now." She gave him a theatrical scowl. "What you got in the bag?"

Chastened, Lummie stood back a step. "I got some beer. Gordon told me he likes to have a beer."

Louise Grove made a face of scalding disapproval. "Not those 40s?"

"No, Missus Grove. Just regular 12-ouncers."

She wrinkled her face and gave him a hard look, refusing to budge. "You know he got heart problems, Lummie. I'm a nurse on the cardiac floor. I hear all the time about men giving themselves heart attacks when they drink too much."

"I'm sorry, Missus Grove. I will only let him have one. I just got to see Gordon right away. Can I come in?"

In her late forties, Louise Grove had a narrow face, thin lips that were equally adept at a scowl or a bright smile. Right now, Lummie was getting the scowl. "You know I don't put up with no drunks, Luther," she said. "It's Gordon's day off. He might like a beer, but just one. I got to worry about his heart, since he won't. The TV news is upsetting."

"Upsetting to me too, Missus Grove."

She looked him over, deciding. "Don't get him excited. I don't need him dropping dead on me."

Lummie nodded. "Yes, Ma'am."

She opened the screen door. "He in back watching the television."

Lummie Malcolm walked through the door as if he were entering church. Mrs. Grove's living room was dark and cool. Heavy drapes in a maroon brocade blocked sunlight. The room was formal, as if no one ever used it. He passed two orange and yellow and green floral couches with plastic coverings. On end tables stood lamps with large bell-shaped shades in sea-foam green. The couches were arranged in an L around a large white coffee table, centered by a covered glass bowl of Hershey kisses. Pastel couch-art decorated the walls. Scenes of Paris—Notre Dame from the Seine, the Eiffel Tower, and a winding street lined with quaint shops. The colors of the room were so jarring, Lummie wondered if Louise was color-blind.

Lummie knew better than to cross a black woman in her own house. He was on his best behavior. He tiptoed past the kitchen and dining room, down a short hall to a family room.

Garden was nearly flat on his back in a red leather Barcalounger. He had the television tuned to Channel 4. Garden was proud of his 36-inch color Trinitron ("Best you can get"). He glanced up at Lummie and pointed to a chair. "This is some bad shit, Luther."

Garden Grove looked pained.

Lummie took a beer can from the bag, popped the top. "We just saw OJ last night." There was a pleading tone in Lummie's voice. He handed the beer to Garden. "I saw the news about the wife and rushed right over."

"Can you fucking believe it?" Garden asked, without taking his eyes off the television. He tipped the beer to his lips for a sip. "Got to be a mistake. They had him in cuffs a few minutes ago. Now he's in the cop car, going downtown. To Parker Center, I suppose."

"What you think going on?"

"I think they made a big mistake," Garden said, his mouth turned down in a frown. "Man's wife is killed. They put him in cuffs 'cause he a black man. Man's got to be grieving, but they treat him like a dog."

"Yessir. Yessir." Luther Malcolm bobbed his head up and down in agreement. "Woman gets killed on the street in front of her house.

Could be anybody. But no, they got to go get her husband. And he wasn't even in town. We watched him go."

"Damn right," Garden agreed. "How can he kill her in Brentwood when he at the airport? This is some nasty shit going on."

Both men stared at the television. Channel 4 anchor Paul Moyer was questioning reporter Phil Shuman, who was standing somewhere near the wife's condo. In video of the scene at the condo, Garden and Lummie could see smudges on the sidewalk leading to a wooden gate.

"Oh, my goodness, that blood?" Luther asked.

"Look like it to me." Garden grimaced. "Look like she coming home or going out and somebody jump her. Probably want her money, she put up a fight. Guy stab her."

"Look like he stab her a lot," Lummie said softly, staring at the screen.

A voice came from behind them. "That white bitch probably really piss somebody off," Louise Grove said. "Could be OJ. She give him endless trouble." She was standing in the doorway, her arms folded, her lips pursed, brow furrowed, scowling in disapproval. "I read the *Globe News*. She call the cops on him all the time."

Garden kept quiet. He might dispute Louise, but not when Lummie was around. She reacted very badly to being shown up in front of guests. Best to keep his mouth shut.

"Maybe she make somebody else mad too," Lummie offered, politely supporting the lady of the house.

Louise sneered. "Maybe he should've been a righteous black man. Picked a black girl. White bitch just want his money," she said. She nodded at her husband and his friend. "Some black men never learn," she said as she turned and walked out.

Garden put his finger to his lips. Luther got it. Don't say nothing.

Lummie waited until he was sure she was busying herself in the kitchen. "What about the bag?" he whispered.

Garden shook his head. "Couple days. He'll be back home. Things'll settle down. I'll get it to him."

4

Three days after the murder, Nicole was buried at an upscale cemetery in Lake Forest, Orange County. The funeral was huge. Closed to the media, but within range of professional camera lenses.

Nicole Brown Simpson was in the casket. OJ Simpson was an unwelcome attendee. Judi Brown, Nicole's mother, asked him directly if he had killed her. "No, no, no, I loved her," Simpson said, through tears. But when he thought no one was looking, he lifted the collar of her dress in the casket to peek at her wounds.

On funeral day, the mere fact that OJ was spotted with the mourners was enough to lead *Nightly News with Tom Jansen* on the NBC television network. The report was filed by Mickey Judge, the junior correspondent in the Burbank Bureau.

Mickey Judge had the network-correspondent look: premature shockingly white hair that always seemed to be both in place and mussed, a face deeply lined from years of chasing the news, and wary blue eyes that said "I've seen it all, so save the B.S."

As his edited story fed from the Burbank Bureau, Mickey Judge watched from the back deck in the control room, hands in his pockets, hoping for the best, expecting the worst. On the front deck, a director was calmly giving orders into a headset microphone; and a technical director, the person who operated the switcher, listened on his own headset. In the playback room nearby, another operator on a headset stood ready to hit the play button on three separate tape machines.

It was a hot roll into *Nightly News,* meaning New York cued Burbank, and the director on the West Coast rolled the tape and for almost two minutes the NBC News flagship newscast was in the control of Burbank. Complicating the situation, Mick's package had been cut into three parts. Three different tapes had to roll in succession at exact times. Three tapes in three playbacks cued up to the first frame. So many ways things could go bad. Nobody liked hot rolls. Too much tension.

Much better if the edited package was finished in time to feed to New York before the Jansen airtime.

But that had been impossible. The edit had been tight. New York took forever to approve the script. Late footage from the Nicole Brown Simpson funeral included a ten-second shot of OJ in dark glasses, holding his daughter's hand, surrounded by mourners with their backs turned to him. Those few seconds had to make the story.

Mick cut a stand-up on the balcony on the third floor with some palm trees in the background that said "LA" to New York producers, but in the end New York wanted other copy added and the package had to be 1:45 tops, so the stand-up got dumped. He simply signed out "Mickey Judge, NBC News, Los Angeles."

But it was another OJ story. The third day in a row he'd made *Nightly*. New York couldn't get enough of the murder. OJ had been seen in handcuffs. Then he was interviewed downtown at Parker Center. Then he was cut loose, but everybody knew the cops liked him for the murder.

On the other hand, NBC News did not like Mickey Judge. Three days on *Nightly* with the Brown-Simpson murder should have improved Mickey's standing. But the vibes out of New York were written in neon: Jansen wanted his own guy on this story ASAP.

Mickey had been on the job as the junior correspondent in the Burbank Bureau for a year, coming on board just before the Northridge earthquake. Even with his coverage of that disaster, he'd never had three days in a row on *Nightly*. He'd never had two days in a row. Once a week for a few weeks would have been enough for a party. And he wouldn't have caught the assignment these last three days if it hadn't been for the fact that the senior correspondent in the Bureau, Johnny Furness, was on a bird-watching vacation in Costa Rica.

Mickey Judge almost never made *Nightly*.

It was the kind of thing everybody noticed. He was on a shit list. Somebody in New York didn't like him. Maybe Tom. Maybe some faceless suit who wanted to suck up to Tom and had never signed off on Mickey's hiring in the first place.

Consequently, despite the fact he looked the part of a network correspondent—war weary, skulking the globe in a worn trench coat—he was in a constant state of quite reasonable fear that it wasn't working out with NBC News, that he wouldn't be renewed on his upcoming anniversary, the network's window to drop him. This run of stories on OJ's wife's murder might save him. So he hoped.

Tom Jansen came back on the screen, added some random fact to the OJ story. His package over, Mickey Judge was done for the day.

Hovering over his shoulder, Alison de Groot, the tall blond Australian who was the Burbank Bureau chief, wrapped an arm around his shoulder and gave him a squeeze. "Good show, Mick my boy," she said in a rah-rah tone. "That's how you show those wankers in New York. Crisp. We like crisp. Come, now, let's go hoist one across the street."

"Across the street" was code for Chadney's, a bar-restaurant and jazz club which was the favored post-*Nightly* drinking spot for the NBC Bureau.

"It'll take more than one," Mickey said, his shoulders sagging in relief. "That was a fucker."

She had a big laugh, always dialed up to blast. "Write short sentences. Get to the fucking point. Do that, and your team down here will get the pictures in. Three genius editors saved your ass today," she said, emphasizing her point with a friendly wag of her finger.

"I hate doing shit that way," Mickey said. "Wimple had the script for hours. Jammed me up taking his sweet-ass time. What the fuck?"

She smiled at him and put her hand back on his shoulder. "It's why we have three editors available, my boy. When they give you fifteen minutes to slap together a network package, that's how it's done."

"New York makes life miserable," Mick said. "And we're supposed to pretend it's okay. It's bullshit."

"My boy, you deserve a libation," she said, turning to head back to her office. "Give me fifteen minutes to give those jollybobs a ring, collect your attaboys, and I shall join you and the troops over yonder." And off she went, headed for the stairs back up to her office.

Mickey walked down the hall and stuck his head in the edit booths to thank the three different editors who had jammed together separate chunks of his package.

He headed back toward the same staircase de Groot had used, but he clattered down the stairs instead of up. On the second floor, he went through the door into the Channel 4 newsroom, a warren of cluttered cubicles that had been his home for three years before he took the job upstairs at the network. He made a beeline straight for the assignment desk.

In every newsroom, the assignment desk rules. It's where

reporters get their orders, it's where the police radios and the wire services and the feeds from the network, and the monitors tuned to the competition, are all under the vigilant eyes of the assignment editor and his or her assistants.

His buddy Danny Bowls sat in the boss chair at the desk. As always, he was holding a phone to his ear with his shoulder. Arrayed before him was a bank of monitors. Channel 4's air feeds from the field, the internal feed of *Nightly News.* The desk had four workstations, computers, multi-line phones, a printer, and a pile of Thomas Brothers map books. But, as was often the case, Bowls was manning the desk alone.

Bowls was a classic assignment editor. Intense. Focused. Unflappable. He'd been a reporter, gotten older, lost some hair, gained some weight; but he knew how to chase stories from a phone, and he had cop sources out the yingyang.

It was Danny Bowls who'd told Mickey Judge "don't do it." Don't go to network, stay here in local. The job is safer, management loves you, the crews think you're cool, you make air every night, why jump? But Mickey jumped anyway; and every time he dropped in on his buddy, Danny Bowls had a look on his face that said *"I told you so."*

"Good piece," Danny said, putting the phone in its cradle. Mickey sat in a task chair and rolled over next to him.

"You saw it?"

"Yeah. The net feed."

"Pig fuck," Mickey said. "An absolute shitshow."

"Lemme guess. New York?"

"Oh, hell, yeah. That dick Wimple took two hours to approve the script. Left me fifteen minutes to jam it together."

"Noticed the stand-up dropped," Bowls said, sipping his late-afternoon coffee, eyes on the feeds.

"Had to. Wouldn't make time otherwise."

Bowls nodded. Shrugged. "Network," he said, as if Mick's aggravations were the most predictable thing.

"So, whattaya got?" Mick asked. Meaning: what were Danny Bowls's cop friends telling him.

"They got his ass. Bloody glove at the house. Blood in his Bronco. Blood drops on socks on his bedroom floor. Serology tests under way, but it's going to be hers and the boyfriend's."

A big exhale sigh from Mickey. Danny Bowls looked up at his pal, wide-eyed. "What's your problem? Stuff like that is what will keep you making *Nightly.*"

"Just the opposite, actually," Mick said.

"Why's that?" Danny asked, surprised.

Mick took a deep breath and patiently began to explain. "Because any minute, this will no longer be OJ's ex-wife killed on the street by god-knows-who."

"Obviously. So what?"

"Any minute now, this will be OJ Simpson charged in a murder case. A death-penalty case."

"Yeah. So?"

"The instant that happens, there's going to be a 747 loaded with network *big-foots* wheels-up from JFK," Mick said, reminding Danny how the network rolls. "They'll fly in first class, land at LAX half in a bag, limo to the Beverly Wilshire all tweaked up. They'll be running up big dinner bills on the Peacock, lots of wine. Swaggering around here like roosters among the hens. They'll be hogging every tidbit of the story. Anything involving the letters O and J they will declare to be their property." Mick paused for the punch line. "When it comes to me, I'm going to be told whatever you got, hand it over. The big boys are in town. They will be taking over the story."

Danny winced. "Dude, sorry. Network. But you knew that going in, right?"

Yeah, Mick did know that. He'd seen it before. "And I'll be sitting in my office, looking for a way back into the story; but even if I find something interesting, they're going to make me give it to whoever has been sucking up to Tom good enough to be the chosen one." Mick waggled his eyebrows at Bowls. "Bottom line, hand-to-hand network news combat. I'm going to have to fight my way through this."

"Sorry, man," Bowls said. "Sympathies. Honest."

"You were right. Never shoulda jumped," Mickey said under his breath. "But I swear," he turned and looked Danny in the eye, "I'm gonna break through this shit."

Danny was quiet.

"What?" Mick asked.

"I've always wondered. Why did you jump to the network? You knew about this stuff. We've all seen it. You had a good gig here in local. You were never going to get fired. You were set. Why'd you jump?"

Mick thought about the question. It was a good question. He didn't have to take a chance on the fickle, unstable network. He could have stayed at local.

"It's the big show," he said finally. "When I got into this business, it was to work at the network, to be a network correspondent. When I got the job, Shuman said to me 'You're a network correspondent now. Nobody can ever take that away from you.' It was a big deal."

Danny laughed. "Shuman was wrong. They *can* take it away. And they just might. You got an anniversary date coming up, right?"

Mick nodded yes. He did indeed. That was the date the network could drop him.

"And you know there's no going home again, right?" Danny jerked his thumb back toward the News Director's office. "Kaufman filled your spot with a young blonde. He's been working on ways to get more young blondes on the air. You helped him out when you quit."

Mick wrinkled his nose like something stunk. He knew. He'd seen his replacement on the Channel 4 roster of street reporters. Blond. Big eyes. Straining the fabric of her clothes top and bottom. Beautiful. Deep as a thimble, but beautiful.

The ambition to be a network correspondent had trapped him. Now he was learning the downside firsthand.

"I'm going to Chadney's," Mickey declared, his challenge in the network civil wars bringing on the need for a drink. "If OJ hangs himself or blows his brains out, page me. I can make *Nightly* once more before the 747 lands."

"No problem," Danny Bowls said.

Out on the street, Mickey Judge waited for traffic to clear, then trudged across Alameda Boulevard to Chadney's. He joined a late fifties balding producer named Charley Barnes in a red Naugahyde booth. Charley Barnes was always the first to arrive. As soon as possible after *Nightly News* signed off at 3:30 Pacific time, Charley liked to tip up his first scotch. As Mick slid into the booth, Charley was signaling the waitress for a second.

"Well, young man, you did good today."

The "young man" comment referred to his status as the new guy. Mickey was on the cusp of forty. Maybe fifteen years younger than Charley, but hardly a young man.

"Charley, this is how I size it up. When this becomes an OJ murder case rather than the ex-wife's murder, I'm going to get big-footed right out of existence."

Charley lit a cigarette and confirmed Danny's take. "That's the New York way," he said. "Tom's probably doling out the good assignments right now. A line of bootlickers at his office door."

Mick asked the waitress for a vodka soda. "But surely Tom knows they're bootlickers. He's not stupid."

"No, he's not. But Tom likes bootlickers."

Mick lit a cigarette and looked at the bright side. "When the bootlicker comes to town, it's going to free me up to work the story on my own. I promise you I'm going to find something that will force them to let me back in."

Charley nodded, exhaling smoke like a dragon. "Sometimes being ignored works to your advantage. With a little time and nobody breathing down your neck, you might find something nobody else has."

Cheering himself up, Mick raised his glass. "There's a fuse burning somewhere, Charley."

They clinked their glasses. "A toast to the evildoers who keep us employed," Charley said. He took a long pull on his scotch, set the glass down with a wet upper lip.

"Lucky for us, the devil provides," Mick agreed, draining his drink and signaling the waitress for another.

So far, he had nothing; but Mick had blind confidence that something good was going to drop into his lap.

5

Two days later, the chief correspondent in the Bureau, Johnny Furness, was still on vacation. Mickey Judge was still the *de facto* lead correspondent.

But this was the day the network brass called Furness back from his bird-watching because of a cascade of head-snapping developments.

At 8:30 in the morning, Simpson's lawyer, Robert Cohen, got a call from the LAPD telling him to surrender Simpson.

Danny Bowls learned the fact almost immediately and dispatched a reporter to Parker Center to see Simpson's arrival.

At 9:30 a.m., Cohen arrived at Robert Nazarian's house in the San Fernando Valley, where Simpson was staying, and informed Simpson that he would have to turn himself in by 11 that morning.

Murder charges against Simpson were filed at about the same time. An arraignment was scheduled for the afternoon.

The 11 a.m. scheduled surrender time came and went. Simpson did not surrender.

Once again, Bowls got word of this from his police sources. Channel 4 did a bulletin, interrupting programming in progress.

Shortly after noon, Cohen got a call from the LAPD telling him that unless he informed them of Simpson's whereabouts, they would have to announce that Simpson was a fugitive. Cohen gave them directions to Nazarian's house.

Police arrived to find Cohen, Simpson's doctor, and others waiting and were told that Simpson and his friend Al Cowlings had quietly absconded from the house.

At Channel 4, Bowls got another heads-up, and Furnell Chapman did a shot into the noon news from the camera location in the newsroom. Bowls got the Channel 4 chopper in the air. A desk debate ensued between Bowls and news director Nathan Kaufman as to whether the chopper should head downtown or toward the Nazarian house.

At 1:50 p.m., LAPD Commander David Gascon went before cameras to announce that Simpson had not surrendered as promised and was a fugitive from justice.

Channel 4 went to continuous coverage. Kaufman stood over Danny Bowls's shoulder at the assignment desk, second-guessing every decision.

Upstairs in the network edit bays Mickey Judge rushed a piece for *Nightly* with all the latest.

Mickey could have saved himself the trouble. It would never make the air.

That was because at 3 p.m., District Attorney Gil Garcetti appeared at a news conference to say anyone helping Simpson flee would be prosecuted as a felon. "We will find Mr. Simpson and bring him to justice." He added that prosecutors had not decided whether to seek the death penalty in the case. *Nightly News* execs in New York dumped Mick's package and took the feed of Gascon live.

An hour and forty-five minutes later, an arrest warrant was issued for Al Cowlings.

At 5 p.m., Cohen held a news conference at which longtime friend Robert Nazarian read a letter from Simpson. "Don't feel sorry for me," the note ended. "I've had a great life, great friends. Please think of the real OJ and not this lost person. Thanks for making my life special. I hope I've helped yours. Peace and love, OJ." The letter was instantly assumed to be a suicide note.

The network desk sent Mickey downtown to Parker Center to "stand by."

Within the hour, Simpson made a 911 call from a cell phone in his Ford Bronco. His location was traced to the Santa Ana Freeway in Orange County near Lake Forest, where Nicole was buried.

The CHP began pursuit.

Al Cowlings got on the phone with police to warn them to stay back. He said OJ was in the back seat with a gun to his head.

At 7:30 p.m., the Bronco turned north on the San Diego Freeway headed toward Brentwood. Crowds gathered on the overpasses, cheering OJ on.

Just before 8 p.m., Simpson arrived at his estate in Brentwood. Negotiations began for his actual surrender.

An all-clear was issued forty-five minutes later, as Simpson was taken into custody.

At approximately 9:45 p.m., Simpson arrived at Parker Center in downtown Los Angeles in police custody.

For Mickey Judge and every other newsperson in the country, June 17 was a mad dash, a frantic scramble to keep up with developments. Mick was left deeply frustrated. With an abundance of news, he should have made air, and if he had stayed at local he would have. But the network job was different. The updates came so fast, he was pushed aside and Tom took events live.

Mick was ordered back to the Bureau to prepare an OJ piece, with the warning that Johnny Furness was on a plane and if he made it to Burbank, the *Today Show*'s executive producer, Bernie Sugar, wanted Furness to front the story.

Mick was teed off to be shoved aside again. He and Danny met on the balcony for a smoke. "This story is going to break in my direction, I can feel it," he grumbled to his friend.

"I hope so," Danny replied. But he kept to himself his own feeling that he couldn't really see how.

Meanwhile, for Garden Grove and Lummie Malcolm, the events early in the day just added to their anxiety about OJ.

Garden and Lummie met in the parking lot at the Fabulous Forum in Inglewood at 5:30 p.m. It was NBA Finals night. The Forum had the game up on big screens, and the bars were open. Knicks and Rockets. Patrick Ewing and Hakeem Olajuwon. Both Garden and Lummie were Laker fans, of course, but the home team had had a crap year.

Garden would like to have been in his Barcalounger, but Louise had been a downer lately. She wouldn't stop talking about that "dead white bitch" and her "dumb-as-dirt black-ass ex-husband," OJ Simpson.

Worse, he'd made a big mistake. He'd told Louise he'd retrieved a lost bag belonging to OJ and planned to give it back to him. She brutally chastised him for getting involved. "It's a murder case now!" she bawled at him, bending herself all out of shape. Garden had had enough of it. He needed to get out of the house.

Worse still, the day had not gone well for Garden's personal devotion to OJ Simpson. OJ was scheduled to surrender to police to be arrested for the murder of his wife. Garden was shocked.

"They going to railroad the man," Garden said to Lummie. "You watch. They going to railroad his ass."

A disastrous turn of events followed. OJ had not surrendered as promised. He was at large, "on the run," and the police were looking for him. Even worse, if that was possible, just as Garden was leaving the house, OJ's friend, a guy named Nazarian, was on television reading what sounded like a suicide note supposedly written by OJ.

Garden didn't believe a word of it. But he had to escape Louise. The NBA finals at the Forum was as good a place as any. It was just a couple of miles from his house in Inglewood. He called Lummie and said let's meet up there.

"You see the lawyer reading the suicide note?" Lummie asked, cautiously, when they were together in the parking lot. His friend looked to be in a foul mood.

"Bullshit. They make the man sound crazy." Garden shut off the topic with a scowl and a sharp tone.

Lummie changed the subject. "You still got the bag in the trunk?"

"Damn right. Haven't touched it," Garden replied. "And I ain't gonna."

"Tell Louise?"

"Hell no," Garden blatantly lied. "Think I'm crazy?"

"Not looking so good for the Juice", Lummie said.

Garden was out of sorts. He was taking OJ Simpson's problems personally. "He go to the funeral and they all turn their damn backs on him. Man trying to mourn his wife, and all those white people treat him like a field hand spoiling their party." The two men walked across the parking lot to a ticket window. The Forum charged for entry just to watch the game on TV. They paid their money.

Inside, they headed for the bar and concession stand. Garden got a double rum-and-coke and a tray of chips and queso. Lummie got his favorite items: the Forum footlong dog, and double Jack and soda.

They took seats in an empty section so they could be alone. The screen had the game on already.

"And another thing," Garden said, picking up where he'd left off. "Day before yesterday, he go down to Parker Center to talk to the cops and his lawyer come outside and talk to reporters. That ain't right. The lawyer supposed to stay with his guy while the cops talk to him. That little son of a bitch let OJ sit in there with the cops alone. God knows what they got him to say."

"That ain't right," Lummie agreed.

"Course it ain't. What the fuck that lawyer up to?"

Lummie let Garden cool off before reminding him that there was a new lawyer. "Guy named Cohen his lawyer now."

"Whatever, Cohen, whoever, don't matter. OJ got to get a black lawyer," Garden insisted. "Somebody who know how to deal with the motherfuckin' LAPD. Think these rich white lawyers got black guys the LAPD trying to railroad? *Hell the fuck no!*"

Garden sipped on his rum-and-coke and seethed. He hardly paid attention to the game. Lummie bit down on his footlong, slathered in mustard and relish and sprinkled with onions.

On the big screen, Patrick Ewing and Hakeem Olajuwon were banging off each other like NFL linemen. Marv Albert was talking too much.

Just before 6 p.m. everything went wonky. The big screen was tuned to Channel 4, the NBC station carrying the game. But suddenly the game was gone. In its place was a picture of a white car on the freeway somewhere. Tom Jansen's voice filled the arena.

"What's this?" Garden asked no one in particular.

Lummie squinted at the screen. "I need glasses. Looks like a freeway chase."

Both men concentrated on the screen. Indeed, it did look like a freeway chase, but very slow.

"Holy fucking shit," Garden said in stunned amazement. "It's OJ."

Tom Jansen had just said those very words. OJ Simpson was in a white Ford Bronco. His friend A.C. Cowlings was at the wheel. Tom Jansen said Cowlings had called 911 to tell the cops to back off. *OJ had a gun to his head!*

A phalanx of CHP and LA County Sheriff cruisers were following. The Bronco was on the move, cruising a circuitous route around the LA freeways.

For a few minutes, Channel 4 kept the NBA game on in a split screen, the game in a smaller box, the Bronco chase in a bigger box. But that didn't last long. Soon the game went away entirely, and the big screen was locked on the white Bronco.

Tom Jansen reported that OJ was headed to his house in Brentwood because he wanted to see his mother. The motley crowd that had come to the Forum for the game began cheering for OJ.

Stunned, Garden and Lummie stared at the screen with wide eyes. Lummie called out the locations the Bronco passed. "He got off the 91 at Torrance. He's coming up the 405 now," he said. "Passing LAX."

"Fuckin' guy right over there," Garden said, jerking his thumb over his shoulder.

They watched in transfixed horror as the Bronco crossed overpasses crowded with people cheering him. Some even had time to make signs: Go Juice Go.

The Bronco took the off ramp from the 405 at Sunset, and

meandered west into Brentwood. It drove into Simpson's driveway and parked there.

The helicopter hovered over OJ's house. Simpson's son Jason was throwing a fit in the driveway. The cops took him inside.

After a few minutes of what looked like police negotiations, Simpson emerged from the Bronco. He didn't have a gun in his hand. The cops took him into custody a little before 9 p.m.

"Doesn't look like you'll be able to drop that bag off to him," Lummie said.

Garden was disgusted. "I get it to him eventually. He's innocent. You watch."

The two friends walked across the parking lot, dejected. They parted with grunted see-ya's and drove home.

OJ Simpson was in an LAPD squad car, boxed in by a platoon of LAPD black-and-whites, police helicopters directly overhead, followed by a V-shaped squadron of news choppers, headed downtown. He was headed to a cell at Parker Center.

6

The Bronco chase was an agonizing day for Mickey Judge. He did a voice-over package for *Nightly* that fed at 3 in the afternoon, Pacific time. New York killed the stand-up, added copy; but by 3:30 in the afternoon it was hopelessly outdated. Mick felt like someone didn't want him to be seen.

Then he did an update at 6 p.m. for the West Coast feed, but that never aired either. The balance of the evening was the entire Bronco chase. Mickey Judge was sidelined.

The Bureau's senior correspondent, Johnny Furness, had been called off his Costa Rica vacation. He had twenty-five years experience with the network, all the way back to the Vietnam war. He was always the number one correspondent out of Burbank. Mickey was standing by in the Bureau to voice the *Today Show* package. But he got called off. Furness hit the ground running and went straight to the edit bays to put the finishing touches on an extravaganza for the *Today Show*.

There was a knockout young woman named Jane Bell who was doing live shots every few minutes for the NBC affiliate stations across the country. In LA, the Channel 4 reporters were everywhere, all over the story. One, Mickey's friend Conan Nolan, even managed to catch up with the Bronco and reported by cell phone from his news van right behind the show-of-force phalanx of CHP cruisers.

Before he was called back to the Bureau, Mick had been at Parker Center in downtown LA. He stood around at the door of one of the Bureau's live vans with nothing to do, watching the feed. The network didn't need him. The affiliates were covered. The locals were too busy to talk to him. When he called Danny, he got a "Dude, gotta run. Later."

To make matters worse, "the 747 of big-foots" landed at LAX and he got a voice page from his nemesis, the New York producer who had put him through hell over his scripts, Bart Wimple. "Dude, Tom put me in charge of coverage. Bev Wilshire breakfast 7a."

The Beverly Wilshire. Breakfast. Seven in the morning. He'd been summoned.

Feeling helpless, the biggest news story of his career unfolding before his eyes, he sat in his office at the Bureau and watched replays of OJ arriving at Parker Center in the middle of a military-style convoy. An escort of police helicopters and news choppers circled overhead. Symbolic of his new inmate status, the vehicle carrying Simpson swooped into an underground garage, and the sports and movie star vanished from sight.

OJ was officially under arrest and charged with a double murder (OJ's ex-wife Nicole Brown Simpson and her friend Ron Goldman). It wasn't long before mugshots were released: a front view and a profile, with the booking board in the lower third of the photos that read "BK4013970061794, Los Angeles Police, Jail Div."

Normally, this would have been the end of the story. But this day was so hot, Channel 4 stayed with it as "continuing coverage" until Leno came on after the 11 p.m. news.

At midnight, Mickey emerged from his office to check in. The Bureau was a scene of frantic activity as producers pulled together whatever they could for the Johnny Furness *Today Show* blockbuster. Mickey was emphatically not needed.

"Go get some rest, sweetheart," Alison de Groot counseled sympathetically. "You have a big meeting with his highness at seven bells. Be fresh."

"Says he's in charge of coverage," Mickey said. "Should I expect to be part of the plan?"

She frowned. "Afraid not, my dear. Even Johnny will be in a subordinate role, I've heard," she said. "They're bringing in David Moody, the flavor of the month. Tom wants his star to blaze."

Mickey might have let his disappointment show. "So what's the meeting in the morning all about?"

"Pick your brain, sweetheart. He just wants to pick your brain. Be a good soldier. Salute and march. Things will work out."

Mickey let out a long exhale. It was about as bad as it gets.

He wandered into the Channel 4 newsroom, looking for Danny Bowls.

Danny was hunched over the desk, phone to his ear, a pencil in his left hand, scribbling notes. He glanced up at Mick, waggled his eyebrows, pointed to a chair. Mickey watched him write. It was OJ details. One of Danny's cop friends.

When he wrapped it up, he looked up at his friend. "Tits on a bull tonight?"

Mick nodded. "Pretty much. Except I got a 7 a.m. with the guy in charge of net coverage."

"A good friend?"

"Not even close."

Danny shrugged. "Network," he said.

Mickey went home to slug down a couple of vodkas and crash. "Home" was a studio apartment a mile down Riverside near the Equestrian Center. He'd been holed up there since he and his wife split up. Furnished. Pool. Cheap. Coffee machine. Refrigerator with bottles of seltzer and microwave pizza and coffee cream. Fine enough. At another point in his life, he might have felt it was lonely. But right now he relished the solitude. He got a mailbox at a shipping center, so nobody knew where he was living except Alison de Groot, and she promised to keep it secret. It was a hideout. A bolthole. A place he could spend evenings brooding about his tenuous career, his divorce, his messy life.

Usually he also had a vodka soda. Or two. Sometimes three. Tonight he went slow. It was an early alarm, and he had to be on his toes with the New York guy.

His phone buzzed. He glanced at the number and smiled. His daughter Kelly.

"Dad, I saw you on the news two days in a row. That's good, right? Things are better?"

Kelly Judge was sixteen. Mick wasn't quite sure how it had happened, but she was turning out to be the kind of girl he should have married. Pretty, smart, feet squarely on the ground. Not anything like the two women he had married.

"Yeah, you're sweet. But that run ended tonight. Got bumped three times, I think. I don't know. Lost count."

"I noticed. Didn't see you. Thought I would. Sorry, Dad."

Mick hated it that his daughter was caught up in the ups and downs of his chaotic career.

"Oh, honey, it's fine. Remember, it's just TV news. It runs hot and cold."

"I like you being on the network news. I can watch you down here." Kelly lived in Santee, a suburb of San Diego, with her mother Sonja. Mick had tried for custody during the divorce a decade ago, but the nature of his work weighed against it, at least in the mind of the judge. "But when I don't see you for a few days, I worry."

"You shouldn't worry about me. I'm good. It's a big story and a lot of people are in the mix. I'd like to have it to myself, but that's not reality."

"Why wouldn't it be better if you were back in local news?'"

She had always been a "why" baby, asking why this and why that. At sixteen, her questions were more mature, and to Mick a lot more scary. He instinctively felt he shouldn't let his daughter see the dark underside of his business, the sharp elbows, the back-stabbing, the uncertainty, life on the bubble. He could barely take it himself; a sixteen-year-old girl shouldn't be so invested.

"Maybe. I liked local news—"

"Maybe you could get a job in San Diego," she interrupted, with a hopeful smile in her voice. "I could see you every night."

"If something opened up down there, I'd take a look at it," he lied. In truth, Mick had no desire whatsoever to work in the San Diego market, even if it put him closer to his daughter. The news environment there was run-and-gun, and deeply, deeply shallow. Moreover, it would put him in the same town as his first wife, Kelly's mother. "I always wanted to be a network news correspondent, so here I am. I have to take the good with the bad."

As soon as the words were out of his mouth, he felt regret for putting his job over his daughter. He hoped she didn't see it that way.

"I worry about you," she said again.

"Worry about your grades and your mom. I'm fine."

She was quiet for what seemed a long minute. "Mom is getting crazier. Now I see why you left."

"Hon, that's not a good thing to say. Just hang in. You're doing good in school. The swim team is awesome. A year or two and you're off to college. I hate to see you sad."

She perked up. "I'm not sad. She's out of my hair, mostly. Out at night on her job," she said, meaning her mom's PR work at music clubs. "I'm looking forward to college. Can't come soon enough."

Mick was hit with another jab of guilt. Leaving his crazy ex-wife all those years ago had relieved him of some strain, but over the years he saw the pressure simply get transferred to his daughter. For years, the little girl was bewildered by her erratic mother. As a teenager she had become resigned to her reality. She counted the days until she could step away, just like her father.

She changed the subject. "What are you doing now?"

"Chasing a really good story."

"An OJ story?"

"Well, yeah, everybody's chasing that one."

"What's the one you're chasing."

"Big." It was a lie. He had nothing.

"Can you tell me?"

"I don't want to jinx it. When it comes time, I'll tell you before anybody."

"Promise?"

"Promise. You'll be the first."

They ended the call with *love-you*'s.

Mick tried to make the two-and-a-half-hour drive to Santee to see Kelly as many weekends as he could, usually driving her to swim meets. She was a dedicated swimmer, hours upon hours each week in the pool. And he knew part of her determination was that every hour in the water was one hour less with her mother.

Sonja Judge kept his name after the divorce, just to needle him and continue to associate herself with him. He moved away from San Diego in the divorce, and never considered going back.

As for daughter Kelly, he was very proud of her, while at the same time feeling deeply embarrassed about having ever married her mother. He chalked it up to his own youth and stupidity. The only good that had come of it was his daughter, but his ex-wife never failed to inject difficulties into his life. More than once, a news director or assignment editor had asked: "Who's this woman throwing your name around, trying to get her client on the air?"

Ugh.

With these worries haunting his sleep, Mick now got a few hours' rest.

He left the apartment at six the next morning. The drive over the hill for his meeting was easier on surface streets than the freeways. He took Riverside west to Olive, past the Disney Studios' Merlin Hat and the glowing peacock at NBC. He went under the Hollywood Freeway, turned left on Cahuenga, crested the hill, and rolled past the Hollywood Bowl. He stayed on Highland to Wilshire and turned right to the Beverly Wilshire Hotel. At that hour, traffic was a breeze and he enjoyed a pleasant drive with a coffee and the pink sunrise over Beverly Hills.

Just off Wilshire he found a parking spot. He put an NBC News placard on the dash, hoping the Beverly Hills meter maids would be cool. He strolled past the doormen at the ornate entrance to the Beverly Wilshire Hotel. He was sitting at a table with coffee in the breakfast bar when Frederick "Bart" Wimple walked in at 7:30 a.m., half an hour late.

Wimple was balding, treadmill-thin, dressed in five hundred dollars of slacks, designer shirt, and cashmere sweater in shades of black and gray. "Buddy!" he boomed as he approached the table. He called everyone "buddy."

Frustrated with having to make nice with someone so at-ease with betrayal, still Mickey stood and shook his hand. He had his best phony smile on. It made no sense to make more enemies, or to make old enemies even more hostile. He followed Alison's advice and played the good soldier.

The salute-and-march was simple: Bart wanted to know everything Mickey knew about the story. Who the players were, how to reach them, who might be a soft spot to work on, who were the *money gets*, meaning booking the big names. Mickey emptied whatever was in his brain into Wimple's notebook. Salute and march.

"What evidence they got?"

Mickey had to be careful. The good stuff came directly from Danny Bowls, which meant he couldn't just give it away.

But, still, he could generalize. "They have blood at the scene. They have blood at OJ's place. They probably have blood in the Bronco. I suppose there might be bloody clothes." Adding, "if the cops found them."

Wimple nodded along, soaking up information, his gray eyes dancing at the possibilities. "What's the number-one piece of evidence that would nail the case down?"

"Oh, easy," Mickey said. "The knife."

"The knife. Of course," Wimple said, trying to cover the fact that this hadn't occurred to him.

"If they find the knife and it has Nicole's blood, Goldman's blood, and OJ's prints or blood? He's on death row," Mick added. "I suppose they got other ways to convict him. But if it came down to a single thing? It's all about the knife."

"And do they have it?"

"Not that I know of," Mickey said. "But if they do, we'll know soon. They'll have to tell the defense. But so far, nothing."

Wimple had that faraway look in his eye that said he was dreaming big.

Mick knew what it was: he was conjuring up something huge to bring to Jansen on a silver platter. Something that would ensure his spot on the untouchable list at NBC News for decades.

"Jesus, wouldn't it be awesome if we could find that knife?" Wimple asked in his dreamy state.

Mick restrained himself from laughing in the New Yorker's face. "It would take a mountain of luck. It's a long shot for the cops, and they got badges and guns and search warrants and all that shit."

Wimple nodded, dropped the idea. "Yeah. Probably just a wet dream."

Mickey went along. "The longest of long shots."

"Just remember," Wimple added. "Whatever you get, blast it straight to me. I'm under orders to make David Moody a star."

David Moody. The mere mention of the name made Mick's stomach churn. Handsome. Wide-eyed. A mop of tousled dark hair hanging over his forehead. Neon-green eyes, dimples, expert at faking the network correspondent look of studious seriousness. Banging the production assistants at 30 Rock. Boy wonder. Flavor of the month among the Jansen mafia in New York.

Mickey furrowed his brow. "I'm not working the story; I'm probably not going to have anything you'd need."

Wimple shook his head no. "Look, you may be in reserve," he said, using a slimy euphemism for "on the bench" and meeting Mick's eyes in a stare that meant business. "But who knows what may drop in your lap. When it does? Straight to me. Got it?"

"Sure thing," Mick said.

But he was thinking *go fuck yourself.*

7

Seven days after the murders, Mickey Judge was picking up some of the slopwork on the biggest story in America.

On the Sunday after the Bronco chase, Wimple wanted him sent out to keep an eye on the men and women from CalTrans and the LAPD and the LA County Sheriff's office as they searched the sides of the road on Sunset Boulevard from Rockingham to the 405 freeway. Others searched the southbound side of the 405 freeway to the Sepulveda exit leading to LAX. Still more searched the roadside along Sepulveda into the airport.

Channel 4 had its chopper up. Local put crews on the ground along the freeway.

Mickey Judge stood by in a chase car on the entrance to the freeway at Sunset with a handset radio waiting to hear from any of the crews if something was found. Danny Bowls was wired into Parker Center, as usual.

If anything was found, they would know. And with any luck, they might even get some video.

A big reason this was such a shit assignment was he had to stand up his daughter. He was supposed to be on the 405 down to Santee. Instead, he was sitting on the edge of the freeway waiting for a break in the story that he had a terrible feeling was just not going to come.

Mick punched in Kelly's number and listened to the rings. Maybe it would go to voicemail and he could take the coward's way out with an apologetic message.

No such luck. She picked up. "You on your way?"

"No, honey, I'm sorry. I'm tied up on this OJ thing."

The silence on the other end was awful. Sometimes he wished she would get angry. Instead, she was just crushed with disappointment. He wondered if she knew how much that hurt him.

"Well, it's your job," she said finally. "What do they have you doing? Will I see you on TV tonight?"

"Frankly, I doubt it. I'm sitting at the edge of the freeway waiting to see if the CHP and Caltrans find the murder weapon on the side of the road."

"Do you think they'll find it?"

"That would be too easy. Can't believe he'd be dumb enough to just dump it on the side of the road."

"He sounds pretty dumb."

Mick snorted a laugh. "He does indeed, honey. He's one of those people who gets famous and thinks he can do anything."

"I'm glad you're not like that."

"I'm not famous."

"Well, kinda. You're on TV."

"I'm not a multi-millionaire movie star."

"You're not? I thought you were."

The radio squawked his name. "Yeah, I'm here," he said. "What's up?"

Bart Wimple's voice came on. "You got anything?"

"Nothing here, Walter. Back to you."

"That's funny shit, Judge. Call me if something pops up."

"Will do."

Kelly heard the exchange. "That your boss?"

"Yeah, a guy named Wimple from New York."

"You don't like him, do you?"

"Why do you ask?"

She groaned. "If it was obvious to me, it was obvious to him too. Maybe you should dial it back. You don't need to get fired again."

How'd she get so smart? he wondered. Can't be from her mom, and doubt it's from me.

"You should go do your job. You'll come down when you're free."

"Love you."

"Love you too," and she hung up.

Wimple called him three more times over the next few hours. "Come on, buddy, make it happen," he demanded over and over. As if Mickey could make the search parties find something useful to Wimple and wonder-boy Moody.

Mickey seethed but could do nothing more than say "I'm on it," like he meant it, which he didn't.

By dark, at nearly 8:30 p.m., the results were in. There was no knife, or pile of clothes, or bag or backpack or anything that had to do with Simpson anywhere along the route OJ's limo had taken the night of June 12th. Most especially, no knife.

At the end of Sunday, the possibility of finding the crucial evidence along OJ's path to the airport was officially over.

But the LAPD had two detectives on a plane to Chicago. They

would search a patch of wooded area behind the airport hotel where OJ had checked in, where he'd received a phone call from LA detectives informing him of his wife's death, and where he'd made a dozen calls himself and eventually vacated in a rush for a return flight to L.A.

This was a day Mick missed Kelly's swim meet, just to throw it away on nothing. He called her to apologize again, got her voice mail.

"Sorry, baby. OJ required my presence. Talk later. Love you."

8

Garden was sitting in his Camry in the parking lot of the liquor store at Cedar and Manchester. He had two mini-bottles of Smirnoff vodka. One was gone; he was unscrewing the cap on the second. Garden was agitated. He was thinking about the video from last night that showed search crews coming up with nothing on the side of the roads OJ had traveled to the airport. They were looking for the very bag he had in the trunk of his car.

He paged Lummie from a phone booth and waited for the callback. "Come meet me," he said. "I gotta show you something."

"Okay, where you at?" Lummie asked.

"Not here," he said, as if Lummie would know his location. "Someplace else. You know where Buckwheat's grave is at Inglewood Cemetery?"

"You want to meet at Buckwheat's grave in the cemetery? What the fuck?"

"Somewhere very private. That's good enough."

"Garden, for chrissakes, I ain't hangin' out at Buckwheat's fucking grave."

"All right, all right. Sugar Ray's. You know that one?"

Lummie sounded reluctant. "Sugar Ray's. Okay."

"Can you come?"

"Give me twenty minutes," Lummie said.

Garden hung up. He swilled the rest of the mini down. The phone booth smelled like urine. He left the mini bottles on the shelf in the booth and shuffled back to his car.

The Camry almost wore down the battery before it fired. Garden drove west on Manchester, turned south on Prairie, cruised alongside Inglewood Park Cemetery. At Florence he turned right, and a short distance farther made a right turn into the cemetery. He followed the winding cemetery roads until he found what he was looking for: the grave of Sugar Ray Robinson, the boxing great.

The tall stone rested on a granite pedestal. It was about four feet high. A towering sugar pine shaded the grave. The rose-colored granite was inscribed *Our Champion, Sugar Ray Robinson*, with his birthdate and the day he'd died in 1989.

A color image of the boxing legend was engraved into the stone against a robin's-egg-blue background. Below the picture of Ray, bare chested and in boxing gloves, the words *God Loved You and I Will . . . Always Forever Your Wife Millie*. It looked to Garden like there was room below Millie's name for her own inscription and picture when she passed.

Garden appeared to be just a fan of the boxing great, stopping to pay his respects. No one would bother him in the cemetery.

Shortly, a '72 Chevy Monte Carlo slid up to Garden's car, nose to nose. Lummie unfolded his large frame from the driver's side and walked over to Garden's side. He put his hands on the door and leaned over. "Jesus, man, you been drinking already?"

"Just a little," Garden said. "Back up and let me outa here."

Garden pushed open the door and emerged from his Camry on unsteady legs. Lummie took his arm, but Garden shook him off. "I got it, man. I got it."

Lummie stood back to let his friend have some room. "What's the matter with you, man? This ain't like you."

Garden stopped at the trunk of the car. "I gotta show you something."

He popped the trunk. In the center of the otherwise completely empty trunk was the small backpack he'd retrieved from the garbage and promised to return to OJ. The zipper was open. "Don't touch the bag, man," Garden said. "But you see those chop sticks? Use them to open the bag a little so you can see in."

Garden stepped away, to give his friend room. Lummie frowned at Garden. He stepped forward and found two Chinese-restaurant chopsticks on the floor of the trunk. "These?" he asked.

Garden nodded. "Damn thing giving my heart flutters."

"Flutters again? Man, you just have to go to a doctor."

"Just look. I'll worry about my heart."

Lummie took a stick in each hand. He reached in and held one side of the bag down while he used the other to pry open the backpack.

Inside, he could make out something, but it wasn't immediately clear what it was. "You got a flashlight?"

"It's fucking noon, man. Plenty of light."

Lummie pulled the bag open a little more. The object inside became visible. He couldn't tell what it was right away, because there was something dark covering it. But after a few seconds, he recognized the object.

"A motherfucking knife," he said, looking back at Garden.

Garden nodded. "And it's covered in blood. All the way up to the handle."

"Damn."

"And when I looked closely at it, I think I could see fingerprints in the blood on the grip."

Lummie dropped the chopsticks and stood up straight to face his friend. "It's *the* knife? OJ's knife?"

Garden reluctantly nodded yes. "Sure as hell looks like it. Unless he was cutting up a pig for a luau. Looks really bad for OJ."

"Holy crap, Garden. You got the knife," Lummie said as he slammed the trunk lid down. "You got OJ's knife. You got the motherfucking knife he did his wife with."

Garden bobbed his head slowly. "Looks like it."

They stared at each other for a few long moments.

"What'll you do with it?"

Garden gave the question some thought. "I been thinking about that." Garden sighed. He looked depressed. The knife in his trunk seemed to connect directly to his hero. It was the bag Lummie had seen on the trash can where OJ was standing waiting for his claim check from the Skycap. How many other people standing right by that particular trash can were under suspicion of murder with a knife on that particular night? Had to be zero.

He didn't know why OJ had killed that woman, but maybe the young stud with her was a good reason. "Right now I ain't doing nothing with it."

Lummie tilted his head and squinted at his pal. "Give it to the cops?"

Garden shook his head vigorously. "That is exactly what I'm *not* doing."

They stood quietly, each staring at the trunk of the Camry as if it might suddenly pop open on its own.

Finally, Garden broke the silence. "I called in sick."

Lummie nodded. "Don't blame you. I just might do that too."

"Want to get a drink?"

Lummie shook his head. "Can't do that, man. We gotta get you some coffee. You get pulled over with vodka on your breath, they gonna poke around in your car, you gonna have to explain that knife."

"Oh, shit," Garden said. "Didn't think about that."

Lummie nodded. "Until you can get that thing someplace safe, you need to play it straight."

Garden nodded. "Where can we stash it?"

9

Armen Shabaglian sat at the bar at the Delerium Restaurant in Glendale. The restaurant was an annex to the Delerium Ballroom, a favorite site for glamorous upscale events such as weddings and anniversaries among the Armenians of Glendale, California.

Shabaglian was drinking with a man in his late forties named Garit "Gary" Minasian. It was a courtesy meeting. Armen Shabaglian's parents had asked Minasian's boss to have someone see the young man. Gary Minasian had drawn the short straw. He looked Armen over with hooded eyes. Minasian's gray-flecked black hair was thinning, and his owlish face was set off by a rapidly graying goatee beard. The public knew Minasian as the owner of a car wash a few blocks away. In reality, he was one of the men who "took care of business" for the most respected—and perhaps the most feared—man in the Armenian community, the owner of the Delerium Ballroom, Harut "Harry" Sarkissian. Harry had a legit business in the Delerium Ballroom. He also had other businesses that were not so legit. Gary Minasian was his second in command in both.

The two men had beers, and they smoked. Armen was going slow. He was trying to impress Minasian. Getting drunk wouldn't help.

Shabaglian's dark complexion and rugged facial features made him a favorite of young women, not just Armenian women, but the Southern California blondes too. He was a handsome young Armenian man, fit, confident, and charming. He'd played football at Glendale High School. He'd gone to junior college for a year. He had a job with the LA Sanitation Department, and he was sick of it. He was hoping Minasian could help him get something better among the Armenians of Glendale.

"I can do anything, Mr. Minasian," Armen said. He was trying to convey that he understood there were activities Minasian and his boss ran that were not completely kosher, but that he would be quite willing to participate in.

"You mechanically inclined?" Minasian asked casually.

"Yessir. I do all my own work on my car. Everything under the hood. I've replaced quarter panels, just about anything."

"What car you got?"

"Sixty-eight Mustang, Coupe. 289. Automatic. Lime Gold."

"What's Lime Gold?" Minasian asked, mildly interested.

"Light green."

Minasian nodded that he understood. "Sometimes we look for a guy who knows his way around cars. Somebody mechanically inclined."

There's a clue, Armen thought. They might be running a dismantling business. Good money in that. Especially good money if the cars were boosted.

"I'm really good at taking stuff apart and putting it back together," the young man offered. Armen knew that sometimes chop-shop operators put together a wrecked car from stolen parts; and sometimes they just stripped the car of whatever parts would come off with a wrench or a torch and stockpiled the parts for later sale. Either way, he was good with it.

Minasian was noncommittal. Naturally cautious, he held back further discussion that might reveal what kind of operation his boss ran. But Armen took it as a good sign that the important man was willing to spend time with him.

Minasian shifted back to talking about things more mundane. Minasian asked him about his parents, where he had grown up, what he wanted to be. Armen was born in Fresno, a slightly different Armenian community, but one the Glendale people felt protective of. As for what he wanted to be, Armen Shabaglian emphasized that he wanted to *be* somebody. A guy who had things, who people looked up to.

Gary Minasian nodded along as if he'd heard it all before. He had. He'd said the same things thirty years ago to another important Armenian, now long dead.

The television behind the bar was on, the sound down. Armen noticed it was a noontime news report. The subject was the OJ Simpson murder case. A preliminary hearing was set to begin in a few days. An actual trial was still months away.

"Funny thing happened at the airport the other day," Armen said, looking up at the television. "Might have something to do with the OJ case."

Minasian's ears perked up. He knew that an Armenian lawyer named Robert Nazarian was a close friend of Simpson's. Minasian and his boss didn't much like Nazarian. Nothing terribly serious.

They just felt Nazarian shied away from them, didn't show them respect. Maybe because of their unconventional businesses. Like he was afraid to be seen with them. Nazarian hardly ever came to Glendale, preferring his Hollywood friends, like Simpson.

"What was that?" Minasian asked, slightly interested, and only because of the Nazarian connection to Simpson. He was actually looking for a way to wrap the interview up and be on his way. The boy might prove useful, but at the moment he couldn't think of anything in particular.

"A couple of guys chased down my truck and made us stop. They're ramp guys, I think. I see them around. They said OJ Simpson lost a bag and it might be in the trash. So I let them go in the back, and sure enough they found that one of the trash bags had a backpack kind of thing they said was OJ's."

"Really?" Minasian remarked. "Strange."

"Yeah," Armen agreed. "It was weird."

But Minasian's interest rose imperceptibly. The boss's thing about Bobby Nazarian meant any gossip that came along was worth reporting.

"When was this?"

"It was the night OJ flew to Chicago. I was making the trash pickups about eleven o'clock."

Minasian frowned, stroking the whiskers of his goatee. "This the night before they found his wife?"

Armen nodded. "Yeah, that night. In fact, they say she was murdered an hour or so before these guys said they saw him at the airport."

Now Minasian was very interested. "You believe them? The two black guys?"

Armen hadn't mentioned they were black. But he guessed it was obvious. He shrugged. "Sure. Why not? Next day, the news said he was at the airport right about then."

"Let's back up. What's this about chasing you down?"

"I picked up the trash at Terminal 4, American Airlines, then headed down the way to Terminal 5. That's where one of them caught up and insisted I let him look for something in the compactor."

"And he found something?"

Armen nodded. "Yeah, it was in the bag I'd just thrown in from the American terminal. There was a small black backpack right on top.

The guy said it was OJ's, said he was going to return it to him."

Minasian thought it over. "Funny coincidence, huh? Next morning, the guy is in handcuffs. And you had something of his in the trash?"

"Yeah, weird," Shabaglian agreed.

"How'd it get there? How'd it get in the trash?"

Armen could tell that the tone of the conversation had shifted. Minasian was interested in him, and it had come on suddenly. "That's the really weird part. The two guys said OJ was right there at the Skycap stand checking bags. They said he had a duffel bag and the small backpack on top of the trash can. They said it looked like the backpack was his, but he went to the plane without it. They figured he lost it."

"They said he 'lost' it in the trash? That make sense?"

"Actually, no," Armen said, shaking his head. "The trash cans have a lid with a solid top, and openings on the sides. You can set something on top. If the backpack was on top one minute and then it was in the trash can the next minute, somebody had to put it through the openings. No way it could just fall in."

Minasian took the information with interest. He slid a bar napkin over to the younger man. "Let me have your number. We'll see what we can do to help you out."

Armen Shabaglian happily wrote his number on the napkin. "That's my pager," he said. He shook Gary's hand and excused himself, feeling that Minasian had signaled the interview was over.

Gary Minasian tucked the napkin with the phone number away in a shirt pocket. He sat at the bar, smoking another cigarette and finishing his beer. He decided he had to go upstairs and tell the boss about this conversation.

The clicking of Gary Minasian's heels echoed as he walked through the Delerium ballroom, an enormous gold-and-white event center. The room had high ceilings, mirrored walls, and gold and crystal chandeliers and space for a thousand people at dinner tables. Ten at a table, a hundred tables. He went through the cavernous catering kitchen, and up a set of stairs in the back.

The office of Harut "Harry" Sarkissian was at the top of the stairs, above the kitchen. He kept another office on the second floor at the front of the building for ceremonial visits, deal closings, and the like, but the one in the back was the working office.

Cheryl Bedrosian, a middle-aged woman with jet-black hair, horn-rimmed glasses, sharp hazel eyes, and a prominent nose, was behind a desk that faced the door. She was the gatekeeper. A phone pressed to her ear, she signaled Gary with a nod to go ahead into Sarkissian's office. She continued listening to someone on the other end of the call.

Harry Sarkissian was behind his desk, his feet up on an open drawer, watching a television. Harry was in his mid-sixties, a little on the paunchy side, his fleshy face clean-shaven, his black hair turned perfectly white. He had the eyes of a falcon: intense, focused. The eyes were on the television screen, a quick shift to Gary Minasian and back to the screen. "What's up?"

"Your boy Bobby got some drama."

"No shit," said Harry. "Looks like that *schwarz* buddy of his is in deep."

Gary laughed. "You think saying *schwarz* is better than *nigger*?"

Harry looked up, surprised. "It isn't? I stopped saying nigger years ago. I thought schwarz was much nicer."

"Black people don't think so. They think it's the same."

Harry shrugged, pulled his feet down to the floor. "It's German for black, that's all."

Gary sat down, changed the subject. "Heard a bit of interesting gossip about OJ."

"Yeah? Gimme."

Gary related the story the kid had just told him.

"A backpack?" Harry asked, intrigued. "Interesting. Think OJ dumped it?"

Gary Minasian made a *who knows?* gesture. "What the kid said was: no way the thing could have got in the trash can by accident. Somebody had to put it in."

"And you're thinking it was OJ?"

Gary lifted his shoulders in an exaggerated shrug. "I'm not thinking anything except the kid was there the night OJ flew to Chicago at about the same time. And these two black guys claimed the backpack they pulled out of the trash was OJ's. And the kid says if it was OJ's for real, then OJ probably was the one who threw it away. That's it."

"That's a lot," Sarkissian mumbled. "I've been watching this thing. They put on a big search for the knife. Up and down the 405 from Sunset to the airport. They're sending guys to the landfill. Got cops going to Chicago to check the hotel. And this kid says OJ threw something away?"

Minasian nodded.

"But the kid doesn't know what was in it?"

"Right. He says the black guys didn't open it in front of him. They just said they were going to return it to OJ."

Harry thought about all this for a long moment. "What if it's the knife?"

"You mean the murder weapon?"

"Yeah. What if it's the knife, what if there's blood?"

Minasian's eyes widened. "I'd say the knife is worth a lot of money to Bobby Nazarian."

"I'm thinking the same thing."

"Maybe millions."

"OJ got that kind of money?"

"I'm sure. Still makes money in movies. Got that big estate. He seems to be on a hiring spree. Already got a bunch of lawyers."

Harry Sarkissian thought about the situation. "You got the kid's number?"

Gary Minasian nodded. He pulled the napkin from his pocket. "Right here."

"What's the kid want?"

"A job. Hinted around he was a good mechanic."

"You didn't tell him what we do."

"Of course not."

"But he seems to know."

Minasian raised his hands, palms up, another *who knows?* "Maybe he's heard something. I don't know. But I guess we can keep him in mind."

"Okay, give the number to Cheryl," he said, pointing to the door. "I'll have her bring him in for an interview. But in the meantime, why don't you call him back, tell him you've arranged an appointment with me, he'll get a call. And tell him to find the names of those two guys. Tell him I'm a friend of Bobby's, and Bobby will appreciate getting in touch with them."

Gary nodded. "A friend of Bobby's? You want me to lie?" he said with a smirk.

"Aw, just fucking do it," Harry said, dismissing him with a wave.

"Sure thing," Gary said. He got up and headed out. "I'll get right on it."

10

Garden and Lummie walked out of a Pack 'N Ship on Manchester Boulevard in Inglewood. Inside, a television was tuned to the OJ preliminary hearing.

"You hear that?" Garden asked, disgusted. "They want to yank a hundred hairs out of his head now? They torturing the nigga."

"I hate that word," Lummie griped. "Don't understand why black people use that word."

"Don't get touchy, okay? Fine. They torturing his black ass. Better?"

Lummie shook his head at his friend, but dropped it. "What they need a hundred hairs for?"

"It must be they must have hair from the murder scene. They trying to nail him for murder. So they gonna yank a hundred hairs from his head. They just torturing the man."

Lummie nodded. "Sure sounds like it."

They had a box, the size used for packing up books. Plus a short roll of packing tape and a bag of Styrofoam peanuts. Garden had just paid the clerk $4.35 for the supplies.

They went over to Garden's Camry and popped the trunk. They put a length of tape along the flaps to close the bottom of the box, then poured in a layer of Styrofoam peanuts to form a cushion in the bottom. They carefully laid the backpack on the bottom, then covered everything in more peanuts. They closed the folding lid and taped it shut.

Garden had a black sharpie. He drew an arrow pointing to the sky on the side of the box. He wrote "This side UP." Without thinking, he scribbled "OJ" on the top.

"That's stupid," Lummie said, pointing to the "OJ." "That just make someone want to look inside to see what it is."

Embarrassed, Garden regretted writing the letters too. He scratched some lines through the "OJ."

Lummie shook his head but said no more. "You know this stuff ain't keeping the knife from moving around in the backpack," he said.

"I know that," Garden replied, his tone put out. "I just think if it's like this, there's less chance the knife jostles around and ruins the evidence."

Lummie scowled. "What the hell you care if it's ruined? You ain't giving it to the cops anyway."

Garden slammed the trunk lid closed. He stared at Lummie with a peeved eye. "Lookit here. The lawyers ain't the only ones who'll get some of that big money OJ got in the bank. We getting some too."

Lummie turned his mouth down, an expression of surprise his friend had turned mercantile. "You think OJ's lawyers will pay you for it?"

"Yeah, I do. They want to make sure the cops never get hold of it, for damn sure. They probably dump it in the ocean. I give a fuck. I just want it in good enough condition that they know they *must* buy it. Understand? They got to think it got the blood and shit all over it and they got to buy it to save OJ's skin. Understand?"

Lummie nodded. "Okay, you think if it's all fucked up they won't have to buy it?"

"Precisely," Garden said, with obvious satisfaction. "I'll say to one of them lawyers: Hey, look, if this knife were to fall in the wrong hands, ya know?"

"Don't get cute. Better threaten to give it to the cops."

Garden scrunched his face. "Hate to even think of that."

"Hey, man, if you don't say you will . . . they don't have to give you no money." Lummie was adamant. "Only leverage you got is to say yo' next call is to the cops."

Garden didn't like it. There was something about even threatening to turn over the damning evidence to the police that just didn't sit right. It felt like snitching.

"Let's get it over to the house before Louise comes home from work."

Garden and Lummie drove two miles to Garden's house. Garden carried the box inside, and he and Lummie picked a spot in a cabinet in the family room, under the television.

"Louise don't ever get in this cabinet?" Lummie asked, shocked that his friend would pick such an obvious spot. "Maybe put it in your garage instead?"

Garden shook his head. "Kids rifling around in people's garages all the time," he said. "Much safer in the house. And she never go in here. It's where I keep my VHS tapes, and she don't give a shit about those."

Lummie looked. Yeah, there was a ton of tapes. In fact they had to take them out, slide the box in, and then put the tapes back, on top of the box.

Garden was satisfied with the arrangement for safekeeping.

"Okay, now how you goin' to get a message to the lawyer?" Lummie asked.

"Just wait," Garden said. "Let's see what happens with his lawyers. He already got rid of one. Let' see who's in for the long haul. We make our move in a while, not right now."

11

The two guys from the sanitation truck were in a '68 Mustang, Lime Gold. The radio was tuned to the OJ Simpson preliminary hearing in a courtroom downtown. Neither man was paying attention. Their minds were elsewhere.

Armen Shabaglian was driving, his partner Marcus Blake squeezed in beside him. Marcus had the passenger seat pushed all the way back, and still his knees were pressed up against the dashboard. His head bent forward. "You got a low roof in this piece of shit," he said.

"It ain't a piece of shit. It's a classic."

"Classic piece of shit. What's this? Twenty years old?"

"Twenty-six, but it's in showroom condition. I keep it perfect."

"Perfect would have some fucking room," Marcus grumbled.

The sanitation-truck partners were on Prairie Avenue in Inglewood, looking for a street called Manchester Terrace.

Even though they were working together today, both Marcus Blake and Armen Shabaglian were keeping a secret from each other: what each planned to do with the backpack when they got it back.

When the cops showed up at the sanitation yard, Armen and Marcus had already agreed to say nothing about the two black guys and the backpack. The cops asked if they'd noticed anything about the trash they picked up that night. Both men shook their heads no. Just trash. "We never look in the bags," Armen offered. Marcus just stayed quiet. He didn't like talking to cops, whatever the subject.

With the cops out of their hair, they made plans to retrieve the backpack.

Armen Shabaglian was looking for a way off the garbage truck. He hoped the backpack would help score a good job through Harry Sarkissian.

Marcus had a different agenda. He knew his brother Jumbo Blake would want it, especially if it had something to do with the Simpson murder. Jumbo ran a Crips set in Jordan Downs in Watts. Even though his brother was trying to transition from the drug business to the music world, he was in trouble with the DA and the

Feds. The DA had a grand jury looking to indict Jumbo Blake, and the Feds were waiting in the wings, ready to pounce. Jumbo needed something to trade.

Marcus was always trying to prove himself to his big brother. In fact, trying to prove himself to Jumbo was how he'd gotten kicked off the USC football team. They'd said he had gang involvement. When the school suits claimed that they'd just learned of his gang "connections," Marcus thought they were idiots. Who didn't know the biggest gangster in the city was his brother?

As for Armen, at first he'd puzzled why Gary Minasian was so interested in the story of OJ's backpack. But then it came to him: one of OJ's best friends was Robert Nazarian. Of course! The Armenians would be taking care of each other.

Then Gary paged. When Armen called back, Gary said Harry Sarkissian wanted to meet him. It would be a huge score if Armen could walk in with OJ's backpack. Mr. Sarkissian would love to be the one to hand it to Bobby Nazarian, Gary said. So whatever you can do. Armen got the point.

Armen had scouted the situation at LAX and figured out that the guy who retrieved the backpack was Gordon Grove—he knew the man as "Garden"—that he was a ramp supervisor, and that he lived in Inglewood. Armen did a simple phone-book search and found the address.

"You just back me up," he said to Marcus.

Marcus was a big man. Four or five inches taller than Armen, and thirty pounds heavier. He had sleepy eyes, a wide face, puffy lips, and a mouthful of teeth.

"So, I'm just here to be muscle?"

"No, man," Armen objected. "I just figured I'd be able to explain why we wanted it back. The bullshit story. Turn it in to lost and found."

Marcus didn't know what Armen's game was. He hadn't bothered to ask what Armen thought he wanted to do with the backpack. But it didn't matter. When they found the backpack, he was going to take it to his brother Jumbo, and the Armenian white boy could just go fuck himself.

And to make sure that happened, he'd brought along his nine, tucked into his waistband under the three-X shirt that hung to his dick.

Armen turned left onto Manchester Terrace, and he drove slowly looking for the right number. He found it, painted on the curb, in front of a pale yellow bungalow house with a concrete driveway leading to a garage in back.

"This is it," Armen said. "Let me do the talking."

Marcus grunted. He was quite certain it was eventually going to have to be a conversation black man to black man. But the Armenian kid wouldn't quite get that until the black guy told him to go fuck himself. That's when Marcus would step up.

Armen stood at the screen door and pushed on the bell. Marcus stood behind him like a granddaddy oak, tall and ominous.

A woman came to the door.

Louise stood behind the screen door, giving the two young men a jaundiced eye. "Yes?" she said.

"Ma'am, we're looking for Garden," Armen said, politely.

"Ain't no Garden here. There's a Gordon."

"Sorry, Ma'am. Yes, we came to see Gordon."

"Well, he ain't here either. What you want with him?"

Armen looked a little disappointed that Garden wasn't at home. "We kind of work with him over at LAX. I thought this was his day off."

"It was," she said. "But he got called in for overtime, so he's either there or he lied to me and he's drinking in some bar down on Manchester. You can go look for him either place."

She stepped back as if she were going to close the door.

"Ma'am, it's kind of important," Armen said. "Gordon brought something home that I've got to return to lost and found. Wondering if you've seen him bring home a small black backpack."

Louise was instantly irritated. Damn Gordon had picked up that thing belonging to OJ. She knew it would be trouble.

This dark-haired white boy was pissing her off. "Don't know nothing about no backpack. You go find Gordon—"

With that, Marcus had had enough. He pulled out his nine-millimeter, pushed Armen out of the way. He yanked open the screen door, brandishing the weapon. He was marching Louise backwards into her own living room before she could react.

"We're just going to look around for that backpack, moms," he said in his gruff voice, pointing the gun in her face. "You just park yourself on the couch."

"You can't—" she started to say, but his big black hand covered her mouth.

"You don't want to get hurt, just keep quiet." He pushed her onto the plastic-covered floral couch. "Just sit tight."

Suddenly, Louise was uncharacteristically docile. She sat quietly but glaring at the big man.

Armen came through the door, pale and scared. "I'm sorry, Missus Grove. My friend is just very anxious to return that item to lost and found. It belonged to OJ Simpson. I'm sure you've heard of him."

"Shut up," Marcus yelled from the next room.

"We'll try not to mess anything up," he said to Louise, apologetically. "But we've got to find that backpack."

Armen hurried back to where Marcus was opening drawers and cabinet doors.

"Don't leave her alone, peckerwood," Marcus said to him. "Go keep an eye on her."

When Armen returned to the living room, he found Louise on her feet pointing a pistol-grip short-barreled shotgun at him. "Oh, shit," he whispered. The business end of the barrel looked big and mean.

Louise waved the gun toward the couch. "Sit," she said in a soft voice.

They waited.

Then Marcus's voice boomed through the house. "Well, look at this!" He began laughing.

He walked back into the living room, holding a box. "Damn thing says 'OJ' right on top," he said, chortling. Then he looked up and stared down the barrel of a Mossberg 12-gauge.

"Oh, now, lady," he said in a make-nice voice. "You don't want to be doing that."

"Shut up," she said. "Drop that silly-ass nine on the floor."

Marcus did as he was told. "See, no gun anymore," he said. "White boy, take this," he said, and he tossed the box to his partner. Armen caught the box.

Marcus was hoping the sudden motion would distract the woman so he could grab her gun. But she didn't flinch.

Armen inched toward the door.

Louise shook her head at Marcus. "You know what I learned from the Inglewood police department after I got robbed about six times?" she asked him.

"What that, moms?" Marcus asked, a sneer creeping across his face.

"That's the second time you called me 'moms,' but I ain't your mama."

Marcus started to speak, but she cut him off by raising the barrel of the shotgun to his face. "I learned that you can go to jail for murder if you shoot the son of a bitch outside your house."

"Uh-huh," Marcus said, starting to be a little alarmed. "No doubt."

"But if you shoot the bastard inside your house, you practically get a medal."

Marcus raised his hands for her to stop. "Lady, I promise you. You don't want to shoot me. My brother Jumbo? He run the Jordan Downs set. You don't want him coming round."

"I don't?" she asked. Then she answered herself. "Actually, I don't care. You come into my house with a gun? What you expect? Cause I'm a woman, I just have to take it? And then you threaten me with your big brother and his gang? Tell you what. If shooting your ass brings him out here so I can shoot him too, then that's what I'm gonna do."

The Mossberg went off like a cannon. Big Marcus flew back into the wall, a hole the size of a basketball blossoming red in his chest. Gunpowder smoke filled the room.

In two panicked steps, Armen bounded out the door. He sprinted across the lawn to the Mustang.

Caught by surprise by her twitchy trigger finger, Louise tried to shake the ringing in her ears. She stepped forward and peered through the smoky room at the big dead man crumpled against a wall.

"Damn," she mumbled to herself. "Trigger too delicate." Then she remembered the other guy, the white boy. She spun around and stepped over to the door in time to see a pale green coupe racing down Manchester Terrace.

"Shit," she said to herself.

It was at this moment that Garden Grove's Camry bounced into the driveway.

Stepping out of the car, Garden saw Louise at the door, the shotgun still in her hands, smoke curling out the barrel.

Garden's face sagged at the sight. "What the fuck, Louise?" he implored. He walked past her, looked at the body of Marcus Blake slumped against the living room wall. And blood smeared down the wall.

"Bastard pointed a gun at me. Came to get that thing you had of OJ's."

Garden's face froze in shock. His eyes rolled around in his head. He turned to his wife. He tried to ask her what had happened. The words wouldn't come. He wanted to ask if the OJ box was gone, but he couldn't make his lips and tongue form the words. His forehead began to sweat. He felt dizzy. He felt like he had to throw up. His arm hurt, his back hurt. In the next moment, a train hit his chest. He groaned loudly, fell backwards clutching his chest, a look of shock on his face.

Louise stepped forward and leaned over to look at him closely. "Gordon?" she asked. "Gordon?"

Gordon didn't answer. She kept repeating his name, to no avail.

The widow could hear sirens. They seemed to be getting closer. Momentarily they were at her driveway.

An hour later, Danny Bowls set the phone back in its cradle at the assignment desk in the Channel 4 newsroom in Burbank.

"That was weird," he said quietly.

"What's that?" Mickey Judge asked. He was sitting in the next chair, scanning a computer screen.

"A home invasion in Inglewood. Lady of the house blew away the intruder with a shotgun."

"Good for her," Mick mumbled. "Justice is done."

"Weird part? He had a white accomplice who got away."

"That *is* weird," Mick agreed. "Hardly ever hear of that."

"Yeah, and this one doesn't have such a happy ending. The woman's husband comes home, finds her with the gun, body on the floor, blood on the wall, and he has a heart attack and dies."

Still concentrating on the computer screen, Mick frowned. "Terrible. Is that going to make air?"

"Stringer video and a reader, I'm guessing," Danny said. "Any idea how many black men are gunned down in Inglewood in any given week?"

"A bunch, I suspect," Mick said, taking his eyes off the computer and swinging around to face his friend. "Meanwhile, anything new on OJ?"

Danny Bowls shook his head. "Just the crap we put on TV."

12

It was an hour later, at 2:30 in the afternoon, when Armen Shabaglian pulled into a parking spot at Gary's Car Wash on Elk Street in Glendale. Armen's hands were shaking and his heart was racing. Sweat ran down his forehead into his thick black eyebrows and oozed into his eyes. He rubbed the salty sting out of his eyes and sat back in the car to take a few deep breaths.

"Holy shit," he said to himself in a soft voice. "What a clusterfuck."

He had called the Delerium from a phone booth when he got off the 134 freeway on North Brand. He asked for Gary Minasian, and the lady told him Gary was at the car wash, so he had come here. He didn't know what else to do. Seeing Marcus blown away was a nightmare. Hearing Marcus tell Mrs. Grove that his brother ran the Jordan Downs Crips set scared the shit out of him. He had no idea what he'd gotten himself into. He needed help.

The damn box with the letters "OJ" scribbled out on the top was next to him on the passenger seat. Armen desperately wanted to get rid of it. Maybe no one would remember he'd ever had it. But then he caught himself. That was stupid. Of course Mrs. Grove would remember. Maybe she'd tell the cops. Maybe she'd tell Marcus's brother. What was his name? "Jumbo," he said out loud. "Fuck me," he thought to himself.

Armen got out of the Mustang and moved the box to the trunk. In a fog, he stumbled inside. His stomach felt queasy, like he had to throw up, but he knew he had to be tougher than that to work for Minasian and his boss. He stiffened himself and walked on with a single purpose: stay cool, show cool.

Ten people were in the waiting room. A few were standing at the big soapy window, watching their cars move through the wash. LA's oldies station KRTH oozed softly from speakers in the ceiling. Most customers were sitting in chairs, thumbing magazines, one talking in a low voice on his phone. The man's cell phone caught Armen's attention. He wished he could afford a cell phone. A pager would have to do until he was making real money. He went to the back and knocked on a door that said "Employees Only." A voice inside said "Yeah," and he walked in.

Gary Minasian looked up like he was expecting him. "Cheryl said you called over at the restaurant. What's up?"

Armen sat down, uninvited. He noticed his hands were still shaking, which is not what he wanted to show. His throat was dry. When he tried to get some words out, he could barely speak.

Gary Minasian noticed. "What's up?" he repeated, this time not a casual greeting but a serious question.

A nervous laugh escaped Armen's lips. "I guess the good news is I think I have the bag for Mr. Sarkissian."

"The OJ bag?" Gary asked.

Armen nodded. He was having trouble swallowing.

"And the bad news?" Gary asked. Obviously there was bad news. He tossed Armen a bottle of water. "Take a sip and tell me."

So Armen told him, pretty much in the correct order of things: how he'd avoided telling the cops who came to the sanitation yard about the backpack. How he'd enlisted his co-worker Marcus to go get the thing, because he'd thought it would be good to be with a black guy going to see a black guy. How he'd started the conversation with Mrs. Grove real nice, and then Marcus had gotten tough, brought out a gun, and pushed his way into Mrs. Grove's house.

"Jesus," Gary muttered.

And then Armen told the rest. Mrs. Grove suddenly had a shotgun. She'd caught Marcus unawares. "Marcus had the box. He tossed it to me, maybe hoping she would turn the gun on me, I don't know, but she didn't. And then she blew him away. Just boom. A huge boom. Caught him right in the chest. A surprised look on his face. And I ran."

"Jesus fucking Christ," Gary muttered.

They sat looking at each other for the longest time.

"Jesus fucking Christ," Gary said again.

Armen cleared his throat. "One more thing."

"Oh, for chrissakes, what?" Gary said, disgusted. What more could there be?

The boy was slow to cough it up. Gary had to prod him again. "Come on. what?"

"This guy Marcus works the garbage truck with me. I didn't know much about him, except his pager number. But he says to the woman, Mrs. Grove, that he's got a brother who's a Crip."

Gary leaned forward, elbows on the desk. "He say the brother's name?"

Armen nodded. "I think I heard him say his brother's name is Jumbo."

"What's Marcus's last name?"

"Blake."

"Oh, for chrissakes, the brother is Jumbo Blake?"

Armen didn't know what to say. Gary was obviously alarmed. "I guess."

Gary sat rubbing his forehead for a long minute. Some of Harry Sarkissian's illegal activities overlapped with black gangs', but generally he and Gary tried to steer clear of Jumbo Blake. "Where's the box?"

They went outside to Armen's Mustang. He opened the trunk.

"That's it?" Gary asked.

"That's it. See the 'OJ' on the top, scratched out?"

"That wasn't so smart," Gary mumbled. He had Armen take the box to his own car, and put it in the trunk.

"What should I do now?" Armen asked. "Go home?"

"You don't want to be there when Jumbo Blake shows up," Gary said. "You better disappear for a while."

"Oh, Jesus," Armen moaned. "That bad?"

"Damn right," Gary said. He thought of the mayhem he'd seen Jumbo Blake leave behind. "Go home. Pack a bag. Call me. I'll tell you what to do next."

"What do I tell my girlfriend?"

"Do you have to tell her anything?"

"You know how girls are. I say I'm going somewhere, she'll want to know where."

"Do you live with her?"

Armen shook his head. "No. Not yet."

"Got a roommate?"

Armen shook his head.

Gary approved. At least he didn't have to worry about Jumbo's crew kidnapping an innocent. "Can you pack a bag and tell her something later?"

"She's at work now."

"Okay, go do that. Then call me." Gary gave him a slip of paper with his pager number scribbled on it.

Gary Minasian watched the green Mustang make the corner at Glendale Boulevard. "What a mess," he mumbled to himself.

Fifteen minutes later, he and Harry Sarkissian were staring at the box on Harry's desk. Minasian had walked in carrying it with paper towels on his hands. He didn't even want his fingerprints on it. Now it was Harry's problem.

Harry looked at the scribbling on top. The letters "OJ" were marked out with a few jagged lines.

"This could be nothing, you know," he said to Minasian.

Gary Minasian shook his head. "Cops came to see the kid, asked about it. The kid lied so he could bring it to you."

"Still might be nothing," Sarkissian repeated.

"Probably not nothing if the guy got blown away over it."

Harry put paper towels on the top of the box so he could hold it down without leaving fingerprints. The damn box could turn out to be the centerpiece of a murder investigation. But he wanted to know what was inside. He cut the tape with a penknife, used paper towels to gently pull open the flaps of the box. Inside, white Styrofoam peanuts. He reached in with a paper towel, felt something big, and slowly pulled it out.

"Oh, Christ, it's a backpack," Gary said.

Harry put the backpack down on his desk. Using paper towels over his fingers, he carefully pulled the zipper until the backpack was open.

"Jesus Christ, it's a knife," he said.

"It's a bloody knife," Gary added, bending over to look. "It's a fucking bloody knife."

Harry let go of the bag and flopped into his chair.

Gary sat down. They stared at each other.

It took a long time for either one to speak.

"Let's go over this again," Harry said. "Why would we think this is OJ's knife?"

"I'm confused," Gary confessed. "Let me page the kid, tell him to get in here. Go over this one more time."

"Don't bring him here," Harry said. "Meet up back at the car wash."

Forty-five minutes later, Armen was in front of Gary Minasian's desk at the car wash. Once again, he went over the story of the backpack, the two black guys fishing it out of a garbage bag in the back of his truck, swearing it belonged to OJ Simpson.

Gary Minasian gave him five hundred-dollar bills and an address in Selma, California, a four-hour drive north, about thirty minutes south of Fresno. "Tell your girlfriend you got a job up there for a week. Go to this place. See a guy named Billy Paboojian. He'll be expecting you. He does a little auto dismantling. You can help."

Armen was quietly elated. This was his "in." A chop-shop operation up in the valley. Things could be way worse. "I'm really sorry about Marcus," he said, though he wasn't really.

"Not as sorry as you'll be if his brother catches up with you."

That shut Armen up.

"Do what Billy Paboojian says," Gary continued. "Keep your head down. No running around getting drunk and crazy. Stay quiet. Keep your pager on. Work on whatever Billy gives you till I get back to you."

Armen Shabaglian thanked his new boss and did as he was told. Four hours later, he pulled into a gravel driveway on the outskirts of Selma. Billy Paboojian was expecting him.

Back in Glendale, Harry Sarkissian put in a call to Robert Nazarian's office.

He was thinking the knife had to be worth a million.

13

It had been days since the Bronco chase and OJ's official arrest. He was locked up tight in the LA County Men's Jail, walking down linoleum halls to meet with his lawyers in sneakers with no laces.

The LA County officials in charge of the jail were taking no chances that their most famous inmate might decide to kill himself. The sheriff, Sherman Block, couldn't see why he wouldn't. "Fucking guy was king of the world a couple of days ago. Now he's eatin' baloney sandwiches and wearing a jump suit," he barked at his staff. "Keep him under constant watch. And I mean fucking *constant*. No fuckups! It'll be your ass if something goes wrong."

But at the Channel 4 assignment desk, Danny Bowls was not informed of the Sheriff's actual quote. His source just said OJ was under close supervision.

Bowls and Mickey Judge were sitting side by side, reading the wires on computer screens. "Don't you have an office upstairs?" Bowls asked without looking up from the screen. He picked up a ringing phone, grunted "desk," and listened. "Okay," he said and hung up.

Mickey was looking at him, obviously wanting to know what that was. "Nothing," Bowls said. "Crews going to lunch."

"Yeah, I have an office upstairs," Mick said, returning to his computer screen. "But every time I sit at that desk, the phone rings and it's either my divorce lawyer or her divorce lawyer."

"What's this? Divorce number two, or three?"

"Fuck you. It's only two."

"So far," Bowls grunted. "By the way, that's the private office of a network correspondent," he said, mock scolding. "Look at these grunts out here in cubicles from hell."

"I'm an ingrate, I know." Mick doubled down on the kvetching. "But upstairs, New York people are crawling all over the place."

"So you're hiding out down here, hoping you can pick up a lead?" Bowls enormously enjoyed needling his friend. The downside of life as a network correspondent was a rich vein of material.

"Of course." Mickey nodded furiously, his mussed white hair bouncing. "That prick Wimple told me flat-out, anything I get comes straight to him. No fuckin' way."

"So you're okay with disobeying direct orders from your superior?"

Mick looked up at his friend with a furrowed brow and a frown. "Just between you and me, yes, indeed. I get the sniff of a lead, I'm gonna work it. I'll quit before I hand over my work to that prick."

"Attaboy," Bowls approved, thrusting his fist in the air. He went back to his screen and the phones. The ringing never seemed to stop.

A little later, Mickey got up to go. "I better show my face upstairs. Make a pain in the ass of myself."

"Hey, wait," Danny said. "Before you go, cover me for a few so I can take a piss and grab a smoke. I got nobody else around."

"Sure," Mick said. "Take your time."

The buzz of the Channel 4 newsroom was picking up, as crews and reporters came back from the field. Reporters went to work banging out scripts, then disappeared into edit rooms. Show producers were flitting around like bees, barking at writers, prodding editors to go faster. The usual stuff.

The phones never stop. Mickey answered the calls. He either blew off callers or transferred the call to someone who could handle whatever the issue was.

But one call caught his attention. "You guys completely screwed up that story," the voice said. "Just missed the whole thing." The caller sounded a little drunk.

"What was that?" Mick asked absently, purposely expressing little interest. Nut jobs were frequent callers.

"The brother that got blown away in Inglewood. That was all about OJ. You guys missed it." The words were coming out slurred.

Mick quickly glanced down at the caller ID screen on the phone console. He scribbled down the number on a phone message pad. "What'd we miss?" He ripped off the message slip, held it up looking at the number.

"You said it was just a home invasion," the caller said. "Just another brother shot in the 'hood. But you missed the real story, man." And he laughed. "You missed the fuckin' story." The voice laughed again, taunting. "Bunch of ignorant white peckerwoods. Just let the real story pass over top of your heads."

"What's your name?" Mick asked.

"My name?" the man laughed. "I'm Mister . . . Gone." Click. The line went dead.

Mick stared at the number on the message slip. He copied it over to his reporter's notebook under the name "Mr. Gone." He wadded up the message slip and tossed it in the trash can.

Area code was 213. Big area. But definitely not the beach or Orange County or the Inland Empire. Los Angeles. Could be anywhere in LA, but definitely LA.

He thought about what the voice had said. Mentioned OJ. Said we missed the story. Which story? Was it that one he and Danny talked about briefly a couple of days ago? The home invasion? The black guy killed by the homeowner? Supposedly a white accomplice who got away? That one?

Mick did a search of scripts on the computer. He found the story of the shooting two days earlier. He scribbled down an address on Manchester Terrace in Inglewood and the names of the two deceased. Marcus Blake and Gordon Grove.

Danny came back: as always, a man in a hurry. "What'd I miss?"

"A seven point three in Pasadena," Mick said.

"You're a dick," Danny smirked. "Nothing?"

"Just the usual cranks and reporters wanting transfers. How come they can't remember the producers' extensions?"

Danny shrugged. "Reporters. Brain-dead half the time."

"Hey, that home invasion shooting in Inglewood couple days ago?"

"Yeah, what about it?"

"Ever send a reporter down there?"

Danny shook his head no. "Think we ran a reader. On the five," Danny answered. "Probably a thirty."

That confirmed what Mick had found in the script file. Thirty seconds for the entire story. No wonder the guy said we missed it, Mick thought. A thirty misses everything.

Mick got up to leave. "You good?"

Danny grunted "uh-huh," already focused on his screens.

Mick felt bad—but only a little—for not telling Danny about the call. But maybe it was nothing. So maybe it didn't matter. Still, he knew it was kind of shitty to not say a word.

But it was a lead. He needed one. And hadn't Danny cheered him on with an "Attaboy" when he'd vowed he was going to work any lead he came across?

Upstairs at the network assignment desk, Mick scooted a chair up to the bank of phone books. Paul Dimmick, the desk guy, was answering phones, keeping the log on the computer. Paul was bald, tall, pear-shaped. He'd been on the Burbank network desk for twenty-five years.

"Mr. Judge, what are we working on?" he asked without looking up. The "we" always amused Mick. Technically, Paul never worked on anything. He just wrote down what others were working on, and called producers and correspondents to tell them what New York wanted them to do.

Mick knew better than to tell the truth. Paul was entering whatever he said in the log. The letters O and J could not be posted on the log without the entire network getting a heads-up.

"Gang shooting in South Central," Mick answered. He pulled the reverse phone directory from a row of heavy reference volumes and a seemingly endless lineup of LA phone books.

"For what show?" Paul asked, confused. He knew nothing of any of the NBC News programs wanting a gang-shooting story.

"Just something to keep me busy, Paul," Mickey said. "Who knows? Might turn into something."

That was good enough for Paul Dimmick. "Very good," he said, typing *Correspondent Judge, gang shooting, 'enterprise'* into the log.

Flipping through the pages of the reverse phone book, Mickey located the number. He wrote down the address. Inglewood. Made sense. The guy was gunned down in Inglewood. Maybe this might turn into something.

Half an hour later, Mick pulled up in front of the house. The address was on East Tamarack in deepest Inglewood, just off South LaBrea behind a fleet truck yard. It was a small house with a concrete lawn. The house was just a few blocks away from the location of the home invasion shooting on Manchester Terrace. This was starting to feel like something.

Mick parked at the curb, walked to the door, and rang the bell.

A tall black man answered the door. "Yeah?" he said through a crack in the open door. His eyes were wary.

"I'm with NBC," Mick said. "Were you the Mr. Gone who called to say we blew the story on that shooting a few blocks over?"

"Naww, man," the man said, but nervously. "I ain't no Mr. Gone, and I don't call no news."

"Look, the guy said the news missed the story. Had something to do with OJ. You know anything about that?"

The man looked even more jumpy now. "Naww, man. I don't

know nothing about OJ. Why would I?"

Mick bore down. "Somebody at this address using the phone in this house called the newsroom and said we missed the OJ connection to that shooting. What was it?"

"Naww, man, I know nothing about that."

"What's your name? I'm Mickey Judge." Mick extended his hand to shake. The man ignored it.

"Really rather not say. I gotta go." And he closed the door.

There was something about this exchange that just screamed *follow me* to Mick. That guy knew something. Mick just had to stay on him.

The house looked inexpensive, the kind a working man might afford to own instead of rent. Mick figured the guy's name might be on the tax records. He sat in the car with his flip phone looking through his combo phone book and daily calendar. He flipped through the pages until he spotted the scribbled name and number he was looking for. It was a woman he knew in the clerk's office downtown who could look things up in the tax records. She pretended to be bothered by his call, but she quickly looked up what he needed. She reported that the house was owned by a person named Luther Malcolm. "Don't be a stranger," she said before hanging up.

Grace Russell, he said to himself. He tried to picture her again. Petite. Chestnut hair. Did he have that right? He remembered a knowing smile and warm eyes. What color were they, again? He couldn't remember.

Mick moved his car farther down the block, where he could keep an eye on the house but might not be noticed.

He waited an hour. Nothing. He was about to leave when he saw an older Monte Carlo back out of the driveway. The tall man, probably Luther Malcolm, at the wheel. The car came directly at Mick.

Mick sprawled across the front seat so he wouldn't be seen. When he raised himself up, he saw Luther Malcolm's car turn left on La Brea. Mick fired up his Blazer, hung a U-turn, and followed.

He kept the Monte Carlo in sight, but there was a point at which Mick could not go further. It was the employee parking lot at LAX. Mick lurked outside the exit gate. He knew that an employee bus would come out soon. He wanted to follow to see where Luther Malcolm worked.

His patience paid off. A bus spewing diesel smoke eased through the gate, headed south on Sepulveda to the El Segundo side of the airport. Mick could see Luther Malcolm on the bus, but again he could only follow so far. The bus entered the airport at a secure gate.

Judging by the gate and the others aboard the bus, Mick figured Luther Malcolm was some kind of tarmac worker. Baggage or something.

The guy would get off work in about eight hours. Mick had to decide if he wanted to follow Luther Malcolm home tonight or stake him out in the morning.

Mick thought about whether there was an upside in bothering the guy late at night after a long day at work. He decided the morning would be best.

But the next two days—Saturday and Sunday—Mick staked out Luther Malcolm's house to no avail. The tall man came out twice to make a beer run. Otherwise, he was tucked away inside. Probably watching the Dodgers. It was a terrible way to blow a weekend, especially one when his daughter Kelly was swimming in a meet in Oceanside. He left her a voice message to do good.

On the third day—Monday—at six in the morning, Mick was sipping a 7-Eleven coffee in his spot down the block from Luther Malcolm's house. After a couple of hours, he was about to make a gas station run to take a piss when he saw the tall black man come out of his house dressed in a black suit.

This time, Luther Malcolm drove his Monte Carlo north on Tamarack, turned right on Manchester, and then a quick left on Prairie. He wound up at an address on Manchester Terrace. Mick checked his notebook. It was the location of the home-invasion shooting.

A limo was parked in front. Luther went into the house, and shortly emerged with a woman dressed in black. She seemed to be bickering with him, harping bitterly about something. It looked like they were dressed for a funeral.

The stretch limo was waiting for them.

14

Inside a small two-story house in the 4500 block of Anzac Street in the Jordan Downs district of South Central Los Angeles, bad news arrived by telephone.

The aspiring music mogul was listening to a demo tape from a kid who took the *nom de rap* "187Boi." The young man sat in a chair designed to make the sitter look up at the boss behind his massive desk. The kid's name was Jamal. There was a last name, but the boss didn't know, or didn't care. At first listen, Jamal seemed talented. He rapped about guns and drive-by's. The beat was good. The lyrics were okay. The performance was . . . well, the boss didn't hear a single.

The president of Bozman Records thought 187Boi was simply not good enough, but he tried to keep his options open. The kid sitting right there might turn into a star. Who knows? Best to keep the boy tied up.

"You wanna do some bodyguard work for me while you're working on your stuff?" he asked Jamal.

"Sure. That would be great," Jamal said. It was obvious to the boss that the kid was disappointed. What Jamal wanted to hear was the boss to be blown away by his tape. But the boss wasn't blown away. Bodyguard work sounded like the farm team.

The boss was well aware that there was lots of competition. Good competition. Dr. Dre and Snoop Dog were on fire, hits pouring out of their studios. And meanwhile his own productions were going nowhere. He desperately needed a hit; but reality was cruel: it sounded like 187Boi was not going to be the one.

The mogul was worried. He'd been counting on the record business to cut him loose from the drug business. But for now it appeared he'd have to carry on with the cash machine that was his drug organization. Drug money was what allowed him to try to jump to music.

If he hadn't already had enough worries, his lawyer reported that the District Attorney's office was empanelling a grand jury to look into his drug organization.

His troubles were piling up. And more were about to come.

The bad-news phone call interrupted 187Boi's music and the

boss's distracted thoughts. The boss held the phone to his ear, listened, his face sinking into a deep frown.

Julius Caesar Blake, the boss, set the phone back in the cradle, glaring at the device. His nickname was Jumbo, and he hadn't gotten the name by accident. He was a huge man. Six feet, five inches, just shy of three hundred pounds. His eyes were lidded, giving him a permanently wary look. His chin had disappeared into the folds of his neck years ago. When he scowled, brave men trembled. He was scowling now.

He ignored Jamal, the hopeful 187Boi rapper.

"Solomon, get in here," he shouted. Jumbo was seated behind a massive desk that was so large, it seemed to have a horizon. His office was a study in the fine art of overdoing it. The room took up half the second floor of the small house in South Central LA that served as his headquarters. Outside his door was an office for the overworked and much-abused Solomon, his assistant. There were no windows, because Jumbo believed in cameras instead. "You never hear about somebody getting his ass shot through a camera," he liked to say.

His office sported wall pieces Jumbo thought of as art. Jumbo's taste in art was highly personal: he liked splashes of color thrown at a canvas from across the room. They reminded him of blood spatters. He had a lot of those.

As a rap-music impresario, Jumbo also had the requisite music executive sound system. Stacks of speakers, turntables, reel-to-reel tape machines, cassette machines, and a video monitoring system linking his office to the recording studio on the floor below.

One corner of Jumbo's spacious office was set up for meetings at a long conference table. Another corner was arranged for more casual meetings on heavily upholstered couches around a massive coffee table, where one could roll fat blunts or lay out lines of coke.

"Solomon, get in here," he shouted again. Impatient.

Jamal tried to sink out of sight in his chair. The boss was angry.

Solomon Morgan hurried into the room. He was a lean but muscled man in his late thirties. He wore a graying goatee and kept his head shaved bald. He had a lined face, a thin nose, and a mouth he had learned to keep shut. He dressed in bright colors that seemed to leap off his dark skin. Today he was in Santa red slacks and a loose-fitting chartreuse silk shirt. Solomon Morgan was Jumbo's man, his most important man.

"You know what the fuck I just heard on that phone?" Jumbo asked, pointing at the phone.

Solomon glanced at Jamal, wondering if the rapper should hear whatever was coming next. He shook his head. "No, sir."

"The fucking cops. They say Marcus got himself killed." In Jumbo's manner of speaking it came out *Marcus got hisself kilt.*

Solomon recoiled. "Killed? Marcus? How?"

"In a home invasion. Lady of the house blew him away."

Jumbo's brother dead? Jamal pressed himself even lower in the chair. Trouble was brewing.

"Oh, man, that horrible," Solomon said with genuine sympathy. "I'm so sorry, man."

"You hear me?" Jumbo didn't seem to be in the mood for condolences. "They said a home invasion."

Solomon wrinkled his forehead. "A home invasion? Over in Beverly Hills?"

"No. Not Beverly Hills. Not Bel Air." An expression of deep revulsion descended over Jumbo's big face. "Fucking Inglewood."

Solomon jerked his head back in surprise. "Ain't no money in Inglewood."

"No shit," Jumbo agreed. "But they said he pushed his way into the house with a gun. Lady blew him away with a 12-gauge."

"Ooof," Solomon winced. "They sure it was Marcus? Don't sound like him."

The boss scowled. "Course it sounds like him. Hothead. I went to all that trouble to get him on the Sanitation Department, and he goes and does this."

The sanitation department? The boss's brother? Jamal immediately thought better of the bodyguard gig.

"But are you absolutely sure it's him?" Solomon asked again.

"Matter of fact, I'm not," Jumbo shook his head. "Can't figure out what he'd be doing over there. The cops want me to come to the coroner and ID the body."

The expression on Solomon's face turned to deep skepticism. "Careful. Might be a trap."

"I thought of that," Jumbo said, wearily. "Get Fink on the phone."

Solomon rushed out. Jumbo noticed Jamal, remembered what they had been doing only a few moments ago. "I don't know, man," he said, waving the young man off. "Hang around downstairs. Write some things. See what you come up with. I may need you from time to time for other stuff."

Jamal figured, considering the circumstances, getting to hang around was about the best he could expect. Relieved he wasn't just thrown out, he quickly disappeared.

In a few minutes, Jumbo was talking with his lawyer, an experienced attorney named Byron Fink. He specialized in criminal defense for black men from South Central who paid in cash.

"Cops might just be fucking with me," Jumbo brooded. "Chickenshit thing to do while identifying my dead brother."

"Sorry about your brother," Fink said soothingly. He was good at soothing. He had frequent occasions to console a client who had lost someone near and dear to bullet holes. "But I wouldn't worry too much about them pulling something. Even if they want to, it isn't time. The grand jury is nowhere near an indictment."

"You think I can go over there without ending up in a cell?"

"I think so. But if you do, call me."

Julius Caesar Blake pondered the short, violent life of his brother Marcus Anthony Blake. It was just like Marcus to go and get himself shot. Jumbo often wondered why something along these lines hadn't happened already.

"I still wonder if they running a scam on me," he mumbled to Solomon.

"But they Inglewood cops. You got no business in Inglewood."

Jumbo had to agree. That was true. The death of Marcus was very strange.

An elevator carried him down to the first floor of his headquarters. Sounds of a beats track escaped the studio door. Ordinarily he might have stopped in, but his mind was elsewhere. He walked out back to his car.

Sitting in his car smoking a blunt, Jumbo pondered his brother. He'd always hoped his brother could join the empire Jumbo had worked so hard to build. But Jumbo hadn't let Marcus in yet, because Marcus didn't seem to understand either the business of drugs or the rap business. The younger Blake demonstrated no finesse. He was all pushy muscle, violent; and much as that was sometimes needed in Jumbo's businesses, it also had to be held in check for the right moment. To Jumbo's great regret, little brother Marcus never could figure out the right moment.

Jumbo's HQ was the picture of gang and drug paranoia and security. The house at 4526 Anzac, near the Jordan Downs

Recreation Center, was a two-story stucco structure with a few bullet holes that needed patching. The house and a large parking area were secure behind a steel gate and a high fence topped with razor wire. A guard shack would have been a sitting duck in this neighborhood. Anybody could have shot it up. Instead, Jumbo configured the street side of the first floor as the lookout position for his guard team. His security men could see who was at the gate and activate the open/close function behind darkened ballistic glass. In fact, the first-floor walls were extra thick because behind the wall board, Jumbo had installed thick mats of soundproofing for the studio, which turned out to have the additional benefit of slowing down, in some cases stopping, bullets.

In most respects a normal-looking ghetto house, but in fact a bunker carefully designed for Jumbo's safety and security.

Anything but inconspicuous himself, Jumbo Blake drove an up-armored gold Mercedes E Class; he wore enough gold rope to tie up the Queen Mary; and he waddled his three hundred pounds around in tailored suits of iridescent colors that cost more than most of his nearby renters made in a year. Today's color theme was banana yellow.

The security gate rattled open, and Jumbo eased the Mercedes through, still second-guessing himself: Should he have brought Marcus into the business? Looking back, he supposed Marcus could have fit in somewhere. After all, Jumbo had employees who worked corners and alleys selling dope, and managers who managed them, and other managers who managed the managers. He modeled his operations after corporations he admired run by white people. Layered and delegated and accountable, his organization was the picture of modern business, from CEO Jumbo down to the street salesman.

And as far as the rap business went, Marcus could have scoured the streets for young men and women who wrote lyrics and made beats, but Marcus didn't seem to have the talent for that either. To Jumbo's lasting frustration, Marcus always seemed unsuited for Jumbo's business. He was impulsive, too often ruled by explosive anger. Worst of all, Jumbo suspected that Marcus resented his older brother's success and authority.

In a great swath of South LA's tired and threadbare black neighborhoods, Jumbo's drug operations encompassed Nickerson Gardens, Avalon Court, Hacienda Village, and Imperial Courts, the neighborhoods around his Jordan Downs home turf. In earlier years, he'd lusted for more territory; but to avoid jealousy of the other set bosses in South Central, he expanded out of town. He set up satellite drug-provider operations far away from LA, in Oakland and Sacramento and Riverside.

Jumbo knew the drug business always ended in sorrow. So he was looking to sell some turf to other more ambitious young men. And for himself, he was counting on rap music to rescue him. Suge Knight went around bulldozing people and managed to stay on top in music for years, but he also ended up in Pelican Bay State Prison. Jumbo had ambitions to become a prince of peace in the violent and tumultuous world of drugs and rap. He didn't want unnecessary fights. Gang murders were unproductive. Mostly.

So Jumbo couldn't figure out how his little brother had managed to get himself killed over in Inglewood. It didn't make sense.

He drove to the Medical Examiner's office near the LA County Medical Center to identify the body.

The Inglewood cops who were waiting seemed to be looking to the big brother for answers. But Jumbo's face was wrinkled in genuine confusion. A home invasion? In lower middle-class Inglewood, over by the cemetery? What would be the point of that? "No money over there," he mumbled. "Makes no damn sense." But when they pulled the curtain back, there was Marcus, dead as dead can be.

The detective thought Jumbo had had something to do with it, of course. He pressed Jumbo on whether Marcus was working for him. Most times, Jumbo's interactions with cops were an exercise in playing dumb. This time, he was sincere. He had no idea what his little brother had been doing.

Jumbo stood at the window, staring at Marcus's dead face, thinking of the promise he'd made to his late mother to take care of Marcus. He was shaking his head. He'd done the best he could. Now he'd have to figure out how this had happened to Marcus, for his dead mother at least.

After confirming that the body was his brother, he called Solomon from the gold phone in the Mercedes. He ordered a big funeral, "best casket you can find." He told Solomon to get a good spot in the Inglewood Park Cemetery.

On the other end of the call, Solomon hesitated. "Considering it happened over there, maybe you don't want to bury him in Inglewood. Maybe you want to think about Rosedale or Forest

Lawn. You know, the big-name cemeteries for dead white people."

Jumbo shook his head. "No. Some of the greats in Inglewood. Big Mama Thornton is there. T. Bone Walker. Murry Wilson." He stopped to think. "Sugar Ray's in there," he said. "That's where I want Marcus."

"Okay, boss." Solomon paused. He wanted to ask something. Jumbo could tell.

"What?"

"But . . . who Murry Wilson?"

"The father of the Beach Boys, dummie. If we aim to do things in the music business, you got to keep up."

Chastised, Solomon retreated. "Okay, boss, you right, you right." But he was thinking: *Who the fuck cares about the Beach Boys?*

Jumbo drove home trying to puzzle out the mystery. He knew who'd killed Marcus. That part was easy, and he'd certainly make arrangements for that bitch. But what the fuck was Marcus doing in Inglewood?

Home was a haul across town from the coroner's office down by the horror show people called Los Angeles County Medical Center. Jumbo couldn't get out of there fast enough. More suited to a man of means, Jumbo lived in the Hollywood Hills. Not a fact he liked advertised in the neighborhoods where he did business. Down there in South Los Angeles, it was best that he was as much a mystery as possible.

Home was a gaudy white-columned monstrosity perched on a hill in a small Hollywood neighborhood behind a gate on a street called La Gorda. As ostentatious as an aspiring rap mogul might envision for himself, the house looked down on the Capitol Records tower, and on a rare clear day he and his baby mama could see the bridge in Long Beach. But he was there for much more than the view. He had plans to conquer the music business. The house was his foothold in Hollywood.

It was also conveniently placed on an outcropping that looked down on the gate to the street. A well-placed camera on Jumbo's property allowed his household security team to keep an eye on who was coming and going through the main gate. Just a precaution.

As a player in the drug business, Jumbo had a lot of experience with cops. He knew how they worked when they investigated him. He'd spent years intimidating witnesses, and until recently had been one step ahead of the cops. The current grand jury investigation was jarring evidence that his methods of staying ahead of the law weren't always reliable.

However, he had learned a lot over the years about how the police conducted an investigation. Their techniques came down to a simple method: contact a lot of people and squeeze them for information.

But Jumbo was not into the shoe-leather part of detective work. Instead, he parked himself on the custom-built oversized chaise situated in a rose garden that used to be a pool before he had it filled with dirt. Jumbo didn't swim. He was scared to death of drowning. "I don't do pools, lakes, or oceans," he told the confused contractor he hired to fill in the pool. "But I like roses. Fill it in."

Comfortably ensconced next to blooms in red, yellow, white, and lavender, he called people on his cell phone. He had some white girls who brought him finger food and refilled his champagne glass. (His girl, a former maid to rich people, enjoyed having white girls working for her. "About time," Lashanda liked to say. "Them bitches can just wait on *ME* hand and foot for a change.")

Jumbo barked into the phone and sent people out to gather facts and report back. In a short time, information began to flow. He learned that the woman who had shot his brother was black, she worked as a nurse's aide at Centinela Hospital over near Hollywood Park and the Forum, and she and her husband lived nearby. And he learned that her husband, the late Gordon Grove, had returned to his home to find the wife with a smoking shotgun and a dead Marcus. The shock of it all was too much: Gordon Grove had dropped dead of a massive heart attack. So Mrs. Grove, too, had a funeral coming up.

In a crucial and confounding bit of information, one of Jumbo's best men reported back that Mrs. Grove had told the cops that Marcus had a white accomplice. Which also made no sense at all. Jumbo promptly sent a man to drop by the Sanitation Department yard to see if it might have been someone Marcus worked with.

Solomon also dispatched someone else to ask some questions among Louise Grove's co-workers at the hospital. He had yet another guy go to LAX to ask questions of Gordon Grove's co-workers.

There were some bumps—people who had to be persuaded to talk. But within a few hours, Jumbo Blake had learned a lot. And he was ready to see Louise Grove.

The woman who had shot Marcus would know best why he was there. Jumbo wanted to question her immediately after the Marcus funeral. To facilitate the meeting, Jumbo decided on what he thought was a clever course of action: he would donate funeral services to the grieving widow, including a plot in the same cemetery where he planned to put Marcus. God knows where a woman with a dead husband and a low-paying job would end up burying the man. Jumbo thought it would be convenient to have her within easy reach on a timely basis. He didn't want to dawdle on discovering what the hell was going on with Marcus.

Jumbo had a minister from the AME church approach the widow with the anonymous offer of a proper funeral for her departed husband.

In a further advance of his plans, Jumbo assigned his stretch limousine to Mrs. Grove's house to take her to her husband's funeral. She didn't need to know it quite yet, but afterwards the limo would take her downtown to his HQ and studio, where Jumbo could make further inquiries of her, where special methods could be employed if necessary.

That morning of the funeral, Louise Grove was in her usual mode: complaining. She was suspicious of the rather generous donation of the funeral expenses from someone she didn't know. "Who would do that, and what the hell they want from me?" she demanded of Lummie.

"Don't complain, Louise," Luther scolded her. "Somebody being very nice. You should try it for once."

Cranky was Louise Grove's normal. Didn't matter the target of her ire was dead. She redirected the bickering at her late husband's best friend, Lummie. But even the shrew was pleasantly surprised when she saw the stretch limo. That was a nice touch. She'd never been in a stretch limo. The limousine made her feel important.

Privately, Lummie also wasn't so sure of the overly generous gift. Somebody had purchased a plot in an expensive cemetery. Someone had picked up the tab for the casket and the funeral services, the hearse, the flowers, the works. Lummie was confounded. Who could it be?

After the burial, they both learned the truth, to their regret.

15

Three days into his stakeout of Luther Malcolm in Inglewood, Mickey felt that things were finally moving.

A stretch limo was idling in front of Louise Grove's house on Manchester Terrace. Mickey was down the block in his Chevy Blazer, slouched down in the seat. He had his binoculars pressed to his eyes, focused on the license plate of the limo. He scribbled down the letters and number.

He didn't possess much information, so even a little was something. He had that phone call mentioning OJ that he'd picked up at the Channel 4 desk. Plus that brief contact with Luther Malcolm at the house the call had been made from. And of course he had the address where the lady of the house had blown away a home intruder and her husband had died of a heart attack. As the husband's heart attack was evidently caused by shock at arriving home to the bloody scene, one could say that she'd killed two men with one shot.

Now he had a limo license number. Not that it seemed to have any relevance. But when grasping at straws, it was Mick's personal rule to not let any straws get away.

He observed two figures emerging from the yellow house. Luther and a woman, Mick presumed the widow. She was chewing on Luther, who was taking it, looking very much like a henpecked husband. They were dressed in black. Evidently it was funeral day.

They started to walk toward the older Monte Carlo, but the limo driver called them over. They talked to him for a few moments, then got into the limo.

Left to assume someone had sent a limo for them, Mick noted their surprise with interest. Why wouldn't they know in advance that a limo would be picking them up? Strange.

Now he had something. A buzz of excitement sat him up straight. "Rather be lucky than good," he muttered through clenched teeth.

Mick followed in his Blazer, a discreet distance back, keeping the limo in sight, allowing other motorists to get in between.

It was a very short drive to Inglewood Park Cemetery. He followed, but caution required that he stay out of sight. Mick parked near another funeral gathering, a large number of African Americans. He got out of the car, slipped on the black blazer he kept hanging in the vehicle for stand-ups. With black jeans and dark glasses and the jacket, he coincidentally looked like a funeral attendee. Or a limo driver.

Mick intended to walk past the cluster of people waiting for a funeral to begin, get up near another small burial group where he could see Luther Malcolm and the widow.

But before he could start, he was stopped.

"Dude, you can't be here," came a voice behind him.

He turned to find a white guy dressed in a dark suit. Mick immediately recognized the guy as a cop he knew. His name was Bristow. First name had slipped his memory, but he thought it might be Larry.

"Hey, man, what's doing?" Mick knew this cop from covering the occasional crime scene or emergency in West LA where the guy worked out of the station below Santa Monica Boulevard, west of the 405 freeway. Bristow spoke in hushed tones. "I gotta get you outa here before the client arrives."

"Sure, no problem. What's up?"

Bristow looked nervous. "I'm working private security for a funeral home. I gotta chase you off. This group is very private."

Mick shrugged. Better to get along with cops than alienate them. "No problem," he said again. "I'm headed over there," he nodded toward the smaller gathering a hundred yards farther on.

Bristow was a ruddy-faced Irishman, red hair, blue eyes. "Good. Can you do me a favor and just move your car up there a bit? This bunch is super paranoid and private."

"Sure," Mick said. "Who is it?"

Bristow nodded toward the crowd. "The fuckin' thing is crawling with gang-bangers with a gun in one pocket and a demo tape in the other."

"Why?"

"It's Jumbo Blake. Guess he's a wannabe music big shot. He's puttin' his brother in the ground. I had no idea it was him." Bristow grimaced. "If I'd known I'd be doing security for a heavy-duty gangster, I would have bailed. But I didn't know till I got here."

"Jumbo Blake? Don't know the name."

"You're better off. He does a lot of badass shit in South Central. His brother got blown away over here a few days ago."

That clicked in Mick's mind. "The home intruder?"

"Yeah, that one," Bristow said. "Do me a favor and just drive off. It'll look like I'm doing my job."

Mickey got back in his Blazer. "And one more thing," Bristow added, leaning in the window. "Please do not mention you saw me here. The captain and the LT would exile me to the late show in a heartbeat."

"Got it," Mick said. The late show. Eleven p.m. to seven a.m. Shitty shift. He started the Blazer and drove fifty yards farther on, backed into a turnout.

So that was interesting, he thought. Jumbo Blake burying brother Marcus the same day in the same cemetery that the widow who killed him was putting her husband in the ground.

Mick didn't believe in coincidences. Now his news radar was flashing red.

It seemed like the very minute he moved his car, he noticed a gold Mercedes roll up to the group of people he'd just left. A very large black man emerged from the car, and the crowd of people parted. He was dressed in black, and he was wearing gold chains, a gold medallion the size of a fist, and gold rings. The whole works so big that they gleamed in the sun from fifty yards away.

This was the guy Bristow was worried about. Jumbo Blake, downtown gangster, brother to shotgun victim Marcus Blake. "Hate to see that guy pissed off at me," Mick mumbled to himself, sinking lower in the driver's seat.

Peeking over the edge of the driver's window, Mick used the binoculars to spot the license plate. He wrote it down next to the limo plate. It was BOZMAN1.

He turned his attention back to Luther and the widow. It was a small gathering. Maybe ten, twelve people. A few women. Mostly men. Must be co-workers of both. An African American minister in a black suit, a maroon clerical shirt with a reverse collar was reading something from a bible that was so worn, it hung over his hand limp as a towel.

Mick called the Channel 4 desk. Danny picked up.

"You heard of a guy named Jumbo Blake?"

"Hell, yeah. Stay clear."

"Why?"

"All kind of bad shit in South Central trace back to him. Dangerous guy. Why do you ask?"

Mick lied to Danny again. "No reason. Somebody told me he was to be avoided. I figured you'd know if the guy was full of shit."

"The story I hear on him is he has a drug organization that the cops and the feds are determined to break up. Meantime, he's one of those South Central guys trying to cash in on gangster rap. Considerably less success there, but Jumbo Blake should be number one on the LAPD's most-wanted. At least that's what I hear."

That didn't sound right. The guy was walking around free as a bird. "If they want him so bad, why don't they pick him up?"

"They will. The second they can pin something on him. Believe me. Hey, gotta jump."

The next call was to the woman who'd gotten him Luther's name. Grace Russell was a mid-thirties brunette he'd struck up a conversation with at the courthouse a year or so back because she was attractive and he couldn't help himself. When he'd learned she was in one of the records departments, he got her number. She may have thought he was going to call for a date, but he had other reasons. When he eventually did call, it was for a favor: he'd needed her to look up something in the records she could access. She did. So she became an invaluable source.

Mick thought he knew Grace's type. The women who worked in the dark recesses of local government offices were either married with kids and a normal life, or they were single women who had a hard time meeting men other than cops and lawyers because of the nature of their bureaucratic jobs. They were desk widows. He'd pegged Grace Russell as one of the latter.

Mick kept the contact fresh by calling her occasionally, just to say hello, by sending her things every once in a while. A box of See's Candy out of the blue. A card at Christmas. She seemed to like the attention, but if she harbored a thought that he might be angling to bed her, he smothered that with the truth: he was married. "I don't date married men," she would say. Later, he didn't bother to tell her that the marriage was over. Last thing he wanted to do was to ruin a source by dating her. His personal relationships tended to go sour.

"What do you want now?" She liked to pretend she was put out. But in fact, she liked talking to the guy she saw on television. That white hair, the sympathetic eyes, the lean face. And he was tall. She liked tall.

"Didn't you tell me you had a friend at the DMV?"

"You're such a putz. I told you my sister is at DMV. Do you

remember anything I tell you?"

Not really, but he ignored the question. "I got the plate. I just need an address."

"Give it to me." Grace was quick.

Mick read off the letters. B. O. Z. M. A. N.

"Why didn't you just say 'bozman'?" she muttered.

"While you're at it, try this one too." He read off the plate number of the limo. No particular reason. He had it. Grace was willing to score one plate for him, why not two?

"You at the same number?" she asked.

He said yes, and she said she'd call back.

Mick had the Blazer backed into a turnout. He could keep an eye on the Jumbo Blake funeral and the other funeral too. Flipped through his notebook. "There's the name," he mumbled to himself. The Gordon Grove funeral.

After spending long moments shaking the widow's hand, hugging her, offering condolences in lowered voices, one by one the mourners drifted away. But Luther and the widow stayed in their seats, watching as the cemetery workers covered the coffin with dirt and replaced the grass turf on the surface.

Grace called back.

"Okay, here's what you need." She read off an address on Anzac Street, which Mick recognized in a vague way as being somewhere down by Jordan Downs.

"Something else you should know. The car is actually owned by an LLC called Bozman Entertainment Corporation. The president is Julius Caesar Blake."

Mick assumed that would be Jumbo. Entertainment? Did this guy think being a drug kingpin teed him up for the entertainment business? He guessed it was possible. Hollywood was bursting at the seams with gangsters out of South Central angling to be recording stars.

"And the corporation owns a lot of property around that address. In fact, it appears it owns an entire two blocks."

"Wow. This a residential area?"

"Uh-huh. Looks like houses, couple small apartment buildings."

Interesting. Jumbo surrounded himself with hand-picked neighbors. Guy was smart.

"Something else," she said.

"Yeah?"

"That other plate you gave me?"

The limo. "Yeah?"

"It's owned by the same LLC. Bozman Entertainment. Funny, huh?"

Actually, not so funny, Mick thought. Was Jumbo planning that the limo would take Luther and the widow home? Or take them somewhere else? Did they know the limo was his? More importantly, did Jumbo just want to exact revenge on the lady who'd killed his brother, or did the two of them know something Jumbo wanted? Like what was Jumbo's brother doing at Gordon Grove's house?

Was he after the same information Mick wanted? The OJ connection?

"One other thing I ran across in our totally awesome cross-reference computer program," Grace said.

"What's that?"

She paused.

He waited.

"Hello?"

"I'm here."

"What was it?"

Another pause. Then she spoke.

"Your wife's divorce petition."

Oh, shit. Mick was stopped cold. "That. Yeah." Mick stammered a little. "Things have been ugly lately."

"It's not all bad news. I don't have to worry about dating a married man now," she said brightly. "So, dinner is good. What night?"

There was no getting out of it now. It would ruin his contact with an important source if he tried to weasel. "Tomorrow?"

"Good," she said. "Perfect. Seven-thirty?"

"Yes. Call back, I'll let it go to voicemail. Leave your address and your cell number."

"Fantastic. I'm so looking forward to this." She sounded to Mick like she was actually excited to go to dinner with him. He called up her image in his mind. Attractive, for certain. Something intriguing about her smile. A petite woman. A way about her.

Okay. Might be interesting.

The line went dead, and as it did the limo returned, gliding by Mick's Blazer. The driver stopped a polite few feet back and let Luther and the widow watch the completion of the burial without being pressed.

Mick got out of the Blazer and walked up to the gravesite. He tapped Lummie on the shoulder. "Hello, Luther."

Luther Malcolm was stunned to see him. "You should leave us alone," Lummie said, instantly smoldering. "This is a damn funeral, man."

"Who are you?" Louise snapped. She seemed the kind of woman whose temper was set on high.

"He's a reporter. Been bothering me," Lummie griped.

"You should introduce me to the widow," Mick said. "I'm here to save you from something bad."

"I know you," Louise said, recognition in her voice, squinting at Mickey. "You used to be on Paul Moyer's news. Where'd you go?"

"I went to the network. Mickey Judge," he said, extending his hand.

"That a better job? Can't be. I don't see you no more," she said, scolding. "I'm Louise Grove." She shook his hand. "Save us from what?"

"Don't get in that limo."

Lummie took immediate offense. "The man brought us over here. What we supposed to do? Walk?"

Louise was also reflexively ruffled. "The young man was very courteous. Name is Laquan. He treat us real nice. He said he take us right home when we ready."

Mick shook his head. "Maybe not. That limo is owned by a guy named Jumbo Blake."

"Oh, shit," Lummie said.

"Oh, shit what?" Louise demanded of Lummie.

"He's the seriously dangerous brother of the guy you shot, Louise."

"So?"

"We can't get in that car."

"Well, what we do instead?"

"Come with me," Mickey said. "I'll get you out of here."

It was a slick reporter's trick he'd learned from an old veteran at the Associated Press. A smooth move Mickey always wanted to pull off himself.

The way the old guy explained it, to nail down an exclusive, always try to kidnap the story.

Get the person who is the center of the story into your car so nobody else can get to them. Then drive around and get him talking. In this case, Lummie and Louise.

When they clicked the seat belts in his Blazer, Mickey thought he'd pulled it off.

He didn't take into account the difficult widow.

16

"You know, I used to like you when I watched Paul Moyer's news program," Louise Grove said, gazing out the window at passing traffic. "Is this what you did when you worked for Paul Moyer, abduct people? Or you learn this now that you a big shot for the network?"

Things were not going so great inside Mickey Judge's Blazer. He and Luther and Mrs. Grove were headed east on Florence Boulevard, away from the Inglewood Park Cemetery. Mickey had a vague plan of just driving around asking questions until either one of his guests broke down and decided to tell him what was going on.

It wasn't working out like he hoped. One of his star witnesses—Louise Grove—was trying to bolt. And he was trying to talk her out of leaving.

"Mrs. Grove, I believe Jumbo Blake is a very dangerous man, especially for you. You killed his brother," Mickey said, looking up in the rearview mirror to see her face. "That's number one. Then I find out . . . luckily I find out . . . that the limousine you rode in," he paused to dramatize his point, "that limo is owned by Jumbo. It was actually sent by Jumbo Blake. That's his car. If you two got back into that car, no telling where it would take you."

Now it all came together for Lummie. He put his head in his hand and groaned. It was Jumbo Blake who had paid for the funeral. It was Jumbo Blake who had gotten them in a spot where he could trick them into his web. Lummie didn't want to say it in front of the reporter, but he realized—to his horror—that they'd been conned by a murderous thug.

Lummie was in the front passenger seat. He turned to look at Louise. "He right, Louise. Jumbo dangerous fella anyway. I'm guessing way more dangerous now cause of his brother getting killed."

"Lummie, shut up," she snapped. "You don't even know this here guy. He could be lying."

Lummie sighed. "Louise, it's not a chance we should take. You killed Jumbo's brother. He's OG Crips. He got to maintain his respect. He got to get even with you."

Louise Grove was not moved. "I want to go to my house. Mr. TV reporter, are you taking me to my house?"

Mickey could feel a migraine coming on. This isn't how things were supposed to go.

"Missus Grove, why did Marcus come to your house? What was he looking for?" Mickey asked, hoping to get her mind off the idea of going home. It didn't work.

"You going east on Florence. You need to turn around and go back west. My house back behind us."

"Okay. I don't think it's a good idea, but I'll take you home if you like."

"I like."

"Louise, I don't think it's a good idea either," Luther said again. "That man will come get you. And the cops took your gun. You think you can protect yourself, but you ain't got that gun anymore."

"Lummie, shut up," Louise snapped at him again. "I want to go home. I'll figure out how to keep that thug out of my hair. You and that dumbass husband of mine are what got us into this mess, bringing that OJ thing home, so just stay the hell out of it."

Mick lit up. *Bringing that OJ thing home!* There it is!

"What was it you brought home?" Mick asked Luther.

"Nothing. It was nothing."

From the back seat, Louise popped a rueful laugh. "Lummie, you lying through you damn teeth."

Lummie spun around in his seat. "Garden told me he didn't tell you nothing about it, Louise," Luther said, angry. "So you don't know nothing."

She got right up in his face. "The hell I don't. Gordon told me it was a little backpack belong to OJ that he found at the airport, in the trash. He was all proud of himself for finding something belong to OJ. He was strutting around like a rooster bragging he was taking it back to OJ Simpson. I know that for damn sure, cause I saw a backpack belonging to OJ Simpson with my own damn eyes."

Lummie couldn't believe Garden had lied to him. He turned back around, shaking his head.

Louise immediately shifted her focus back to Mickey and returning to her house. "If you don't take me home, I'm going to call 911 and tell them I'm in a car with a TV reporter and I'm getting kidnapped." She pulled a cell phone out of her purse. "Don't make me do it."

Mickey didn't want to let her go, but he really had no choice. If he didn't pull over, she really would be able to bring the cops, and that wouldn't help him at all.

"Stop the damn car," Louise shouted. "There's a cab right there will take me home."

A yellow cab was idling in a loading zone in front of an auto-parts store.

"Missus Grove, I really do advise you, don't go back to your house," Mick said, pulling the Blazer over to the curb. "I really think you must get out of town. Go someplace where he can't find you."

"How long I got to stay away from my house, Mr. Smartguy?"

"I don't know. But I wouldn't go back there today. He just buried the brother you shot."

Mick turned to Lummie. "Can you take her to Vegas or something?"

"I don't want to go to Vegas or anywhere but my own damn house. And Lummie, you just shut up. Caused enough trouble already."

Lummie looked at Mick and shrugged. "What can I say?"

"Okay, since you insist," Mick said. "But when you get close to your house, please look around for strange-looking cars. If you see one, tell the driver to keep going. Luther and I will wait here till we hear from you that everything is okay. If it's not," he stopped to emphasize the point. "If it's not okay, or if you have a bad feeling, just have the cab bring you right back here." Mickey gave her three twenties. And he scribbled his cell phone number on a sheet from his reporter's notebook. "Here's my number."

"Louise, I'll come with you," Luther said.

"No, you just ride with the white boy," Louise Grove said, sliding out of the back seat. She opened the door and stepped out. She waved at the cab to pull over. Then she came to Luther's open window. Louise Grove was one angry woman.

"Lummie, you are the man who got me in this trouble. You and that thick-headed husband of mine. You brought that OJ thing into the house. That's what brought those two idiots to jack me up. Which is what led to me shooting that one."

Her eyes were narrowed to bloodshot cuts. "So always remember, this is your fault. All of it. And if the big thug comes to kill me and I die, I want you to think about what you did that led to all this. Okay?"

"Louise, don't be like that. Just let me come back with you."

"I don't want you coming home with me. You forget I'm a grieving widow. But here's what I want you to do," she said. "Just remember this is your fault." Stabbing a finger in his face. "All. Your. Fault. Period."

Then she turned and stalked off. She jerked open the cab door, got in. Slammed the door.

This wasn't the way Mick had planned for things to work out. Now he had to worry that Mrs. Grove would end up dead or disappeared, which he assumed were the same things.

But. A backpack. This was new.

"So, what was in OJ's backpack?" he asked Lummie.

Luther Malcolm shook his head, disgusted with everything. "Why should I tell you?"

"Might be the only way to keep you alive. Marcus's brother might be looking for you too."

"So even if I knew, how's it help me to tell you what is in the backpack?"

Mick skipped that question. The answer he had right at hand wouldn't be very convincing. He needed to come up with something better. "So, you found a backpack that OJ left at the airport? Is that it?"

Lummie glanced away. Mick took it as a yes. "So what could be in it that was so important?" he asked, not expecting an answer.

But the answer came to him. "Luther, was it the murder weapon?"

Lummie's expression didn't change. He stared straight ahead. Again, Mick took it as a yes.

"Holy crap, you had the knife? Holy fucking crap." He stared at Lummie for an answer, but the tall man just turned away from him.

"What were you two going to do with it? Turn it over to the cops?"

Lummie shook his head. "Never do that."

That was as good as a confirmation to Mickey. The knife! It had been found. Now he knew he had a monster story. "Where is it now?"

Lummie let out a long breath. "I don't know. We had it in a box. Packed up good. The guy with Marcus took it, I guess."

"Who is that guy?"

"Don't know his name. Louise said a white guy but dark skin. Like Greek or something. Egyptian, maybe. Assume it was the guy who worked with Marcus on the garbage truck. Never knew his name."

Idling at the curb, Mickey thought about what he'd just learned. The knife was in a backpack of OJ's, which was now packed in a box. Likely in the possession of a white guy who came to Louise Grove's house with the now-dead Marcus Blake.

This was a huge story. A monster. It potentially ended the OJ trial before it had even begun. If the prosecution had the knife, the Simpson defense would have to punt with whatever plea deal they could get. And it probably wouldn't be a good deal. Life, if he was lucky.

His phone buzzed. Caller ID said it was Kelly. He knew he couldn't talk right now. With a pang of guilt, he let it go to voicemail.

He would call her later.

This development was big. Really big.

It didn't take long for Mickey to realize that he was the only one outside of Lummie and Louise and maybe the mysterious white guy who knew OJ's knife had been found. Maybe even the white guy didn't know.

But if OJ's team discovered this fact, they would be in a panic. Whatever defense his lawyers were planning could be blown out of the water by the discovery of the murder weapon.

His mind racing, Mick realized something else: if something happened to Lummie and if something happened to the white kid—whoever he was—no one would ever know the knife had been found.

At that moment, his next move became obvious: he had to get Lummie on tape.

Not just for himself, but certainly that part of the equation was enormous. *Nightly* couldn't keep him off the air if he had the knife story. But also for the case against Simpson. If he was the one who killed his wife and that guy she was bringing home, the knife would put him away.

Mickey pulled away into traffic.

"Where you goin'? We gotta wait for Louise to call," Lummie objected.

Mickey needed fudging the truth to work one more time. "We got to get you on tape, Luther. Maybe the only thing that will keep you alive."

"I ain't goin' on TV." Lummie looked at Mickey like he was asking him to jump off a building.

"I didn't say you'd be on the air. We just need to get your story on tape. Then we hold it to make sure nobody comes after you."

"Come after me? Who would come after me?"

"Whoever doesn't want the knife to be found. Getting you on tape might save your life."

"How?" Lummie asked the question staring at Mick with wide eyes.

Mick was afraid he was going to ask that. Skittish interview subjects often asked how going public would help them. Truth was, Mickey didn't always have a good answer. Most times, going on tape or going live was not in the best interests of witnesses or people who had information. Sometimes just the idea of being on television was enough to pull them in. Lummie wasn't one of those people. One glance, and Mick could see he wanted no part of being on television.

"I promise we won't air it now. We'll just keep it locked up. But we need to let people know you already told your story and it's on tape so there's no point taking you out." It was a stretch, but what Mickey lacked in logic he made up in fast talk.

"Who would want me dead?"

Great question. Obviously not the police or prosecutors. They'd probably rush him into protective custody. "Most likely it's OJ's people," Mick said. "The knife puts him away. Those people are your problem."

Lummie sulked. He hadn't thought of that. Maybe the reporter was right.

The 110 freeway was dead ahead. Mick swung a left into the northbound lane. It seemed like the freeway was enveloped in a brown cloud. Out the windshield, a river of cars as far as the eye could see. On either side of the freeway, storage units, gas stations, workout clubs, and fast food franchises marched alongside traffic in a repetitive stream. He was heading for the Criminal Courts Building. The trip was going to take a while.

A plan was forming in Mick's mind. If he could get Lummie on tape, he might be able to corroborate Lummie's story in some way. If he could do that, he might avoid being forced to turn the story over to that asshole Wimple. The prick was determined to keep Mickey off the air. But the knife story might be big enough that *Nightly* would have to carry Mick's reporting, face and all.

There were immediate problems. At this stage, Mick knew he couldn't call the desk and ask for a crew. They'd want to know what it was for. That would alert Wimple. He couldn't ask his friend Danny for a crew, for the same reason.

But there was something he *could* do. He knew that Alison de Groot put on a retired cameraman as a day hire to do the live shots at the courthouse for out-of-town reporters who dropped in depending on the day's events in the preliminary hearing. Mick knew that cameraman. He was old, slow, a guy near the finish line just going through the motions. After he lined up the shot and hit record, he never paid the slightest attention to what was going on in his viewfinder. Mick had actually seen the guy sitting in a tall director's chair behind the camera, sound asleep. It could be the Lincoln assassination: he wouldn't notice.

Mick checked his watch. The guy was still on the clock at the courthouse, doing midday live shots. All Mickey had to do was get there, put Lummie in front of the camera, and roll the tape. Then clear out of the area before other reporters or crews overheard what was going on.

It would be tricky, but he had to try. Lummie was going to slip through his fingers soon. Getting him on tape was now or . . . probably . . . never.

Lummie was brooding in the passenger seat. "I don't want to be on TV," he spoke up. "That sounds more dangerous than being an anonymous person."

"Just the opposite. First off, it's just tape. Not on TV yet. But the point is: OJ's people won't think of taking you out if they know there's already tape of your testimony."

Lummie wasn't convinced. Gloom descended over his shoulders.

From Florence and the 110 to the Criminal Courthouse where the Simpson preliminary hearing was under way was a thirty-minute drive, best case.

Mickey kept talking all the way. He hammered away on two points: Lummie was in danger; people would want him silenced. They might want to snatch him. His best defense against bad things happening was getting his story on tape. Bad people had to know that it would do no good to touch him. They had to know what Luther Malcolm knew, what he'd seen—OJ's knife—was already banked, tucked away for use if anything should happen to him.

Mickey knew Lummie had to feel fear, and Mickey poured it on. "We got to eliminate the incentive for grabbing you. Or taking you out. These guys don't play around."

Lummie wasn't sure he should trust this white boy. But he was susceptible to fear. And he knew that he had information that somebody would want.

"I don't think OJ's lawyers would kill me," he said in a sullen tone.

"OJ's side," Mick responded. "Maybe not his lawyers. Let's assume they're honest. But how about all the people who don't want him convicted? His fans, his friends. People who depend on him for money, the entourage people, the hangers-on? They're the ones who got the problem of the knife. They cannot have that knife show up in court."

Lummie grunted, wavering.

Mick pressed forward to close the deal. "Maybe that explains Jumbo. Maybe they already hired Jumbo."

"Maybe I should go to the cops. They would protect me."

Alarm bells rang in Mick's head. "No way, man," Mick said, arguing against perfect sense. "They take your story down, send memos to the prosecutors. Then they cut you loose and you're out in the world, a sitting duck. You know, Jumbo kills people and they never find a trace."

Lummie wasn't convinced yet, but he was close. "We gotta get back to Louise," Lummie said.

"Hey, she made her decision. Let's save you first, then we'll double back and see if we can help her."

Somehow Mick was getting it into Luther Malcolm's head that videotaping his story would save him.

Mick's thinking leaped ahead to what else he'd need. He knew he'd have to get more than just Lummie's interview to be a network-quality piece. He'd have to try to track down who had the knife. He would have to prove the story was true. Otherwise, New York would think Lummie was just a guy trying to angle a few minutes of TV fame by cooking up an outlandish story.

But getting Lummie on tape was a start.

At the parking lot downtown behind the Criminal Courts Building, Mickey scanned the row of cameras on the back balcony where reporters from the networks and the locals were doing live shots on the Simpson Preliminary Hearing. Wasn't even the trial yet, and the media was a circus.

Luckily, the NBC camera Mick was looking for was at the end, in the worst spot next to traffic noise, out of the shoulder-to-shoulder crowd of light stands and cameras on tripods that stretched farther down the balcony toward Spring Street.

Mick walked Lummie up the stairs at the end of the balcony. His interview subject was intimidated by the media scrum. "Don't let those people know who I am," he whispered.

"Believe me, last thing I want," Mick whispered back.

"Hey, Mickey, what's up?" the ancient Leon Butcher greeted him, surprised to see him. "I thought you were off this story." He worked half a day, but even that wore him out. He was gray, pale, and stooped.

Mick could see Butch had already pulled the lines from the camera to the microwave truck. Perfect.

"Butch, I'm on something else. I need a quick interview. Just line up a shot for me and hit record. I'll be outa your hair in ten minutes," Mick said.

"I gotta pack up, Mick," Butch said, giving Mick his Sad Sack look. "I'm supposed to be off the clock."

"It's okay," Mick assured him. "Nothing fancy needed. Just hit the record button and you're done. Go ahead, pack up your gear. I'll get this guy in the shot, get him interviewed, wrapped before you need to get the camera off the sticks."

Butch was hesitant, but he relented. "Okay, make it quick."

Mick clipped the lavalier mic on Lummie's shirt. He moved him to the X marked in gaffer's tape on the floor. Butch said "rolling" and turned away to pack up the rest of his gear. Crucially, Mickey noticed Butch didn't have his earpiece in. With the nearby traffic on Broadway, he wouldn't be able to hear a thing.

Mick had Lummie state his full name and where he worked. He confirmed that he worked with the late Gordon Grove, and the two of them saw OJ Simpson at the airport on the night of June 12. Then he told how he and Gordon Grove had suspected that a backpack of OJ's that was on top of a trash can had wound up in the trash, and they retrieved it.

"You're sure it was OJ's backpack?"

"I saw him put it on the trash can while he waited for his bag checks. Had a duffel over his shoulder."

But the money quote came as a relief to Mickey.

"Garden had me open the bag and look."

"What was inside?"

"A knife. A knife covered in blood."

Mickey tried to conceal his delight. It was a network sound bite. Short. Succinct. Devastating.

He asked more about what Lummie had seen in the bag just to get him to repeat himself and add some details. "I could see a fingerprint in the blood on the handle."

Then Mick decided he'd chanced exposing his exclusive enough. If he hung around too long, someone on the crowded back deck was going to come over to say hello and might overhear.

Mickey shut down the interview. He popped the tape from Butch's camera, gave the cameraman a big thank-you, and hustled Lummie away.

He and Lummie were back in the Blazer. "We better get back to Louise," Lummie said.

"We're on our way," Mick said.

The tape was in the seat pocket. Gold.

Mick was high on the adrenalin that was pumping through his body.

Through persistence, determination, and a little trickery, he had the big interview. Now he had something important. Not enough for air. Not yet. But it was a very good start.

17

Jumbo Blake was furious. "What you mean, they gone?"

Solomon was at the wheel. Jumbo was in the back seat of his gold Mercedes, speaking on his gold phone. Marcus Blake's mourners were driving away. The cemetery workers were filling the grave with dark brown dirt. Jumbo was watching them but focused elsewhere. His mind was on the two people who were supposed to be in his limo right now, on their way to his HQ downtown where he could work his magic and pop out some information. His thoughts were on this major-league screwup.

"Did you get the plate on that car?" He listened, then slammed the phone down. "For fuck's sakes," he muttered.

Solomon's eyes darted up to the rearview mirror. "What happened?"

"What kind of name is Laquan, anyway?"

Solomon shrugged. The boss sometimes obsessed on the strangest things. "All the baby mamas making up names like that. They think it sounds African."

Jumbo slipped off his gold-frame sunglasses. "Laquan," he began, with studied disdain, "Laquan said he was waiting for the two of them to get into the car; he looks up and a gray Chevy Blazer going down the road. Moving fast. He didn't want to damage the limo chasing them down, so he let them go." The bossman was furious. "Where we get this kid, anyway?"

"Lives in Crenshaw. Dorsey High."

"Okay. Well, we get nobody from there now. Maybe they all stupid. Why didn't we use Jamal?"

"He was busy in a recording session."

"Damn, my shit comes before his shit! What the fuck?"

"Sorry, boss. Thought we'd give Laquan a try. He got some good raps too."

Jumbo stewed. "Solomon, do I got to make all the decisions around here? I put you in charge of that, and what I get out of it? Fucked, that's what."

"Sorry, boss."

An angry silence fell over the interior of the Mercedes. Marcus,

Solomon, Jamal, Laquan. Surrounded by fuckups. "What we got on the guy Marcus was going to jack up? The name was Grove, right?"

Solomon bobbed his head up and down, sunlight flashing off his polished head. "That's the dead guy. But we just got word back that Marcus worked on the garbage truck with a white boy. A guy named Armen Sha . . ." he stumbled on the name. "Funny name. Armen Shabag . . ." he stumbled again. "Sha-bag-li-an, I think."

"Shabaglian?" Jumbo asked as if it were a revelation. "You know what that is?"

"No. What?"

Armenians," Jumbo grumbled. "Damn Armenians!"

He shook his head as if he should have thought of this already. "Let's go, Solomon. *Giddy the fuck up*."

His man was confused. "Go where?"

"Glendale, Solomon," he shouted. "Glendale! Where all the Armenians are!"

Solomon did the best he could, but figuring traffic it was still an hour from the 405 and Manchester Boulevard in Inglewood to the 134 and Brand Avenue in Glendale.

"Fucking Armenians," Jumbo muttered, over and over. "Fucking Armenians."

Eavesdrop on any automobile in LA with two occupants, and you overhear a heated debate on the question of which route would be the quickest and easiest. Of course, Solomon and Jumbo were no different. They quarreled about the way they should go. Jumbo wanted to go south on the 405, just below the airport pick up the 105 eastbound, then take the 110 north through downtown, connect to the 5 north and then go east on the 134 to Glendale. Solomon thought that was totally wrong. He gently insisted on going north on the 405, taking the 10 downtown where he could get the 5 and connect to the 134 into Glendale. "If you want to get there the quickest way."

They did it Solomon's way, but Jumbo seethed in the back seat as the endless diorama of Los Angeles apartment buildings, concrete office towers, strip malls, and off ramps clogged with automobiles slipped by his window.

The gold Mercedes slid to a stop in a yellow zone in front of the Delerium Ballroom. "Bring the iron," Jumbo said to Solomon. For himself, he took a Glock 9mm out of the rear-seat center console and dropped it in the pocket of his black mourner's jacket.

During Jumbo's long drive to Glendale, upstairs in Harry Sarkissian's office Harry and Gary Minasian were reviewing a tape recording of Harry's call to Robert Nazarian. As expected, Nazarian didn't believe the claim that Sarkissian was in possession of OJ's knife.

"Don't bullshit me," Nazarian's voice squeaked out of the small speaker.

"Ask your fucking client if he dumped a backpack with the knife in the trash at LAX. I got guys who said he did, and they retrieved it. Now I got it."

The tape ended abruptly. Nazarian hung up without another word.

Sarkissian smiled at Gary Minasian. "He knows OJ will say yeah, he did."

Gary nodded yes, he supposed so.

When Nazarian called back, it was obvious that Simpson had confirmed the information. Nazarian had a simple question:

"What do you want?"

"A million."

"Dollars?" Nazarian squealed.

"Fucking A," Harry said. "A million bucks and you can have the knife back. Otherwise, I sell it to TV, and they'll eventually turn it over to the cops after they milk it for ratings."

"You're a fucking prick," Nazarian said.

"Hey, it ain't your money. And we both know he got it."

"You're still a prick. I'll get back to you."

Harry clicked off the speakerphone. "What you think?" he asked Gary.

"Maybe he'll go for it. You didn't say how long he had."

"I don't hear back in a day or so, I'll make another call."

As the two men discussed the possibility that Harry was about to come into an easy million dollars, they didn't know what was happening downstairs. Jumbo and Solomon walked into the restaurant, breezed right past the hostess. Something about their look told her to shut up. They crossed through the kitchen to the staircase leading to Harry Sarkissian's office.

In deference to the boss's funeral, Solomon had toned down his wardrobe. He was in gray slacks and a black-collared sweater. Black wraparound sunglasses hid his eyes. His shaved head gleamed in the kitchen fluorescent lights. He looked South Central badass, just a little less badass than the boss, who was badass cubed.

They banged open the door to Harry Sarkissian's outer office.

Seated at her desk on the phone, Cheryl Bedrosian rolled her eyes. "You again?" she mumbled.

"I need to see him," Jumbo said as he and Solomon blew by her and barged into Harry's office.

Gary Minasian and Harry Sarkissian were discussing the chances that Nazarian would come up with the money. The racket in the outer office stopped the conversation.

The box containing the backpack and the knife was nowhere in sight, of course, locked in a safe house a few blocks away.

That precaution was because Harry knew that after the extortion demand, Bobby Nazarian might send some heavies around to just snatch the knife. After all, it's not like Harry could call 911.

But Harry wasn't expecting Jumbo Blake. He didn't even have his Doorricade door bar in place. It should have been across the door, but the security bar was hanging on its hinge, forgotten.

Both he and Gary were startled, but not truly surprised. The two men had discussed what might happen when Jumbo Blake discovered that his brother had been killed in the company of Armen Shabaglian.

Gary Minasian rolled his chair around to the corner of Harry's desk, facing Jumbo and Solomon. He figured it was unlikely that Jumbo would pull out a gun; but if he did, he might have a chance to draw his own.

Harry's eyelids drooped in a *what now* expression, and he opened his hands as an invitation for Jumbo to take a seat.

"I ain't sittin' down. I got some questions having to do with the fact you the king of the Armenians."

His brown eyes shaded by white bristle eyebrows, Harry waited.

"My brother Marcus got killed in a nothing little house in Inglewood a couple days ago. Lady of the house blasted him with a shotgun. I have no idea what Marcus was doing there."

"My condolences," Harry said, quite insincerely.

"I give a fuck for your condolences," Jumbo said. "Here's the deal. Marcus had a white guy with him. Now I find out he worked with a white guy on the garbage truck, probably same guy. And that guy's name was Sha . . ." he stumbled over the pronunciation. "Shabag. . . ."

Harry filled it in for him. "Probably Shabaglian. Common name. So what?"

"Any funny shit goes down in LA with a Armenian involved, it comes back to you. Who was that guy, and why was he and my brother pulling a home invasion?"

Harry Sarkissian knew this was about the box. And he certainly was not going to admit to knowing anything about it.

As for the Shabaglian kid, Harry reacted as if that was the last thing in the world he would know. "I don't know every single Armenian in LA, no more than you know every black kid with a gun."

"Listen here, Harry," Jumbo said. He put his palms down on the desk and leaned over, menace radiating off his enormous body. "My little brother and some Armenian guy were into some kind of shit, and I want to know what it was."

Harry Sarkissian needed to be both cool and fully duplicitous. "I have no idea," Harry lied. "I don't know a Shabaglian who worked with your brother."

Jumbo could smell lying. "Lookit, I stay out of your way, Harry, you stay out of mine. We got an arrangement. But this is different. My brother Marcus, he is in the ground this morning, not walking around like he should be. And the only thing I know is that he and some Armenian guy name of Shabaglian was doing something together. I want to know what the fuck it was."

Confirmed, Harry thought. He doesn't know about the knife!

Now Harry knew he had a huge advantage in this conversation. He simply shrugged again. "I don't know, Jumbo." Harry Sarkissian was good at lying with an honest face, not that Jumbo was taken in.

Jumbo Blake didn't like being told he was at a dead end. "Tell you what, Harry," he said in a soft but ominous tone, "you Armenian people got a school over here called Chamlian, I think."

Harry's eyes opened wide. That was over the line. Chamlian was an Armenian private school, eastern Orthodox. Many of Southern California's Armenian parents sent their children there. "Stop right there, asshole!" Harry jumped to his feet, poked his index finger like a gun at the center of Jumbo's forehead. "You know better than to threaten kids."

The big guy stood up straight and proclaimed his innocence. "Harry, I didn't threaten any kids."

"Don't play with me. You brought up a school. That's a threat when it comes from you."

"Harry, calm down," Jumbo said, his hands gesturing *stop*. "Look,

I got to do something to make you move!" Jumbo seemed almost apologetic. "I know you got grandkids. Sure, you're sensitive about kids. I got some babies here and there myself. I love kids. I think it's just best if you find a way to answer my question and bad shit never happens."

Harry's temper was rising. "Just leave the fucking kids out of it. You don't want cars and houses blowing up on those blocks you own downtown."

"See?" Jumbo said. "This is how wars start. You don't want a war. Me neither. So how about you just figure out which of your Armenians was with my brother and what the fuck they were up to. It's pretty damn simple."

Harry grimaced and seethed. Demands he could ignore. Threats were different. But Jumbo was right about one thing: he certainly did not want a war. Jumbo's goons rampaging around Glendale spraying houses with hot lead would eventually come back on Harry Sarkissian. What kind of crap was the local boss up to if he brought a war to Glendale?

"If the situation was reversed," Jumbo continued, "and you wanted to know what some black kid was up to when some Armenian got killed, I could find out what my guys were doing in a couple minutes."

Harry shook his head. "Never heard of the fuckin' guy."

"Well, you think about it. Make some calls," Jumbo said, pointing at Harry with a fat finger. "And you get back to me. *Com-fuckin-prende?*"

Jumbo and Solomon didn't wait for an answer. They were done. They both turned and stalked out, leaving Harry Sarkissian and Gary Minasian looking at each other.

"Think he's serious?" Minasian asked.

Disgusted, Harry Sarkissian nodded *of course he was*. "Always has been in the past. No reason to think he's not now."

"What are we going to do?"

Harry grimaced. "I don't want to, but we may have to throw him a bone."

"Give up Shabaglian?"

Harry shook his head. "That would be pointless. He'd learn about the backpack, and he'd want to know what the fuck that was all about."

Minasian gave his boss a cockeyed look. "You mean you're gonna pay him off to go away?"

Harry shrugged. "Maybe he doesn't need to know about the knife itself if he'd be happy with the cash. Maybe the price just doubled. Bobby Nazarian is just gonna have to deal with the new situation."

The two men were quiet, thinking. Harry broke the silence. "Let's get Risoroni on it. I need to know if Jumbo's got a weak spot."

Felix Risoroni was a private investigator Harry sometimes used when he needed deep background on someone. The guy was an expert snoop.

"I'll give him a call," Minasian said.

18

Lawry's Steak House on La Cienega in Beverly Hills was one of the places rich people lunched. Robert Nazarian was soon to be a familiar face to the millions who followed the OJ Simpson case on television. Jet-black hair with a white streak swooping back from his forehead, he had a face worn down by fixing other people's problems, not entirely unattractive, well-preserved—lotions and facials—but ordinary.

His seatmate in the upholstered booth was an African American lawyer, also soon to be known to millions watching the Simpson saga on television. Jimmy Cheatwood and Robert Nazarian had business to discuss about OJ even though it would be weeks before Cheatwood officially joined the Simpson defense team. The delay wasn't that Cheatwood was playing hard to get: he just needed to make certain that the trial would be downtown where he could get a black jury. And he had a plan for that.

This meeting was about something else entirely. Nazarian had been contacted by an Armenian acquaintance with a startling demand.

"He says he has the murder weapon. OJ's knife," Nazarian said, leaning forward, whispering.

"What?" Cheatwood's drink stopped halfway to his mouth. "OJ's knife?"

"He wants a million." Nazarian relayed this news with a straight face and a serious tone.

"Well, that's absolute bullshit," Cheatwood said. "How could some guy have the murder weapon? Don't forget, we're going to argue it does not exist, because OJ didn't kill anybody."

"Jimmy, it's Bobby," Nazarian said, a little exasperated. "She was knifed by somebody. There is a knife somewhere. If it turns up and it's OJ's . . . it's a problem. We might have to take this serious."

Cheatwood gave Nazarian an eye roll. He was impeccably turned out in a three-thousand-dollar suit the color of bronze, a five-hundred-dollar peach shirt, thousand-dollar diamond and ruby cufflinks, and a two-hundred-dollar floral tie in shades of green. Clothes, cars, houses, women: nothing but the best for Jimmy

Cheatwood.

"Bob, seriously. You've never done one of these cases. I have. The nut jobs come out of the woodwork. Honestly."

They had drinks in front of them. Menus were open. Neither earned their attention.

"Look, let me explain something about these guys," Nazarian began, patiently. "These are badass Armenians. I don't hang with them, because they got all kinds of funky illegal shit going on. That's number one. They're real."

"Who?"

"Harry Sarkissian and his guy, Gary Minasian. They run chop shops, insurance scams, swindles of all kinds—"

"Not even close to South Central," Cheatwood interrupted dismissively. "They kill people? They shoot up cars? Drive by houses, blasting away with AK-47's? Do they leave people on the side of the road in the desert with broken bones because they're a little annoyed?"

Nazarian started again, with a deep breath. "They might. Not a lot. Only if they have to. And they never do it themselves. They got somebody who contracts Russians so it never comes back on them. But they're real. They're serious. I think we have to look into this."

Cheatwood picked up his drink. Johnny Black and water. He took a long sip. "So we're going to assume for argument's sake our guy did the killing."

Nazarian nodded. "Regrettably."

"Let's start at the beginning. How do they say they've come by this knife?"

"What they said was one of their people works at the airport picking up garbage—"

"Garbage?" Cheatwood interrupted, startled. He was not expecting that answer.

"LA Department of Sanitation. And he picked up trash from American Terminal 4 the night OJ went to Chicago. And a small backpack containing a bloody knife was found in the trash."

"What's that got to do with OJ? LAX is a big place. Lots of people throwing away things."

"I know. But they say it was the very trash can OJ was standing next to as he was checking his bags. They say he dumped it. Expecting it would be in the landfill by now. But, instead, they have it. And they want money. Big money."

A serpent smile wriggled across Cheatwood's lips. His teeth flashed bright in the darkened restaurant. "Do you have any idea how I would tear that story apart in a courtroom if the DA brought that in as evidence and put some garbage man on the stand?" His eyes twinkled behind his gold-rimmed glasses.

Nazarian nodded in complete agreement. "I've seen you work. I get it. But what if …", here he paused.

"What if . . . what?" Cheatwood asked.

"What if the knife has blood and the blood is Nicole's. And Goldman's. And OJ's?"

Cheatwood paused to take a bracing draught from the drink in his hand. "Nicole's blood, Goldman's blood, no problem. OJ's blood? That would be a problem, but I'm sure I could get it thrown out."

There was no doubt that would be the tack Cheatwood would take, Nazarian admitted to himself. But still. "What if the world hears about that knife way before a jury is empanelled. We don't buy it, they sell it to the *National Enquirer* or Court TV. Every person in LA will have that knife stuck in their mind. It could be a disaster."

Cheatwood took a deep breath. "If the DA and the judge—whoever it turns out to be—or the Bar Association got word we were trying to obtain a piece of evidence to drop it in the ocean, it might be even worse."

The waiter came to take their order. Each man ordered a salad. They both knew they were going to be on television soon, and they wanted to look good.

"What should I do?"

Cheatwood took another slug from his drink. "First thing. What's OJ's real financial picture?"

Nazarian winced. Cheatwood's fee was going to be through the roof anyway, but there was no point in giving him privileged information that would jack it up even more.

"His accountant just bought him a giant annuity in case this thing goes sideways."

Cheatwood shrugged. "Probably just as well. Whatever else he's got will get chewed up keeping him off death row."

There it was. The lawyers were going to strip OJ down to his underwear, but they might save his life.

"So, how much is liquid?" Cheatwood asked.

Bobby Nazarian took a deep breath. "All in, probably twenty, counting a quick sale on the estate."

"He might be able to keep that for a few minutes, but not long," Cheatwood said. "So you think if we had to throw a million at this knife problem, we could do it?"

"As long as you weren't planning to clean him out."

That remark was taken as an insult and caused an uncomfortable pause in the conversation.

After a few moments of silence, by which Cheatwood made his hurt feelings known, Nazarian restarted things. "So, what should I do?"

Cheatwood had been thinking about it. "String 'em along," he said. "Don't say yes, don't say no. Say we have to see it. Dribble the ball. Let me think about it."

Reluctantly, Nazarian agreed. He didn't want to deal with the criminal Armenians, but he was worried they might actually have what they said they had.

19

Louise Grove either ignored or forgot Mickey Judge's advice. She did not look around for strange vehicles when she arrived on her block, as a precaution. Louise Grove was just too bullheaded for that.

She just handed over all of Mick's money to the cab driver and hopped out.

Louise didn't even make it to the front door.

She was teetering along her sidewalk, her nose buried in her purse searching for her keys, not looking where she was going. It was broad daylight. It was a sunny day. Visibility was perfect. But no one in Louise's neighborhood saw a thing.

Because they knew what was good for them.

In an instant, three men were on her. One clapped a gloved hand over her mouth, another took her under her arms, and the third picked up her ankles. As she squirmed and emitted some sounds that might have been screams had she not been muffled tight, they carried her to a waiting limo and had her prisoner in seconds.

The men gagged her, zip-tied her hands and ankles, and sat her on the banquette seat.

They put a bag over her head. They drove for about an hour. When the car came to a stop, Louise was fairly certain they were in South Central. She couldn't tell exactly where, but she had an eye on the compass in her head. She felt the car going north on the 405 and then east on the 10. She'd done it a million times. Whoever the driver was made no attempt to confuse her. They took her out of the car and into a building. From the sounds of booming hip-hop on the street, she knew she was in a black neighborhood. Pushed forward, she was taken in a building, then restrained in a chair with tape around her wrists and ankles. Then activity stopped. She waited a long time. She heard what she thought were the muffled sounds of music coming from somewhere. Eventually, she heard footsteps of men returning to the room. They took the bag off her head.

She looked up into the barrel of a Glock 9mm in the hand of Jumbo Blake.

Her eyes widened slightly at the barrel of the gun, but when she raised her gaze to Jumbo they narrowed to smoldering slits.

"I got you gagged so you'll have to listen," Jumbo said slowly. "I know you be mad at me. But I just don't want to hear it right now." Jumbo lowered the gun. "You just stay calm, because I am going to take the gag off and let you talk in a minute. You got that?"

Of course Louise was angry. It was in her nature. She got angry about a lot less. But it only took her a few seconds to realize she had no choice. She would have to save the tongue-lashing for Jumbo Blake until he took off the gag. *If* he took off the gag.

So she nodded *okay.*

"So, lookit here," Jumbo said. "You killed my brother Marcus. Shot a big ol' hole in his chest. What you got? A Mossberg? Damn, makes a mess, don't it?"

She glared. Jumbo noticed.

"Hell. They didn't even try to save him at the hospital. Believe you work over there at Centinela Hospital, right?"

Louise nodded. Reluctantly.

"Yeah. Well, they roll Marcus in there and took one look at him and called the coroner. The embalmer took more time than the emergency docs."

Jumbo shifted the gun from hand to hand, thinking about Marcus.

"So I think I got a right to kill you," he said, serious as a preacher. "But I also know Marcus did bust in your house waving around that nine of his, so I guess you had a right to shoot his ass. Though I must say, since it was my brother and since I promised my mother I'd take care of him, and since you essentially broke my promise, maybe I still got good enough reason to kill you."

Louise grunted. Jumbo thought he could make out a muffled "fuck you."

"Okay, so you want me to go fuck myself. But here's the thing. I know Marcus was a hothead. Hell, I didn't even let him work in my own enterprises. I made him go work a garbage truck. So I understand your point in shooting any son of a bitch who comes barging in your house with a gun. I get that. I'd do the same."

Now Louise gave him the one-eye squint that said *What you up to?*

"So here's what I'm going to do. I'll take off that gag so you can tell me what it was that Marcus and his white boy thought was so important that they come in your house with a gun. What was they looking for? And more important, did they get it?"

The room was rather plain. Louise glanced around and realized it was probably a soundproof cell. Maybe a torture room. Except there seemed to be guitar cases, and drums against one wall.

"So let me just add before I take the gag off," Jumbo said, as he reached for the gag, then pulled his hand back. "Nobody can hear you. I could fire a gun in this room, and nobody outside would hear a thing. Don't bother screaming. Save your breath."

He reached his hand to the side of her head, gave a tug to the blue Crips bandanna tied around her mouth, and it fell in her lap.

She stretched her mouth. The gag left marks on the edge of her mouth and across her cheeks. She glared at him. "If you didn't have that gun and I didn't have these things around my hands, I'd claw your eyes out."

Jumbo shook his head. He had to accept that she would be a hard case. "I don't have to explain again what I want, do I?"

She sneered. "Why would I tell you anything? You'd just shoot my ass the second I told you what I know."

"Let's get something straight, first," Jumbo interrupted. "Do you know anything?"

"Damn right I know something," she snorted. "It was my late husband who got us all into this mess because he found something. It was important and he brought it home, and that's why your brother was there."

"What was it?"

"I can't tell you that," she said, as if he'd just asked her something perfectly stupid. "If I tell you that, you just kill me. I don't think you even care if you get blood all over the walls and the floor, do you?"

Jumbo shrugged. "A little blood isn't a problem. But I hate it when bits of skull get stuck in the walls."

She gave him a peeved look. "See? Why would I give you what you want? Next thing you'd have pieces of my skull in your walls."

"But I ain't going to shoot you."

"I got no reason to believe that. You have to figure out some way to offer me a guarantee that after I tell you what I know, you won't kill me."

Jumbo's sunny expression turned into a mean, threatening glower. "What if I just apply pain? What if I put you on a table and pull a strip of skin off? What if I put hot irons some place delicate? What if I gouge out your eyes? What if I let men do things you can't imagine?"

Louise pursed her lips. "I can imagine a lot. Maybe I live through it, maybe I don't." She had a look on her face that said she was ready to face the worst he could bring.

"So, you gonna make me do the bad things? I got the water thing ready to go. People hate drowning."

"I ain't gonna tell you nothing till you untie me and make me feel safe that you ain't gonna kill me when you know what I know."

Jumbo shrugged. "Have it your way," he said.

"I was an Army nurse in the Gulf War," she said. "I had torture training in case Saddam fucking Hussein got hold of me."

"Let's just see how much you can take," he said, sadness in his voice.

"Let's just see how much you can dish out," she said, defiance in her voice.

He shook his head. "You one crazy bitch."

20

Mickey Judge and Luther Malcolm rolled up to Louise's house on Manchester Terrace and parked behind Luther's Monte Carlo.

Mickey shut off the Blazer. "Don't do that," Luther said. "You best be on your way. You done enough today."

Luther's air was quiet resignation. He wanted to get Mickey Judge out of his hair. Mick could tell Lummie felt betrayed. "Let me come in with you to check on her."

Lummie shook his head. "That will go very badly. She already mad at me. She hate you. Best be on your way."

"You think she's okay?"

Wearily Lummie answered. "Probably. Jumbo no fool. He not going to fuck with her the day he bury the brother she shot. What the Italians say? Revenge best served cold? He not gonna do nothin' for a while. Maybe we got time to get her out of town to relatives someplace. She must have some people somewhere who could put her up till Jumbo forget about it."

"You think he'll forget about her shooting his brother?"

Lummie winced. "Probably not. You right. Maybe she can sell the house and move someplace where he can't find her. I don't know. I gotta talk to her."

"Sorry, Lummie, but remember all I did was keep you two from getting in that limo."

The tall man slumped a little. "I know. But somehow it seem you did more. All this trouble come down on us when you show up."

Mick thought that was unfair. He wasn't the one who'd retrieved OJ's bag out of the trash. He wasn't the one who'd found the murder weapon and kept it in Garden's house. He wasn't the one who'd blown Jumbo's brother through a wall.

But there was no point in debating the matter. Mickey fired up the Blazer, and Lummie got out. "Let me give you my number," Mickey offered.

"Naww, man, I don't want that number." Lummie turned his back and walked toward Louise's house.

Reluctantly, Mickey pulled away from the curb and drove west on Manchester Terrace.

Lummie stopped and watched him go. He let out a deep sigh and continued up Louise's walkway to the porch.

Along the way, he noticed something in the lawn. The grass was long, overdue for a mowing. He bent down and picked it up. It was a lady's black high-heeled shoe. "Louise!" he said out loud.

Lummie hurried to the front door, pressed on the bell. No response. He pounded on the door and called her name. No response.

"They grabbed her," he said to himself.

He took the shoe and walked to his Monte Carlo. Louise would need her shoe.

He didn't like going down to South Central, but today he had no choice. He was sure Louise was in Jumbo Blake's headquarters deep in the hood, near the Jordan Downs. Supposedly it was a recording studio, but Lummie was sure there would be guys with guns.

21

In the aftermath of the frantic rush to get Lummie on tape, Mick felt as he often did when he got what he wanted. The elation he felt over confirming that there was an OJ knife and that it was in the wind—a huge story—was counterbalanced by a guilty funk about how he had left these two people. Louise was angry; and while her bitterness was most likely because her husband was dead, he couldn't help but feel that her anger had something to do with himself.

Then there was Lummie. He'd been weaseled into giving an interview he didn't want to give, make admissions he didn't want to make. Mick had a sharp feeling of regret over having just made things up in order to scare Lummie into the interview. And even though getting the man on tape was great for Mickey Judge, he felt a squirming guilt about putting the guy in that spot.

But he'd been through this before. It came with the job. A reporter often had to weigh the demands of the work—finding out stuff—against the reality that revelations weren't always good for the people who told what they knew.

The truth about the news was that it was never good news. It was always bad news for somebody.

Mickey believed the best way to shake off the discomforting feeling was to press ahead. Move along, put your regrets in the rearview mirror. Make trouble for somebody else down the line, and you'll forget the trouble you made for someone else who came before.

Burying the grief he caused had always worked before, but it wasn't working so great at the moment.

But so it goes.

He glanced at his watch. Still a couple of hours till the normal quitting time for working folks. He needed to find out something about the white guy who had come to the Grove house with Marcus. All he knew about the guy was that he was white and he worked for LA Sanitation.

He spotted a phone booth and jerked the Blazer to the curb. Phone booths were starting to become uncommon. The poor parts of town still had a few scattered around strip malls. The richer areas were starting to lose them. People with money were buying cell phones.

Mickey thumbed through the book and found the LA Sanitation Department. He placed a call and asked for the location of the yard near the airport. It wasn't far.

He found an LA San yard just south of the airport, where the trucks rested until trash pickup runs began in the early morning hours. Mickey knew there was no point in going into an office and straight up asking about Marcus Blake and his partner. HR would have rules about discussing employees. Instead, he pulled into the parking lot and waited.

Within an hour the shifts changed. As drivers and helpers streamed out of the facility, Mick looked for black men. He figured they would be the individuals most concerned about what had happened with Marcus.

Within twenty minutes, he'd talked to five African American men coming off shift. All of them said nobody had the same partner all the time, but they identified Marcus Blake's most consistent partner. He was a white guy named Armen Shabaglian.

So now Mick had another name. At this point, still no way to find him. Until he remembered his upcoming date with Grace Russell.

"Grace, I got your message with your address," he said when she picked up. "I was calling to see what time would be good, and what kind of place you'd like to go to."

"No, you're not. What else do you need?"

What was it in his voice that gave him away? Mick wondered. Maybe the girl was just smart.

"Actually, I was going to ask you to look something up, but I really did call about a place. You're in the Valley. Ever been to Casa Vega?"

She warmed a little. "I pass it all the time on Ventura, but I've never been. Sure, love that."

"Or would you rather go over the hill? Nicodell's down on Melrose. Across the street is Lucy's El Adobe."

"They sound nice too."

"Nicodell's is at the gate to the Paramount Lot. Next door to KHJ. Sometimes see a star or a deejay in there."

"That'd be fun."

"Then there's Musso and Frank's in Hollywood. Been there?"

"Oh, I'd love that," she enthused. "I went once. It's fantastic."

"Musso's it is. I'll make the rez for eight, pick you up seven-thirty.

We'll have time for a drink before."

"Fantastic," she repeated. She sounded really pleased. "I was looking forward to tomorrow night. Now I'm really *really* looking forward to it."

Mick wondered if that meant she planned sex. If so, he better pick up his apartment. Stack the newspapers and take out the garbage. Spray some Fabreeze here and there.

"So, what was the other thing you needed?" Her tone changed. Now she sounded more than happy to help.

"Oh, it's not terribly important. I'm trying to track down a guy."

"What's the name?"

"Shabaglian, first name Armen," he said, reading from his notes.

"Oh, an Armenian. Bet its Glendale."

"Why's that?"

"Lots of Armenians in Glendale. Around the courtrooms, even talk there are Armenian crime gangs, if you can believe that," she added absently, while she clicked the keyboard.

Armenian crime gangs? Mick asked himself. Better ask Danny about that.

She found an address for a Department of Water and Power account under the name Armen Shabaglian. Sure enough, Glendale.

On the way to locate Shabaglian, Mickey first stopped at the Burbank Bureau. A paranoid thought had hit him hard: maybe he should make a copy of the Lummie interview, a safety copy.

Getting the big interview was no good if something happened to the original. He parked in the lot and hurried into the building, hoping to avoid running into anyone who wanted to stop to chat. He used the staircase, ran up two at a time, walked purposefully down the hall of edit bays, giving a little wave to the people working. He sneaked into a vacant edit bay, popped the Lummie tape into a machine, cued it up. He put a blank tape in another machine, hit record, then started the playback machine. The dub took ten minutes.

Two tapes under his arm, he bounded up the stairs to his office, a man in a hurry. People tended to let you breeze by if you seemed purposeful and in a rush. He locked the original Lummie tape in the drawer of his desk and hurried out again before anyone noticed him or stopped him. He slipped the dub of the Lummie interview under the driver's seat of the Blazer. If the Burbank Bureau collapsed in another earthquake—a repeat of Northridge, let's say—he had a copy in the car. If his car caught on fire, he had the original in the Bureau.

He left the Bureau, his mind at ease. He had a safety. He was sure he was covered if disaster struck. The Lummie interview was protected.

Off to Glendale, a short drive from the Bureau. The Shabaglian apartment building was on Orange Grove, just east of Glendale Boulevard. Two stories, a pool in the center court, orange trees in front. Armen Shabaglian was the resident of unit #104.

Mick patiently rang the bell over and over, but there was no answer. The guy was gone. He rang another bell and got a woman to come to the door. The neighbor recognized him from TV and was glad to tell him Shabaglian said he'd be away for a week or two.

That was it. Dead end. The day's work was over. Mick would say three quarters successful.

On the success side of the ledger, Mick had Lummie on tape confirming that there was a knife and why he believed it was OJ's. That was big. Actually huge.

He also had the name of the person last seen with the knife. The Shabaglian guy. Lummie said it was in a cardboard box that he and Gordon Grove had personally taped up. But that box and the last person seen with it were gone. The knife was on the loose.

It was a good day, despite Mick hitting another wall. If this Shabaglian guy was gone, and there was no way to track him—at least no way Mick had access to—then he was at a dead end. For the moment.

Mick quickly realized he was going to have to reach out for some help. Of course, cops might have some way to track down Shabaglian. His acquaintance Bristow was probably too far down the food chain to be able to help.

Maybe it was time to confess to Danny. Maybe *his* cop contacts would lead to something.

But how to tell Danny he'd lied to him without the guy shutting down?

It was a problem.

22

South Central Los Angeles is just part of a vast city, but even a mere fraction is a big place. Luther Malcolm had a general idea that Jumbo Blake's headquarters was in the area of Jordan Downs. But he had no idea exactly where. What he did know was that everybody down there would know. All he had to do was ask.

After slogging through a thousand traffic lights straight east on Manchester Boulevard for more than an hour, Lummie found his way to the Jordan Downs Rec Center. The Watts neighborhood seemed to be bungalow houses on small lots with brown lawns and two-story housing projects interspersed every few blocks. He parked the Monte Carlo near the Rec Center, figuring there would be lights on after dark, in case he didn't make it back for a while. There was a small chance it wouldn't get stolen while bathed in bright lights. A small chance.

He asked the first older black man he encountered, and discovered Jumbo Blake's place was just a couple of blocks away. He walked over.

Lummie thought it was one of the strangest-looking houses he'd seen. It was behind a high fence and a serious steel gate, for starters. But the house itself was weird and ugly. There were big blacked-out windows on the first floor. He assumed that was where Jumbo's guards were. It was the only location in the house that had an unobstructed view outside. The rest of the ground floor had little windows that looked like nothing more than gunports. It was stucco. There were bullet holes here and there. The second story had no windows at all, just a bunch of pockmarks. And it was painted an ugly dark color. Might have been blue at one point, but the dust and air pollution had discolored the stucco. Now it was the color of mud.

Lummie leaned on the buzzer at the gate. A voice came on. "Move along, asshole. You got no business here."

"Yeah, I do," Lummie said. "I want to see Jumbo. Tell him the name is Luther Malcolm, and I'm here about Louise."

The intercom went silent. Lummie waited.

It took a few minutes before things started to happen. The motor on the gate cranked up, and the gate rolled slowly to the side.

Lummie stepped in, stopped, and waited. The gate rolled closed. Still, Lummie waited.

Then the door on the side of the house next to the blacked-out windows opened and three large black men emerged. They were wearing black jeans and black T-shirts and black muscles stretched their clothes.

One faced Lummie while the other two patted him down. "No weapons?" he said to Lummie.

"Naww, man, I don't do that."

"And you come round here?" the man muttered. "Some men born fools."

If that was supposed to get a rise out of Lummie so they could beat him down, it didn't work. Lummie just waited for them to finish their security check, and he followed the leader into the house.

He was led down a hallway on the first floor. He could hear the muffled sounds of a bass guitar and a bass drum coming through the walls. They arrived at a windowless room. There were cases and drums and an electronic keyboard pushed to one side. Lummie assumed it was an instrument storage room. Louise was in a chair. She was taped to the chair at her wrists and ankles. But she didn't have a gag in her mouth; she could talk, and she started in on Lummie immediately.

"Look who rode in on his white horse!" she mocked him. "What the fuck you doing just walking in?" she demanded. "I thought you might come to rescue me, but you got to have come with some troops, man."

"Got no troops, Louise, you know that."

"Well, fuck of a lot of good it do to just be another prisoner here."

"He torture you yet?"

"No. But he says he will. Wants to peel skin off. Said he'd let me sit and think about it a while."

"I don't think it'll happen."

She laughed at him. "What you mean you don't think? He torture you too, fool!"

"He won't torture me."

"Well, ain't you Mr. Crystal Ball," she said with all the scorn she could muster. "How you going to get out of torture when the fat son of a bitch decides he wants to torture you? They tape you to the chair, just like me, and then they pull your fingernails out and waterlog you and all that shit. And like a big dummy, you just walk into it."

"Ain't pulling no damn fingernails out, Louise. Ain't peeling skin off. Ain't doing nothing. Just relax."

"Relax? Easy for you to say. That big son of a bitch ain't come in to tie you up yet. But he will. Just watch."

The door opened. Jumbo Blake walked in, his face in a scowl that was more inquisitive than threatening. Solomon Morgan and Jamal the rapper were behind him, looking ominous. Jumbo walked straight up to Lummie, got right in his face. "I got a crew out looking for you, and you just come swaggering in?" Jumbo was perplexed. "What you think you doing here?"

"I come to get Louise," Lummie said, standing up straight.

"Oh, did you?" Jumbo raised his eyebrows like the arches under a bridge. "Well, why don't you take that tape off her hands and legs, and you two can just walk on out of here?"

Lummie nodded. "I know you're fucking with me now, but I'm here to give you what you want so Louise and I can just go."

"Since you know what I want, why don't you just tell me what I want." Jumbo sat down in a lounge chair and waved his arm for Lummie to take a seat. "I'm interested in you informing me what I want." Jumbo managed an air of both cordiality and menace.

"Lookit," Lummie said. "I know who you are. I'm not here to fuck around with you or try to squeeze a deal out of you. You want to know what was in that box your boy wanted when he stormed into Louise's house with that gun."

"Don't tell him, Lummie," Louise barked.

"Why the fuck not, Louise? What's the point of keeping it secret from him? We don't care. He wants to know. When he finds out what it is, he's going to be grateful enough to just let us go."

"Says who?" She spit out the question like something foul was in her mouth.

"Because he knows he can always come kill us later if he wants to kill us. Ain't that right, Mr. Jumbo?"

A smile crept across Jumbo's face. "Maybe you should tell me what you know, and we'll see how it works out."

Lummie nodded. "That's fine. I know what was in that box the white kid made off with, because I was the one who taped the box shut. Inside is a small backpack that belonged to OJ Simpson. Inside the backpack is a knife." He stopped to let the news sink in. "A knife. And it was covered in blood." He stopped again.

An incredulous expression crossed Jumbo's face. "OJ's knife? OJ Simpson's fucking knife? You lying?"

"No, I ain't lying." Lummie continued. "Louise's late husband Gordon and me, we put it in a box with those Styrofoam peanuts, and we taped it up," he continued. "Gordon put it in a cabinet in his house because he thought Louise never went in that cabinet because he had it full of his VHS tapes. But evidently she did, and I guess he told her what was in the box, because she knows."

"Wait." Jumbo stopped him, a deeply skeptical look on his face. "How you know it was OJ's knife?"

"I feel like I've told this too many times," Lummie said, as he took a deep breath. "Louise's husband Gordon and me were getting off work at the airport. We heard OJ was at the curb checking bags. So we went to meet him. I saw him with a duffel bag and a small backpack. The backpack was on top of a trash can right where he was waiting for his claim checks. Then I saw him go to the plane and he was not carrying that backpack. Then your brother and the white boy came and picked up the trash. We realized OJ had lost the backpack. We chased down your brother and his white boy and looked in the back of his truck and found that backpack."

The situation began to dawn on Jumbo. OJ's knife. The evidence that would put him away forever. "What were you going to do with it?"

"Gordon was going to return it to OJ when he got back from wherever he went. Well, now we know it was Chicago. But me and Gordon never got the chance."

Jumbo took it all in with a slightly surprised look and pursed lips. OJ Simpson's knife. "I want to understand this correct. You mean the one he killed his wife with?"

"That white bitch," Louise mumbled.

"I guess," said Lummie. "What else could it be? He left it at the airport the night his wife was killed. Would be in a landfill if it wasn't for Garden and me."

Jumbo turned to Louise. "This is important, Missus Grove. That box your friend describes. Is that what the white boy took from your house?"

"Why should I tell you that?" she snapped.

"Louise, for chrissakes," Lummie interrupted, raising his voice at her. "Tell him what he wants to know so we can get out of here. That's why I'm here. To get you out. Don't make it so damn hard." Luther Malcolm was angry, his eyes wide, his arms flapping the air in emphatic frustration.

Jumbo didn't say a word. He just slowly turned from Lummie to Louise. The look in his eyes said "Well?"

Louise was still angry, but softened. Lummie said he'd come to rescue her. That actually meant something.

"You came to get me?"

"Why the fuck else would I be here?" Lummie asked, exasperated.

Jumbo kept his eyes on Louise. His eyebrows tilted to one side like he was asking *Yeah. Why else?*

"Okay, fine," Louise said in a calm voice. "Yes. The box the white boy ran off with is the one Lummie and my husband put in the cabinet under the TV. Gordon told me it was OJ's backpack. I made him tell me what was inside, but I didn't see it. A knife. A bloody knife. That's what he said."

Jumbo nodded, taking it all in. He looked over to Lummie. "So the white boy had the box and inside the box was OJ's backpack and inside the backpack was a bloody knife. That what you telling me?"

Lummie nodded. "That's it."

Jumbo thought about it. The damn Armenians. Sarkissian, that asshole, undoubtedly lied about not knowing the Armenian kid. He had the box. He had the backpack. He had the knife. He was probably going to sell it to that Armenian asshole who was OJ's friend.

I'm going back to Glendale and I'm going to get OJ's knife, Jumbo thought. I'm going to take it away from him.

"Who else you told about this?" Jumbo asked.

Lummie squirmed. He was embarrassed about being talked into the interview with Mickey Judge, but at the moment Mickey's argument maybe made sense: telling his story on tape might protect him.

"I told a reporter."

Louise yelped. "What?"

Jumbo frowned. "What reporter?"

"A guy from NBC. I taped a interview with him. I explained the whole thing." Lummie fished around in his shirt pocket. "Here's his card."

Both Louise and Jumbo stared at Lummie. Neither one could understand anyone talking to a reporter.

Jumbo looked at the card. Mickey Judge, NBC News, Burbank.

"You mean the one who took us from the funeral?" Louise asked.

Lummie nodded yes. "That one. Yeah."

Jumbo's antenna went up. A reporter was the one who snatched them before they could get in his limo? Little reporter son of a bitch was looking for the knife.

"Yeah. Same one," Lummie continued, explaining himself to Louise. "He said it was an insurance policy against anyone trying to shut me up. My story was on videotape. Kind of made sense."

Jumbo shook his head. Lummie getting played wasn't even worth a comment. What it meant to him was that a reporter was on the case, same as himself. "Did the reporter know who had the box?"

"He knew it was a white boy. But I couldn't tell him more than that. I don't know who the guy is," Lummie said.

"I seen the guy on TV before," Louise volunteered. "Used to be on the Paul Moyer news, but he said he work for the network now."

A reporter was on the trail, but Jumbo was slightly relieved. He seemed to know more than the reporter. He knew the kid was an Armenian and, considering how the Armenians stuck together, that meant chances were good Harry Sarkissian had the box with the knife.

He stood up. He signaled Lummie to stand. "Why don't you get that crazy bitch out of my hair," he said, and he lumbered out of the room.

Solomon and Jamal followed him out. Solomon figured Jumbo might do something to Lummie and Louise sometime, just not right away.

Jamal saw an opportunity to impress the boss. Jamal knew how to blow up a house.

Lummie unwrapped Louise's wrists and ankles. They walked down a hall to the door. The gate opened for them. They walked a couple of blocks to his Monte Carlo, and they drove back to Inglewood.

Louise was quiet the whole way. She knew she should thank Lummie. He'd taken a chance, coming to get her. She owed him a thank-you at the very least. But it was just something she didn't say very often. She really didn't even know how.

So she stayed quiet while Lummie drove west on the 10 freeway and south on the 405 to Manchester Boulevard. It was a long time to stay quiet.

23

The gold Mercedes eased out of the gate on Anzac Street. Jumbo was at the wheel, a burning blunt in his right hand, his left hand on the wheel. Like Lummie, he also headed west. But Jumbo didn't return to his mansion in Hollywood. Instead, he drove along Manchester and took the 110 north. The Mercedes proceeded within the speed limit and glided through the interchange to the 10 freeway west. Fifteen minutes later he exited on La Brea. Jumbo continued north to Hancock Park, one of LA's most exclusive neighborhoods. He made his way through the leafy enclave of slate roofs and deep green lawns and shimmering swimming pools to Hudson Street along the west side of the Wilshire Country Club.

He pulled the Mercedes to the curb, got out, and surveyed the rich white neighborhood. This is where he wanted to be. But he knew Jumbo the drug kingpin would not be welcome. Jumbo the entertainment impresario might, provided he made his past disappear. He had goals.

He walked along an impeccably manicured hedge to the front door of a Tudor-style mansion. He announced his arrival by banging on the door with an ornamental knocker, and waited.

He figured there must be at least three cameras on the front door area. Jumbo waited patiently. He knew he was being examined.

A little time passed. The porch light snapped on. A man answered the door. He was tall, stoop-shouldered with graying hair, a middle-aged man's paunch, and a cautious eye. Lawyer Byron Fink gave Jumbo a quizzical look.

"Mr. Blake. What's up?" he asked, a little on the nervous side. His gang kingpin client didn't just show up on his doorstep absent a problem.

Jumbo arched his brows. "Do we really want to stand out here with the neighbors watching?"

"Right, right. Come in." Byron Fink stood aside for Jumbo to enter. His client was right. No point in the neighbors seeing this.

He led Jumbo to a library just off the main entrance. "Cigar? Drink?"

"Naww, man, this will be quick. It's business."

"Okay," Fink said, offering Jumbo a chair. He sat down heavily, even more stooped sitting than standing. "Tell me."

"I think I know how to get the DA and that grand jury off my back," Jumbo said.

Byron Fink was a little surprised. "Oh? How?"

"I need you to go tell them what I got and get a promise to end this bullshit case against me."

The lawyer winced. "They don't do a lot of that, especially at the grand jury stage." He gave Jumbo a game smile. "But it's always worth a shot. What you got?"

Byron Fink was a criminal defense lawyer whose clients tended to be both rich and guilty. Those two facts made Byron Fink rich as well.

"I'm sure all the lawyers in town want a piece of that OJ case," Jumbo said, his voice burbling out from the loose folds of his neck. He kept his eye on his lawyer for any sign of weaseling. "You in on it?"

Fink shook his head no. "Cohen is leading the OJ team. He called them all in for advice. A regular war council. He said all West Side Jews. I wasn't invited. I'm with the mid-Wilshire Jews, I guess. Not involved."

Jumbo nodded. He appreciated straight talk. "You think they got him nailed?"

Fink shrugged. "Not really. They got a bunch of circumstantial evidence. Don't get me wrong. He probably did it. But I expect Jimmy Cheatwood will end up on the defense and he'll make it a racism case. White cops, black celebrity. He'll find a white cop to be the bad guy." Byron Fink shrugged his shoulders and waved his hands in front of him as if to say *it's obvious*. "That sort of thing."

Jumbo nodded again. "That good enough to beat it?"

The lawyer in Byron Fink liked discussions of legal issues. He warmed to Jumbo's question. "Jimmy will do something dramatic like convene a meeting with black civil rights leaders and Garcetti— the DA . . . ," he added, as if Jumbo might not be familiar with the DA's name, "and he'll get the trial moved downtown where he can get a black jury."

"Why wouldn't the trial be downtown anyway?" Jumbo asked, surprised that was even an issue.

"The murder was on the West Side. Trial should be in Santa Monica. But for Jimmy it's a matter of too many white people out there. Jimmy would go through half the town trying to find one or two black people for the jury, and they'd be virtually white anyway. You know what I mean."

Jumbo did know what he meant. OJ was virtually white. Lived in the white world, owned a white mansion, slept with white women, married a white woman. White people thought of him as white. They'd never think of Jumbo as white.

"So, bottom line, the DA needs everything he can get his hands on to get his black ass convicted?"

Byron Fink winced at the expression, but nodded in agreement. "Yeah. Jimmy gets a black jury downtown? He's practically a god, as you know. Nailed the cops on the Louis Foster case. That was huge. Did Rollins. I don't need to tell you. Black people love him. If he says cops framed OJ, most likely they believe him."

In the silence that followed, Byron Fink was confused. "You agree? I'm sure I'm right."

It took a few moments of ruminating, but Jumbo eventually spoke. "Yeah, I do agree. So I got something, or I will soon have something, that will help the DA close the deal."

"And you want to trade?"

"Damn right."

Shaking his head, Byron Fink found himself confused. "No offense, Jumbo, but what could you possibly have that would help the DA that much? It would have to be something that would ensure a conviction."

"The knife. The bloody knife," Jumbo said.

"The *what*?" Byron Fink leaned forward to make sure he was hearing right.

Jumbo spoke slowly. "Shortly I will have the knife OJ used to kill his wife and that horny white boy."

Fink looked at Jumbo a long time, blinking his eyes, and then laughed heartily. "No way. You can't just give them a bloody knife. It would have to have her blood on it and the guy's blood on it, and OJ's blood on it. It would have to be the real knife. No bullshitting on this."

"I understand."

Byron Fink cocked his head, looking closely at Jumbo. He leaned forward in his chair and spoke in a soft voice. "And you have the knife?"

"I know where it is, and I'm going to get it. I want you to open negotiations to have them drop the charges."

Fink was trying to get his bearings in this conversation. "Wait. Let's talk about the knife you think is OJ's knife. Why do you think it is the knife, the real knife?"

The Fink library was dark, comfortable, quiet. Jumbo let his eyes wander over the shelves of leather-bound books as he tried to organize his thoughts. "Look, my brother got killed trying to get his hands on it. I'm told it's in a box. Was in a house in Inglewood. Long story, but my brother got shot and another guy ran off with the box."

"And the box contains the knife?"

"I've been told that in the box is a backpack of OJ's, and in the backpack is the knife."

Byron Fink interrupted. "Why do you think the knife is OJ's?"

Jumbo took a deep breath. Sitting in a wingback chair, he leaned forward, his hands on his knees. He told the story that Lummie Malcolm had related to him just an hour earlier. OJ at the airport going to Chicago. Checking his bags. The backpack on a trash can, OJ standing beside it. OJ goes to the plane, the backpack is in the trash. The two guys retrieve it from the trash, look inside, see there's a knife. Most certainly OJ's knife. "That's what I know."

Byron Fink rolled his eyes and rubbed his forehead. "That's a lot of stuff. You sure about it?"

"I'm sure of what I told you. I talked to the guy who saw all that."

"And he told you he saw the knife?"

Jumbo nodded.

"And he told you he saw blood on the knife?"

Jumbo nodded again. "That's what he said."

For a criminal defense attorney like Byron Fink, this was a bombshell. An unprecedented situation. He wasn't even sure how it would play out. A lot of people seemed to have been involved. That always complicated things. "Just so I have it straight, from what you know, since OJ Simpson lost possession of the box or the backpack— the knife—how many people have handled it?"

Jumbo scrunched his face, thinking. "I'm not absolutely sure, but. . . ." He paused, going over the list. "The guys who found it, then the guy who took it from the house when my brother was killed, then at least one more who has it now. Then me, when I get it. Which I'm going to do shortly."

The lawyer blinked at Jumbo. Stunned. "Wow," Fink said. "The DA is going to want to talk to the guy who found the backpack. Can you produce him?"

"I know where he is, yes," Jumbo said, even though he was a little startled to hear Lummie would be needed. That news complicated his plans for revenge.

"Let me think," Fink said.

They were quiet for what seemed to Jumbo to be a long few minutes. Finally, Fink broke out of his thoughts and spoke. "For starters, if I tell the DA you got something like you describe, they'll get a warrant, bum-rush you, put you in a wagon and tear apart everything with your name on it. They'll think they have a perfect right to seize it."

"So how do we do it?"

"We could go to them and say you have information that could lead them to this piece of evidence. That would be helpful, but I don't think that would be strong enough to get them to send the grand jury home."

"So?"

"So it's best if I don't say anything until you have the . . ." Fink paused, struggling with uttering the word "knife" . . . "the piece of evidence in hand. In your possession, I should say," he added quickly. "Not in your hands literally. Definitely not your hands. Don't touch it."

"Yeah, I know about evidence," Jumbo said, waving him off.

"At that point, I would open a negotiation. And at that point, you would have to stay secreted someplace unknown to me until the negotiations were over. Otherwise, they'd make me reveal your location, and, like I said earlier, they'd grab you and seize the evidence."

"Bottom line, I got to get my hands on the knife."

The lawyer held up his hands in the stop position. "Again, whatever you do, don't touch the knife. And if possible don't touch the backpack. The thing is worth nothing if they can't connect it to OJ, either by his blood or fingerprints or hair or something."

"So if I can locate the box it's in. . . ."

"Careful with that too. They'll want to establish who handled it by taking prints."

"But I need to check to make sure the backpack is inside and the knife is inside that? Right?"

Rolling his eyes, Fink thought about that. "Look, ordinarily I'd tell you to just bring the box in and let them handle everything from then on. However, in this case you want them to drop that grand jury investigation. If you walk in, hand over a box, and it's empty, bang. Your deal goes poof, we're back to square one, facing indictments. Understand?"

Jumbo nodded his big head up and down. The downturned mouth, the narrowed eyes, the flaring nostrils meant he understood. "Got it."

"So, try to get the crucial piece of evidence in your possession without disturbing it too much," Fink said. "Her blood, the guy's blood, OJ's blood? It's a winner. It's the Mega Millions if they can find his print on the knife. So be very, very careful.

"One more thing super important," Fink added. "Chain of custody. Very important."

"What's that mean?"

"Usually refers to who in the legal system possessed the piece of evidence. From the cop to the lab to the storage room, that sort of thing. But in this case, very important we can produce the two guys who got the backpack and put it in the box."

"One's dead."

"Okay, but the other one needs to stay alive. We'll have to hand him to the DA along with the box."

Shit, Jumbo thought. I came close to killing the guy.

Jumbo glanced at his diamond-encrusted Rolex. "I figure this session has cost me about five hundred bucks at your rates, so I'll go now."

Fink waved him off and let go a nervous laugh. "You get that knife, this session is free. I'll make up the fee, plus some, just in face time on television."

24

In the afternoon session of the OJ Simpson preliminary hearing, a witness named Sukru Boztepe took the stand. He was called to testify because he was the first person to see Nicole Brown Simpson's body, lying on a pathway to her condo in a grotesque pool of blood.

He described being led to the scene by Nicole Simpson's Akita dog, which attracted attention because it was loose on the street after dark, barking.

The Akita stopped and seemed to point with its gaze. Boztepe looked where the dog was looking. He saw Nicole's body. He said he saw a woman "laying down horizontally, face turned to me."

What else did you see? Marcia Clark asked. "A lot of blood. I just turned around and never looked there again," Boztepe said.

Twelve miles from the Criminal Courts Building on West Temple in downtown LA, Mickey Judge watched testimony from his office in the NBC Burbank Bureau. The producers who picked sound bites for the network package—the boy wonder David Moody's package—were pretty much in agreement that today's *money bite* was the witness who described Nicole's dog barking as *"a plaintive wail."* Mick thought Sukuru Boztepe describing seeing Nicole's body and the blood was better: *"I just turned around and never looked again."* That was the quote that encapsulated the horror of her slaughter.

But Mick's judgment was often out of step with the groupthink. Of course a dog would wail plaintively if its owner had just been savagely butchered on the sidewalk in front of her home. Dog owners—there must be hundreds of millions of them—would relate to that.

Mick stewed. Maybe his ear for a better bite explained why he didn't fit in with the network people so well.

Such was the thinking. The "plaintive wail" was the day's news. The wires said so. The other nets said so. The local television anchors said so.

What was killing Mick was the knowledge that the sound bite of the day should have been Luther Malcolm's: *"I opened OJ's backpack and saw the knife. It was covered in dried blood. I think I could see a fingerprint."*

That was a sound bite that would blow the windows off the Bureau.

But Mick couldn't let it out yet. He had to figure out some way to establish that what Luther Malcolm said was credible. That was the lowest bar. Mick didn't think he had to prove that it was truly the murder weapon. Was there a box, was there a backpack matching the one OJ had, and was there a knife inside? Those were the questions to be answered before the story was worthy of reporting.

The network wasn't going to air Lummie without confirmation of some sort, and while Danny and the locals might (the locals were more likely to run with a sensational but unconfirmed angle), making Danny's day would not necessarily help Mick.

He had the name of the guy who supposedly had run out of Louise's house with the box that supposedly held the knife. He had Armen Shabaglian's address. But the guy was MIA.

He needed a confirmation from Shabaglian and information on the location of the box, the knife, now. He was working the Shabaglian angle without any luck. He blind-called Armenian restaurants, the Armenian churches in Little Armenia—the Hollywood and Western area of Los Angeles—even Armenian grocery stores. Sometimes he would ask if the owner or manager knew an Armen Shabaglian, or if it was a restaurant he'd just ask for Armen Shabaglian cold, in the blind, hoping the guy was sitting at the bar. He knew it was a longer shot than a lottery ticket but (a) he had no choice, and (b) it kept him looking like he was busy.

He felt useless. A reporter was supposed to have ways of finding people. It's basically all a reporter was good for. Find a person who could tell you something. If you couldn't find a person, you couldn't get information.

He was stymied, and there were moments he wanted to put his fist through a wall.

Pushing his luck, he called Danny Bowls. "Let me pick your brain quick," he said. Mick hated making this call, but he was out of options.

"Shoot," Danny replied.

"Somebody told me there are Armenian crime gangs. Like in Glendale. That true?"

"Yeah. I don't know if you'd call it a gang, but a guy named Harry Sarkissian is supposedly the *capo di tutti* over there."

Mick scribbled the name. "What do they do?"

"It's not like drug gangs. The cops think they got chop shops, run some insurance scams, muscle in on real estate deals. They don't do drugs or girls. Very little gunplay, at least as far as I've heard. Kind of a higher-class gang, if you know what I mean. Why? What ya got?"

"Oh, just a sniff. Thought it might turn into something. Since I can't make air with OJ, maybe something else."

"Keep me posted. I'm sure we'd want anything you get. Sarkissian is well known. Runs the Delerium Ballroom. Plays golf at Chevy Chase. Saw him there once."

"Chevy Chase Country Club, Delerium. Those two places?"

"Wherever Armenians hang out."

"Thanks."

"Don't forget to let me know."

"You got it."

Except he was fudging again. Mick felt bad about picking the guy's brain with no intention to reciprocate, at least for a while. Maybe this Harry Sarkissian was a connection to Armen Shabaglian, though it seemed like a long shot. Sarkissian sounded rich, connected. Shabaglian was a kid on a garbage truck at LAX.

But. Couldn't hurt to go poke around.

First thing Mick drove to the Delerium Ballroom in Glendale. A big garish mirrored gold-trimmed wedding or party venue. The restaurant looked interesting. He asked the hostess for Harry Sarkissian.

The girl made a call, and momentarily a pleasant-looking middle-aged Armenian woman was standing in front of Mick. She said her name was Cheryl Bedrosian and she was Mr. Sarkissian's assistant. "Can I help you?"

Mick handed her a card, introduced himself, and said he was trying to locate a man. "I was hoping Mr. Sarkissian could help."

She cocked her head, as if this was a strange request. "Who is it you are trying to locate?"

"A young guy named Armen Shabaglian."

Cheryl Bedrosian knew better than to appear to recognize the name, but in fact it sounded familiar. Was that the name Gary had given her, to bring the guy in for an appointment? "Why would Mr. Sarkissian know the man?"

Mick shrugged. "I'm just taking a shot in the dark. Mr. Sarkissian knows a lot of people in the Armenian community, I would think."

"What does this Mr. Shabaglian do?"

Mick had been afraid she would ask. "My understanding is he works for the LA Sanitation department."

She smiled. "Mr. Sarkissian is supposed to know a garbage man?"

He could feel she was shutting him down. "I thought he might, for some reason."

"Mr. Sarkissian is not the village priest. He doesn't know everyone." She extended her hand. The meeting was over.

"You have my card," he said. "If something occurs to you, I'd appreciate a call."

"Certainly." She turned and walked away.

Mick felt like an idiot. And he felt like a drink.

He walked into the bar and took a stool. The bartender brought him a vodka soda. He sat thinking. What next?

"The boss ever come in the bar?" he asked the bartender, a young dark-haired woman.

"Not on Wednesday," she said. "Golf."

Danny mentioned Chevy Chase. "He like Chevy Chase, Oakmont?"

She popped a derisive laugh. "He's trying to buy Chevy Chase so Armenians will have a place to go. Oakmont's a joke. Think he plays LCF."

"LaCanada Flintridge?"

"Until he gets Chevy Chase bought, yeah. Think so."

Hurrying out to his car, Mick stopped in his tracks at the front door. On the wall, a large portrait of a white-haired man. "Your host, Mr. Harry Sarkissian," a sign below said. Mick studied the face. Prominent nose, a strong confident stare, bushy white eyebrows, and a glorious pompadour of white hair.

It was a twenty-minute drive up in the canyons toward Flint Ridge, LaCanada.

Mick valeted the Blazer at the clubhouse, and told the lady at the check-in desk that he had an appointment with Harry Sarkissian.

"He and Gary are supposed to finish soon. Are you joining them for lunch?"

"Yes, I am," Mick said. They might not know it yet, but . . . "Yes, exactly right," he repeated.

Mick was seated at a table in the dining room when he saw a guy he was sure was Harry Sarkissian arrive with another man he assumed was Gary. The hostess brought them to their regular table, where Mick was waiting.

"What's this?" Harry Sarkissian said to the hostess, gesturing toward Mick.

"Your lunch appointment. I seated him already."

"I don't know this guy," he said to her, and turned to Mick. "Who the fuck are you?"

Mick was standing, extending his card to both men. "Mickey Judge, NBC News Burbank. I just wanted to have a quick word."

Gary Minasian puckered his mouth, his eyebrows joined in consternation and his sharp eyes sizing up Mickey.

Harry Sarkissian nodded to the hostess that she could go. "What do you want?" Harry did not take a seat. He intended to make this quick.

"Mr. Sarkissian, I'm trying to locate a certain man. As an important figure in the Aremenian community, I was hoping you might know him, and might be able to put me in touch with him."

"NBC in Burbank. Are you the network, or Channel 4?" Sarkissian was shifting his eyes from Mick's card to Mick's face.

"Network news."

"You think I can help you find a guy?"

"I was hoping you might help."

"Why would you come to me?" Sarkissian's suspicions were rising, not diminishing.

"The young man I'm trying to get in touch with is named Shabaglian. Armen Shabaglian. I thought he might be someone you would know, considering your extensive relations with the Armenian community."

Gary's stare at Mick became even more intense.

"You think I know every Armenian in LA?"

"Not at all. I was hoping to get lucky. That you might know this particular guy."

"Shabaglian is a name I've heard, of course. But I don't believe I know the one you're talking about."

"I figure he's about twenty-five. Works for LA Sanitation."

Sarkissian laughed. "You come ambush me at my lunch, asking about a garbage man? Get the fuck out of here."

Mick reddened. He didn't mean to insult the man. "Look, I'm sorry if you take offense. I thought I'd ask you because you are such an important figure in the community—"

"Bullshit. You come to me because some cop said Harry Sarkissian has his finger on everything that has an I A N at the end of the name. I'm an honest businessman, and I've just about had it with the constant insinuation that I'm involved in some sort of underworld activity."

"Whoa. Mr. Sarkissian, I said no such thing."

"The fact you're coming to see me looking for a fucking garbage man with an Armenian name tells me you've been talking to cops and they've been slandering me again, as they always do."

"Hey, Mr. Sarkissian, no offense intended."

"Yeah? Well, offense taken. Get the fuck out. Please."

Mick held up his hands in a gesture that said *no problem.* "Sorry to disturb you. When you have a chance to think things over and you can help me out, you have my card."

"You're not going to hear from me. Please leave us to our lunch."

Harry Sarkissian stood his ground, with his *consigliere* at his side, both staring daggers at Mick, waiting for him to retreat from the clubhouse.

"It was good to meet you," Mick said. "Have a good day."

Walking back to the valet, Mick thought *Damn, that didn't go well at all, did it?*

Gary Minasian and Harry Sarkissian watched Mick go. They waited until he was out of the building before they sat down.

"Holy fuck," Gary said. "How'd that asshole get that name?"

"You sure you got that kid somewhere he can't be found?" Harry asked.

"Nobody's finding him at Billy Paboojian's. He's hidden in a sea of grapes."

"Better be," Sarkissian grunted. "At least until I get the money for that knife."

The two men ordered drinks and fell into silence, thinking about the sudden and troubling appearance of a reporter asking about the Shabaglian kid. Could the reporter know about the knife? Harry Sarkissian couldn't see how. Even the kid who'd brought the box to him didn't know what was inside. How could this reporter?

Still, it was troubling.

Back at the bureau, Mick went straight to his office and mulled his situation. No further along finding the Shabaglian guy, and managing to piss off an important man in the process. While tempted to forget the whole thing as a swing and a miss, it was nonetheless troubling. One thing to make no progress. Another to seem to be going backward.

The annoying Bart Wimple stuck his head in Mick's office. "Buddy, find anything new?"

Startled by the sudden appearance of his nemesis, Mick just shook his head no. "I'm working on non-OJ stuff," he bald-faced lied.

"Come across anything OJ, pick up the phone. I'm always available," he said, before ducking out as quickly as he'd ducked in.

"Will do," Mick said.

But here he was, sitting on a major development and definitely not keeping Bart Wimple up to date.

The tape of Lummie telling what he knew, the all-important interview, was locked in a desk drawer right under Bart Wimple's nose. That tape was just too important to not lock up. Who knows if a guy like Wimple might walk into Mick's office to look around when Mick was out?

After the Jansen broadcast, everybody decamped to Chadney's for the drink or two or three that unwinds. Mick didn't go. Too uncomfortable. Not just for him, but he knew it would be for everybody. He was the only one who wasn't in on the only story that counted in the Burbank Bureau.

Alison de Groot stopped by his office on her way out to join the others. "Ola, my boy. Care to wander over for a libation?"

Whatever else was annoying or tense in the network bureau, the Chief was a sweet woman who was always trying to make life a little easier for her people. She noticed when one of her charges didn't drop by to hang out in her office, check in with her. People often did, if for no other reason than to take the temperature of a news division that was subject to constant turmoil.

"Thank you for the invite," Mick said. "But believe it or not, I have a date." He smiled. But it was forced. He was fuming about being benched. She wasn't fooled.

"Jolly good. You need a little TLC," she said, taking a seat. "So, are you all right? Haven't seen you much out of your cave."

Mick appreciated her concern. He didn't want to lie to her, but he didn't dare tell her what he was doing. It would just put her in an uncomfortable position of holding something back from Wimple and Moody. Or, worse, betraying him by informing them.

"I saw on the log you were working on an enterprise involving a gang shooting. What's that?"

That damn log Paul Dimmick kept. Everybody read it.

"It was just something I went to take a look at, to appear to be busy, to be honest."

"Turn out to be anything?"

He shook his head. "A nothing-burger," he lied, and he hated doing it. "I just went down to Inglewood, took a peek, and came back. Just a gang shooting. Nothing for network." He hoped she was unaware he'd spent his weekend staking out Lummie's house.

She wasn't buying it. She was smart, and she'd been dealing with bullshitting correspondents and cameramen for a couple of decades. She could smell the dodge.

"You seemed to be MIA a long time."

Mick didn't panic. You can't panic if you're lying.

"You caught me. I stopped downtown at the courthouse to go to lunch with the woman who has been helping me out. She's nice. I asked her to dinner."

That particular lie seemed to do the trick.

"Oh, right, your date. A dolly for Mickey!" she lit up in a big smile. "A little romance back in your desolate life. That's sweet," she said, getting up. "Anyone we know?"

"I doubt it. A woman who has been kind enough to supply me with information from time to time. She has access to records at the courthouse. I kind of got ambushed. I asked her to look something up for me. In the process, she ran across my divorce filing."

"Oh?" Alison asked, expecting more.

"I was kinda trapped. She said it was time I took her to dinner, since she would not be going out with a happily married man."

Alison laughed. "I see. Hoist on your own petard. Well, try to have a good time."

The bureau was suddenly quiet. When *Nightly* wrapped, everybody but one desk person was free to clear out. Most nights, anyway. Sometimes people had to hang around to update *Nightly* for the West Coast. Not tonight.

Mick sat in his office, thinking about lying to Alison. Lying to Danny. Reporters often held back their best stuff until they got details nailed down. But it was another thing to just plain fabricate what he was doing, keeping his boss and his buddy in the dark.

He left the bureau to escape his guilty feelings. He had a couple of hours before it was time to pick up Grace Russell for dinner. He decided to shoot down to Inglewood to check on Lummie and Louise.

25

Lummie opened his door at Mick's knock. "Shit," he said. "You again?" His arm stretched across the door opening, blocking Mick from stepping in.

"Who is it, Lummie?" Mick recognized Louise's voice coming from inside.

"It's that reporter," Lummie tossed back over his shoulder.

"That little sonofabitch?" she said, and in an instant she was at Lummie's back. She slipped under his arm to get into Mick's face.

"You lying little sack of shit," she said, spittle flying as she poked Mick in the chest. "You said you were coming back for me, but you didn't. You ran off with Lummie. You took time to go all the way downtown to get him in front of a camera. Had to get a interview. You a selfish bastard. You left me to get kidnapped by that thug Jumbo."

"You got snatched?" Mick immediately felt guilty. She was right. But then again, she seemed to have escaped Jumbo's clutches.

"Damn right. I would have been tortured to death if it hadn't been for Lummie coming to rescue me."

Guess I missed some drama, Mick thought. "But you look like you're all right."

That seemed to amp her up. "Because Lummie came to get me," she repeated. "If it had been up to you, I'd still be a prisoner in that crack house." Louise was in a simultaneous tizzy of anger at Mick, and—weirdly, considering her cantankerous nature—evidently grateful for Lummie's efforts in extracting her from Jumbo's grip.

"I have Lummie to thank for being alive and well, not some selfish white news man with ulterior motives." Her face was alternately grimacing at him and glancing to Lummie with warmth.

Mick looked at Lummie. "What happened?"

Lummie shrugged. "Jumbo had her picked up. He wanted to know what was in the box. Said he was fixin' to torture her or something. But I just went down there and told him what was in the box. No point keeping it secret." He dropped his arm over Louise's shoulder, protectively. She did not object.

"Well, I'm glad things turned out all right," Mick said, sheepishly.

"That was very bold of you, Lummie. Things could have gone badly."

Lummie beamed, proud of himself. "He just wanted to know what was in the box."

"So he doesn't have the box," Mick said.

"Not yet," Lummie said. "But I expect he will. He seems to want it. And he's the kind of guy who gets what he wants."

Louise still had that puffed-out-lips look of defiance and injury on her face. "I still can't go back to my house. Luckily, I got someplace to go where he can't find me if he still wants to kill me. No thanks to you."

Mick took her onslaught for what it was. She was just attacking him to be attacking him. He had nothing to do with her jam with Jumbo Blake, but she was the kind of woman who would place blame wherever she could.

Lummie looked sheepish. "We going to stay out of sight here for a little while. Just to see if Jumbo's calmed down."

"Are you sure it's a good idea to stay here? You're just a few blocks from Louise's house, from where—"

"From where I shot that black bastard?" Louise interrupted.

"Yeah, from there," Mick agreed. "Maybe you should get out of town for a little while. Go out to Lake Havasu or something. Somewhere it's not so easy to find you."

Lummie looked at Louise. She shook her head, almost imperceptibly. "I think we're good here," Lummie said.

Mick took a card from his shirt pocket, handed it to Lummie. "Any problems, call me, okay?"

Lummie took the card. "I gave the other one to Jumbo," he said.

Uh-oh. "Jumbo knows about me?"

"Damn right," Lummie said with a sly grin. "He knows the white boy has the box, he knows the knife is in the box, and he knows I did that interview with you and you got a tape."

"Why'd you tell him that?"

Lummie's grin widened. "Why not? He wanted to know. And I wanted to get Louise out."

"But you didn't have to tell him about me."

Now the grin turned into a sneer. "Why not? Didn't you tell me if bad guys knew my story was on tape, I'd be safe?"

"But telling him it was me puts me in a vulnerable spot." Mick winced, hearing his own voice say those words. Lummie could hit him back.

And Lummie did. "So? You did that to me. I did something back to you." He stepped back, Louise still under his protective arm, and he closed the door in Mick's face.

Mick walked back to his car with unsettled thoughts. Okay, so now Jumbo knows I'm on the trail of the knife. He knows I did an interview with Lummie. He knows I know about the knife. And he probably figures I know he doesn't have the knife yet.

We're about in the same spot, Mick thought. And I need to stay ahead of him.

It was an hour fighting traffic back over the hill to the valley.

He had a little time to kill. He stopped at a flower shop on Ventura Boulevard and picked up some roses for Grace Russell. He picked yellow. Red would have been a little presumptuous.

Mick drove out Ventura Boulevard to Reseda, found the correct address, and knocked on Grace Russell's door. She had a nice house on a nice street. It looked like she was the picture of normality. He made up his mind to try to be normal too, though that was often chancy at best.

Grace answered the door with a gleaming smile and bright eyes. She was petite, chestnut hair to her shoulders, mischievous hazel eyes, and tanned arms. She was dressed in a tight blue skirt and a sleeveless white shirt, and mid-height espadrilles. Her legs were tanned and firm. She gave him the kind of hug that is meant to say "hello" and not much more.

Beaming, she said she loved the roses. She invited him in while she put them in water.

He glanced around the living room. Comfortable couch, deep blue. Large coffee table, looked like mahogany. Art on the walls, appeared to be nice stuff, perhaps a tad expensive. Pleasant colors all around. The girl had good taste.

"You want to have a drink first?"

Mick glanced at his watch. "Why don't we have that drink over the hill?"

"Perfect," she said. She grabbed a light jacket and her purse, and locked the door.

They drove through the Cahuenga Pass from the San Fernando Valley into Hollywood, chatting about her work and commute times and the fire season and a little bit about the OJ circus in her building, the Criminal Courts Building. "The elevators are impossible now," she said. "I have to give myself an extra half hour."

By the time they were seated at Musso's, she'd gotten down to the real stuff.

"So, why the divorce?"

His vodka and soda looked good. He took a deep pull before answering. "It was time to go. So I went."

"Oh. It was you who did the deed? The fifty ways to leave your lover?"

"Yeah, but I think she was doing the passive-aggressive thing. Setting it all up for me to go."

"Any kids?"

Mick played with his drink straw, thinking about the answer. It wasn't time to talk about the first wife. Too messy. She might bolt. Therefore, not time to talk about his daughter. "We don't have kids. But she has taken over raising her niece."

"How old?"

"Ten."

"Why does she have the niece?"

"The mom, my ex's sister, OD'd."

She winced. "Oh. Sorry. That's bad."

He wanted to get off his marriage details. Too ugly to get into and expect her to hang in. "How about you? You must have an ex-husband lurking around somewhere."

"I turned him in."

Mick laughed. "Like he was a car? Turned him in, like trading in a car?"

She smiled back. Mick found himself liking her a lot. She was very pretty, a sparkling personality. She charmed him like she had a fistful of pixie dust.

"No. I turned him in to the FBI." She smiled again.

"What?" Mick laughed again, a little louder. "You did *what*?"

She shrugged, like saying *what was I supposed to do*? "He was a crook."

"Aren't you supposed to be the loving wife? Protect your husband, can't be forced to testify against him?"

She flashed him that thousand-watt smile again. "I might have, if he hadn't failed to file taxes for five years, and if he hadn't been embezzling from his bank, and if he hadn't taken us so far down the road that I was in legal jeopardy too." She sipped her drink. A Cosmo. "He got what he deserved."

Mick sat back thinking, maybe his first wife wasn't such a horrible story. She hadn't teed him up for jail. "I had you pegged for a little more tender-hearted than that."

"I am tender-hearted," she objected. "But I'm not going down with the ship." There was that smile again.

Like he'd just been thinking, this was probably a good opportunity to bring up wife number one and his daughter. But still he let the moment pass.

A waiter appeared. Mickey ordered the grilled pork chops, a Musso Frank's specialty. She ordered the swordfish, grilled. They got sides of creamed spinach and potatoes au gratin. They got side salads. Ordering food provoked chatting about other things. Restaurants they liked. Places in LA to hang out. Vacation spots that were good. They both liked Kauai. Eventually, she got around to asking him about his job. "I like watching you on TV. I miss you on the Paul Moyer news."

He had to laugh to himself. Paul Moyer was the anchor. The program was called the Channel 4 News at 5. But civilians always called it the Paul Moyer news.

"It's frustrating right now," he admitted. "The network is a snake pit. They brought in a correspondent from New York. I'm out of the big story."

"I take it that bothers you."

"Bothers the hell out of me, yes. For one thing, not very likely I can keep a job if they won't use me. Secondly, telling stories is what I do. Somebody stops me, I feel bottled up."

"Do you have a plan?"

Mick nodded *yes, of course*. "I'm working my way back into the story even while they're trying to keep me out. Actually think I'm ahead of anybody else. A little skullduggery on my part, with some help from you, thank you. I think it will work out." He smiled. He wanted to project confidence.

"Oh, I almost forgot," she said, brightening as she remembered something. "I found a couple pieces of information for you." She dug into her purse.

She unfolded two pieces of paper.

"What you got?" Mick asked.

She pointed at the one on top. "The guy you wanted an address for? Bozman Enterprises? He's got a house in the Hollywood Hills he's hiding under another LLC called Bigboz Enterprises. Seems fixated on being the boss."

Impressive. Probably more likely to find Jumbo Blake at the Hollywood place than a drug house in South Central. "That's very interesting. Thank you."

"And between us," she whispered, leaning forward across the white linen tablecloth, "he's the subject of a grand jury investigation right now."

"Really?"

"Yes. Got a lawyer named Byron Fink. Ring a bell?"

"Heard the name."

"Big criminal defense guy."

"What's it about?"

She shrugged. "Drugs, I would think."

Mick was pleasantly surprised. This woman was very attractive, effortlessly amusing, charming, sexy—and she evidently kept him in mind at work. Looked up things without him even asking. How could you beat that?

"Plus one more thing," she said, pointing to a second paper she put in front of him. "See that?"

Mick looked it over, hard to read in the low light.

"That's your boy Armen Shabaglian. He got a speeding ticket a couple of days ago. Up by Fresno."

The paper seemed to levitate off the table into Mick's hand. It was a copy of a speeding ticket. Shabaglian was doing 60 in a 40 zone. The ticket had his car's make and model and year, and the license plate. Most importantly, it showed the address where the CHP officer had stopped the car.

Mick looked at her in stunned disbelief. She had just handed him the way to find Armen Shabaglian. If his luck held.

He had a lead at just the moment he'd thought he was stymied.

Mick looked up into the face of his dinner date, a woman who was becoming more beautiful by the moment. "Is it too soon to say I love you?" he asked.

She laughed, those bright teeth flashing, her eyes dancing. "You can say you love me, but I'm not going to bed with you." She paused. Smiled again. "Not yet, anyway."

They parted at her door with a kiss. Sweet, a little tender, a hint of lusty. Just one. And not too long. Just enough for both of them to communicate *Yeah, I'm interested.*

Back at his apartment still thinking about Grace Russell, Mick absentmindedly flipped on the TV. A breaking story grabbed his attention. Phil Shuman was down in Inglewood, standing in front of the smoking ruins of what looked like a small house. He was saying something about a gas explosion. He said property records showed the house belonged to a Luther Malcolm.

Mick's fingers were shaking as he punched in the numbers for Danny Bowls.

"Does Shuman have the name right? Luther Malcolm?" he said the moment Danny picked up.

"Sure does. Got the name myself."

"Jesus," Mick mumbled. He was feeling sick. No question Jumbo Blake got his revenge.

"Another thing that's funny," Danny said. "A second body. Identified as the woman who shot that home intruder a week ago."

"Louise Grove," Mick said softly.

"Yeah. How'd you know?" Danny asked, surprise in his voice.

"Bad luck just seems to follow some people," Mick said as he ended the call.

26

Harry Sarkissian and Gary Minasian were seated on a couch, huddled around a coffee table in Sarkissian's office. Each was holding a report with a velum cover. Both were reading intently.

On the opposite side of the coffee table was a short man in a mauve suit, a green dress shirt, and, to complete the clash, a yellow tie. He had a glistening bald head, a long overhanging lip that hid his upper teeth, and thick black eyebrows slanted into devil eyes. A shabby half-grown beard clung to his face like gray moss.

His name was Felix "Happy" Risoroni. His company did private detective work. He'd been hired by Harry Sarkissian to gather information on Jumbo Blake. Sarkissian and Minasian had long experience with Jumbo Blake, but it was intermittent. They felt they needed a refresher course.

"What's this grand jury thing?" Harry asked, not moving his eyes from the page.

Minasian looked up at Risoroni, his eyes scrutinizing, his mouth set in a frown. Grand juries were scary things. They worked in secret. A guy could have an indictment drop on his head out of the blue.

"That's my big score," Happy Risoroni said. "I got a guy on the grand jury. Your boy likes to portray himself as a rap music entrepreneur. But of course his real deal is drugs. Has been for years. So they're after Blake for his drug business. It's all up and down the state, highly stratified operation. District managers supervising street managers who are supervising street salesmen. His highest-ranking men make six figures, his lowest-ranking salesmen do a little better than slinging a rag at an auto detailer. Despite his activities trying to find, and sign and promote, rappers, he's kept close watch on the drug operation. It's where the money comes from."

Sarkissian bobbed his head up and down. He got it. "Jumbo likes to say he got out of the drug business, music more his interest now."

"It's bullshit. Of course he'd like to do well with rappers, but he's getting blown away by everybody out of Compton. Not to mention the East Coast dudes, Biggie Smalls and Diddy and Jay-Z, all of them doing much better than Jumbo Blake."

"So he's still spending a lot of time on his core business?"

"Until just recently, he was on the road constantly," Happy said. "Oakland, Sacramento, Marin City, Fresno, Bakersfield, and of course a big operation in South Central. I don't think people outside his operation quite knew how it stretched up and down the state. The Feds and the DA's office are working together. The DA goes first, get him on state charges, then the Feds are going to jump in with a RICO indictment."

Harry liked what he was hearing. The Racketeer Influenced and Corrupt Organizations Act. They could put Jumbo away for a long time on that.

"Whatever the state stretch is," Happy added, "the Feds will be waiting when he's out."

Harry Sarkissian puckered his lips, thinking. After a moment, he had a question. "You said 'until recently' he was on the road. What happened?"

"This thing with his brother getting shot seems to have slowed him down. He's shaking trees all over town, trying to get to the bottom of it."

"Has he?"

"Gotten to the bottom of it?" Risoroni shrugged. "That I don't know. What I do know is he's kind of on a rampage."

Sarkissian nodded that he was well aware. "How's the chances he beats the charges?"

"He's got Byron Fink on his side, which is good for him. Except Byron has to sit tight. He can't be in the grand jury room, so the prosecutors are in there running wild, as you would suppose."

"Why do you think they're so focused on Jumbo? Lots of drug dealers around, right?" Harry asked, still studying the page.

"The only thing it could be about," Risoroni said, "both the DA and the Feds want to make an example out of him. He's been way too bold for a drug dealer. He's acting like he's a legit business. Lots of people work for him; lots of people means there's always some willing to talk. So they're burrowing in, finding the weak characters, getting testimony, stashing witnesses where Blake can't get to them. He's in a world of hurt."

Harry was thinking of the trouble Jumbo was giving him over the Shabaglian kid and the box. What with all this trouble in Jumbo world . . . *well, fuck him then.*

But Harry hadn't gotten to where he was by not thinking ahead.

This was such a moment. What if Jumbo got to somebody who knew there was a box and what was in the box? What if Jumbo knew the OJ knife was in play? Could he be angling to make a deal with the prosecutors? A trade? The knife for the grand jury case to go away? Maybe.

Worse, what if Jumbo figured out the knife was in Harry's possession?

In Harry's mind, those two possibilities only made sense.

"Can somebody make that grand jury work faster?" he mumbled. "Get that sonofabitch in an orange jumpsuit?"

Happy Risoroni smirked. "I can work miracles. But not mega miracles. That's out of my hands."

That annoyed Harry. "You charge a lot for not being able to do things," he muttered.

"Harry, calm down. I did good for you."

Sarkissian flipped the pages. "What's this about seasickness?"

Risoroni was hoping Harry would notice that nugget of information. "That's why you pay me the big bucks." Happy's face lit up. "Interesting fact about Jumbo. His baby mama wanted to go on a fancy vacation. They took a cruise out of somewhere in Florida, cruising around the Carib islands."

"Yeah. So?"

"Mr. Blake got sick. Almost the first hour."

"People get sick on cruise ships all the time. They're a floating box of disease. So what?"

"Yeah, but not this time. This wasn't one of those poop cruise deals. This trip, just a few people got sick. This was seasickness brought on by plain fear. Never came out of his cabin. When the maid staff or the room service guy came to the cabin, he was in the bathroom with the shakes. Lashanda told her girlfriends he was the most miserable he's ever been."

"You spent money getting shit from her girlfriends? Why tell me this? Some people don't like the ocean."

Risoroni reacted defensively. "For one thing, the seasickness is a symptom. He's afraid of water, lakes, rivers, oceans, swimming pools; bathtubs too, I suppose. It's called aquaphobia, and he got it bad."

"Fear of water. This is what I pay you for?"

"Hell, yeah. It's the personal information that makes a report like this come alive. This is the sort of thing that gives you a fuller picture of the man. You should appreciate it."

Sarkissian scowled. "I pay you for information that does me some good. The fact the fat guy gets seasick is fucking useless."

"Well, that's all I got," Risoroni said, getting to his feet. "And you're a fucking ingrate."

Harry Sarkissian closed the book. "Okay, Happy, you did your job. I got both the useful and the useless. If anybody ever calls you to look into my business, call me. I'll have their legs broke, understand?"

"You tell me that every time I see you." Happy Risoroni shook hands with both men and left like smoke drifting out a window.

The room was quiet for a few moments. Harry was looking at the report again, lips pursed.

Gary Minasian spoke up. "That bit about seasickness got me thinking."

The boss looked up. "Yeah. What?"

"Look, we got the box stashed in a safe house, but maybe these places we got around here aren't safe enough. Considering the guy seems to be ocean-phobic maybe you should move the box someplace a little safer."

"You mean run it over to Catalina?"

Gary nodded yes.

"Think that trip across the channel is really going to stop him from trying to rip us off?"

"Not really. Might slow him down a little. First, the place really is a secret. Second, he can't just roll up. He'd have to get a boat, he'd have to jump through a few hoops."

Harry thought about it. It was true. He had a safer safe house over on Catalina Island.

And it wasn't just Jumbo he needed to worry about. No telling what that shitheel Nazarian might try to pull to avoid paying money for the thing.

"I see your point," he said to Gary. "I'll take the rest of the day off."

Harry Sarkissian drove a few blocks away, used a key to enter an attractive home in a middle-class neighborhood. The place was both furnished and empty. Harry kept it as a place to stash people and things if the need arose. The box was in a closet bedroom. He took the box marked "OJ" on the top and placed it on the passenger seat in his Escalade.

He drove down the 110 freeway, proceeded straight south all the way to Long Beach. In an hour, he was parking at the Long Beach

Marina. He walked down a ramp and through a locked gate onto the floating dock.

His boat was halfway down. He went aboard, unlocked the cabin door. He put the box down below on one of the bunks. He changed into jeans, T-shirt, a windbreaker, and deck shoes. It was a beautiful blue-sky day. He put on a wide-brim hat and sunglasses. Couldn't be too careful about skin cancer.

He fired up the twin diesels. He flipped the tie lines off the dock cleats, coiled them on the deck. He took his place at the wheel and backed the big boat away from the slip.

Harry cleared the breakwater and set a course for Catalina Island. The box would be safe there. Safer, anyway.

Jumbo wouldn't know Harry had a house on Catalina. Nobody did, except for Gary Minasian. Not even Harry's boyfriend knew. It wasn't a party house. It was a lay-low house. A hiding spot.

For a guy with a propensity for aquaphobia, there would be that big channel between the mainland of California and Santa Catalina Island. Perhaps it was enough ocean to give Jumbo Blake the yips.

Harry opened up the twin diesels. It was a calm day on the channel. Stretched before him was a couple dozen miles of blue glass. *"Twenty six miles across the sea, Santa Catalina is waiting for me. . . ."* The song was wrong. Twenty-nine point three miles, in fact.

He took off his hat and let the wind whip through his silver hair.

Harry wasn't fooling himself. Jumbo could get people over to Catalina even if he wouldn't go himself. But the channel was just another obstacle the big guy would have to deal with.

Plus, when it was time for an exchange—the box for cash— whether it was Jumbo Blake or Bob Nazarian, the situation was easier to control for Harry Sarkissian if the handoff was on the island. The wharf crowded with tourists at Avalon would be perfect.

In Harry Sarkissian's estimation, neither of the two potential buyers would do anything weird in front of so many witnesses.

27

The copier spit out sheets of paper. Mick turned to another page of the Thomas Brothers map book for Fresno County. Three in the morning in the Burbank bureau, Mick was grinding off the map pages he would need when he got to Selma. But he was preoccupied with guilty thoughts. Lummie and Louise blown up in Lummie's house. Supposedly a gas leak.

BS.

Jumbo. Mick was sure of it.

It also bothered him that Jumbo Blake, noted drug lord, seemed to be so intent on getting his hands on the knife. Mick completely understood his hostility toward Louise. She had killed his brother, after all. But what was the knife to him?

Unless it had something to do with what Grace had mentioned: a grand jury on Jumbo's case.

But his thoughts returned to Lummie and Louise. He wondered if blowing up in a gas explosion was painful, if they'd been conscious, if they'd suffered. He had no idea how he was going to get back at Jumbo Blake for this, but he was sure there must be a way.

Justice would have to wait. He needed to get up the road to Selma. It was straight up I-5, join Highway 99 at the foot of the Grapevine grade, and a couple of hours beyond Bakersfield. It would take him three hours. He wanted to arrive at dawn, see if he could spot Armen's Mustang somewhere in the area where the speeding ticket had been issued. It was a long shot, but the only shot he had.

He gave himself a three-hour nap. Now a little after three in the morning, he had a tall go-cup filled with hot black coffee, and map pages. The Blazer was gassed for a thunder run to the small town that billed itself "The Raisin Capital of the World."

Driving in the dark, the passing suede hills were invisible. But Mick knew they were there. He'd been over the Grapevine on Interstate 5 many times since he'd been a little boy. But his thoughts drifted back to Lummie and Louise. Why had they thought they were safe just a few blocks from where Louise had killed Jumbo's brother? Why wouldn't they listen to him? It would have been easy to disappear somewhere. Bullhead City was just a few hours away.

The gold country, a five-hour drive. Everybody hides out up there. Arizona, even. Somewhere.

And why would Jumbo bother killing them? They couldn't hurt him. Mick could come up with no other reason than he was just vicious.

True, Louise had killed Marcus. But Jumbo's brother had it coming. And Mick was sure Jumbo knew it.

In the black night of Highway 99, the Bakersfield sign loomed, blinding bright and startling. Red, green, blue, orange, yellow neon. A surreal object and a surreal message. *"Bakersfield. Fun. Sun. Play. Stay."*

Mick was in a depressed and cranky mood when he arrived in Selma at 5:45 a.m. First thing, he pulled into a McDonald's. He ordered a tall black coffee and four cheeseburgers. He ate half of one, and gave up. Crap.

With Thomas Brothers map sheets spread out on the passenger seat, he found Rose Avenue, where he exited Highway 99. He drove east to the corner of DeWolf Avenue, the north-south cross street where the speeding ticket had been issued.

He could picture it, even though he had no other information than the fragments on the speeding ticket. But that was a lot. A light green '68 Mustang. Twenty-something kid with a twenty-six-year-old car. A 289 could get up and go. Probably ripping down this straight country road, rows of grapevines whipping by, figuring there wasn't a cop for miles.

He was wrong and got nailed.

It was clearly raisin country. Well-tended houses were separated by even better-tended fields of Thompson Seedless grapes, the variety that became raisins. The grapes on the vines at the first of July were small. By early August, they would be plump. They would be cut from the vines, laid out on paper trays in the sun. Dried into raisins. Mick knew. He'd worked the fields, picking grapes during a summer in high school.

Mick passed houses that looked like the modest castles of raisin kings, each separated by what seemed to be vast rows of vines, exploding in green, upward of forty acres in size, neatly tended. It was easy to tell the owners' homes from the help houses. The owners tended to carve out an acre or two from the grapes, build a modern three- or four-bedroom home, landscape it handsomely, add a pool. Examples could be found every quarter mile or so.

Generally, houses that looked like they would fit in any middle-class suburb. Basketball hoop in the driveway. The only difference would be the view: a sea of grapevines.

Mick drove down Rose Avenue a couple miles, looking over the houses, looking for a green Mustang. Thank god the kid had picked a distinctive car. He could spot both the hood and the rear lines in his sleep.

He came back to the corner of DeWolf Avenue. He turned south. More vines, row after row after row. The sun was just coming up. He noticed some stir on the properties. Crews were showing up in vans to do some sort of work in the fields. Too soon for harvest. Probably pruning.

Half a mile south of Rose on DeWolf was a small older structure that looked like it might be a foreman's house. Not as new as the one he figured was the owner's house on the other end of the property. The one that had a mailbox with the name "Paboojian."

Behind this foreman's house, equipment sheds stretched a couple of hundred yards down a gravel access road. Farm vehicles of various sorts—pickups, flatbeds, tractors—were parked in the area of the barns and sheds in the back. Cruising by slowly, Mick thought he caught a glimpse of what he was looking for.

He went a little farther, turned around in the middle of the road, and drove back. He stopped where the gravel driveway met DeWolfe. He lifted his binoculars to his eyes. There in the far back, partly obscured by a John Deere tractor, was the front end of a green Mustang.

Mick couldn't tell if it was the exact vehicle he was looking for, but he thought chances were good. How many quarter-century-old green Mustangs would he find tucked away in raisin country? He thought not many.

The Blazer made a light crunching sound in the dirt road. Dogs came running to meet his car. Before they started barking, Mick threw his leftover burgers out the window, and the mutts forgot about him. Mick stopped in front of the Mustang and checked the plate. It was Armen Shabaglian's car.

He put the Blazer in PARK and shut it down. There was activity in the house, lights in what must have been a kitchen. But it was a hundred yards back toward the road. So far, it didn't seem he'd been noticed.

Stretched out before him was a series of buildings. Clearly the first two were barns, and the third in the row seemed like it might be a bunkhouse. Mick walked to the first building, pushed back a sliding door. Inside were tractors, trailers, and other farm equipment he didn't recognize. It seemed to be a repair shop.

Mick was making his way back to what he thought was a bunkhouse, figuring he might find Armen Shabaglian asleep. But along the way, he paused to slide back the second barn door to take a peek. Barn two was as large as—and almost identical to—the first. Metal roof, metal panel siding, an oversize sliding door. What he saw inside stopped him cold.

A little morning light through the open door clearly revealed a chop shop. Mick slipped through the narrow opening of the big door. To his left, rows of heavy-duty steel shelving held auto parts of various sorts. He saw water pumps, and power-steering units, full engines, pistons, cams, short blocks, radiators, fuel injectors, all in multiple iterations.

He walked along the shelving, marveling at the array of parts. At the back, he found an enclosed box with ventilation tubing to the outside. Hanging beside it were respirators, heavy rubber gloves, and long-sleeved hazmat suits. Five-gallon buckets contained hydrochloric acid. He recognized a rust-removal station. The process was called pickling.

In the center of the room, two vehicles were in the stages of dismantling by torch. Two "nose" units were already cut away, waiting to be moved off. Mick knew a little about the chop-shop business, sometimes known as the illegal "auto dismantler" industry. His father was a San Francisco cop who had worked the auto-theft detail for a while. The old man had taken the kid along once in a while when they went off to inventory a chop warehouse after the owners were arrested.

A chop warehouse was exactly what Mick was looking at. The "nose" was the front end of an '83 Camry, which Mick knew to be one of the most popular for chop owners to order stolen. A chop called in an order for a certain model, stealers would go out to find one and bring it back. The chop would then strip out the parts, or cut off the nose to put on the front end of a wreck. Slap in some parts, throw on some paint, and the result was a running car ready to head to a ship for the Central American market.

Mick walked along the rows of steel shelves. He looked over the parts stacked in the dozens. He wasn't enough of a mechanic to recognize precisely what they all were, but the mere fact that someone had pulled these pieces off a car surely meant they were worth money.

In all, a lot of money.

He thought it was odd that this setup would be smack in the middle of a sea of grapes, but maybe that was an excellent cover.

It was all very interesting, but he realized he was wasting time. He needed to find Armen Shabaglian.

Mick turned to walk back out and resume his search. But he didn't get far.

As he turned around, a fat fist came out of the dark and hit him square between the eyes. It was his last conscious image before total darkness.

Three men stood over Mick's splayed body. Two were looking down on him. One was agonizing over the punch. "Fuck fuck fuck," the man squealed. A squat man with an overhanging belly, hairy arms, and a bald head, he shook his right hand and danced around in pain. "Damn guy has a head like a slab of rock," Billy Paboojian whined. Billy's round face winced in pain. His brown eyes, hidden under a heavy brow, were squeezed shut. "Damn, that hurts," he moaned.

"Break your knuckles?" Manny Meza asked. Manny was Billy Paboojian's foreman. A fifty-year-old Mexican dressed in Wranglers and a blue long-sleeve work shirt, he wore a sweat-stained straw cowboy hat and Western boots with rubber soles covered in mud. His job was to oversee the fields of Thompson Seedless; but more importantly, he supervised the auto-dismantling operation, the lucrative part of Billy Paboojian's enterprises.

"I don't know," Billy said. "Hurts like a son of a bitch, I tell ya." He held his hand out to Manny. "I can't look."

"Knuckles might be swelling. Blood in the way," Manny said, sympathetically. "Lemme get it off." He gave Billy's hand a wipe with a red shop rag pulled from his back pocket.

"Go easy, willya?" Billy squawked. "Fuck, that hurts."

Behind the two men, Armen Shabaglian was watching, eyes darting from Paboojian and his foreman to the body on the floor. He was holding the shotgun Billy had handed him just before he punched Mickey.

Young Armen was alarmed. He was supposed to be just lying low, out of the way of Jumbo Blake. Now they had some guy knocked out cold at their feet. Armen wasn't sure what Billy might do to the guy.

After all, the guy had come sneaking around Billy's very illegal auto-dismantling operation. He'd only been on the Paboojian farm a few days, but Armen was already wracked with second thoughts about volunteering to do "anything" when he was begging Gary Minasian for a job. This chop job in the middle of grape fields was big-time. Belatedly, he realized he could go to jail.

Billy cursed himself. "I shoulda just shot the guy. Now my hand is all fucked up."

A chill went up Armen's spine.

Manny scoffed. "Can't just shoot him. This ain't Texas."

Billy shook his head. "Shoot him. Punch him. Makes no difference. Either way, he gets pickled." Billy shook his injured hand, as if that would help. "Damn, this hurts."

Pickled? Armen's ears burned. What's that?

"Better make sure he's not a cop before you do anything to him," Manny mumbled.

"He ain't a cop. Ain't how they operate. Probably some nosy insurance investigator," Billy groaned. "Long as there's no LoJack on his car, nobody ever know he was here," he added through gritted teeth. "Pickle him, nothing left but sludge."

Manny shook his head. The boss was so impulsive.

"Then chop the car," Billy continued. "He was never here. We know nothing." In excruciating pain, Billy grunted out the words through gritted teeth, rolling his eyes into his head.

Manny picked up Billy's hand again. "Boss. Bad news. You got bone poking through the skin."

"Jesus, I broke my hand on that fucker's head?"

"You shoulda hit him in the jaw. Straight punch to the forehead: that's tough bone there."

Billy reacted badly to criticism. "You shoulda been the one to punch the guy out. I'm the boss. What were you doin' hanging back like a pussy?"

"You didn't give me time, boss," Manny said.

Armen shuffled back a step or two, as if a little distance would help him deny that he was involved.

"We gotta do something about your hand," Manny said, hoping to get Billy Paboojian off the blame game.

The pain clouded Paboojian's thoughts. He wasn't thinking clearly. "Like what?"

"You gotta get it looked at. Bone coming through the skin.

Infection. We gotta go somewhere."

"A hospital?"

"Either that or a vet."

"I don't want a vet fixing my hand. I'll end up with a hoof."

"Okay, so let's go to the hospital."

"I don't want to show up in town with this. People ask questions."

"We can go to Fresno. Twenty minutes."

Billy Paboojian thought about it, cursed himself and the guy with the hard head. "Just get some zip ties on the guy," he finally agreed. "Then we'll go."

Left alone while Manny stepped away for the zip ties, Billy turned to Armen. "You stay here. Hold that gun on the guy so he knows you're serious. I'll deal with him when I get back."

Armen nodded. Much too tentatively for Billy's taste. "Hey, kid, you got it?"

"Yessir," Armen stammered.

"Don't fuck this up," Billy warned him. "I don't like fuckups."

Unbeknownst to Billy Paboojian and Manny Meza and Armen Shabaglian, Mickey Judge was listening.

He had been unconscious for a moment; but as he regained his senses, he heard a man's voice talking about what to do with him.

His head hurt so bad, he thought he might throw up. Pain radiated from the bridge of his nose to the back of his head and down his spine. Despite the agony, he had the sense to stay quiet.

Manny Meza returned with white plastic zip ties, secured Mickey's hands and ankles. "Good enough?" he asked Billy.

"Better tie him to something or he'll get up and hop around," Billy ordered. "Let's get it done. I gotta get moving."

Now Manny had to find a rope. Then he had to lift Mickey by the shoulders. Mick groaned, but to Manny and Billy it seemed involuntary, that the guy was still out. Manny and Armen dragged him to a post. Manny wrapped the rope around Mickey's chest and the post. "I don't think he's going anywhere," he said.

"Who the fuck is this guy, anyway?" Billy asked as they walked out.

"Lemme check his car," Manny said.

Billy Paboojian got into the passenger side of a dusty Silverado 1500 pickup. "Come on," he shouted at Manny. "Step on it."

Holding a lanyard dangling a collection of plastic ID cards, Manny jumped into the driver's seat. "He's a fucking reporter. Looks like

NBC News. In LA."

"Aw, shit," Billy moaned.

"Can't vat this guy. Gotta figure out something else."

"Why not?" Billy shot back. "If he's dissolved, he's dissolved. We chop the car. It disappears. We know nothing."

Manny fired up the truck. "You gotta think about it. It's not like vatting some dumb immigrant nobody ever misses. This guy goes missing, there's going to be a manhunt. God knows who he talked to, who he told where he was going."

"Fuck that," Billy said. "If he's gone, he's gone. Not our problem. Get me to the fucking hospital. This is killing me."

Manny shook his head. "Boss, think about it. We got a ways to drive. Think about it."

Billy waved him off. "Just fuckin' drive."

Ten minutes later as they sped up Highway 99 toward Fresno, Billy had calmed down. "Okay, we don't pickle him. We just keep him locked up until we can get all that shit out of that barn."

"Take it where?"

"The barn over in Mendota. Better there anyway. It's out of the way."

Manny agreed. "Take us a day or two to move everything."

"It's okay. The guy can just chill. When we've moved everything, we'll drive him and his car into a field and leave him there."

"Let him go?"

"Yeah. He might say he was at our place, but who cares? We'll be clean by then."

Back at the chop shop, Armen didn't know that his excitable boss Billy had changed his mind. Armen was still wondering what Billy Paboojian had meant when he'd said he was going to pickle the guy.

Mickey opened his eyes when he heard the pickup skitter out the driveway on loose gravel.

He tried to blink the pain away. Didn't do much good. He wanted to rub his forehead, but his hands were tied.

"You're Armen Shabaglian, aren't you?"

Armen was sitting on a folding chair, holding the shotgun across his lap. He didn't want to be talking to the prisoner, but there wasn't much choice.

"Who are you?" he asked.

"I'm Mickey Judge. I'm a correspondent with NBC News in LA."

"Oh, shit," Armen said.

28

Armen stared at the man tied to the post. The guy was already showing signs that he would have two bodacious black eyes. And now Armen realized he'd seen this man on television in LA. He wasn't bullshitting. He was a television reporter. Now what?

"I'm Mickey Judge. I'm a correspondent with NBC News in LA," Mick repeated. "Do you have any idea what that means?"

The boy was disoriented. "What are you doing here?"

"In a minute. Let's talk about you," Mick said, squirming to sit up straighter. He held his hands up to show Armen the zip ties. "You going along with this? Those two guys are talking about killing me. You going along with that?"

"You really should shut up."

"No, seriously. Let's talk about you on death row. Cause that's what'll happen. They're talking about pickling me. You know what that means?"

"Means nothing. Just a joke. Can't pickle a whole person."

"Not a joke. You don't even know what pickling means, do you?"

"What?"

"It's steel pickling. Hydrochloric acid. They're talking about putting me in a vat of acid till my body dissolves to sludge. There's nothing to connect them to my murder. They're talking about chopping my car. Like no one will know I was ever here."

Armen swallowed hard.

"Problem. Everybody knows I'm here," Mick said, in the tone of a teacher speaking to a lazy student. He lolled his head back and forth, trying to swipe away the pain. "The assignment desk in Burbank. My bureau chief. The producer back in LA. The woman who gave me the speeding ticket you got that showed exactly where you were, about two hundred yards from this spot."

"So?" Armen wanted no part of a killing, and he was hoping Billy Paboojian was just mouthing off. "Billy isn't going to kill you. You're hallucinating."

"What's he going to do with me, then?" Mick asked. "Let me go. Let a network news correspondent run back to LA and tell the camera crew to come to Selma and find a chop shop that probably is responsible for half the car thefts in the Central Valley? Think that fat little guy who punched me is going to just say 'Hey, ya got me fair and square, I'll just go to jail'?"

Mick let it sink in a moment. He needed the time to will the pain away. Or try. Wasn't really working.

Mick figured his best bet was to scare the kid with the bullshit story that he'd soon be involved with a murder. Mick didn't know anything about Billy Paboojian, but he was willing to believe the guy wasn't stupid enough to kill a network news correspondent. The ensuing shit storm would be a wonder to behold.

But the truth would get in the way of scaring the shit out of Armen Shabaglian. "Let's get serious. He's going to have to kill me and try to pretend I was never here. And ya know what? He's going to get caught, and so is the other guy. And so are you."

Armen shook his head. "You're letting your imagination run away with you."

"Hey, kid, you already saw one murder when Mrs. Grove blew away your buddy Marcus. Luckily for you, you have no culpability there. You gonna stand by for another and take the fall this time?"

That hit home. Armen's mouth hung open and his brow furrowed, and he began to perspire as his heart picked up speed. "Who are you? Why are you here?"

Mick stared him down for a tense moment. "I'm here to ask you a question. Who did you give the box to?"

A look of horror crossed Armen's face. Now he realized the situation that faced him. He'd been found. A trail to the box had led to him. His first reaction was denial.

"I don't know anything about a box."

"Yeah, you do. Your friend Marcus got killed. Just before he took a shotgun blast to the chest, he got that box to you. You took it somewhere. Who'd you give it to?"

Cornered, Armen chose further denial.

"I don't know what you're talking about."

"Yes, you do. Look, Marcus's badass brother already knows who you gave it to, so you don't need to protect anybody anymore. I just want to get to that person and help them out. Whoever it is will be a lot safer if they can tell their story. Marcus's brother already killed two people who got in the way last night. You hear about that?"

"No," Armen shook his head.

"One of them was that lady."

"What lady?"

"Mrs. Grove. The one you tried to jack up. The one who killed Marcus."

"No. How?"

"Jumbo blew up the house she was in."

"Shit." Armen's head swiveled around, looking for a way out.

"And now you're with two other guys with a harebrained scheme to kill another guy. Me. And you're in the middle of it. See your problem?"

Armen wanted the bad stuff to go away. "You're just going to make trouble for me."

"I'm making trouble for you? Those two guys talking about killing me? They're making trouble for you. You better get your ass over here and get me out of this stuff before they come back and things get really, really bad for you."

"You're full of shit," Armen said in a weak voice.

Mick shifted back to why he'd come here. "Look, I know what's in the box. Whoever you gave it to knows what's in the box. Do you know?"

"I don't know what you're talking about."

"Yes, you do," Mick repeated for the third time. "You know there's a backpack in the box belonging to OJ Simpson. But do you know there's a knife in the backpack, and it's probably the Simpson murder weapon? Do you know that you handled the murder weapon?"

Armen Shabaglian's eyes widened and stammered something incomprehensible about knowing nothing about a murder weapon.

"Look, you don't have a lot of time. Let's look at what you have to do right now to save your ass."

The kid's mouth clamped shut. He decided it was time to listen.

"First, get me out of this stuff, otherwise you're a kidnapper and an accessory to murder. Death-penalty case. Second, tell me who you gave the box to. And third, most important, get in your classic Mustang and get as far away as you can. Go to Reno, go to Canada, go somewhere that you can't be found till all this blows over." Mick raised his hands. "Start with the zip ties."

Five minutes later, both Armen and Mickey were outside at their cars.

"This is it," Mick said, rubbing the ligation marks off his wrists. "Who'd you give the box to?"

Cornered, Armen sputtered. "I gave the box to Gary."

"Gary who?"

"Gary Minasian."

"Where is he?"

"His carwash."

"You gave it to a guy at a carwash?" Mick asked, incredulous.

"Gary wanted it for his boss Harry. Harry is going to help me get a job. Get off the sanitation truck."

"Harry?

"Harry Sarkissian. He's a big deal down there."

"You gave the box to Gary, who gave it to Harry?"

"Yes."

Son of a bitch. Harry Sarkissian lied to my face, Mick thought. His next thought: Right, they all do.

Mick got in his car. The keys were under the seat, where he always left them. Right alongside the safety copy of the Lummie interview. His credentials were gone. So Billy Paboojian knew who he was. That couldn't hurt.

Armen got into his Mustang. Mick rolled down his window with one last message for the young man. "Take my word for it. Don't be found."

It was three hours back to LA. He wanted to go see Sarkissian right away, but after checking the mirror he decided he needed to stop at a Walgreen's for the biggest pair of dark glasses he could find. Maybe another stop at the Bureau. Maybe the makeup ladies could cover the black eyes. They made him look like a cartoon burglar with a raccoon mask.

A pair of giant dark glasses fixed to his face, he swung into the Bureau parking lot. He crossed the parking lot without running into anyone. Inside, he had to make a choice: elevator or stairs. Most people used the stairs. The elevator was slow, but chances were good he'd be alone. He punched the elevator button. The doors slid open. He slipped inside and hit the button for floor three.

Bad luck. Bart Wimple stepped into the elevator just before the doors closed.

There was no hiding. Wimple stared at him, his eyes widening. "Buddy, what the fuck is under those shades?" he said. Then he laughed. "You look like a bar fight gone very bad."

Mick cursed himself for not taking the stairs. "Dark room. Bumped into a low beam."

Wimple laughed again. "Well, you sure as shit don't have to worry about being on TV for a while. Not looking like that."

29

Cheryl Bedrosian sat in front of Harry Sarkissian's desk, staring down the square barrel of an ugly Glock 9mm in the hand of Jumbo Blake.

Jumbo's attention was on Harry Sarkissian's art collection hanging on the walls of his office. Jumbo had just barged in and forced Cheryl into Harry's office at the point of the gun.

The artwork fascinated Jumbo Blake. "What's that one?" he asked Cheryl. Jumbo was staring at a picture on the wall of Harry Sarkissian's office at the Delerium Restaurant and Ballroom. The painting depicted ships in a cannon battle in the age of sail. Bright orange explosions against a night sky leapt off the canvas.

"That's Aivazovskiy, The Battle of Chesma. He was Russian. Famous for seascapes."

"Russian? Not Armenian?"

"No, Armenian. Russian. Armenian." Cheryl sounded rattled. "When he was alive, same thing."

Pleased with her discomfort, Jumbo Blake nodded that he understood. "I personally don't care for old-style art like that," he said, but pointed to another painting. "And who's that?"

"Arshile Gorky. Called the father of Abstract Expressionism. Died in 1948. Hanged himself."

"Damn," Jumbo said. "Hanged himself. One depressed motherfucker, I guess." The painting was a riot of bright, contrasting colors and odd shapes, some vaguely human.

"I suppose so," Cheryl said, distracted.

"So Harry got nothing but Armenian artists on the wall?"

"Pretty much." Her tone indifferent, her mind elsewhere.

"And who that?" He pointed at a portrait of a man, seated.

"The artist is Minas Aveteryan. Terrible thing with him. His studio burned. Most of his canvases were lost."

"Hmmmm. Shame. Real shame." Jumbo turned his attention to a framed photograph. "That a relative of Harry's?"

"No, that's the novelist William Saroyan. Very famous Armenian novelist. Wrote plays too. From Fresno."

"I like to have art in my office too," Jumbo said, opening up, gesturing expansively. "But I go for the wild stuff. You know, where they pour the paint out of buckets?"

Cheryl nodded, though she neither approved nor cared. But Jumbo was interested in the art, so she was damn well going to keep talking, distracting the big man. "Then there's Karen Aghamyan," she said, pointing to another. "She did that piece just a couple years ago. And next to it is Hovep Pushman. It's called 'Youth,' painted about 1920 or so. And next to it Martinos Saryan. He was painting at the turn of the century. It's called 'On the Way to the Well.' He was Russian too."

"You Harry's art expert?"

She shook her head no. "I help. But Harry knows his stuff."

"If he ain't here, where is he?" Jumbo asked, turning his attention away from the art on the walls.

Jamal, aka 187Boi, stood beside the office door. He was on bodyguard duty, arms folded across his boyish chest, his eyes hidden behind wraparound dark glasses. He held a Beretta 9mm in his right hand.

Jumbo Blake had commandeered Harry Sarkissian's office, collapsed in Harry's fancy leather chair behind Harry's ornate desk. He was making himself at home, perusing the art collection, while making Harry's assistant, Cheryl, extremely nervous.

Jumbo Blake was waiting for Harry Sarkissian. He had come to get OJ's knife.

"What's that rock thing?" Jumbo said, pointing the Glock at a stone sculpture on a credenza.

"It's called a khachkar. Khach is cross. Kar is stone. It's a stone cross."

"Oh. Religious." Jumbo absentmindedly let the gun drift. It swung away from Cheryl, then it swung back toward her.

"Honestly, Mr. Blake, he didn't say where he was going. He just left."

"You wouldn't lie for the boss, would you?"

"Not with that gun in my face," she said. "No, sir."

Owing to the nature of her boss's business, Cheryl Bedrosian was not completely unfamiliar with men brandishing weapons. Still, no amount of experience offsets the anxiety of the dead eye of a gun barrel staring at your forehead.

Grunts of disapproval rumbled up from Jumbo Blake's throat. He looked over his prisoner. Cheryl Bedrosian was a woman in her middle forties, a little on the heavy side, dark hair, and dark circles under her eyes. She kept a pack of Marlboro Reds and a lighter in her hand. She lit a cigarette.

Jumbo frowned, waving the smoke away with a big hand. "Do you have to?"

"You're the one sticking the gun in my face." She exhaled a cloud of blue smoke. "To be honest, I'm nervous."

"Cigarettes bad for you."

She snorted a derisive laugh. "I'm sure you smoke those blunts."

He scowled, scooted the desk chair back from her smoke. "Where he like to go when he just disappears? The movies? Card house? Titty bar?"

"This isn't golf day. He might be on his boat," Cheryl said, taking a deep drag. "He likes his boat."

"Fucking boat," Jumbo mumbled. He let the gun drop to his ample lap. "So where's his boy Gary?"

"At the car wash, I suppose," she said. Now Cheryl Bedrosian relaxed a little, clearly relieved to have the gun out of her face.

"Okay, you page him. When he calls back, tell him Harry wants to see him and get his ass on over here."

Cheryl did as she was told. She picked up the phone on the boss's desk and called Gary Minasian's pager. She punched in her own number for a return call and waited. She didn't volunteer the possibility that Gary Minasian and Harry Sarkissian might be together, in which case the call would tip them something was amiss at the office.

Jumbo leaned back in Harry's chair. He had two men with him. Jamal stood to the side like the khachkar, stony-faced and silent. Solomon Morgan was outside in the gold Mercedes. He was both lookout and backup.

It didn't take long for the phone to ring. "Harry wants to see you," she said, appearing to not give away her situation. But she knew if the two bosses were together, they would figure it out. She hung up.

Jumbo grunted. She had done nothing to raise his suspicions.

"Am I a hostage?" Cheryl asked.

Jumbo shrugged. "You can't go anywhere. Does that make you a hostage?"

"I think so," she said. "Can I call my daughter and have her get some money together so you'll let me go?"

Jumbo's scowl darkened the room. "Hell, no," he said, cross. "I'm not here for your money."

"What are you here for?" Cheryl was genuinely curious.

"I'm here to get that box from Harry."

Cheryl took another deep drag. "What box?" she asked, perplexed. First she'd heard of a box.

"Don't play dumb." Jumbo was incredulous. This was Harry Sarkissian's assistant. She had to know what her boss was doing. "There's a box. I want it."

Cheryl was confused. "I know nothing about a box. What's the box?"

"Some kid named Sha . . . Sha. . . ," he stammered, trying to pronounce the name.

"Shabaglian?" she asked. The name rang a bell. That young man Harry had had her call to come in for an interview. The one the reporter asked about.

"Yeah. That's it. Kid named Shabaglian gave Harry the box."

"What's the box?"

Jumbo ignored her question. "OJ got a Armenian friend, right? That guy Nazarian?"

Cheryl nodded *yes, that was true.* "So what?"

"So that's the connection. The box. Nazarian. Harry probably figure he can get one or two of those millions OJ got stashed."

"He got millions?" the bodyguard asked. Jamal was young. Barely remembered OJ Simpson. Something about football. Or movies. Something.

Cheryl looked from Jumbo to Jamal. What on earth were they talking about?

Jumbo gestured with his gun, waving it around like it was a pointer in the hands of a professor. "Jamal, that's actually a good question," he replied. "We all just assume he got millions from all those years playing football and being on TV and in the damn movies. But," he continued to wave the gun to emphasize his next point. "Maybe he do. Maybe he don't. You see?"

Jamal was confused. "I guess."

"Jamal, this is a lesson for you. Money has a habit of slipping away. Money is not loyal. It will run off with anybody. So we don't know yet if he still got that money." He turned his attention back to Cheryl. "Your two bosses, they squeezing Nazarian to squeeze the cash out of OJ. And they can do that because . . ." he paused for the punch line. "Because . . . they got the damn box!"

The room was quiet as Jumbo frowned and gave the situation some thought. "However . . . big problem! Big problem," he repeated. "That box rightfully belong to me!"

She met his stare and shook her head. "I don't know what you're talking about," Cheryl Bedrosian said. "I haven't heard about any of this."

"Sheee-it," Jumbo said, annoyed. "If you really don't know, I'll explain. My little brother Marcus got killed fetching that box for me. But when Marcus got shot, some Armenian kid he work with run off with it."

Cheryl nodded. "So?" she said, still confused.

Jumbo continued. "So the obvious. The little bastard brought it to the Armenian boss of all Armenians, Mr. Harry Sarkissian."

Befuddlement descended over Cheryl's face. Box? Brother? Killed? What was all this?

Jumbo's bodyguard Jamal nodded his approval. "Exactly right," he mumbled. "Damn thing rightfully yours."

Sucking up to the boss was Jamal's way of giving himself a soft landing. Hoping to impress Jumbo, he'd created a gas explosion at the house where Louise Grove was staying. The house of the guy who'd come to save her at Jumbo's headquarters. Then on the way over to Glendale, he'd overheard the boss tell Solomon he needed to keep that Luther Malcolm guy alive. Something to do with the DA and the grand jury investigation. Jamal was pretty sure that guy had been in the house with Louise Grove when it blew up. Jamal was nervous, and right to be.

"Damn right," Jumbo agreed with Jamal, aggrieved by the injustice. "I shouldn't be screwing around with Mr. Harry Fucking Sarkissian about that box. It should have been in my hands three days ago."

The room was heavy with Jumbo's wounded sense of fairness, an obvious personal affront. Cheryl didn't say a word.

Jamal's thoughts wandered. He wondered if he could be pinned for the house explosion. He couldn't see how. But even if he were somehow found out, he planned an appeal to Jumbo: *I was taking care of business so you wouldn't have to.* After all, how did he know the boss needed that guy alive? He'd sure sounded like he wanted him dead when he let the two of them leave the Anzac house.

At that moment, they heard the outer office door open. They all turned their eyes to the doorway.

"Maybe Mister Harry has arrived," Jumbo said in a low voice, a malevolent grin flowering on his fleshy face.

He pointed his gun at the door. Jamal stood back and raised his gun to the door.

30

Thirty miles away, at the Long Beach Marina, Gary Minasian sat at a picnic table with a clear view of the slip where Harry Sarkissian was easing his boat into place. Sarkissian jumped off the boat, put the tie lines over the dock cleats, and hopped back on. In a few minutes he'd changed his clothes, locked the cabin door, and walked up the gangplank to terra firma. He spotted Minasian and let out a sigh.

"What are you doin' here?"

"We got a problem."

"What's that?"

"Cheryl paged me. When I called back, she told me to come to the office. That you wanted to see me."

Harry scowled. "I didn't tell her any such thing."

"That was obvious," Minasian said. "You're here. Not at the office. So that means something bad is going on."

"Like what?"

"Like Jumbo Blake is back. Like he's sitting there with a gun on her, waiting for me to walk in."

Harry winced. "What's he want you for?"

"I assume he wants to force me to bring him to you. It's you he wants. Actually, it's that thing he wants," Gary added. Meaning the knife.

Harry grumbled. "Well, he can't have it."

"But here's the rub," Gary Minasian said. "He's figured out you have it. And just playing dumb, pretending you don't ain't gonna cut it anymore."

"That knife is a lot of money to me."

Minasian waved him off. "Sure. So forget about Nazarian. Fuck him. He's a prick anyway."

"I hate kissing off a customer."

"But you still have a good customer. Get the money from Jumbo Blake. He's sitting on a ton of cash, and Risoroni says he's got his ass in a sling with the DA. He needs that knife to make a deal."

"You think Jumbo is our best customer?"

"Of course."

"But I was about to jack up Nazarian another million."

"Don't get greedy."

Sarkissian thought about the problem. Under normal circumstances, he wouldn't deal with complications he was facing now.

Minasian pushed him along. "Right now you need to make a call and get Cheryl off the hook. I have a plan. Just listen."

31

As soon as the makeup ladies finished trying to cover his black eyes, Mick hit the freeway to Glendale. A glance in the rearview mirror confirmed what they had told him when they finished: "There's only so much we can do." He still looked like a raccoon.

Now he knew for a fact that Harry Sarkissian had the box. And he knew for a fact that Sarkissian had lied to him, but that was irrelevant. Of course he would lie.

The point now was to talk Sarkissian into letting him get a couple pictures of the knife. That would be enough for a story. If Sarkissian wanted to say a few words on camera, that would be fine too, but his main priority was to see that knife and get a picture.

Mick carried a Nikon Cool Pix happy snap camera in his coat pocket. Best case, he could talk Harry into a full-on interview. He would call for a crew. Worst case, he'd get a couple photos. Well, worst case was Harry telling him to fuck off, but he thought he could argue his way out of that.

What he was really hoping was that he could deal with Sarkissian and get what he needed. He did not want to be in the position of asking Jumbo Blake for help. That guy was too scary. At least Sarkissian was just an asshole, not a killer.

He parked in the Delerium parking lot and hurried inside. He strode past the hostess with a curt "appointment with Mr. Sarkissian" and found the stairs to Harry's office.

Without knocking, he went through Sarkissian's outer office. He expected to find that woman Cheryl at the desk, but her place was empty.

Inside Sarkissian's private office, Jumbo and Jamal heard a voice on the other side call out: "Hello? Anybody here?"

They aimed their weapons at the door to the office.

Cheryl cocked her head at the voice. It didn't sound like either Harry Sarkissian or Gary Minasian.

Mick heard a voice from the other side of the door to Sarkissian's office: "In here."

Jumbo and Jamal and Cheryl heard footsteps. The bodyguard tensed. Jumbo Blake sat a little taller in his chair, gripped the gun a little tighter, gave the door a squinty stare.

Cheryl scooted her chair back, frightened at what was about to happen.

Outside, Mick put his hand on the doorknob and turned. It was unlocked. He pushed the door open.

Inside Harry's office, three people held their breath and watched Mickey Judge walk in.

"For fuck's sakes," Jumbo said, as he dropped his gun in his lap. "It's that asshole TV reporter," he said to Cheryl, like it was her fault.

Mickey Judge immediately realized he'd made a terrible mistake. There sat Jumbo Blake, dwarfing the furniture. The very son of a bitch who had killed Lummie and Louise.

He glanced to his right. A tall thin black man was staring at him, holding a handgun. He guessed it was a Beretta 9mm, but who knows? The skinny guy looked like he didn't know much about guns. He held it sideways, gangbanger style.

Groaning on the inside, Mick cursed himself. He shouldn't have been in such a crazed hurry to get to Sarkissian. He should have looked around outside. Undoubtedly the gold Mercedes was out there like a huge stop sign, and yet he'd missed it.

Cheryl Bedrosian's face registered surprise and pity. What sort of schmuck has such bad luck to walk in on a thug holding a hostage?

From Mick's position, there was no option but to play it straight. He took a business card from his shirt pocket, handed it to Cheryl. "Mickey Judge, NBC News in Burbank. I'm sure you recall. I'm here to see Harry Sarkissian."

Mocking laughter burst from the big man with the gun. "Do it look like Harry Sarkissian sitting behind his desk?"

The bodyguard joined the boss in mirthless laughter.

Harry's assistant stared at Mick. "What happened to your eyes?" Cheryl asked.

Pointing the gun at Mick, Jumbo shifted from mocking to quizzical. "Somebody kick your ass?"

"I don't think we've met," Mick said, ignoring the jibe. Nothing unusual here. Just two scary guys with guns. "I'm Mickey Judge," he said, extending his hand.

"Fuck that," Jumbo said, waving the gun toward a chair. "I seen your sorry face on TV. Sit your ass down."

The bodyguard gave Mick a push in the back that sent him stumbling into a chair.

Glancing around the room, Mick confirmed his initial impression that this was bad. He was pinned down. Armed man at the door. Behind the desk, the very ominous Jumbo Blake casually waving a gun at him. No way to hotfoot it out without risking either one blasting off a shot. He noticed two windows, but probably a long drop to the street—at least a leg-breaker, most likely—not to mention getting sliced up diving through glass.

But he also noticed one more thing: the door he came through. On the left side, a Doorricade door bar was hanging unnoticed to one side. Mick guessed Harry Sarkissian was concerned about an office invasion, which was probably smart if he was even half the criminal some people said he was.

Cheryl Bedrosian stared at Mickey's card, but owing to the tension she couldn't quite focus to make out the words. "I know I met you once. But who are you again?" she asked.

"I know who he is," Jumbo interrupted her. "This cracker is a TV reporter. He want to talk to Harry. Same as me. That right, boy?"

So there it is, Mick thought. Jumbo Blake admitted he was on the trail of the box, but didn't have it yet. "Yes. I came to see Harry," Mick nodded.

"Well, he ain't around," Jumbo said. "Maybe you got bad timing."

"You think Harry has the box? That's why you're here?" Mick asked. He knew for a fact Harry had the box with the knife. Shabaglian had told him. But did Jumbo know that?

"What I know is you in no position to ask questions," Jumbo grunted in a rasping voice. He was looking Mick over closely. "You look like a damn cartoon burglar. What happened to your face, boy?" he asked. "Somebody musta punch your lights out."

"A little tussle," Mick shrugged. "So, where's Harry?"

The big man's reaction to the question was to ask one himself. "You know why somebody punched you out?" Jumbo asked. "Because of shit like that. Nobody likes assholes messing in other people's business."

"What about the box? You made a deal with Harry yet?" Mick pursued the point.

"See what I mean?" Jumbo sighed. "Nobody likes the news. And that right there is why. Y'all a bunch of nosy, pushy assholes."

Mick rolled his eyes. "I'm sure we all agree rap moguls ripping off black kids and secretly dealing drugs are way more likeable."

The gangster snorted in disgust at the effrontery. He turned to

Cheryl. "Can you fucking believe this white dude insulting me to my face? Saying I exploit black people?" Jumbo looked over at Mick with disdain.

"You're charging black kids to record their raps in your studio, knowing you won't be signing most of them; and if a good one comes along, you wrap him up tight and take all the money for years."

Jamal's ears perked up.

Jumbo took the bait. "They getting a shot. Nobody else do it for them."

"While you take their money for the shot. And they're probably out robbing other black people to pay you."

His temper rising, Jumbo stood up and pointed the gun at the top of Mick's head. "Ain't nothing next to the way white people keep them down. Like you. You the one tricked Mr. Luther Malcolm into a interview about the box. Didn't even cover up his damn face. You even give a thought to the fact doing a TV interview might not be so healthy for him?"

"So you're saying Lummie died because he did an interview with me?" Mick asked, looking up at the gun barrel.

"Ask yourself that question," Jumbo said, still menacing Mick with his gun.

"I have. My conscience is clear. How's yours?"

Jumbo scowled, ignored the question. "That reminds me. I want that tape."

Mick shook his head no, mocking the guy with the gun. "It's at the bureau. But you can't have it anyway. NBC property."

"I want it."

"Fact of life, we can't always get what we want," Mick said. "Why would you want it anyway?"

"That's not your business."

"You want my exclusive interview with the guy who taped the box closed, the guy who saw what's inside, an interview everybody in this town would kill to get their hands on. But it's none of my business," Mick scoffed. "Right."

"What's the box?" Cheryl interrupted.

Incredulous, Jumbo and Mick looked at each other wordlessly, asking *Harry didn't tell her?* "You really don't know?" Mick asked.

"This is the second time I've heard about a box. I have no idea what you two are arguing about."

Mick took a deep breath and, keeping an eye on Jumbo, he told Cheryl the truth: "Harry has a box. It's very important. I want to take a picture of what's inside. Jumbo here, he just wants to take it."

Jumbo didn't object.

"What kind of box? I haven't seen a box."

"A shipping box. Like you get at Office Depot. Put something in it. Ship it."

"Okay. So what?"

Mick let a dramatic exhale loose. "Inside the box is OJ's knife," he said. Blunt.

"OJ's knife?" she reacted with a snort. "What's that?"

"The murder weapon," Mick said, drawing his finger across his neck. "The one he cut his wife's head off with."

Involuntarily, Cheryl put her hand to her own throat. "You think Harry has OJ's knife? Impossible. You're dreaming."

"No, I'm not," Mick said. "I'm damn sure your boss has it."

Jumbo sat down, put his gun on the desk. Listening to the exchange, he decided there was no point in staying out of the discussion. "I admit I was stumped at first. Couldn't figure what Harry want that knife for anyway. Then I realized he probably figured he'd sell it to OJ for real money. Bank."

"OJ's in jail," Cheryl said. "He can't buy nothing."

Jumbo looked at her and squeezed one eye tight. "You damn well know what I mean. OJ's people. OJ got a Armenian lawyer, that Nazarian fella."

"Yes. I've heard Mr. Nazarian is a friend of OJ's." She butted out her cigarette, but not completely out, because her fingers were shaking. The ashtray continued to smoke.

"See?" Jumbo said, turning to his bodyguard. "The Armenians sticking together. Sarkissian plan to sell the knife to Nazarian. Then he'll go dump it in the ocean."

At this point, something Mick had been puzzling about led to a realization. Why would Jumbo want to kill Lummie? Thinking it over, he realized he might have made a mistake in assuming Jumbo purposely killed Lummie. An accident, maybe. But not on purpose.

"I think I get it now," Mick interrupted.

He waited until Jumbo turned his attention to him. "Your lawyer explained chain of custody."

Jumbo's expression turned sour, but he said nothing.

"If you offer the knife to the DA," Mick continued, "you would need to also give them the guy who put the backpack in the box. That's Mr. Lummie Malcolm. But bad luck, because . . ." Mick said, putting on a theatrical frown, "because you killed him."

Jumbo jerked his head back. "Why would I do that?"

"Revenge. You wanted to kill Louise. But you got Lummie too. By mistake."

"I didn't kill either damn one of them," Jumbo said. "The house blew up. Gas leak or some shit."

"I don't believe that, and I'm sure the DA won't either when they realize Louise killed your brother."

Jamal held his gun on Mick. He was tempted.

"You pretty damn smartass for a guy who don't have the gun," Jumbo said. "Where that tape?"

"You need the tape of Lummie because you screwed up and killed Lummie. The interview with him establishes chain of custody."

"Where's the tape?"

"I told you. At the Bureau. About three miles that way," Mick said, pointing west. "At the NBC lot. Just tell security I sent you. They'll take care of you."

"You one annoying smartass." But Jumbo didn't buy it. "Jamal, get his keys and go check his car."

The bodyguard patted Mick down. No keys.

"He probably leave them in the car. Go look for a Blazer."

Before Mick could ask how he knew what kind of car he drove, Jumbo answered.

"My limo driver saw a Chevy Blazer zooming away with Lummie and Louise," Jumbo explained. "You ain't invisible. People see what you doing."

"I'm not hiding. I'm looking for the knife. And I'm not the one killing people."

Shaking his head and waving his gun at Mick, Jumbo turned to Cheryl. "It's so upsetting to be falsely accused."

She gave him a sympathetic but entirely insincere nod.

He had more to say. "This little shitheel figures he will get the knife. Why do he want it? So he can be all boy scout and turn it over to the cops. He's hoping to be a celebrity."

Mick shook his head no, frowning. "The fact that the knife has been found is a story," Mick said. "It's a huge story."

"Oh, what a load of crap," Jumbo said, shaking his head in

disgust. "I watch the damn news. You people usually totally ignorant about what's really going on. But that doesn't stop you from pretending you know." He paused, giving Mick a look of thorough disdain. "You go on TV parading around as a big shot who finds the damning piece of evidence," here he made air quotes with his fingers, "the evidence that solves the crime or uncovers the crooked politician." Jumbo made mocking air quotes again. "People see you on TV all full of yourself. You think we don't see through your game? Mostly you pushing a load of crap," he repeated.

The two men stared at each other. Mick couldn't outright agree; but true, the news business was messy.

However, this whining from a gangster, drug lord, probably a killer, was absurd. Whatever rough spots in gathering and broadcasting the news—and there were plenty—there was no equivalency with the deadly business of heroin and gang murders. And yet here he was in a room with a man with a gun and a chip on his shoulder about the news.

How exactly had Jumbo Blake been wronged? Mick couldn't remember ever seeing a story about Jumbo and his business, and Mick knew why. Reporters, even black reporters, had almost zero interest in going into "the hood" to dig up facts on people like Jumbo Blake. It was just too dangerous.

But those were his private thoughts. Across the desk Jumbo continued, on a roll. "All you guys do is make yourselves out to be high and mighty, the ultimate good guys. But I know what goes on."

"Everybody's a critic. We do our jobs anyway," Mick said with a shrug. "It's the news business." Explaining his job to Jumbo was pointless.

"But you know fuck all about my business," Jumbo shot back, angry. "You like to believe it's something unsavory, criminal. But I got up-and-coming rap stars. I entertain people by the thousands."

"I heard you got a grand jury on your case and it's not for your 'rap business.' You're waiting for Harry so you can grab that knife. Because you're hoping they want to nail OJ way more than they want to nail you."

"You don't know shit."

Mick pushed harder. "You realize helping the prosecution will make you the biggest snitch in the country?"

Jumbo slowly raised the gun and wrinkled his face like he smelled something foul. "Nobody's going to call Julius Caesar Blake a snitch."

"That's what I'll be reporting."

The glower rose on Jumbo's face again. "Maybe I should just make sure you don't report anything."

"That's a joke," Mick interrupted. "Kill a network news correspondent? You'd get crushed."

Jumbo interrupted. "Don't get all drama queen on me. Maybe I just make sure nobody believes you about anything."

Unable to contain himself, Mick laughed in Jumbo's face. "You? Damage *my* credibility? Don't be absurd."

Jumbo shook his head in disgust. Looking Cheryl in the eye, he gestured to Mick. "I guess I'm getting no respect here. The motherfucker says over and over I'm a drug dealer. Now, if I'm a drug dealer like he says, why couldn't I plant a brick of dope in his car, in his house, someplace it make him look dirty as fuck. After that, nobody believe him about anything."

"Okay, you are a drug dealer. So much for the phony rap-mogul dodge," Mick said. But he took a new tack. "What're you all worked up about? This is a big story, really big. If you're the star of it, the guy handing the key piece of evidence to the LAPD, that makes you a hero."

Frustrated, Jumbo leaned forward on the desk and looked Mick in the eye. "You just finished telling me that I'd be the country's biggest snitch. Now you trying to put me on TV so everybody knows I put him away? You ain't making sense. Do you even listen to yourself?"

"Worried about being fingered as a snitch?" Mick asked. "Okay. But look at it this way."

This guy don't know when he's beat, Jumbo thought. He put his chin in his right palm, elbow on the desk, absently spinning the gun around on the desktop with his left hand. He stared at Mickey waiting: how was this bullshit artist going to talk his way out of this?

"Follow me," Mick said, leaning into Jumbo's space to make his pitch. "Black people don't think of OJ as a guy from the hood," Mick began. "He lives in fucking Brentwood, for Chrissakes, which is white as white can be. The wife he killed was super white, fake tits, nose job, fake blond hair, fake puffy lips, the works. His new girlfriend is white. Haven't you noticed? OJ is fucking white."

The big guy with the gun threw up his hands in frustration, jerking the pistol back at Mick's forehead. "Cracker, do I look that stupid?"

Mick sat back in his chair. "The guy is white. Nobody cares about dropping a dime on a white guy."

Jumbo cocked the pistol. "I guarantee you black people are going to think he's black," he snarled. "You need to stop trying to sell me bullshit!"

Jumbo went quiet, almost daring Mick to speak again, to beat the dead horse again. The air crackled with tension. Cheryl glared at Mick, the shit disturber.

Jumbo took a deep breath. He let the hammer down slowly. "Where the fuck is your boss?" he asked Cheryl.

"I really don't know," she said softly, glaring at Mickey. "And Mr. Judge, I wish you would stop provoking the man."

Jamal walked back in, carrying a tape. "Found it. Under the driver's seat," he said, handing it to Jumbo.

The label was marked "LM-safety". Jumbo looked at the tape cartridge. He'd never seen a professional ¾-inch tape. "What is this?"

"It's a field tape," Mick said. "You need a pro machine to play it."

"You don't have VHS tapes?"

"We're NBC News, not Blockbuster," Mick said, like Jumbo knew absolutely nothing.

"Well, fuck," Jumbo groused. "How can I tell if Lummie is on this tape?"

Mick shrugged. "Who knows? I got lots of tapes in the car."

"Fuck you," Jumbo growled. "You wrote Lummie on the tape. It's Lummie."

"Says L and M. Could be anything," Mick said and slumped down in his chair.

A tense silence fell over the office. "Is that guy ever going to show up?" Jumbo complained. Gary Minasian had been summoned. He should have been here by now.

Cheryl pursed her lips and nodded. "I'm sure he will."

32

The phone on Harry Sarkissian's desk rang. Cheryl Bedrosian looked over at Jumbo, who shifted his eyes to the phone. "Pick it up."

"Harry's office." She listened. "Okay," she said.

She extended the phone to Jumbo. "He wants to talk to you."

Jumbo leaned back in Harry's executive office chair. "Yeah," he said into the receiver.

"Look, here's the deal," Harry Sarkissian's voice came down the line. "That knife you want so bad? I planned to sell it to OJ's people. But I'm happy to sell it to you. However, one important condition."

"What?" Jumbo asked.

"It'll be at the bottom of the Catalina channel in twenty minutes if you don't let Cheryl go right now."

Checkmated in the first move, Jumbo's face slumped in disbelief. He shook his head. "No, you won't. Too much money for you."

"But I will. Cheryl's my sister. Can't worry about money when it's my sister."

"Your sister?" Jumbo felt a headache coming on.

"Yeah. Married Alex Bedrosian. She doesn't use my name anymore."

It wasn't quite clear to Jumbo if he should believe Sarkissian. "If I don't get that knife, I really will shoot her right in the head."

"Do that and you really don't get the knife. I sell it to Nazarian, he drops it in the ocean and you're out of luck."

His mind racing, Jumbo tried to quickly calculate if he had a move to make.

"Look, I know why you want it," Harry continued. "Gets you off the hook. I know all about the grand jury."

Jumbo sighed. "Okay, okay, so I let her go. What then?"

"You and I meet. We work this out."

Jumbo thought that over. "Let's say I do. How can I be sure the knife is still okay?"

"It just is. I still want money for it. You let Cheryl go and nothing happens to the knife."

"I let her go and you want money? Both?"

"Precisely."

The big man let out a resigned groan. "Where do we meet?"

"You know the Proud Bird, end of the runway at LAX?"

"All black people do. Always big crowd there."

"That's the point. I'll be there in an hour."

Jumbo thought about it. "Okay, fine, I won't kill your sister. But what do I do with this other asshole?"

"What other asshole?" Harry was genuinely surprised. "Who else is there?"

"This TV reporter came strutting in here."

On the other end of the call, Harry looked at the phone as if it had a meter that read true or false. "A TV reporter?"

"Yeah, a real dickhead too."

Harry ran his fingers through his silvery hair, thinking. Remembering his run-in with the reporter, he searched his pockets, fished out a card. "Name Mickey Judge, NBC?"

"That's the prick."

The bastard is relentless, Harry thought. "I really don't care what you do. Just don't kill him," he told Jumbo. "Too much of a mess. It'll come back on all of us. Some bruises and broken ribs are okay."

"I really would rather do him," Jumbo said, staring at Mick.

"Don't. We don't need the cops after us. This knife is hot. And they don't even know about it. That's the beauty of this deal. Just me and you, then you get to bring a surprise gift to the DA's office. They'll be grateful and cut you some slack."

"Fuck."

Cheryl took the phone out of Jumbo's hand, replaced it in the cradle. "Can I go now?"

Jumbo waved the gun, go. She grabbed her purse, paused at the door to look back at Mick. "Good luck," she said. "Don't come back."

Jumbo put the gun barrel to Mick's temple, cocked the pistol. He held it long enough for Mick to feel the cold metal make an impression in his skin.

"Sit here, peckerwood," Jumbo whispered. Mick's hands raised in submission, he nodded okay. The metallic click of the hammer was a potent message. Maybe he damn well could shoot him right there in Harry's office. After all, it would be Harry's mess to clean up.

Jumbo and Jamal stepped over to the door, leaving Mickey in the chair in front of the big Sarkissian desk.

His voice kept low, Jumbo stood in the doorway giving Jamal instructions. "Take Solomon. Take this asshole's car. Go out to those warehouses in Pacoima, you know the ones?"

Jamal nodded.

Mick couldn't hear what Jumbo was saying, but he assumed it was about himself and it was not good.

"Beat the shit out of him," Jumbo continued, his lips close to Jamal's ear. "Work on the ribs. Break a few. Maybe use the bat. Maybe he gets a broke leg."

Jamal grinned. "Got it."

"Not the head. We don't want him dead. I want him—"

Jumbo didn't get to finish the sentence.

Seeing that his opportunity would evaporate in just moments, Mickey sprang from the chair, charged Jumbo from his blind spot. He hit the big man high, knocking him forward into Jamal. Jumbo and Jamal tumbled out through the office door.

Mick slammed the door and flipped over the Doorricade, barring the door from the inside. Thinking the two armed men might shoot, he quickly stepped out of the way.

The shots didn't come at first. Jumbo was screaming at Mick to open up. Then both he and Jamal started firing through the door.

Mick picked up a chair and swept it back and forth through the window. Glass fell in a shower below. He grabbed the tape from Sarkissian's desk. He climbed up on the sill, took a look, and jumped.

What lay below was the outside wedding venue. The grass was thick; the sprinklers had left it soggy. Mick rolled when he hit the ground, feeling some of the broken glass jabbing his hands and shoulders. He surprised himself: maybe a sprain to his left ankle, grass stains on his pants and jacket, some cuts. But nothing seemed broken.

It took a few hard kicks, but Jamal finally broke open the door bar, which had been weakened by gunshots. Jumbo rushed through and ran straight to the window. He watched as Mick hobbled across the wide expanse of lawn, looking like he'd survived the second-story jump.

"You and Solomon take his car, see if you can find him," Jumbo seethed. "If you can, put a little extra into the beating. Then take his car back downtown and torch it."

Precisely an hour later, Jumbo Blake was sitting in a booth at the Proud Bird, fuming. The popular eatery was at the end of the runway at LAX. Every two minutes, another passenger jet whistled by the windows for yet another safe landing.

Harry Sarkissian and Gary Minasian approached the booth. "Me and your boss gonna talk," Jumbo said to Gary. "Mind if you get a drink at the bar?"

Minasian looked at Harry. Yes or no? Harry nodded yes.

"Lookit," Jumbo said when the two men were alone. "You and me got to make a deal here. I need that knife bad."

Harry Sarkissian waited to speak until the waiter got their drink orders. He asked for a vodka tonic. Jumbo said "Rum and coke."

"That thing is worth maybe two million to me," Harry said. "I can't just do you a two-million-dollar favor."

"*Two* mil? You jacked the price?"

Harry ignored the question. "How'd it go with that TV reporter?"

Jumbo scowled. "That's a sore spot. Fucking blindsided me, got away."

"Is that a problem?"

Jumbo shrugged. "Wasn't going to waste him anyway. He got away without a beating, but he had to jump from your window. Probably fucked himself up."

Window? "Did he break the window?" Harry asked, alarmed. "I got a lot of nice art in there."

"Yeah. Actually, the office is kind of a mess."

"Shit," Harry said. He picked up his phone, punched in some numbers. "Cheryl, honey, go back over and see how bad it is. Yeah, Jumbo." He turned to Jumbo. "Don't tell me you shot the place up?"

Jumbo shrugged. "Just the door."

"Fuck. Cheryl, go see what you can do."

Clicking off the call, Harry steamed in silence.

"What could I do?" Jumbo asked. "The asshole is doing a TV story about our deal. I had to do whatever I could to . . . ummm . . . discourage him."

"The artwork is expensive. Some priceless. How bad is it?"

"To be honest, I didn't stop to look," Jumbo said dismissively. "It's a new door and a new window. Let's get down to business."

Harry needed a couple of minutes to work on his anger. When he was ready to talk, he said Nazarian would pay a lot of money. "You're going to have to meet the price."

"They want to put me away," Jumbo said. "The knife gets me off the hook. Not fair of you to jack me up when I'm looking at serious time."

"One thing I'm curious about," Harry said, ignoring Jumbo's plea.

"You'd send the brother to death row?"

Jumbo shook his head dismissively. "Lots of brothers on death row. One more don't hurt nobody. I'm thinking about me. I need that fuckin' knife."

A sneer on his lips, Harry Sarkissian made up his mind. "Fuck Nazarian. The little shit has always been an asshole to me." Just like that, he dumped his countryman. "Fuck OJ. Got two million you can spare?"

Jumbo wrinkled his nose and shook his head. "You jackin' me up asking that kind of money. OJ looking at death row. You can squeeze him. I'm just up for a little drug thing, out in a few years. I'm in a different category when it comes to paying."

"Think they send you to Pelican Bay?"

Jumbo looked disgusted. "That's cold, man."

"You got the biggest drug operation in Southern California. You rack two mil in your sleep. I don't mind selling the thing to you and telling Nazarian to fuck off, but price is price."

Jumbo hated being pressured like this, but he had to keep the deal alive. "Fine. Couple days while I round up the stacks. Just don't let anything happen to that thing. I need it to be perfect."

Harry Sarkissian said he understood. "It's perfect now. It'll be perfect when I hand it to you."

Jumbo got up. "I'll be in touch." He headed to the car valet.

"Don't take too long," Harry said, waving Gary back to the booth.

The big man strode out of the restaurant and folded himself into the gold Mercedes.

Gary slipped into the booth.

"Trust him?"

Sarkissian shook his head. "No, but I bought a little time to jack up Nazarian again." He grinned at Minasian. "I could go for three mil."

"And double-cross Jumbo?" Gary asked, consternation on his face and in his voice. "That'll come back on us."

"It's no double-cross," Harry objected, waving his finger to underscore his correction. "It's a bidding war. That's different." Harry took a sip of his drink.

"How about we do a deal that doesn't keep the war going?"

"You're a pussy," Sarkissian said, sipping his drink.

33

Jamal drove Mickey's Blazer around Glendale for an hour, looking for him. Solomon sat in the passenger seat, shaking his head.

"Tell me again how he got away?"

"Fuck you," Jamal mumbled. "It was the boss who turned his back on the guy."

Solomon laughed. "You're going to find out. The boss never takes the blame."

Jamal cursed his luck and kept going up and down the streets off Brand Avenue, in the neighborhood of the Delerium. He and Solomon never spotted the runaway reporter.

But Mick saw them. He recognized his Blazer coming, and ducked into a doorway out of sight. His car turned right on the next street, and Mick got lucky: a bus was pulling up to a bus stop, and he jumped aboard.

Mick sat in the back of the bus, assessing the damage. His jacket was torn, and he was surprised to find that the knees of his jeans were ripped and bloodied. Must have been the broken glass. He had something happening on his face, because his hand came back with a little blood when he touched it. It seemed he'd come through the jump with a bit more damage than he'd thought at first.

But he had his tape back, and he'd escaped from Jumbo Blake. All in all, a win.

The bus took him back down Brand Avenue. When he saw a cab idling at the curb, he got off and grabbed the cab. "Burbank airport," he told the driver.

At the airport, he went to the Hertz desk and got a car. Then he drove home, pulled off his trashed clothes, and got in the shower.

Standing under the hot water, blood swirling in the drain, he surveyed the last twelve hours. Mick realized he had escaped both Selma and Glendale with his life. He'd started the day not having met either Billy Paboojian or Jumbo Blake. Half a day later, they'd both had a crack at him.

Mick put some iodine and band-aids on his scrapes.

He sat on his rented couch and closed his eyes. Punched in the head. Dodging bullets. Holy crap. Nobody told him a network correspondent would face that kind of stuff. Maybe in a war zone. But not in the Raisin Capital of the World and sleepy Glendale. Holy crap.

He drifted off for a few minutes, but his dreams woke him up. What if he'd been pickled? What if Jumbo had been a better shot? He thought of his daughter. He thought of Grace Russell. Holy crap. This isn't good.

But there was more to do. He dragged himself off the couch. He got into fresh clothes and went downstairs to the Hertz car.

He called the LAPD to report the Blazer stolen. He gave them the license plate number, the year, make, and model. The person he was speaking with wanted him to come down to a station to fill in a report. Mick figured no hurry. He was sure Jumbo's guys would strip it anyway.

In his rental car, gripping the steering wheel with fingers stiff as claws, Mick found himself waiting for the air conditioning to cool off, taking deep breaths. Yes, he'd powered through that horror show as if he had the balls of King Kong, but it wasn't the way he felt.

He felt terrified.

Jumbo was much scarier up close than he'd anticipated. And the son of a bitch was shooting through the door, for god's sakes. "I'm done pushing my luck," Mick said to himself.

Mick took a few deep breaths before he put the car in reverse. He slipped out of his parking spot and chunked it into drive. Slowly, he crept out of the parking lot at the Equestrian Arms Apartments. It seemed his heart was beating too fast to drive fast. Carefully, he negotiated a few simple turns, got on Riverside Drive to scoot back to the safety of the Bureau. Behind gates. Behind guards. Behind locked doors.

Mick felt like a total amateur to walk into a trap like that. He marveled that he'd got through it. He wondered how many times luck would pull him out of a jam.

His pager was buzzing on his belt. He drove on without looking. Mick didn't care. He was too busy coming down from a ledge. His nerves still jangled like he had touched a hot socket.

As he was about to turn into the NBC parking lot, he changed his mind. Instead, he turned into Chadney's lot. It was still early. The valets weren't on duty yet. The place was close to deserted.

Sitting at the bar with a drink, he finally pulled the pager off his belt and glanced at the numbers. It was a lineup of the same number, signaling urgency and frustration. The calls were all from Alison de Groot. There was no way Mick could look at those repeated pages and not conclude he was in some sort of trouble. Good news didn't usually warrant pages five minutes apart for nearly the last hour.

There was no point in calling. He slugged down the rest of his drink and left some bills on the bar. He walked across the street. Exhausted, he got in the slow-moving elevator rather than bound up the staircase.

He stood in Alison de Groot's doorway. "You called?"

She looked up at him with pursed lips and a squinty eye. "Take a seat, my boy," she said, picking up the phone. "He's here," she said to someone on the other end, and she returned the phone to its cradle.

"You look like shit. Are those black eyes? And what are all those band-aids?"

Mick nodded yes. "Long story. If you don't mind, later."

She shook her head and stared at him like he was a rogue child.

Mick sat on the couch opposite her desk. "So . . . what's up?"

She gave him one of those *I'm disappointed in you* looks. "For starters, I don't think I should have to page you eight times before you get back to me."

There wasn't much to do about that complaint. She was right, of course. But he could hardly say he was sneaking around trying to work a story in secret and had been staring down an angry thug with a gun. Those kinds of details are best saved for after the story is done and he's accepting congratulations. "Sorry. I had the pager in the car, and I was . . ." he searched his weary mind for the rest of the sentence . . . "I was out of the car."

"What? You were at the beach?"

"No, I screwed up. It was off my belt."

Her door opened, and a producer named Wanda Nancosta walked in, her face decked out in the sour expression that was her personal calling card. She was a middle-aged, dark-haired, overweight, twenty-year veteran of the bureau whose main skill, it seemed to Mick, was her uncanny ability to spy on colleagues and report to New York.

"Wanda and you will be working together," de Groot said to Mick. His heart sank.

There wasn't much of a greeting to each other besides a nod.

Wanda looked about as pleased as Mick to get this news. "What happened to you?"

"Long story. But in service of the cause."

Alison arched an eyebrow at him. She would want to know about "the cause."

Neither Mick nor Wanda was pleased with their assignment with each other. But they both knew better than to object in front of each other. Mick figured the whiny witch would drop in to Alison's office later to beg off. But with the way his luck was running, she'd get a no.

"What are we working on?" Mick asked.

"Well, it turns out boy wonder Mr. Moody isn't quite as gung ho as he started out." Alison was speaking of David Moody, of course. "Now it turns out he needs to take weekends off and fly home to see honey pie for a conjugal."

He needs to bang the wife, Mick said to himself. If he doesn't get at it, maybe she bangs someone else.

"So I'll be needing you two to take care of weekend *Today Show*. They'll need a live shot and package at seven Eastern, both Saturday and Sunday."

That would be four in the morning Pacific. Mick tried to make sure his inward groan wasn't audible.

"And a repeat at eight ET," she added.

"Who's doing weekend *Nightly*?" Mick asked.

"That would be Burbank's redoubtable Johnny Furness, veteran of wars, tsunamis, earthquakes, political campaigns, and myriad idiocies that have come down from New York over the decades. So don't be upset with your assignment. He's not terribly pleased either." She gave them both the grim smile that meant discussion over, there is nothing to be done except kindly salute and march.

While the prospect of working with a woman who rode to work on a broom and ridiculous weekend hours were both horrific, Mick was actually relieved to find that he wasn't in the trouble he'd half expected.

Wanda suggested that they both adopt a Wednesday-through-Sunday work week, in which they would catch up on the court proceedings on Wednesday, start formulating a piece on Thursday and Friday, put the piece together Friday afternoon, return to the bureau at three in the morning Saturday, do the live shot at four.

What about Sunday, Mick asked.

"We go home, take a nap, and come back Saturday afternoon to cut the Sunday piece. After six Sunday morning when *Today* clears, we're off."

"That sounds about right," Alison said brightly. "Be sure to call if anything seems to be going sideways."

The meeting broke up, Mick and Wanda going their separate ways. The less time he spent around her the better, as far as Mick was concerned. He was positive she was one of the Jansen-ites who rushed to a computer or telephone to tell on him whenever he did something the news god might frown on.

One incident in particular stuck in his mind. A year and a half ago, the fire at the Branch Davidians was raging, everybody in the Bureau gathered in the newsroom riveted to network coverage on ABC, CBS, NBC, and CNN. Jennings was on ABC's air, Rather was on CBS, Blitzer was on CNN, but Jansen was still missing from NBC's air. Several people in the bureau were muttering "Where's Tom?" Mick made a joke. "Probably signing the lunch check at 21."

Nobody laughed. No mirth about Tom. Mick watched Wanda duck out to her office. He just knew she would be tapping out a note to Tom on the new correspondent's heresy. The bitch.

Mick was walking down the staircase to the Channel 4 newsroom when he met Danny Bowls coming up. "I was just going to see you."

Danny didn't look like he was in a good mood. "I'm not even going to ask what the fuck happened to you. You're a mess."

"I know."

"I was coming to see your boss, matter of fact. Might as well take it up with you directly."

"Okay," Mick said, cautiously.

"We got a problem."

Uh-oh. "What?"

"This," Danny said, holding out a small piece of paper. It was the carbon from a phone-message pad. "You know I recognize your handwriting, right?"

Mick got a sinking feeling. Yes, it was his handwriting. And the problem came to him quickly. He had taken the phone call from Luther Malcolm while Danny was out for a smoke. He'd written the number on a phone message pad and inadvertently left a carbon underneath. A stupid error. And one that showed he'd lied to Danny when he said nothing had happened while Danny was out for a smoke.

"I thought this note was odd," Danny said, wiggling the small piece of paper. "The letters 'OJ,' a phone number," he said, "a real mystery."

Mick nodded. Pursed his lips. He knew what was coming.

"I checked the number in the reverse directory. Got the address. Sent Shuman down there to see what it was about."

"Look, Danny—"

"I'm not done," he said, holding up his hand for Mickey to stop. "Shuman meets two people at that address. A man and a woman. He gets names. A Luther Malcolm and a Louise Grove. Later I figure out she's the one who killed the guy in that home invasion, whose husband dropped dead."

Mick squirmed.

"They say they got nothing to add. They already talked to somebody from Channel 4, none other than Mickey Judge. And that Mickey Judge actually already interviewed the man. So leave us alone, they say. Go the fuck away."

"Look, Danny—"

"I'm not done. Then we have a house explosion in Inglewood, two people dead. Turns out the same two people. Now, it could be a coincidence that the house with two people connected to a home-invasion killing and with some kind of OJ intersection blows up in a gas leak, could just be unhappy coincidence for hard-luck people. Or . . . or . . . or maybe there's something more to it." He stopped to take a breath and poke the air with an angry index finger. "In any case, since you got the tip while sitting at my desk, on my phone, I think I have a right to demand you tell me what you got and let me work the fucking story that someone called in to my newsroom."

Danny was hot. He realized he'd been screwed by a friend, and he was pissed off.

"Look, Danny—"

He wasn't having it. "Don't 'look' me. You got a tape of that guy who's now dead, and I want to see it. Now. Where is it?"

"Danny, remember when I said if I got a lead, I was going to work it, and you said 'Attaboy,' cheered me on?"

"Listen, pal," Danny said, assuming his bulldog stance and jabbing an index finger in Mick's chest. "You totally fail at *sneaky*. I actually have some video of you interviewing a black guy on the back deck of the Criminal Courts Building. My crew guys said they saw you show up with a guy trying to be all stealthy, so they shot a little video for the hell of it. And then they thought it was highly unusual to see you do a quick interview and beat it without the customary *hey-how-you-doin'* to all your old friends. So Shuman ID's the guy for me, and now I know it was Luther Malcolm, the guy who died in a house that blew up. I've already done a lot of work on this, and what I've found is crumbs that lead to two people. OJ and you."

Mick had nothing to say. There was no denying.

"So let's go. I want to see that fucking tape."

Mick was trapped. "It's in my office," he said. He had no choice.

"I'm not letting you out of my sight. Lead on."

34

Back in Alison de Groot's office, Mick felt like the accused in a court-martial. She was behind her desk, judge and jury, an expression of deep consternation on her face. Mick was sitting to her right, alone, isolated. On the long couch under the window that overlooked the Burbank lot were Bart Wimple, Mick's New York nemesis; Nathan Kaufman, the news director from downstairs; and Danny Bowls, Mick's angry friend.

The interview with Lummie Malcolm had just concluded on a monitor on the wall. Everybody had had a good view. She popped the tape out of a player and set it on her desk.

During the playback of the interview, Wimple had shot a lethal look Mick's way every couple of minutes. He didn't quite know what to do about this mess.

Kaufman and Bowls were likewise glaring. The news director was a tall, thin man with a bushy moustache and thinning dark hair. He was representing the interests of Channel 4.

"The story came to our desk, and your guy hijacked it. Rightfully, the interview with the guy belongs to us. And I want to run with it." Kaufman broke the silence, claiming first rights.

Alison turned to Mick. "Who shot the interview?"

"Butch," Mick said.

She turned back to Kaufman. "It's my day hire who shot it. It's my correspondent who interviewed. The tape is ours."

Wimple spoke up to Kaufman. "You can't run with this anyway. You got nothing but an interview with a guy claiming something preposterous. You don't know this knife exists. We wouldn't put it on *Nightly* or the *Today Show,* and you shouldn't run it either."

Kaufman wasn't buying it. "We run with shit less than this all the time. On the tape is the guy who called our desk. He says he was one of two people who retrieved a backpack from the trash after OJ put it there. This was on the night OJ killed his wife. He says on the tape he saw the knife. Then he ends up dead. That's a lot, and it's good enough for me."

Wimple shook his head. "Yes, the guy is dead. You have no way to question him, check his credibility. He could have been making this shit up."

It was Danny's time to back up his boss. "Here's the deal. The preliminary hearing is going to be over in a few days. Then there's going to be weeks of jury selection. Damn little news. The knife angle, the mystery of the knife, the suspicious deaths of two people connected to the knife, chasing down all the angles . . . all that gives us a way to stay ahead of the story until the trial actually starts. I can churn this thing for weeks."

"You can't make this cock-and-bull story about a mystery knife last until the trial. That's not till after the first of the year," Wimple scoffed.

Alison interrupted, addressing Bowls. "Wait. Are you saying you'd be willing to hold the story until the prelim wraps?"

Now Kaufman interrupted. "No. I don't want to wait. This story is fucking hot!" He poked his hands in the air in frustration. "Are you kidding me? A guy says he saw the murder weapon, bloody fingerprints, and the thing is in the wind somewhere. And the guy seems to have been murdered. Of course we'd run with that story." He turned to Wimple. "If *Nightly* has such high standards that you wouldn't touch it, just don't. But don't stand in my way."

Mick was getting a migraine. He glanced over at Alison. She met his eyes and gave him a *holy-shit-what-did-you-get-me-into* look.

Wimple sat forward. "You can't do that, because the second you put it on the air, the net is going to have to pick it up, even though it doesn't come close to our standards. So what will happen? I will have to write a script that says *we don't believe our own story, but we're telling you anyway*. That's a steaming pile of crap."

Kaufman turned to de Groot. "We don't want to have to go up the chain of command on this. If we can't come to some agreement in this office, it's going to get ugly. Vice presidents are going to be throwing lightning bolts around, and I assure you that you and I don't want to be caught in the crossfire."

Alison furrowed her brow and clamped her mouth shut. She could imagine the phone calls. He was right.

She turned to Mick. "First off, a public flogging, my boy. You have started an internal ownership fight. The worst kind, because even though we're all NBC News, in reality we have totally different standards on what is ready for air."

Mick squirmed in his chair. He didn't like this "flogging," as she put it, and he was trying to restrain himself from blowing the room up.

"So let's hear from you," she said. "What else do you have?"

Mick took a deep breath. "Here's what I'll say—"

Wimple interrupted. "Jesus Christ, don't you dare hold anything back—"

"Hey, fuck off," Mick shot back. "You're in here big-footing me on two-bit day-of crap with your golden boy, and I'm actually still working the story. I'm not telling you everything so you can just hand it over to the twirp—"

"You fucking well better—" Wimple shouted.

"Calm down, boys," Alison interrupted both of them.

Bowls and Kaufman had two different reactions. Danny was embarrassed for his friend, but also still a little pissed at him. Kaufman was delighted to start an internal fight at the network.

Neither said a word.

Alison de Groot waited for the air to settle. "It's Channel 4's tip, but it's our tape. And my guy has been working the story," she said, evenly. "So I want to hear from him where he is on the story." She looked around the room, engaging each man's eyes, setting down her rules. "So, Mickey Judge, it's time to talk. And please, if your obvious wounds have anything to do with the story, don't leave that out."

Mick took a deep breath. He was determined to not give too much away to this room full of sharks. It was his story to work, even if his ownership wasn't as tidy as he would have liked. Telling about Billy Paboojian discussing killing him and Jumbo Blake shooting up Harry Sarkissian's office was probably too sensational at this point.

"The basic thing is the knife Luther Malcolm described is in a small backpack, and that backpack is in a box. Luther and Gordon Grove put it in that box for safekeeping. I think I know who has the box. But I don't know where the box is. That's what I'm working on. If you all will just stand down for a little more time, I think I can close the deal."

"What's that mean?" Wimple challenged him.

"It means I think I can get video or stills of the knife. If we have video, and we have Lummie's interview, I think we meet the threshold for a story. Until then, all we have is a dead guy's word that there is such a thing."

"Do we need the cops to confirm it's the murder weapon?" Alison asked.

"That would be ideal. But besides me, I know of two other people who want the knife, and I have a guess as to why, but I'm not sure one is willing to turn it over to the cops."

"Well, who else would they give it to?" Wimple asked, his tone pissy.

Mick waited to answer. Just long enough to glare at the asshole. "How much you think the knife is worth to OJ's defense lawyers?"

"Oh, just great," Wimple blew up. "Now we're interfering with evidence crucial to the biggest murder trial the country's ever seen. Fantastic. We're totally fucked."

The Channel 4 guys screwed their mouths down tight. They wanted no part of this argument.

"Not necessarily," Alison said. "We would be revealing that the evidence might exist. Here's a guy who says it's the knife probably used in the murder. Maybe Mick gets a picture of the knife the guy says was probably used in the murder. Proving or disproving is up to the authorities."

Mick saw a flicker of hope. That sounded like she was on his side.

The little prick Wimple stared at her. "You know that's not air-able. How are we going to look when they take this knife and find the blood is from a deer or a cow? We're going to look like chumps. A certain party is not going to like that, I can promise you."

Everybody knew he was referring to Tom. At NBC, all roads led to Tom Jansen.

"We're not going to air until authorities say they're investigating whether it has a connection to the case."

Even Kaufman had to adjust. "You're probably right," he said, backing off his original position. "Regrettably, we'll have to hold off until somebody confirms an official investigation of whether it has something to do with the case." He was clearly disappointed he couldn't run with half a story.

"Wait," Mick interrupted. "What does 'something to do with the story' mean?"

Kaufman threw open his hands. "I'd be happy with a confirmation the police lab is testing it. We'd have a couple days to work it, stretch it out. And every day we'd wrap up with 'time will tell' so we're covered if it turns out to be nothing."

"In other words, you'd milk the cow for a few days without worrying about getting actual milk," Mick said.

Kaufman shrugged. "We do it all the time. It's why we're number one."

Wimple was only partly mollified. "We're going to have to tell New York what's going on," he grumbled. "A whole bunch of people are going to want in on this."

Everybody in the room knew what he meant. Vice presidents of News, vice presidents of Standards and Practices, executive producers of the shows. Mick could picture them all. A bunch of swaggering roosters in thousand-dollar suits.

"Hang on," Alison said. "Let's hear the rest from Mick. Where are you at this moment?" she asked him.

His exhale could be felt across the room. "I have the name of the guy who was last known to have the knife. I'm running him down."

Alison turned to the Channel 4 guys. "How much time before you'll want to show the cops your hand?"

Kaufman glanced over at Bowls, raised his eyebrows in a question mark. "How many days left in the prelim?"

Bowls shrugged. "I'm guessing four, maybe five."

Alison turned to Mick. "Be honest here. Anybody else on this? Do we have competition?"

Mick shook his head, thanking his good fortune he didn't have to tell her Jumbo Blake briefly possessed a copy of the Lummie interview. "No sign anybody talked to Lummie or the late Mr. Grove or the late Mrs. Grove. So unless the guy who's got it is calling reporters, which I doubt, I'd say we got it to ourselves for the moment."

Wimple was shaking his head. "I don't like this."

"Well, what would you do?" Alison asked him.

"First off, it has to be a *Nightly* story; so frankly, Mick, you're out of it."

Mick erupted. "Your boy knows fuck all. I'm not holding his hand while he does my story."

"It's got to be Moody," Bart said, shrugging his shoulders, end of story. "Direct from Tom. That's just the way it is."

Mick turned to Alison. "Seriously?"

"Calm down," she said to him. She turned back to Wimple. "And you'd do what?" Alison asked, trying to move him along.

Wimple rubbed his bald head, thinking. "I'd have Moody take a copy of the tape and have a camera crew follow him as he walked into Parker Center to screen the tape to the cops."

"Oh, for Chrissakes, that's idiotic," Kaufman exploded. "They'd just hold a press conference to announce a major lead. I know those assholes. They'd fucking play the tape in a news conference. Everybody would have it."

"They damn well shouldn't. It would be cop malpractice," Bart shot back. "Besides, you just said yourself you'd confront the cops with what you got."

"I wouldn't hand them the tape," Kaufman snapped.

"Settle down, boys," Alison said wearily.

Wimple took a deep breath and continued. "I'd cut a deal for us. They confirm the knife is evidence in the case. We'd have the exclusive when they had to reveal the knife in discovery."

"You're fucking dreaming," Kaufman muttered. "Discovery? That's weeks away. I'm not going along with that at all. You even think that's what you're going to do, I'm going to air with the interview."

"Hold on, hold on." Alison had heard enough. She called for time out, making a T with her hands. "I have to take control of this. So here's what's going to happen." She looked at each of the men and shifted from her command voice to her calming voice. "You guys are all going to stand down for a few days while Mick continues to work the story. He's got a lead or two, let him work it."

"Local," she said, pointing at Kaufman and Bowls, "can have the story with its own reporter the day Mick is ready for air. Mick will do the story for the *Today Show*." She looked at Mick and nodded, asking 'okay by you?' without actually saying the words. "And Bart, you and Moody can have the story on *Nightly* the night before." She looked around the room. "Channel 4 gets the local exclusive, Mickey Judge gets the *Today Show* exclusive, and boy wonder gets the *Nightly* exclusive. Is that splitting the baby evenly enough for everybody here?"

"So the punk is going to break my story?" Mick asked Alison. "That sucks big-time."

"Hey, fuck off," Bart shot back. "Take it up with Tom and you'll leave the room with your head in your hands."

Alison called for silence again. She addressed Mickey. "Young Moody will credit NBC correspondent Mickey Judge with discovery of the story in his story for *Nightly*. You'll take your bows the next morning on the *Today Show*."

Wimple muttered "Tom's not going to like this."

"I'll deal with him," Alison said.

Kaufman held up his hands in semi-surrender. "No longer than the end of the prelim."

Danny Bowls pursed his lips, looked down at his shoes. He didn't like the compromise one bit. It should have been his exclusive days ago. He felt ripped off.

Bart Wimple nodded. "For now, okay."

Alison turned to Mick. "Before I send you out there, how are you going to do this?"

His fury bottled up long enough, Mick addressed the three men trying to take control of his story. "I just want to remind you all this arguing is about my story. There wouldn't be a story to fight over if I hadn't run this down," Mick said, barely restraining his anger. "Maybe if Danny had been on the desk when that call came in, maybe you would have checked it out. But don't bullshit a bullshitter. You don't let reporters spend any longer on a story than what it takes to get a quick interview and a fact or two for a stand-up." Mick looked at Kaufman. "Remember, I worked in your newsroom. I know how things go. Fact is, I'm the one who went out and blew my weekend and found the guy. I'm the one who got him on tape before he died."

The three men fidgeted, clearly resenting getting called out. "Did anybody even know there was a knife story before I got it on tape? No. You all gave up after they couldn't find it on the side of the freeway. I'm the one who landed the story." He paused to look each person in the eye. "I know I maybe should have told Danny or Alison what I was doing, but you guys ought to be a little more grateful for what I've already done. Instead, I'm sitting here listening to three guys who did nothing tell me I did something wrong and dividing up my story among yourselves. Frankly, I feel like telling you all to go fuck yourselves."

"Now, now, Mickey," Alison scolded.

"No, seriously, Alison," Mick shot back. "I'm the one who is on the bubble here. I'm the one fighting for my job, and I got this pack of vultures trying to pick my bones. Fuck it. I'm going out to work the story, but I'll be damned if I'm going to sit here like a whipped dog. These guys don't want to admit it, but they'd have nothing to fight over if I hadn't gone out and done the work."

She knew he was right. She glanced around at the others, but there were only the averted eyes that said they were not in the least chastised. The capacity for news executives to be embarrassed is very limited. Mick glanced around the room. Pursed lips, eyes downturned, uncomfortable silences.

Alison de Groot broke the silence. "Go find Tony Salt. He'll be your producer. I'll free up Willis and Bill for your crew."

Mick sighed. His righteous indignation was not going to score him points. Now she was adding people to his efforts, probably to keep an eye on him. It was something he had to accept. But the story was getting crowded.

"Get crackin'," she said, dismissing him. "You don't have much time."

It was Mick's cue to leave. "I have no reason to expect it, but you guys should wish me luck," he said to the three execs.

Nobody said a word. Mick stalked out of the meeting, trailing fumes of anger like smoke.

Kaufman and Bowls got up and gave Alison the nods that meant meeting over. There was no need to further emphasize what their limits were. Kaufman had made himself clear.

But he added one thing. "When you hired him, I let out a huge sigh of relief."

She returned a grim smile. Kaufman and Bowls left her office.

When they were alone, Wimple sat with his legs crossed, sharpening the crease in his gabardine slacks with two fingers. "That tirade didn't help."

"Have you guys already made the decision he has to go?" she asked, her voice soft but her tone alarmed.

"There's been talk," he said. "Jesus, did you see those eyes? And the bandages? The guy's been out getting in fights. That bullshit story about running into something don't play."

Alison de Groot frowned, ignored the business of Mick's face. "Let's see how this works out. He isn't the first correspondent to tell New York to go fuck itself."

Wimple scrunched his upper lip against his nose. He didn't agree, but he changed the subject. "Look, I can't be keeping secrets from New York," he said softly.

Alison knew he meant he couldn't keep a secret like this from Jansen and the *Today Show.*

"I know that even better than you," she said. "Sugar already hates me." Bernie Sugar was the exec producer of the *Today Show,* with a reputation as a midget with the temper of a deranged tyrant.

Wimple didn't say anything, which in its own way was a confirmation that she was right about Sugar.

"Okay, so let's do it this way," she continued. "You send a note to himself," she said, meaning Jansen. "Keep it simple. Say we're working a possible angle on the murder weapon, and it will be an exclusive. But leave it at that."

"You think that's enough?" he asked. He got up to leave."It's about all we know for certain, not counting the interview already on tape. Think you can keep that to yourself for now?"

He grimaced. "For now."

As he left, she thought to herself: "Liar." She knew he'd puke up the whole story just to make himself look good to the *Nightly News* god.

The question was whether he'd wait days or hours.

She decided it probably wouldn't even be hours. Minutes, more likely. She thought it best that she beat him to the punch. She turned to her computer screen and began composing a note. It began: "Tom, we have a situation. . . ."

35

The core group of producers and correspondents in the Burbank Bureau—and that included the bureau chief, Alison de Groot—had bonded together in overseas assignments, often in war zones. It was a very tough group to crack. They'd been through things where each other's lives were on the line. It was a group who could communicate with each other by a look, or a single word, imperceptible to anyone else. And the loyalties ran deep.

Mickey Judge was not one of that group, and neither was Tony Salt. Mick guessed Alison was doing him a favor in assigning him a producer who had not worked with Jansen in the Gulf War or the Fall of The Wall or any of the other high-stakes stories where personal connections were cemented.

At least Mick could assume that there was a chance Tony Salt wasn't going to call or send messages to Tom the first chance he got.

Before hooking up with his new producer, Mick went to his office and called downstairs to the Channel 4 newsroom. He got reporter Phil Shuman on the line. "Hey, can you meet me in the parking lot?"

"Sure."

Five minutes later, they were standing at Mick's rental car in the lot next to the four-story building that housed Channel 4 and the NBC News Bureau.

Phil Shuman was a ridiculously handsome man, in Mick's opinion. He had jet-black hair, shocking blue eyes, a chin chiseled out of granite, and a winning smile. Plus he was impressively smart and a solid reporter. A pretty face, but not just that. One of Mick's favorite colleagues.

"The house explosion in Inglewood," Mick said. "Two people died, that one. Remember?"

"Yesterday, yeah. What about it?"

"Anything funky about it?"

Shuman shook his head. "Not really. They said it was a gas leak and probably someone lit a cigarette."

"Was it fire department or cops investigating?"

"Fire," Phil said. "Why?"

"I knew those two people. I don't think either one smoked. And aren't you supposed to be able to smell a gas leak before it builds up?"

Shuman agreed. "That's what I thought. I guess they could have been asleep."

"And someone lit a cigarette?"

"Or maybe an electric spark. Like you flip a light switch."

Mick nodded, sure could be. Still, he was suspicious.

"You got the name of the investigator?"

Shuman pulled a reporter's notebook out of his back pocket and flipped through a few pages. "Here. Dawson. Ronnie Dawson, County Fire, the Manchester station. One West Manchester. Want a phone number?"

Mick took the number down. He had one last question. "Black or white?"

Shuman laughed. "Inglewood, man. Black. Probably lives right in the neighborhood."

Tony Salt was sitting in Mick's office, in his chair, feet up on Mick's desk. "So, I hear you're looking for me."

Tony Salt was tall, probably six-four. He wore jeans and a pullover gray sweater. He had a mischievous expression on his face at all times. He was a charmer. And Tony Salt was black.

"Let's go to Inglewood," Mick said. "Gotta check something out."

Salt stood up, towering over Mick. "That's why you needed me. You're doing black."

"This is a sidebar. Just want to check something out."

"Where should I tell the crew to meet us?"

Mick shook his head no. "Tell them to stand by here. We'll have them meet us somewhere else."

On the drive to Inglewood, Tony was curious about the story, naturally. He said Alison hadn't told him much.

"First thing about this story," Mick said, "is it may turn out to be nothing, complete BS," Mick said. He explained the basics quickly.

Tony Salt could make his eyebrows bend in opposite directions, a facial trick as good as saying *you're shittin' me*. "So, we're looking for OJ's murder weapon. The one the cops couldn't find?"

"Sounds nuts, I know," Mick admitted. "But that's where I'm at. An improbable story that could be huge . . . if true."

They drove by Lummie's house, what was left of it. The roof opened up in a jagged hole, and ugly black burns flared out the windows. When the explosion had ignited, deadly flames had ripped through the windows and blown the doors off.

"Two dead," Mick said. "Luther Malcolm and Louise Grove."

"Damn," Tony Salt mumbled, examining the damage. "That's a bitch."

They drove by Louise Grove's house. Mick was shocked to find that it had suffered a fire as well. The neat little yellow bungalow was a blackened shell.

"Jesus, Jumbo did this one too," Mick muttered.

That name set off Tony Salt. "Wait. Who?" Salt demanded. "Did you say Jumbo, as in Jumbo Blake?"

"Yeah. Did I leave him out of the story?"

"You sure as hell did. What's he got to do with this?"

"His brother was killed in there," Mick said, pointing at Louise Grove's house, "and she was killed in that other house, along with the owner, Luther Malcolm. I think Jumbo did 'em both."

"Oh, shit, this is deep," Tony Salt said, a frown sinking over his face. "Jumbo Blake don't play. You sure you know what you're doing?"

Considering Salt's reaction, Mick thought it best to refrain from revealing the moment he jumped out a second-story window, dancing around Jumbo's bullets.

They drove a few blocks to the county fire station at 1 West Manchester. Ronnie Dawson was at a desk in a cubicle at the back of the building, behind the bright red fire trucks.

"The gas explosion with the two dead. Could be all there is to it. Don't know yet," he said.

Mick was listening. They had agreed that Tony should do the lead. Black man to black man might work out better.

"How does an explosion like that happen?"

Dawson was professional. "I can't get into too much detail. But usually it's a stove. That's the normal assumption. It's July. No reason for the heater to be on."

"But what ignites it?"

"Almost anything. Someone lights a cigarette—"

"Neither one smoked," Mick interrupted.

"That was my information too," Dawson agreed. "Might have been a light switch. Or maybe the air conditioner kicking on. Anything that makes a spark."

"Any sign of foul play?" Tony asked.

Dawson shook his head. "Now you're getting into the

investigation. Can't go there with you."

"Did the victims die from burns, or smoke inhalation?"

"You'll have to ask the coroner. Not my area."

Tony looked over to Mick and shrugged. "You got anything else?"

"Did the house have a crawl space beneath the floor?" Mick asked.

"Yeah, it did," Dawson nodded.

"Could someone crawl under there and tamper with the gas line?"

"I can't talk about the investigation with you." Dawson shut down.

"So there is an investigation?"

"Of course. Two people died."

"What about that house fire over on Manchester Terrace? The lady who lived there is one of your victims."

Dawson eased back in his chair. It squeaked. "I don't mind telling you, that one bothered me. Just because the owner died in the other house. Maybe a coffee-maker started that one."

"But no one was there. Why would the coffee-maker start a fire if no one was making coffee?"

Dawson shrugged. "They just do. Sometimes. We get a lot of fires that are countertop appliances. Coffee-makers. Toasters. Toaster ovens. People should unplug them, but they don't."

Mick and Tony were driving away. "What's this got to do with the story of the knife?" Tony asked. "Aren't we getting sidetracked?"

"A bit," Mick agreed. "But when your main witness dies, I think it's worth finding out why."

At the medical examiner's office near the county hospital, an Asian woman who conducted the autopsy saw nothing particularly unusual about the deaths of the two people. "Looks like they were sleeping," she said. "It was evening. Looks like they were knocked unconscious by the force of the explosion, then they actually died of smoke inhalation. Though they probably would have died of burns even if somehow they'd been rescued from the building."

Mick and Tony were headed downtown, to Jordan Downs.

"Weird they would be sleeping so early in the evening," Mick said.

"Maybe they got it on and dozed off."

"Plausible, I suppose," Mick said absently. But he was wondering about that scenario. Louise Grove didn't seem the type to finish dinner and jump Luther. Luther didn't seem the type to suddenly display seductive powers. But maybe he was wrong.

"Why do you suspect Jumbo Blake had anything to do with it?" Tony asked. "I really don't want to be messing with him over nothing."

"He's got a reputation for revenge," Mick said. "Louise shot his brother. Luther was probably collateral. But Jumbo had a gun in my face."

"When did Jumbo have a gun in your face?"

"This morning," Mick admitted. "We were both in the same place, looking for the guy with the knife. I want him to know network news is on to him so he doesn't come after me."

Tony Salt reacted with alarm. "You think you can scare off Jumbo Blake by waving your press pass?"

"I'm just sayin'. I end up dead," Mick said. "Jumbo Blake did it."

Reluctantly, Tony Salt called the crew and told them the address in South Central. Both the soundman, Willis Gillis, who labored under the obvious nickname *Rhyme*, and the camera guy, Bill Prettyman, were black, but they did not think their skin color was any particular protection in that neighborhood. Tony tried to mollify them. "Just get some exteriors and the street scene, get back in the van, and wait for us."

When Mickey and Salt arrived at the Blake HQ on Anzac, a very large black man came out of the building to see what the white guy and the black dude at the gate wanted. Rhyme and Bill said he'd already been out to tell them "No pictures." Bill had told him he had an assignment and he was damn well going to take pictures on a public street. The guard wasn't happy.

Now the white guy was asking for Jumbo. No, he said, Jumbo ain't here.

Mick could see the gold Mercedes parked in the back. He was pretty sure Jumbo was watching them on a CCTV screen.

He handed his card through the gate. "Just tell him Mickey Judge from NBC News was here to see him. We had a nice conversation this morning. Let him know I'll try to catch up with him later at the Hollywood house."

The guard looked perplexed. "What Hollywood house?"

"Just tell him," Mick said. "He'll know."

Mick told Bill to try to get a shot of the Mercedes.

36

At Roscoe's Chicken and Waffles on West Manchester in Inglewood, Robert Nazarian and Jimmy Cheatwood were dressed in golf slacks and golf shirts. They had finished a round at the Riviera Country Club on OJ's membership, and they drove down the 405 to Inglewood for lunch. They walked into Roscoe's in golf shoes with rubber cleats.

The waitress brought their order. Cheatwood had a plate of fried chicken, collard greens, potato salad with a tomato topping, and cornbread with a dollop of butter. Nazarian had the house special, fried chicken and a waffle the size of a hubcap frosted with butter and soaked in syrup.

They had a table at the back of the restaurant with an unusual buffer of empty tables. They needed privacy, so Jimmy quietly slipped the hostess a fifty for the arrangement.

They both had glasses of orange soda on ice.

Glancing around to make certain he couldn't be heard, Nazarian leaned close. "He wants two now."

"Two? Million?" Cheatwood reacted with genuine surprise.

Nazarian nodded yes, two million. "He called me on the way down. He says the price got jacked because another bidder has entered the picture."

"Who?" Cheatwood set his chicken back on the plate. "Who?"

"A guy named Jumbo Blake."

Now Cheatwood sat back in his chair like he'd lost his appetite. "That dude is a major drug dealer. There's a grand jury sitting on him right now. He gets that knife? He's turning it right over to the cops in exchange for dropping his case."

"They would do that?"

"To nail the OJ case down? Hell, yeah."

"I'm surprised. Let a major drug dealer off?"

"OJ Simpson is the number one prosecution in the galaxy right now," Cheatwood said. "This is not a good situation. You got to get your guy to promise not to sell the thing to him."

Nazarian was about to take a bite. He put his chicken down. The conversation was turning way more serious than he anticipated.

"Chip Trafficant is in charge of the money. He was willing to go for one, but two is really pushing it."

"Does Chip Trafficant want to see his guy on death row?"

"Of course not," Nazarian said. "But he's doling out the money carefully. The legal team is going to end up with some very expensive names. You, for starters. Cohen, of course. F. Lee is in the mix. The motions guy from Stanford. The DNA guys from New York. Investigators, office staff—"

"You," Cheatwood interrupted, adding Nazarian to the lawyers at the OJ trough in what sounded like an accusation.

"Yeah, me, but my rate isn't anywhere near the rest of you," Nazarian replied defensively. "Chip is looking ahead. Long trial. Towering legal costs. He's balking at two million for a knife that may or may not be the real thing."

Cheatwood leaned forward over the table, speaking in a low voice. "This is the deal. I was skeptical of this knife at first. They're going to have blood evidence. I can make the jury question how it was handled, make it white cops framing the black guy. I can spread *gris gris* over all that stuff. Raising doubt is what I do." He paused, poked the air with a fork. "But if that knife is real, if Jumbo Blake gets ahold of it and he makes a deal with prosecutors? It's doomsday for OJ. One hundred percent." He paused again, for dramatic effect. "If they have the knife and it turns out there's Nicole's blood, and Goldman's blood and OJ's blood, I can dump buckets of magic powder on that jury, but evidence like that is going to send our guy away."

Frowning at the seriousness of the situation, Nazarian agreed. "I understand. What do you want me to do?"

Cheatwood went back to his chicken. He bit through the crusty skin and chewed on a savory chunk of white meat. He wagged his finger at Nazarian. "One way or another, the knife has to go away. Either we buy it off your boy, or we make it disappear for real, never to return. Do whatever you have to do."

Nazarian cut into his waffle with a fork. "You don't mean *whatever.*"

Cheatwood nodded *oh yes he did.* "What-the-fuck ever. That knife cannot end up in the DA's office. It's the whole ballgame."

"You can't handle it in the courtroom?"

Cheatwood's annoyance ratcheted up to indignant. "Look, I can make drops of blood sound tampered with. But if that knife is OJ's and if the blood tests out, we're fucked. It just cannot become evidence. Got that?" He ended the instruction pointing a forkful of collard greens at his lunch partner. "No fuckin' around. No knife."

"Suppose I can't stop my guy and he sells it to Jumbo? Can we make a move on him to get it?"

Cheatwood snorted. "First, he got just about as many guns as the LAPD, and we ain't gettin' into gunfights with Jumbo Blake's crew. Second, all he gotta do is tell the LAPD where it at and they swoop down on it. So no, if it gets in Jumbo's possession, we got real trouble. You have to take care of this. No fuckin' around."

Nazarian grimaced as he went back to his lunch. He handled minor stuff for OJ. This was way above his pay grade.

37

For their first date, Casa Vega had been Grace Russell's second choice after Musso and Frank's. For the second date, they met at the venerable Mexican restaurant in Sherman Oaks, one of a string of towns along Ventura Boulevard in the Valley.

"My god, what happened to you?" she asked. She stood in her open doorway, staring at his battered face.

"Some guys decided to dissuade me from my work," he said. "It's okay. Minor scrapes."

"The makeup under your eyes isn't really hiding the bruises," she said, holding his head in her hands. "Poor baby. Did you get a medal?"

At the restaurant they settled in a green leatherette booth, ordered drinks—Margarita for her, Absolut and soda for him—and began nibbling on the chips and salsa that hits the table almost the very instant you sit down. "And some guac" said Mick, quickly adding guacamole to their drink order.

Grace wore black skinny jeans, a crisply ironed white shirt top, and a turquoise leather jacket, which she draped over her shoulders. Her hazel eyes seemed to light up at Mick, and her smile was enough to make Mick forget about the rough day. "I still don't get it," Mick said: "you're really too lovely to be hanging out with me."

Grace gave him a *who-you-trying-to-fool* look. "Is that the best line you've got?" she asked.

"It's not a line. You *are* beautiful. How come you're not taken?"

"Picky," she said. "I'm picky." She picked through the chips for the right size.

"How come you picked me?"

She gave him a frowny look. "Fishing for compliments? Clumsy, I'd say."

"Okay, never mind."

"No, I'll play," she said. "I liked you on TV. You're good-looking, of course. Otherwise you wouldn't be on TV. When did your hair go white?"

"In my late twenties."

"Huh," she said to herself. "Lucky for you. It's a good look."

"You fell for my white hair?"

"No. I thought you had interesting attitude. I was quite pleased when you slithered up."

"I slithered?"

"Definitely slithered. You weren't even sly about it."

"It was only because you worked in the records office. You were too cute to be single. I just wanted information."

"Ha! You had no idea where I worked."

Mick shrugged. True. "Okay, you caught me. I was hitting on you even though I was sure you must be married. I figured I might be able to steal you away."

"Lucky you. No thievery required."

He assumed *he* would be the charming one, if charm were required. Turned out it was the reverse. Their drinks arrived. They ordered dinner. Chicken enchiladas with verde sauce for her, carne asada with red sauce for him.

She sipped her Margarita through a straw. "How come you had time for dinner? I thought you were buried in your story."

Mick shrugged. "I wanted to see you, of course. But I also wanted to ditch the producer."

"Why? You don't like him?"

Mick shook his head no. "He's a good guy. I just feel crowded. At local, it was just me and a cameraman. At network it's a producer, a cameraman, a sound man, sometimes a transmission truck. Lot of people when you're trying to work a story."

"Is he going to be mad that you ditched him?"

"No. He won't know what I did tonight."

"What are you doing tonight?" she asked. "Aren't you here with me tonight?"

"After dinner I was going to go check something out." A fudge. He intended to go back to his apartment and call Kelly. It would have been a good moment to reveal he had a daughter. But he thought about it and decided not yet. A mistake.

She put a theatrical frown on her face. "I wasn't going to bed you tonight anyway, but I thought you'd at least try."

Mick smiled. "If I tried, we'd be in bed."

She laughed. "You think yourself some kind of wonderful?"

"I'm a very persuasive fellow," he said, lightly squeezing her hand.

She snorted out a derisive laugh. "We'll see."

After the main course they shared a flan for dessert, along with coffee. "You asked me about Harry Sarkissian," she said.

"Uh-huh."

"I found more on him."

"Oh?"

"He's the principal in an LLC called Yaravan Entertainment."

Mick's interest piqued. "And?"

"And the LLC has several houses around Glendale. Appears to be rental homes and apartments."

"That's it?"

"No," she said, coy. "There was one property associated with the LLC that caught my attention because it wasn't in Glendale."

"Where is it?"

"Catalina Island," she said. She passed him a piece of paper. "It's a house on Catalina."

38

The men's central jail in downtown LA was a notoriously wretched place. Bobby Nazarian had to go there to see his client and good friend OJ, but he couldn't wait to get out. His visits with OJ were relatively short on most days anyway, because he usually had work to do for the accused star; but on this day he had an important appointment. He spent twenty minutes with OJ before bugging out. Too much of a hurry, in OJ's opinion.

Nazarian had a crucial meeting, and it was definitely in OJ's interest that he make the appointment.

He drove from downtown Los Angeles to Hollywood, along Sunset and up Coldwater Canyon past homes where money twinkled in the windows. At the crest, he turned right on Mulholland, wheeled through a series of turns on smaller streets, and parked in the lot at the Mulholland Tennis Club.

His meeting was a game of tennis with the man Jimmy Cheatwood had told him to see. Eddie Baker was owner of Edward Baker Security, a high-dollar private investigation firm. "My schedule is jammed," he said, "but do you play tennis?"

"I do. Not well, but I do."

"Good. I booked a court. Let's meet there."

Baker was a wiry guy with a wry smile, and an air of competence and expertise. He'd been in the CIA as a young man and managed to parlay that brief experience into a very successful West Coast security firm. Publicly, his firm supplied bodyguard services for celebrities, a highly profitable business. But he also quietly kept an active dirty-tricks arm for those occasions when celebrities and celebrity lawyers needed to spy on each other. Whether it was lawsuits or undermining rivals with negative publicity, Baker's "investigators" were in high demand.

Baker was dressed in white, sitting on a bench on the court waiting for Nazarian. The Mulholland Tennis club overlooked Hollywood and Los Angeles. During the day, the view was muddy with smog; at night it glistened with a zillion watts of light.

Nazarian arrived in blue shorts and a matching short-sleeve blue-collar shirt with the Nike swoosh on the left breast. He set a tennis bag down beside him, shook hands with Baker.

"So, what's this about?" Baker asked.

Nazarian unzipped the racket bag, revealing several rackets and cans of balls. He pulled out one racket, with a blue cover, and held it up over his face, obscuring his lips so his conversation could not be subject to spies with cameras and lip readers.

A crooked smile crossed Baker's face. "You being followed?"

"Never know," Nazarian said. "The media is all over us."

"The media can't get in this place, I assure you."

Nazarian shrugged. "We have a very very sensitive job," he said in a low voice. "Just listen."

Eddie was expecting something sensitive. When he called Cheatwood's office to check out the call for a meeting, he got a message from an assistant that it was important. "Go ahead," he said.

Liberally employing the word "supposedly," Nazarian described the situation with the knife. "Supposedly" a knife, "supposedly" the murder weapon, "supposedly" covered in blood. "We don't know if it's real, but we're in a situation where we can't take a chance."

He explained that the "team" was in negotiations to pay a certain party a sizable amount of money to gain possession of this "supposed" knife, but now a situation had arisen. He explained that "a downtown gangster" was trying to wriggle out from under a major indictment and was bidding up the price for the supposed knife. "His intention is to trade the knife to the prosecutors for dropping the indictment. We need to make sure he never obtains the knife and never has a chance to make the trade."

"Where do we stand at the moment?" Eddie asked.

Nazarian's face soured. "I don't know. But I wouldn't be surprised if things are in motion. No time to waste."

Eddie took the names of the players. Harry Sarkissian. Jumbo Blake. Maybe Gary Minasian, Nazarian wasn't sure. Eddie made a call to his office and spoke to an associate for a solid five minutes. When he ended the call, he gave Nazarian a thumbs-up. "Team on Jumbo Blake. Team on Harry Sarkissian. Separate team on Gary Minasian. If we detect a handoff, we intercept. Done."

Nazarian was a worrier. The swath of white in his black hair seemed to move toward his forehead as he furrowed his brow. "Take this." He put a manila envelope in Baker's tennis bag. "It's cash. Make sure we can say we bought it. Nobody gets hurt, nobody has a claim their property was stolen."

"How much there?"

"A hundred grand. Tell 'em they should be happy to get it. They're both crooks. Hardly the type to go to the cops."

Eddie Baker nodded. Clients often gave him these instructions; he assumed it was to cover their ass. Sometimes it wasn't possible to do things in a clean, completely legal way. He always assumed that the client didn't want to know what it took to get the job done. "What do you want done with the supposed knife when we take possession?"

"I don't want to see it. Handle it, dispose of it," Nazarian said. "You make sure the right thing is done with it. Which is no one ever sees it again."

"Okay. You're here, so let's play." The two men then played a six-game set, Eddie Baker easily taking each game. "Don't ever play for money," he warned Nazarian with a laugh.

The teasing about his tennis skills put Nazarian off. "You know what to do," he said as he packed his racket.

Eddie Baker hurried to his office. His Porsche glided down Coldwater Canyon Boulevard like it was on rails. He slid into his parking space in the basement of a Sunset Strip high-rise. On the eighteenth floor he gathered his researchers. The team already had Jumbo Blake's addresses and had a team with eyes on Gary Minasian, who seemed to be aimlessly supervising a Glendale carwash. So far, they hadn't located Harry Sarkissian.

That flaw in the investigation worried Eddie. "Stay on the black guy. He's going to find his way to Sarkissian. He'll lead you to him."

There were two Jumbo teams. One was in South Central, keeping an eye on the Anzac address. The other was in the Hollywood Hills, parked outside a garish white plantation mansion a researcher had discovered was owned by Jumbo's LLC. Both teams were poised to follow if the gold Mercedes were to appear.

The Baker office, for all its reach, hadn't caught up with Grace Russell. They didn't know about the house on Catalina Island.

Yet.

39

Cheryl Bedrosian looked up from her desk as the office door opened. "Not you again," she said, letting her hands drop on the desk in exasperation.

Mickey Judge grimaced at her. "Yeah. Me."

A crew of repair guys was working on replacing Harry's office door and Mickey's escape window.

Tony Salt stepped in right behind Mickey.

"Is the big black guy your bodyguard?" she asked, nodding at Tony.

"You gonna feel bad sounding racist like that, ma'am," Tony said, feigning insult. "My name is Anthony Salt. I'm a producer for the NBC News Bureau in Burbank assigned to work with Mr. Judge, one of our premier correspondents." He put his card on her desk.

She held the card like it was an invitation from the queen. "An important man, I see! My apologies," she replied, in Tony's mocking tone.

She stopped. Whatever they wanted, they would have to say.

"Looking for himself," Mick explained. He and Tony had to step out of the way of workmen. The floor was covered in a drop cloth, men on ladders reframing the office doorway.

"How'd the artwork survive?" Mick asked.

She gave him a forced smile but didn't answer the question. "You want to see Mr. Sarkissian, you mean?" she asked, then immediately answered her own question. "Well, he's not here."

"Has Jumbo Blake been back?"

"Thank god, no. I was hoping I'd seen the last of all of you." She stopped to think and pointed her pencil at the two visitors. "You know Harry is very cheap, but I'm really going to have to insist we get some security guards."

"Where is Harry?"

Cheryl clasped her hands and sighed. "Normally, I would know. But Harry informed me that if I were to have any idea at all of his whereabouts, I might be put through physical pain to give up the information. So, like a caring brother, he has left me totally in the dark."

"Not knowing won't stop somebody from assuming you do know

and torturing you anyway," Tony said, deadpan.

"Thank you for that advice. I thought of that too, but Harry still wouldn't tell me."

Tony stepped around her to the door to Sarkissian's office. She didn't object. He leaned through the doorway. No Harry. "Don't believe me? You think I'd say he's not here when he's sitting behind his desk?"

Tony shrugged. "What you going to do with those pictures with holes in 'em?"

She rolled her eyes. "My boss is very angry about that."

Mick put another card on Cheryl's desk. "Seriously. He should call me. I think I know why Jumbo wants that knife, and I think he'll do anything to get it. Harry should call me."

"Tell me. I'll tell him."

Mick shook his head. "I do that, he'll never call me. Tell him to call."

She shook her head no. "I guarantee you, whatever you got figured out, Harry figured out a while ago."

Mick grimaced. She was probably right.

In a sidewalk conference outside, Mick showed Tony Salt the address on Catalina. "We should go there. I'll bet anything Harry is over there with the box, waiting to make a deal with Jumbo or somebody."

"No way we're going to Catalina without being absolutely sure he's there. We end up way out of position if we find out the deal is going down somewhere else." Tony Salt was adamantly opposed to taking a flyer on Catalina.

"Look, I would much rather deal with Harry Sarkissian than Jumbo Blake. Jumbo gets the box, we're fucked. He's already shot at me once. No doubt he'd do it again."

"I told you, he don't play," Tony said. "But problem is, he's the way we're going to find Harry Sarkissian. Jumbo will be going to him to buy that box, and our best bet is to follow him."

Mick groaned. Sarkissian was an asshole, but getting told to fuck off was much preferable to Jumbo's gunplay.

The crew arrived, and Tony and Mick climbed in the van to lay out a game plan for following Jumbo.

"Chances are he's at the Anzac address," Mick said, meaning Jumbo Blake's Jordan Downs fortress. "But there's also a chance he's in the Hollywood Hills."

"Remind me again," Billy Prettyman said to Tony. "Why are we following this thug around?"

"The only way I can think of to find Harry Sarkissian," Tony said.

"Why can't we find Sarkissian without Blake?"

"I'd like to, but Jumbo is offering money," Mick explained. "Harry's more likely to surface to collect the cash than to make himself findable for us."

"Do you have any idea where he might be?"

Mick groaned. "Here's the hard part. I have an address for a place he owns. He could be there."

"So why don't we go there?"

"It's on Catalina Island," Tony interrupted. "We'd go there, but I'd like to have some indication he's actually there. Otherwise we go way out of our way, and he surfaces somewhere else while we're out of position."

"But if we had to go over there, how would we do it?" Prettyman asked. "Fly?"

"No flying," Mick said. "We'd go by water." Mick pulled a black combo calendar and phone book from his shoulder bag. He thumbed through the pages until he found a name. He punched in a number. "Decker? It's Mick."

The conversation was about a boat run to Catalina if needed. Tom Decker was a friend. He ran tugs out of Long Beach and was Mick's go-to guy if Mick needed to get on the water for a story.

"How much advance notice you need?" He listened. "I'll get back to you."

Salt was looking at Mick with questions that were so obvious, they didn't need to be asked. "If we must get over to Catalina, he'll take us," Mick said. "Maybe we'll have to, maybe we won't."

While Mickey explained the call, Tony scrunched up his face so his upper lip touched the bottom of his nose. Again. It was his look of skepticism.

Tony Salt arrived at a decision. "We need whatever video we can get," he said. "So let's have Rhyme and Bill go downtown, stake it out." He addressed the two men. "It may be a waste of time. But it's worth the trip. Try to get some video of him, the car, whatever."

The crew agreed, reluctantly. They weren't thrilled to be hanging out in a drug neighborhood in front of the HQ of the drug mogul. But they would go.

Mick and Tony drove to the white mansion in the Hollywood Hills. When they arrived at La Gorda, they encountered a gate and a keypad with a list of residents.

"Should we try one?" Tony asked.

"And say what when they ask who it is?"

"Lie? Pizza delivery? Carpet cleaners? Electrician?"

Mick rubbed his forehead. "These aren't just any schmucks. These are rich people, probably have juice somewhere. We get caught lying to these people . . ." he trailed off.

"Yeah, I know. We'll be in Alison's office."

Mick noticed there was a space on the left side of the gate that a person could pass through. The gate simply kept out vehicles. "How about you go through that opening," he said, pointing to the passage, "and just check to see if his car is there?"

"Why me?"

"I'd go. But a white guy walking up to this dude's house might be more alarming than a black guy."

"You racist," Tony said as he got out of Mick's rental car.

The white monstrosity loomed on a rock outcropping directly above the gate. Mick was unaware that a camera was trained on the gate. Tony also could have been spotted had anyone in the house been paying attention, but no one noticed. Tony slipped through. Mick backed his car away from the gate and parked just off the road near the entrance to the private street.

Tony Salt had to walk up a steep concrete driveway to be able to see the cars parked at Jumbo's house. He went only far enough to see over the crest. A gold Mercedes was clearly visible. Tony Salt hurried back down the driveway and through the passageway beside the gate. He slid into the passenger seat of the rent car.

"Okay, his Mercedes is there. Now what?"

"First call the crew and have them come up to the Hollywood area and stand by. Then we wait," Mick said. He backed his car farther away, to a spot where he would be less noticeable when Jumbo drove out.

Inside the gate, parked in a black Audi sedan farther down La Gorda from the Jumbo Blake driveway, an Eddie Baker team reported in. "A guy walked up the driveway and then quickly backed out," the man said into the phone. "I think somebody else is keeping an eye on our guy."

40

The reason no one in Jumbo Blake's great white monstrosity mansion noticed Mickey Judge's car at the gate, or Tony Salt creeping up the driveway, was Jumbo Blake himself. He had his entire house crew gathered around the rose garden, where he stretched out on his chaise. He was chewing them out for what he considered lackadaisical security.

After a roaring dressing-down, Jumbo dismissed them back to their posts. By that time, they had missed the fact that Jumbo's house was under surveillance by both Mickey Judge and the professional follow team from Eddie Baker's security firm.

Jumbo's cell phone buzzed. The voice on the other end was lawyer Byron Fink. "Come see me."

"When?"

"Half an hour ago. Step on it."

Jumbo looked at his phone as if there was something wrong with it. He hated being ordered around.

He stood up from his chaise and roses. "Fucking lawyers," he mumbled.

Twenty minutes later, Jumbo Blake walked out of the main door of the garage. He was wearing a bright blue tracksuit, several gold ropes around his neck, gold Nike trainers, and gold rings on four fingers. His eyes were hidden behind five-thousand-dollar gold and diamond sunglasses, but the scowl that surrounded the eyewear made it clear that Jumbo was fuming.

The gold Mercedes slid down the steep concrete drive and out the Gorda gate. At the wheel, distracted by the pressure of being Jumbo Blake, Jumbo didn't notice a Hertz sedan slip in behind at a discrete distance. In the rental car, Mickey Judge and Tony Salt, distracted by the trickiness of following a car unnoticed, failed to notice a black Audi drop in behind them.

The three-car convoy made its way out of the hills, over to Highland, and down to Wilshire Boulevard. Just south of Wilshire, Jumbo turned into an underground lot beneath a medium-rise office building. Mick thumbed through his notebook, found a notation of Jumbo's lawyer that Grace Russell had given him. He called 411 and asked for a number for attorney Byron Fink. "That's his lawyer's office," Mick said to Tony. "We'll wait."

Half a block away, the driver of the Eddie Baker crew punched off his cell phone. "Lawyer," he said to his partner. "We wait."

In Byron Fink's office, Jumbo collapsed into a chair in front of Fink's desk. "What?"

The lawyer sat forward in his massive leather desk chair, elbows on the desk. "You're out of time. If you're going to get that thing, you need to do it now."

"Grand jury done?" Jumbo asked.

Byron Fink nodded yes. "A few formalities at the end before they hand down an indictment. I want to end it before that happens. Much harder to get the DA to drop a case if the indictments are issued."

"I need to make a couple calls," Jumbo said.

"Use that," Fink said, pointing to an adjoining office. "I don't want to hear."

Jumbo slouched into the vacant office, seating himself behind an empty desk. His first call was to Harry Sarkissian.

"The money's ready. I need to do this now."

The view from Harry Sarkissian's Spanish colonial on Catalina Island was perfect. The sky was blue, the smog a distant smear over Long Beach on the eastern horizon. The banana trees and rubber plants and hibiscus and the night-blooming jasmine were in their sun-drenched glory. Yachts lolled in Avalon harbor, and a faint murmur of tourist meanderings wafted up from the waterfront bars.

"Call me when you come ashore. I'll meet you in town."

"What town? Where are you?"

"Avalon town. Catalina Island. Call when you land. And don't come if you don't have the money."

Jumbo grimaced as the reality came over him. "Catalina Island? You expect me to come to a *island*? Get your ass over here."

Harry laughed. "I know you hate being on the water. Too bad. Suck it up. Thousands of people do it every year. It's an hour boat ride. And I wouldn't advise the helicopters or seaplanes. They tend to crash."

"Man, you cannot be serious."

"I have a perfect view of the harbor and the landing. I'll be able to watch you come ashore. Don't bring your army. If you do, I won't answer your call."

"How am I supposed to get there?"

"I'm not your travel agent. Figure it out. But here's a pro tip. Angelo's Marine Service in Long Beach. He runs charters. He'll bring you over for a few hundred bucks. Be sure to tip."

The line went dead.

"Fuck fuck fuck fuck fuck," Jumbo screamed.

Byron Fink burst through the door connecting the two offices. "What?"

"I gotta go to fucking Catalina fucking island to make the handoff," Jumbo seethed.

"So go."

Jumbo glared at his lawyer. He didn't want to say he was certain to be sick and freaked out on the ocean. It would make him sound weak. But he had to go.

He called Solomon. He was abrupt. "You got the stacks?" he asked, meaning the money.

"Two mil in stacks is a damn big duffel bag, boss. Weighs over fifty pounds."

Jumbo didn't want to hear it. "Find a place called Angelo's Marine in Long Beach Marina. Meet me there with the bag."

A call to Angelo's Marine in Long Beach got him a reservation and turn-by-turn instructions. Folding the directions into his shirt pocket, Jumbo stalked out of the lawyer's offices.

Down on the street, Mickey and Tony Salt spotted the gold Mercedes exiting the parking structure and heading west on Wilshire. He made a left turn on La Brea, Mickey and Tony following, and the Baker team following both of them.

Tony was driving. Mickey had decided earlier that he wanted his hands free to make calls if he had to.

When Jumbo got on the 110 Freeway southbound, Mick figured it out. "He's going to Long Beach. He's going to cross over to Catalina. That's where they're making the exchange."

Tony Salt shook his head, skeptical. "That's just a guess. Anything could happen in Long Beach. He could stop anywhere between here and there."

But Mick was sure of himself. "It may be a hunch; but if he gets down there and gets on a boat, we better have a boat or we're screwed." He paged through his phone book again. Punched in a number. "Hey, man, looks like we're on. Can you still do it?"

"Hope you're wrong," Tony said, shaking his head. "I hate fucking boats."

"I know I'm right," Mick said with confidence. "I can feel it. Jumbo's going over to Catalina."

Mickey called the crew. He gave them instructions to get to Long Beach Harbor. "Head there. I'll call when we know exactly where we'll be."

Tony Salt kept the gold Mercedes in sight, straight south on the 110 Freeway. This was the vast expanse of rooftops that constituted the suburbs of Los Angeles County and upper Orange County. Mick remembered a description of the area from Richard Henry Dana's *Two Years Before the Mast*. In the mid-1830s, Dana rode by horse from the Laguna Beach area to the pueblo of Los Angeles. Just before the Gold Rush, the entire expanse was cattle-grazing land. Now it was forty miles of concrete and neon.

"Jesus, Tony, it looks like we're doing this." Mick could hardly believe it was happening. "I think the knife is in play, and we're on its tail."

"We don't even know if there *is* a knife," Salt snorted. "We'll see."

Following behind, the Baker team had no idea what was going on, except they sensed something important might be happening because Jumbo was on the move and out of his normal area of operation. Their office could offer no help, because the office knew nothing about Harry Sarkissian's getaway house on Catalina Island. All the Baker controllers could tell the crew was to stay on them.

41

There was no way for Mickey and Tony to know exactly where Jumbo was going. All they could do was follow and hope they wouldn't lose him. All they could tell Rhyme and Bill was to show up in the area of Long Beach Harbor.

"He's not going over by Belmont Shore and Naples," Mick told the crew. "That's touristy. Boat rentals over there are for families cruising around the inner harbor. He has to go over by Terminal Island and find a serious fishing charter."

Mick's guess was right. The Mercedes exited the 110 Freeway at Anaheim Drive and followed an eastbound track until it could make a right into the east basin area of the industrial harbor.

They watched as the Mercedes pulled into the parking lot at Angelo's Charters. Mick called Bill and Willis and gave them the location.

Tony and Mick were so focused on watching Jumbo that they didn't notice the black Audi standing off, keeping an eye on both the Mercedes and the Hertz Chevy.

Mick called Decker. "He's at Angelo's charter in the east basin. Know where it is?"

He listened for a moment before he snapped the flip phone shut. "He's on his way," he said to Tony.

Now, a few minutes later, they sweated the crew. "Where are you?" Salt asked into his cell phone. "Just hurry, man." He turned to Mick. "They're five minutes out."

Next was the nerve-racking chore of waiting. Jumbo was inside, completing the charter for a run across the channel to Catalina Island. The transaction would take a little time. Mick watched the charter office with his binoculars. Jumbo was inside at a desk, talking with a man, evidently making the deal. "He hasn't got his gun out, so it looks like he's going to play this straight."

Another car pulled up next to Jumbo's Mercedes. A trim, muscled black man emerged from the car. He was carrying a satchel that seemed heavy.

"Seems the money has arrived," Mick mumbled. "Wonder how much."

"Where the fuck is the crew?" Tony stewed. He punched numbers into his phone. "Shoot from the van," he said in the phone. "Don't show yourself. Get Jumbo waddling onto the boat. Can't miss him. He's huge. Another guy with him is slim. He's got a bag of money."

One of the two men in the Audi got out of the car and walked to the charter office. He waited inside to be helped after Jumbo. He also wanted a boat, but he was really waiting to overhear where he would be going. It didn't take long for him to discover two things: he was going to Catalina, and he would have to find another charter company. There were no more boats available at Angelo's. He was sent farther back up the basin to a company "next to the Chowder Barge." The man said thanks and left.

The crew van arrived. It pulled up sideways to the charter office. Tony was on the phone with Rhyme, pointing out where to spot Jumbo. Bill slid the side door open a few inches and lined up his shot through the narrow opening. He was able to get Jumbo and the other man walking out of the office, down a ramp to the slips, and climbing aboard a boat called the *Saucy Suzie*.

They got an excellent shot of Jumbo going through a selection of life vests. He was too big for everything they had, and the captain had to scoot back to the office to find one big enough. The large man made the boat list side to side as he moved around on the deck.

"Looks like he's nervous," Mick said quietly.

"Probably hates it," Tony said

"How about you?"

Tony rolled his lips together, thinking about the question. "I don't much like it either. But I'll get through it."

"Bill and Rhyme cool?"

Tony Salt shot Mick warning eyes. "Hey, man, don't say that to them. Bill shot film in Vietnam. He can do anything."

Jumbo's boat was ready. The *Saucy Suzie*'s diesels were chugging exhaust. Jumbo was seated just inside the wheelhouse, looking uncomfortable. The captain backed it out of the slip. The *Saucy Suzie* turned and headed out.

Right behind it, a fast boat called the *Scottish Hammer* slipped into the spot. "There's our guy," Mick said. "Let's go."

Willis and Bill piled out of the camera van and trotted to catch up. Mick and Tony walked quickly to the ramp and down onto the dock.

Tom Decker was idling the engines, holding the boat to the dock with a line around a cleat. Decker was bronzed and weathered from the sun. He had a big grin on his face. "It's always rock 'n' roll with you, Mickey Judge. What're we doing this time?"

Mick climbed aboard. He lent a hand to Tony, and then to Bill and Rhyme and their gear.

"We're on our way to get OJ's knife," he said to Decker.

"The murder knife?"

"The very one."

"The fuck you say," Decker laughed in a whoop. He released the line and backed out of the slip. The *Scottish Hammer* stalked the *Saucy Suzie* out the channel, through the breakwater, and out into the open ocean, pointed toward Catalina Island.

42

At dockside just before boarding, Captain Angelo Granitelli had one last admonition. "Just so I'm clear with you guys, no guns on board this vessel. Absolute rule. Understood?"

"We cool, man," Jumbo said with a serpent smile. "Your boat, your rules."

The *Saucy Suzie* rocked a little when Jumbo stepped on board. He found himself in a room that looked very much like a small apartment. Captain Johnny called it the salon. There was a built-in couch to the left, with a low table in front. Across from the couch arrangement were two chairs and a flat-screen television. The windows were big, the sun streaming in. Forward of the living room arrangement was a kitchen. Jumbo looked over the stove and the oven and the refrigerator and the sinks and the food prep area. He nodded his approval to Solomon. "This a boat, huh?"

"Sure is, boss. Big-ass boat." Solomon checked out the bar. "Hey, your favorite. Courvoisier."

Jumbo looked at the bottle. "Maybe I have some later."

Captain Johnny hurried by him, up a short flight of steps to the wheelhouse. Jumbo followed, ducking his head low. "Nice boat. How much?"

"I picked it up for ninety-five."

"Ninety-five thousand?" Jumbo made a face like he smelled a fart. "For a fuckin' boat?"

"It's an '87 Bayliner 4550, the queen of the sea," Granitelli said. "And if you like it, it's for sale. Same price. Ninety-five K and it's yours." He busied himself checking various readings on his instrument panel and fired up the engines, which gave off a low rumble. "Twin diesels," he said to Jumbo. "We'll do close to thirty most of the way over."

Jumbo took a seat behind the wheelhouse chair on a curved bench. Solomon plopped down beside him.

Granitelli glanced back at them. "You guys might be more comfortable in the salon," he said, jerking his head back down the set of steps. "Make yourself a drink, get a beer, whatever."

"Naww," Jumbo said. "I think I'll feel better here."

"Suit yourself," Johnny said. Captain and owner of the *Saucy Suzie,* Granitelli was a fifty-year-old whose face was mostly white beard. That part of his face which wasn't covered in whiskers was sunbaked to a reddish brown. His eyes had the squinty lines of a man who keeps an eye on the horizon. He was quick with a smile, but cautious in his judgment of people. So many oddballs ended up on his boats. Jumbo Blake was certainly one of those. The skinny guy with him also looked to Johnny like he could be a problem.

But Angelo Granitelli had to pay attention to the tricky business of getting past the breakwater before he could pay any attention at all to his passengers.

A deckhand named Oscar pulled the lines free of the slip cleats and jumped aboard. Captain Granitelli backed the big boat out of the slip and turned it toward the open channel. Under way, the *Saucy Suzie* chugged along at the 5 mph limit past the slips and the yachts and industrial docks. The sun was glistening off the glassy water. They passed boats with groups aboard, dressed for a warm day in tank tops, bathing suits, shorts, and showing lots of skin.

"Lot of white people on boats," Jumbo muttered.

"Lots of black people too," Granitelli said. "This is Long Beach. Black people live here, and they like the water too."

Jumbo wasn't sold. He knew sooner or later his mind would give in to fear and his stomach would revolt.

The breakwater loomed, a line of riprap rock fifteen feet above the water line. Granitelli eased the *Saucy Suzie* through the opening in stone jetty walls that protected the Long Beach inner harbor, and applied power. The *Saucy Suzie* sat back on its twin screws, leaving a spiraling white wake in the blue water.

"Next stop, Avalon," he shouted above the rumble of the diesels. Jumbo nodded, but said nothing more. He squeezed the arms of the bench so hard, his black knuckles seemed to show the bones.

In Angelo Granitelli's eyes, his passengers were highly unusual. First, he'd probably never had someone as large as Jumbo on his boat; and second, he couldn't recall hosting a person as obviously beset by anxiety as Jumbo.

The big man perched uneasily on an upholstered bench to the left of the narrow passageway to the salon and the bar and the kitchen below. Opposite him, Captain Granitelli was on his feet, leaning against a tall captain's chair on a swivel. He had one hand on the wheel, the other on the throttles. Before him was an instrument panel with light switches, gauges showing readings on RPMs, speed, oil pressure, battery condition, water temperature, and fuel levels. His radio was in easy reach. Intermittently he glanced at a compass and a radar screen positioned just ahead of the wheel. His heading was SW, 220 on the compass face.

Johnny glanced back at his passengers. The big guy looked like he was barely holding it together. "What's your name?" he said to the other guy.

"Solomon."

"Keep an eye on your partner for me. He don't look too good."

Solomon nodded okay, but he paid much closer attention to the satchel between his feet.

Granitelli's crewman Oscar, a quiet thirty-something black man, wore an unkempt beard, black-out dark glasses, and a blue knit watch cap. He sat on a bench to the aft, scanning the wake left by the twin screws, watching where they'd been recede from view.

Johnny couldn't help but notice that his client, Mr. Blake, seemed like he was spiraling down. Jumbo was trying to maintain the appearance of ease and nonchalance. But he was breathing heavily, swallowing frequently, and perspiring freely. Granitelli was certain he had a passenger who was going to be heaving up his stomach long before they reached Catalina.

As they cleared the breakwater, several oil tankers moored just offshore came into view. Johnny aimed the Bayliner toward a gap between the huge tankers.

"Mr. Blake, you been over to Catalina before?" Johnny asked, hoping conversation would put the big man at ease.

Jumbo was staring straight ahead at the expanse of water. He pursed his lips and shook his big head no. "I don't like being on the water, if you must know the truth. So I'd appreciate it if everything went nice and smooth." He turned to face Johnny. "I'd hate to have a bad experience."

Granitelli caught his meaning. It was a silly threat. As if the captain could control the weather.

"Mr. Blake, on the other side of these tankers we're going to have about twenty miles of ocean to Catalina," Granitelli said, serious, nodding to the direction they were heading. "It's July. I'm positive we're going to encounter a fogbank. Won't be able to see much. And there's probably going to be swells. The boat is extremely seaworthy. This is my personal boat. I was sure you would be more comfortable on this than on my fishing charters. Still, we're going to be banging over some waves. It's going to get rough."

"How rough?" Jumbo asked, his eyelids narrowed to slits.

"Rough enough that you ought to take this," Johnny said. He handed Jumbo a plastic bag.

"What's this for?"

"That's what you puke in. Don't be puking all over the boat. Puke in that."

Jumbo took the bag, shoved it in the pocket of his jacket.

"Maybe you ought to go below. There's nice comfortable beds. You could lie down flat. Maybe you'd go to sleep and won't even notice."

"The fog you talk about. The rough water. How you know that?" Jumbo asked, suspicious. "Sunny here. The water smooth. How do you know?"

Jimmy pointed out the forward windscreen. "Mr. Blake, from here we can see about four miles to the horizon. It's twenty-seven miles to the island. Beyond that four-mile mark there's a fogbank that we'll be in until about five miles from the island. I know that because it's on the weather maps. Plus boats returning from Catalina have reported the fog and the chop. I'm just telling you that's what we're going to go through before I can land you in Catalina."

"Can you drive around it?"

Jimmy shook his head. "We're going straight through it. You sure you don't want to go below and take a nap?"

"I don't like being closed in. I'll be better here."

"Don't lose track of that bag. I think you're going to need it."

Jumbo leaned back and crossed his arms over his stomach. "Fucking Sarkissian," he muttered to Solomon. "He do this to me on purpose."

43

On Mickey's boat, things were also not going well. Tony Salt and Willis Gillis retreated to the cabin as soon as the *Scottish Hammer* cleared the jetty and Tommy put on the power. Tony apologized. "Hey, man, I don't do well on the ocean," he said before stretching out on a berth. Willis was likewise stomach-aggrieved. He sat in a swivel chair, his head thrown back.

Both men were effectively useless.

Bill Prettyman, the camera operator, was made of tougher stuff. Mickey and Prettyman stood next to Tommy in the wheelhouse as the *Scottish Hammer* passed the moored tankers and slammed over swells. Mickey had binoculars to his eyes, watching the boat they were following. "Are you sure you can keep up with him?" Mick asked.

"I could pass him, if you want," Tommy said. Decker was focused on their quarry dead ahead, throwing a glance at his instruments at intervals.

"I don't think I want that. Should I?"

"Not really. We're going to run into fog. Running ahead of him is a good way to lose him."

Bill and Mickey took seats on the bench behind the captain's chair. "What do you want for video?" Bill asked.

"The most important shot will be the handover," Mick said. "I'm not worried about much else until that happens."

Prettyman was getting close to sixty. He had a face that had seen wars and had been staring at bad things for a long time. "You believe it?"

For Mick, that was the question that had never been resolved. Was it possible that they were on the trail of a true story? Or was it a figment of the imagination of two men who were now dead? Had Mick asked all the right questions of Luther Malcolm before a suspicious gas explosion made it impossible to ask followups? "Bill, I just know what a guy told me," Mick replied. "That's all we ever have until we get to the real thing. So I don't know what else to do except follow up."

Prettyman looked him over carefully. They had worked a couple of stories together, but nothing big, certainly not anything where they were in danger, the kind of situation where a cameraman learned whether he could trust a correspondent. He had nothing to go on except what he was looking at. Mickey Judge was experienced, but it was all local news. He had a good reputation, but now they were on something that seemed slightly deranged. He just had to make a guess about the guy and hope for the best.

"Okay, so how are we going to get close enough for a shot of the handoff?"

Mick shrugged. "Honestly, I have no idea. I think we're just going to have to roll with the situation, whatever plays out. Tony thinks if we keep an eye on Blake, he will lead us to the handoff. I agreed. But I would much rather have been able to approach Sarkissian without dealing with Jumbo."

Prettyman nodded that he understood and agreed. "If we're waiting to move until the handoff, it's going to be pretty damn obvious what I'm doing. Hard to hide that big camera."

Mick agreed. "When we bust you out, we're totally exposed. They'll know what we're doing. Hard to know what happens then."

"What am I looking for?"

"My understanding is that it's a box. A cardboard box. The thing is inside."

Decker hollered out to them. "Okay, we're getting into the fog. I'm going to have to slow down."

"Can you still keep an eye on them?" Mick asked.

"I can see them on the radar. That will have to do."

Mick and Prettyman searched the water ahead. They could see maybe fifty yards. Somewhere ahead was the *Saucy Suzie* and Jumbo Blake.

44

Enveloped in the thick early-July fog, Angelo Granitelli slowed the *Saucy Suzie* to a prudent 7 knots. His radar screen showed boats ahead of him proceeding in the same direction, and boats to his left traveling in the opposite direction. Captain Johnny was confident that all was safe, but he was cautious, carefully keeping an eye on the short length of water ahead that was visible, and an eye on the instruments that could see farther than the human eye.

Seated behind him, Jumbo Blake was not nearly as calm. His big head swiveled around at the wall of gray that surrounded the boat. The brief period of calm while the boat slid over smooth water had evaporated. Now they encountered swells and the heaving-up-and-down that both worried him and played hell with his stomach. Worse, in the fogbank he had completely given in to his claustrophobia.

"Hey, man, you got to get us out of this," he shouted at Granitelli. "What's the way out?"

Johnny swiveled around in his captain's chair. "I *am* getting us out of this. It's straight ahead."

"Bullshit. I can see straight ahead. It's nothing but gray. Where'd the blue sky go?"

Swiveling back forward, Johnny pointed straight ahead. "Blue sky about five miles ahead. We're getting there."

"Hey, man, you even know where the fuck you going?"

"Absolutely. I'm following the compass, keeping watch on the radar."

"Let me see," Jumbo took to his feet, staggered forward, grabbing the back of Johnny's chair. "Show me."

Granitelli pointed at the radar screen. "Those dots? Those are other vessels. See how they're the same distance from us as we move forward? That means they're going the same speed."

"Them dots, they other boats?"

"Yeah. That's what I said."

"They out of this fog yet?"

"No. If they were, you'd see them moving away from us as they pick up speed. Can't go fast in the fog."

"Man, I really don't like this. I never been good on the ocean. I don't like it one damn bit."

"You're perfectly safe. You should go make yourself a drink."

Solomon spoke up. "He's right, Jumbo. Let's go down to the living room where it's more comfortable. I'll make you a drink."

Jumbo turned on his man. "You okay with this, man? We out in the middle of the ocean. Can't see a damn thing. Nothing but water for miles." He stopped to contemplate his situation. "Hey, how deep is the ocean here?"

"About a mile, six thousand feet, more or less."

Jumbo's face drooped at the startling information. "A mile? A mile of water under my feet? Oh Lord, nobody told me that. Solomon, why didn't you tell me that?"

Johnny turned to him. "Mr. Blake, doesn't matter how much water around you. I can guarantee you're not even going to get wet. That's why we have this boat. It's a hundred thousand dollars of safety and luxury."

"You telling me money gonna keep me from sinkin'?"

Johnny nodded yes. "That's exactly what I'm telling you. This is my wife's boat. Brought it out special for you. If I trust it to keep her safe, you should trust it too. Go on downstairs and enjoy the ride. Turn on the TV, play some music, have a drink. We'll be there in a few minutes."

"Come on, Jumbo," Solomon said, taking the boss by the arm. "The guy's right. Let's go down to the living room and let him do his job."

The two men retired to the salon. Jumbo took a seat on the couch and grumbled about the fog. Within a few minutes, the sun began to appear. And then quickly they were back under bright blue skies. Captain Johnny put on power, and the *Saucy Suzie* was soon bouncing over three-foot swells.

Nothing was working in Jumbo's favor. The speed and banging off the waves were too much for him.

Within minutes, Jumbo Blake was retching into a plastic bag and moaning threats.

Solomon wasn't as affected. He stood by his boss with a water bottle and sympathy. It was all he could do.

The deckhand, Oscar, approached. "You'll feel better outside in the air," he said. He offered an arm. Jumbo looked at him suspiciously, but Oscar was black. That helped. Jumbo took his arm. They went out on the aft deck, and Jumbo held the railing with both hands. He took deep breaths of salt air.

Then he hung over the side and puked into the sea.

A few hundred yards behind, the *Scottish Hammer* emerged from the fogbank. Mickey was peering forward through his binoculars.

"Oh, shit," he said. "That's Jumbo throwing up over the side."

"Lemme see," Prettyman said, taking the binoculars.

"Oh, yeah," he said. "I think I can get a shot of that." He turned to Decker. "Can you get closer?"

"I can get right on top of him if you want."

"Not that close," Mick warned. "Closer, but not too close."

45

Harry Sarkissian was growing impatient. He peered into a tripod-mounted telescope on the deck of his home on Stagecoach Road, high above Avalon Harbor.

He watched boats emerge from the fogbank that lay a few miles off Catalina, and he waited for a call from one of those boats. His phone was silent.

Harry could stand the wait no more. He picked up his phone, punched in the number he had for Jumbo.

Harry waited impatiently for an answer. After many rings, a strange voice came on the phone.

On the *Saucy Suzie,* Solomon fished the phone out of Jumbo's jacket pocket. The big man was doubled over the railing, coughing, heaving up more of what little was left in his stomach.

"Yeah," Solomon said.

"Who the fuck is this?"

"It's Solomon. Jumbo's man."

"Well, fucking great to meet you, Solomon. Where the fuck are you guys?"

Holding on to the boss's belt, Solomon straightened up and looked forward. He could see the outline of an island on the horizon. "I see an island. Is that Catalina?"

"Probably. There aren't any other islands out here. So how far out are you?"

Solomon pulled on Jumbo's belt, as the big man was sagging over the edge.

"No idea, man."

"Well, call this number back when you enter the harbor. Think you can figure that out?"

"Hey, fuck the fuck off," Solomon said, punching the phone off.

"Who was that?" Jumbo groaned, straightening up.

"Your asshole buddy. Wants to know where we are."

Jumbo stood tall, his hands still gripping the railing. "Where are we?"

"I see an island out front. Guess we're getting close."

Carefully, Jumbo released the railing, steadied himself on his feet.

The *Saucy Suzie* was still barreling along, making Jumbo's footing shaky. "Let's go see what our Captain boy says."

Inside the salon, Jumbo made for the kitchen sink. He sloshed handfuls of water in his mouth, spit it out. Solomon offered him a finger of whiskey. "This will help," he said. Jumbo tossed it back. Wheezed.

Solomon followed the boss up the steps to the wheelhouse. Oscar the deckhand and Angelo Granitelli were at the wheel, staring straight ahead. Catalina Island rose on the horizon, close enough that they could make out the casino on the north end of the town of Avalon.

"How much longer?" Jumbo asked.

"Ten minutes. Your guy know where he wants to meet us?"

"I'll call now."

Jumbo punched redial. The call went to voicemail. Jumbo's message was simple. "What the fuck, asshole. Where are you?"

Up on Stagecoach Road, Harry Sarkissian was pretty sure he'd spotted the right boat. You could never be sure, but pleasure-boat traffic was light midweek. This particular vessel was bowling along like a rocket sled straight for Avalon, with another boat trailing. Almost like they were together.

Sarkissian made a call. Gary Minasian answered. "The boat ready?"

Minasian answered yes. Everything was ready. Gassed, checked, ready to go. "I'm standing by on a mooring just off the Green Pier."

Harry rang off, immediately called Jumbo's phone again.

"What the fuck, man. I just called, damn voice mail."

Sarkissian ignored him. "Tell your skipper the Green Pier, the dock closest to shore." And he hung up.

On the *Saucy Suzie,* Jumbo put his phone back in his pocket. "He says the Green Pier. Dock closest to shore."

Angelo grimaced. "I'll have to drop you and get off the dock. Can't wait there."

"Wait. What are we supposed to do?" Solomon asked, even before Jumbo could react.

"You go do your business, come back to the dock, I'll swing around and pick you up."

Jumbo pulled up his jacket, exposing a gun in his waistband. "You wouldn't be fucking around with me, would you?"

Angelo looked at the gun. He glanced up at the glowering Jumbo.

He met the eyes of his deckhand Oscar, who shook his head almost imperceptibly.

Granitelli made an instant decision. As soon as Jumbo was off the boat, Angelo would wheel the *Saucy Suzie* around and head back to Long Beach. Jumbo had just broken the cardinal rule: no guns. Bring a gun on board, and Granitelli was done. He especially wanted no part of thugs with guns.

"Everything's cool," he lied.

46

Once the *Scottish Hammer* slowed, Prettyman went below and rousted Tony Salt and Willis Gillis. Both were unsteady, but they managed to get on their feet and come up into the light.

Prettyman and Mick and Decker worked out a plan. They would follow the *Saucy Suzie* in, and wherever the Jumbo boat put in, Mick's crew would disembark and follow. There was no way to know exactly what was going to happen, but what they did know was that they would not be able to see it from water level. They had to get off the boat and get up on the pier to be within sight of Jumbo and the guy with the satchel.

Decker swung the *Hammer* in behind the *Saucy Suzie* as if he was just another boater entering the harbor. There was nothing unusual about two boats in fairly close proximity. As they approached the pier, Decker spoke up.

"You can't tie up at these docks, only drop off. He's pulling up to the last dock. I'm dumping you guys here." He slid the *Hammer* up next to a dock nearest the end of the pier.

Mick and the crew piled off. Mick carefully watched what was happening at the *Saucy Suzie*. Jumbo and his man with the satchel disembarked and took the staircase up to the pier level.

Mick and his crew also went up a set of stairs to the pier level.

On the pier, they watched Jumbo and his partner standing, looking around as a few midweek tourists meandered by them.

Prettyman got the camera on the sticks and lined up a shot. It was a long way off, maybe fifty yards, and people were moving in the foreground, sometimes obscuring Jumbo and the satchel man. But Bill got a good minute of them waiting.

Then they saw a man walking toward Jumbo with his arms wrapped around a cardboard box.

"Is that it?" Tony Salt asked Mick.

"Showtime," Mick said.

Prettyman rolled another minute-plus as the men exchanged the box for the satchel.

Fifty yards away from Bill Prettyman's prying lens, Jumbo gave the box a heft, testing its weight. "Doesn't feel like much," he said to no one in particular. He pulled back a flap just enough to see the backpack inside.

"Mess with the knife at your own risk," Harry Sarkissian said. "This have the full two mil?" he asked about the satchel.

Jumbo nodded yes. "Fifty fucking pounds of hundred-dollar bills, asshole." He hated giving up the money. But in this crowd, there was nothing he could do. "I'll be in touch," he said. "Don't spend it all."

Sarkissian grinned. "No refunds, dude. A deal's a deal."

Harry walked away, down the same staircase Jumbo and Solomon had used. His boat was idling, Gary Minasian at the helm. He jumped aboard, and Minasian backed it around and headed out.

"Call our guy," Jumbo ordered Solomon.

The cardboard box under one of his enormous arms, Jumbo's face sank as he saw Mickey and the camera crew approaching.

Mick held a stick mic, Bill Prettyman right behind him, the Ikegami on his shoulder, Rhyme behind him with a sound-mixing box on a strap around his neck, a mic boom in his hands, headphones clamped over his ears, Tony Salt behind him, towering over everybody but Jumbo.

"Get the fuck away from me," Jumbo snarled at Mickey.

"The knife OJ used to kill his wife is in that box. Let's have a look," Mick said.

"You can go fuck yourself," Jumbo said. "I don't know what you're talking about. You shouldn't be messing with me."

"No, you do know what I'm talking about," Mickey insisted. "Your brother Marcus went to Gordon Grove's house to get that box. He was shot dead there. His co-worker Shabaglian escaped with the box. You've been trying to track it down; now you have it. It's OJ's knife."

"The fuck you say."

"How much did you pay? How much was in the satchel?"

Jumbo thought about shooting the insolent bastard on the spot. But he turned to Solomon. "Where's our boat?"

Solomon pulled his phone down from his ear and whispered to Jumbo. "He said *I told you no guns.* He said *Go fuck yourself.*"

The big man's shoulders sank. "I'll kill the motherfucker," Jumbo growled.

Solomon whispered in his ear again. "He says he ain't coming back."

"Motherfucker," Jumbo seethed. "Fucking chickenshit

motherfucker."

"You lose your boat?" Mick asked.

The answer was a malevolent glare.

"I'll take you back," Mick said.

Jumbo gave Mickey another lookover. "You got a boat?"

"Right down the stairs," Mick said.

"There?" Jumbo wheeled, pointing a massive hand at the staircase. Mick nodded yes. Jumbo headed for the stairs.

Decker slid the *Hammer* into place alongside the dock. He watched the whole crowd coming down the stairway. "Shit," he thought. "That's seven guys. One is enormous."

Mick hopped aboard first and held out his hand for Jumbo, who accepted it warily, and came aboard. He had the box under his arm, and the other hand held the gun, suddenly pointing at the camera crew. "You black bastards stay. Solomon, come on," he said.

"Decker! Gun!" Mick shouted.

Solomon had one foot on the boat and one on the dock as Decker hit the power and jerked away from the dock. Solomon did the splits for an instant, then toppled into the water.

"Hey, fucker," Jumbo shouted at Decker. "Go back for my guy!"

Decker pointed the boat toward the open passage to the channel, the throttle set at a reasonably slow speed. He got up from the captain's chair, stepped past Jumbo.

"Excuse me," he said politely. "I don't do guns."

"What's with these pussy boat guys?" Jumbo asked Mick.

"Drive the boat," Decker said to Mick, and he stepped past. And then he dove overboard.

Decker came up for air as his vessel eased away. "Don't sink her," he shouted.

Mick grabbed the wheel, straightened the course.

He looked back at Jumbo. His gun hung at his side. The box was under his arm. He was one seriously pissed-off enormous black man.

"You know how to drive this thing?"

"Just you and me," Mick said. "Better hope I know what I'm doing."

47

Eddie Baker swiveled in his desk chair to take in the view from his Sunset Boulevard office tower.

He was listening to one of his operatives describing the chaotic scene on the Green Pier.

"It appears the item is on that boat with two people?" Eddie asked. "One black and one white? We know who the black guy is. Who's the white guy?"

He listened a little. "Okay, he was with a camera crew? Means he's a reporter for somebody. But the camera crew was left on the dock?"

He listened again.

"Okay, don't let the guys left on the dock get another boat and catch up. Go now. Get to them first."

He listened. "What should you do?" He shook his head like he couldn't believe the question. "You got flares on board. Burn the fucker to the waterline. Sink that boat. Then disappear."

The Baker operatives were idling at a mooring in Avalon Harbor, observing the scene. They saw the *Hammer* rumbling away from the Green Pier, slowly at first, then picking up speed when it cleared the harbor mouth.

The Baker boys fell in behind.

On board the *Hammer,* Mick was trying to figure out a compass heading. He didn't actually know what he was doing, but generally heading east and a little north seemed about right. Jumbo was at his back. "You just get me across this water back to dry land, understand? No fucking around." He jabbed Mick's back with the gun to make himself clear.

"Put the fucking gun away, or I'll drive us in circles until the police boat catches up. They can't be that far behind."

"Don't fuck with me," Jumbo shouted. "I'm serious. I can drive this thing too, drive right up on the beach. So don't fuck with me. I'll shoot your ass and throw you over."

Since Jumbo's threat carried a certain weight of both their personal history and logic—no doubt Jumbo could do precisely that—Mick piped down and put more power on. The *Hammer* cut through the blue water, bouncing on a low swell.

"Why don't you check that box? See if you got what you paid for."

Mick glanced behind him. Jumbo seated himself on the cushioned bench behind the wheel position. He had the box next to him. He held the gun in one hand, and he lifted a flap of the cardboard box, peering inside.

"None of your damn business, but yeah, I see what I paid for. I ain't messin' with it."

"What do you get out of it?"

"None of your damn business."

"You get out of those charges the grand jury's working up?"

"I told you before. You a nosey son of a bitch."

"No point in not telling me. The DA's gonna say you're a hero recovering a key piece of evidence. I can have a crew waiting for us when we pull in. Do an interview. Get video of the knife. Make you a star. OJ might even take a plea. If that's the murder weapon, he's done."

Jumbo waved his gun at Mick. "Keep an eye on where we're going."

"Fine. I'm watching where we're going. But what about it? I can get you on the *NBC Nightly News* with Jansen. Coast to coast. International. You'll be worldwide, famous."

Jumbo shook his head. "You white boys are so fucking dumb."

Mick was uncertain what he meant. "What?"

"You talking yourself out of what you want, that's what."

"You still worried about snitching?"

Jumbo got serious. "You don't seem to be taking serious enough what happens to a black guy who puts this particular black guy on death row. How fucking dumb can you be?"

"Oh, come on," Mick said. "Look, everybody knows he did it. Even black people."

"Hey, dummy, think it through," Jumbo spit. "Black guy kills white bitch. Black guy facing trial to put him away for life. Black guy has lots of money to hire lots of lawyers to get him off. This black guy teed up to beat the system. Gonna be a hero to black people everywhere. How many other black guys got the green to beat the DA? None."

Jumbo waved his gun like he was writing in the air. "And you want to show the world another black guy rolling up with the key evidence that puts him away forever?"

Of course they'd been through this at least once before. Mick changed tack. "Okay, I keep you anonymous. Just show the knife, the DA has new evidence. We just do it that way."

Jumbo laughed at him. "You just a dumbfuck white boy. There ain't gonna be a story for the news. There ain't gonna be pictures of the knife. You ain't getting shit except a bullet in the back of the head."

"Come on. Don't be ridiculous. How many people saw you and me go off together? You shoot me, and you'll be looking at the same shit OJ is."

"Not if I sink your fucking body and they never find you."

"They'd find me."

"Why you so sure? I watch the shark shows. You should too. Lots of sharks out here. They always hungry. Maybe wouldn't be enough left of you for anybody to find."

"Sharks? Is that why you're so scared of the ocean?"

"Reason enough."

"But if I go missing after being with you, it's on you."

"Maybe you panicked and jumped overboard."

"Why would anybody believe that?"

"Because I said so. And because you a dumbfuck racist white boy in a panic."

"That's your story?"

"Big black guy just doing his thing. Racist white man jumps overboard cause he's so racist, he just assumes the black guy make him a bitch. Maybe you figured you could swim all the way. Who knows? Dumbfuck white boys do weird things."

It was preposterous, but Mick realized it was also possible. It would be hard to stick Jumbo with his murder if his body wasn't found. And a bleeding body in the water probably *would* attract sharks.

But he couldn't keep his mouth shut. "Why'd you kill Lummie and Louise?"

Jumbo sneered. "I didn't kill them two fools. Jamal did. Dumbfuck. I needed that Lummie guy alive."

"Why would Jamal blow them up, except you told him to?"

"I didn't tell him shit. He was just trying to impress me."

"That's your story? You and OJ might be sharing cells."

"Hey, peckerwood," Jumbo shouted. "You in no position to be talking smack. Just keep your mouth shut and hope I'm just fine with you walking away when we get to shore. I got the gun, you got shit. Best you shut your mouth."

48

Baker's men worked up a plan.

There was no point in attacking the *Hammer* in totally clear visibility. Too many other boats transiting the Long-Beach-to-Catalina corridor. They would wait until the *Hammer* entered the fogbank.

On the *Hammer,* Jumbo was fighting his phobia, and his weak stomach. He was on the phone with his lawyer, Byron Fink, barking orders to the lawyer. "Be at the Angelo's Marine in Long Beach. Get moving now. Don't leave me standing around."

"You turning it over to the DA's office today? Soon as we get back?" Mick asked.

"None of your damn business." Jumbo was standing over Mickey, watching how the boat worked. The steering seemed simple. Just like a car. The double handles on the right side of the wheel were apparently the gas. There was a compass device, and it seemed to be set for a general course of northeast.

Jumbo worked up a plan. The fogbank was ahead, looked like about a mile. Force this white boy over the side. Shoot him. Not in the head. He'd want him to bleed to bring the sharks in. So maybe a shot to the upper thigh. Try to nick that artery so he'd bleed a lot and he'd bleed fast. Jumbo thought about the shark shows he watched incessantly. They could smell blood from a great distance. They'd come to feed on the white boy, and nobody would ever find him.

When he got back to Long Beach, he'd say the white boy had panicked and jumped overboard. Racist white boy. Afraid of the black man. Made sense to Jumbo. He wished he hadn't previewed it for the reporter asshole, but it was a plan.

For the first time as a reporter, Mick was feeling like his life was in danger. For one thing, his overreach trying to get Jumbo to cooperate on a story had backfired. Now he was alone with a killer. He was vulnerable. Out on the water far from the view of others, he was helpless in the face of Jumbo's worst impulses. The fogbank was approaching. It would be perfect cover if Jumbo wanted to do something to him. If he went overboard, could he last long enough for someone to find him? He would swim, he could float. So maybe. But even in this warmish water, he'd have to worry about hypothermia. How long before another boat happened by? It was an escape plan, but it was not a chance he wanted to take. Only in a desperate situation.

But there was always going on the offensive. Mick started calculating whether he could dump Jumbo. The only weapon he had was the wheel and the throttle. Could he swing the boat violently, tip the big guy off balance, stagger him to the edge, make a power turn, pitch him overboard? If Jumbo got dumped in the water, Mick would have to drive off and leave him or risk getting shot. For sure he'd drown. And if he did, would Mick be on the hook for a murder, or was self-defense credible?

The two men were sizing each other up, trying to figure out what to do with the other as they entered the fogbank.

They motored along at a slower speed. Both men silently calculated while the *Hammer* glided along for a hundred yards. Each man worked on a decision about the other.

Jumbo's impulse was to waste the guy. Why not? The only reason to restrain himself was this white boy was a higher-profile guy than his usual victim. No doubt there would be consequences. But there was the fuck-it factor. He just didn't like the guy on his back. And would it be such a bad thing to send a warning to others in the snooping business that it wasn't a good idea to be snooping into the affairs of Jumbo Blake? No, it would not.

Plus, Jumbo just didn't like him. The white boy was such an unbearable snotty motherfucker.

Hostility and menace wafted off Jumbo. Mick could smell it. The guy was going to do something to him, and it was going to be soon. Mick began planning his move. He would jam the throttles, and whip the wheel to the right, and then back to the left, teeter the big guy to the rail, maybe push him over. It wasn't a great plan, but it was all he had.

Mick was about to act. Jumbo was about to act. The moment arrived for a struggle to the death in the fog.

But that was the moment the completely unexpected happened.

Announcing itself with a roar of engines, a fast-moving boat appeared out of the fog, making a close pass. A man on the open deck fired something that came at them in a bright whoosh, crashing through the windscreen, showering Mick in splintered plastic.

"Holy shit!" Mick thought, swiveling around to see the attacker. "What the fuck!" Jumbo shouted.

In an instant, the *Hammer* slipped into chaos. Mick had to spin the wheel to avoid a collision. Jumbo staggered, tried to regain his footing. Failed. He crashed onto the deck, screaming obscenities, scrambling to get to his knees. Water sloshed up on the deck. Jumbo was slipping and sliding, grabbing for the railing. He steadied himself on his knees and began firing his weapon at the attacking boat. Another flaming object whooshed overhead, high, but scary.

Another whoosh bounced off the *Hammer* in front of the wheelhouse. Mick caught a glimpse of a man on the open deck of the other boat. He saw him loading a gun of some type. Mick quickly realized the man on the other boat was firing flares.

Flares were damn dangerous, especially at close range. A direct hit from a flare could kill a guy. But perhaps the biggest danger they posed was fire.

Jumbo was on his knees at the railing, screaming useless nasty threats at the attackers. He had his gun out, firing madly into the fog, to little effect.

The *Hammer* was spinning as Mick poured on power and whipped the wheel around, but still the attacker kept coming. Another flare whooshed past Mick's head.

Firing ineffectually, Jumbo ran out of ammunition. He sprawled on the deck, grasping for a handhold. "Stop spinning," he screamed at Mick. "Stop!"

But Mickey and the *Hammer* had no defense but rapid maneuver. Mick had the *Hammer* in a tight turn at high speed. Jumbo screamed like he was on the Veloraptor at Six Flags.

With no returning fire coming from the *Hammer,* the attacking boat closed in and the shooter fired flares at a much closer range. One hit the stern at the engine compartment with a flash of phosphorus and a crashing bang of broken fiberglass. Quickly Mick realized he had a fire blazing aft. He slowed the throttle to idle, yanked a fire extinguisher off the wall, and staggered in the rolling waves back to spray down the fire. Jumbo was on his hands and knees, slipping around the wet deck, screaming incoherently.

The fire flared up, and the whoosh of the fire extinguisher had an effect only for a moment, and not enough. Mick suddenly faced a wall of flame from the engine compartment and the *Hammer* lost power. In moments, the engines died, and they were rolling dead in the water.

The attacker boat made another run. The *Hammer* was a sitting duck. A flare penetrated the fore cabin just above the waterline, then another and another. Mick realized the attackers were trying to sink the *Hammer*.

And they were doing a good job of it. Mick saw he had fires raging fore and aft. He checked for another fire extinguisher abovedecks, but the other was below, where fire blocked him. He quickly made the decision that they had to abandon the *Hammer* and hit the water.

Mick knew his phone would be dead as soon as it was wet. He punched in 911.

"911. What is your emergency?"

"I'm on a vessel in the Catalina Channel on fire. Five miles off Catalina. Two people aboard. We have to abandon the vessel. We'll be in the water. Send help."

Jumbo was in the grip of panic. He'd fired all his ammunition. His gun was useless. The boat was on fire. He was scared to death of the water. He was on his feet, his precious box wrapped up in both arms.

"Where's your vest?" Mick shouted at Jumbo.

The big man shook his head, confused. A vest for a very large man was somewhere, but not on Jumbo. Mick ripped up seat cushions. He shoved one into Jumbo's chest. "This will help you float. When you hit the water, get on your back, hang on to this. You'll be fine. Hang on to it for dear life."

Mick jumped off the burning boat, hit the bracing sea clutching a seat cushion. He rolled over on his back, arms around the flotation cushion. He looked back. Jumbo was at the railing, frozen in fear. "Jump! Jump!" Mick shouted as he frog-kicked backward away from the burning boat.

The attacking boat spun around one more time and roared away into the fog. In a flash of blue paint, it disappeared in the gray mist. Mick realized that the entire attack had happened at such dizzying speed, he wasn't even sure he could describe the boat or the men on board except to say it was a white hull and maybe some blue someplace. And the men were white.

His eyes wide as tea saucers, his mouth open, his tongue licking his lips, Jumbo stood immobile, frozen by fear. He teetered on the deck, right on the edge of the burning boat. He held the precious box in his arms. He wheeled around to face the flames. The fire was impossible to endure. He turned back around to the water. Fear gripped his heart and his head. Die by fire or water, which was it to be?

He was stuck. Frozen. He couldn't move.

But not for long. Quickly the flames and the heat became too much. He tumbled forward into the water. Immediately the box slipped from his grip. His arms and legs churned the water in heart-throbbing panic.

Jumbo forgot Mick's instructions instantly. He didn't roll on his back. He didn't clutch the flotation cushion. The box had slipped away. He thrashed the water, arms and legs whirling to no effect except to waste precious energy. He sank, popped up, sank again, popped up again.

Mick was furious. He had to try to save Jumbo, even though he'd been thinking about how to drown the guy only a few minutes ago. He slipped out of his flotation vest, laid it on the floating cushion. Free of encumbrance, he dove beneath the swells.

Saltwater stung his eyes, but he could see Jumbo's giant frame thrashing a few feet in front of him. He put his lifeguard training from high school to use for the first time. Mick swam to Jumbo underwater. His strategy was to turn the big man around so he wouldn't get caught by Jumbo's arms, take him under his armpits, get him on his back where his mouth and nose would be out of the water in a position that allowed him to breathe.

Underwater, Mick turned the big body so the arms and legs were away from him. He put one arm under Jumbo's armpit and across his chest, the other arm over the big man's shoulder to take his chin in hand and pull him back, stretching out the big man's body flat on the surface. The idea was to allow the drowning person to breathe and relax enough that the lifesaving person could maintain control and subdue the panic.

But the theory didn't quite match up with the facts. Jumbo was much too big and much too strong to simply take control of him from behind.

If Mick had been taking a lifeguard test in a pool with a normal-sized victim, it would have worked. On the open ocean with a panicked giant, it was hopeless.

Jumbo felt the hands on his waist underwater and redoubled his panic. He spun around, clutching at Mick and pulling him into his enormous arms.

In an instant, Mick was the victim, tied up with a muscular giant who was holding on to anything that might save him.

But all his panic accomplished was to sink them both.

Mick and Jumbo were both underwater, the big man going down, taking Mick with him. Jumbo and Mick were face to face, and Mick watched Jumbo's wide eyes, his mouth clamped shut, holding his breath. Mick quickly realized the guy might be able to hold his breath longer, and if Mick remained in Jumbo's grasp he would drown first.

Now there was no choice if he was to survive. Mick had to doom the man he'd tried to save. He doubled up his fist and punched Jumbo in the chest, hard. This one for Lummie, he thought. He punched again. This one for Louise. A third punch. This one for me.

A spurt of bubbles shot out of the big man's mouth and nose. Mick punched again, this time lower, around the diaphragm. And in the next moment, Mick watched as Jumbo gulped in water as if it were air. The first reaction was to hold Mick tighter. Mick pushed in vain against the big man's chest to try to break free. He let out small amounts of air to take the pressure off his lungs, but he knew he didn't have long.

The two men were locked in a death embrace, sinking under Jumbo's weight and as his lungs filled with water.

Mick was starting to black out when he felt Jumbo's arms weaken and then go limp. He felt Jumbo's body sliding down his legs, deeper into the Catalina channel.

He broke free and pushed to the surface, popping into the air with a gasping, sputtering explosion. Mick rolled on his back to take a few deep breaths, regain his breathing, and bring a little strength back to his muscles.

The boat was burning about twenty feet away.

He scanned the water, trying to see over the tops of the swells. *Where is the box?*

To the left he spotted the flotation cushion with his life vest where he'd left it. He paddled over slowly. With what seemed like insurmountable difficulty, he managed to put the vest back on. Zipped up and tight, now he could rest, the life vest doing the work of keeping him afloat.

Fog enveloped him. The light of the burning boat cast an orange glow over the water. Small bits of debris floated past him.

Then he saw it. The box was thirty feet away, the cardboard

soaked through. It was listing to one side, the top flaps open.

Mick summoned the energy to go toward it. He paddled slowly, afraid to create a surface disturbance. The swells were bad enough.

He was within a few feet. It was just out of his grasp. He could see the backpack. But then the box tilted. Water rushed in. It tipped. Then the open box gulped water. It went over. Mick saw the backpack slide out, out of his reach. He watched helplessly as the ocean swallowed it whole.

In an instant it was gone.

49

The last thought Mick remembered was wondering whether the burning boat would attract another vessel. It was his only hope.

When the police rescue boat found the burning hull of the *Hammer,* Mick hardly noticed.

He was delirious with cold, shivering in waves of cramping convulsions, his arms clutching the flotation cushion like claws. He hardly knew how long he'd been in the water. Hours, days, it was all the same.

The one coherent stream of thoughts that replayed in his mind over and over was how he had fucked everything up. Luther was dead. Louise was dead. Now Jumbo was dead. The knife—if there ever had *been* a knife—was gone. The Armenian seemed to have made off with a lot of money. Strangers had tried to kill him. There was no story for NBC News. Alison de Groot would be mad. Wimple would be laughing. Bowls would pity him. He was as good as fired. And he hadn't called his daughter. He hadn't called Grace Russell. That bit haunted him. In the swirling thoughts of his hypothermic mind, he wanted most to talk to both of them and apologize for being so stupid.

But then he felt something tugging at his life vest, and he surfaced from those twisting and turning thoughts. It was a gaff, hooked onto the collar of his vest; then there were arms under him, and he rose out of the water and the shivers struck again, really bad.

Dimly he was aware of people hurrying him belowdecks, and suddenly he was in a warm room. They tugged his clothes off, wrapped him in warm blankets, laid him on a bunk. Everything was warm again, but still he shivered in convulsions. Someone was pouring warm liquid to his lips; he swallowed what seemed like soup. He began to warm from the inside.

Over the tops of the faces leaning in, asking him questions, giving him cups of something to drink, he saw Bill Prettyman and his camera looking down at him.

He was back in the clutches of NBC News. He felt jabs. Maybe needles. The people around him either became quiet or he just didn't hear them anymore. He felt like he was sliding into a deep darkness, not like dying, but a deep enveloping and comforting sleep.

Mick awoke in an ambulance. He could tell it was an ambulance because he'd seen them before. Just never from the horizontal point of view.

There were bags of fluids above him and tubes into his arm. He was groggy and carefree. He slept in an instant, woke with a start, drifted off again.

The next time he woke, it was in a hospital bed.

50

Mick picked up the phone ringing next to his hospital bed.

"Dad, for chrissakes, what the fuck? Are you okay? You're scaring the shit out of me!" Kelly was on the line.

"I'm better, honey. A little scrape with a bad guy is all."

An exasperated sigh. "Dad, you're on the fucking news. You almost died. What the fuck!"

"Where'd you learn to swear like that?"

"You. Mom. The world. Seriously, you okay?"

"Yes. I'm fine. I didn't die."

Silence on the other end. For a long minute.

"Kelly? You still there?"

"I'm coming up."

"I'll come get you."

"You can't. I'll take the train and get a cab at Union Station."

"Just wait till I get back to the apartment. I'll be out of this hospital bed in a day."

"I'm worried about you. I got one parent who's a basket case and another trying to get himself killed. This is not good for my mental health."

Mick laughed, but softly. His broken ribs objected to a real laugh.

"Gimme a day or so, baby. I'll be free of this story, and I'll come get you. We'll go to a Pads game. Go to Coronado Island and stay at that big hotel. You got school. Stay put until I can get there."

"You better. Call me as soon as you get home."

"Love you."

"Love you too."

Tony Salt picked Mick up at the hospital in Long Beach and drove him to his apartment in Burbank. "I'm under orders to make sure you get in your apartment okay and that you have something in the refrigerator," Tony said. Mick assured the producer that he was fine.

They had to get the manager to open Mick's apartment. His keys were gone. Maybe at the bottom of the Catalina Channel.

Tucking Mick in was one thing, the food situation was not. "There's shit in your fridge," he said, meaning nothing. "Bottled water, vodka, hummus, but it's green," he said, tossing the container of hummus in the garbage. "I'll call Gino's for delivery. You can go."

"Your call, superman. I don't spoon feed anybody." Tony Salt left, but reluctantly.

Mick called Grace and got her answering machine. "I'm fine. At home. Going to sleep." He forgot to leave her his landline, a mistake that left her angry and frantic.

The story of the rescue at sea was on television, on both Chanel 4's newscast and *Nightly News*. The essence of the story was that an NBC News correspondent had a close call with death. A boat fire in the Santa Catalina Channel, another person died. NBC had no interest in telling the complete story, the one in which it would have to explain why Mickey Judge was on that boat, and who the other person was. Jumbo was identified as "a J. C. Blake of Hollywood, an unfortunate victim of drowning."

In a near panic, Grace Russell pushed and pushed until Paul Dimmick put her through to the bureau chief, Alison de Groot.

When Grace explained who she was, that she was calling because Mickey's phone seemed to be out of order, Alison remembered her. "Ah, yes. You are the dearie he mentioned to me. I'm sure he'd love to speak with you."

"Thank you for believing me," Grace said, relieved. "I've been running into slamming doors all day."

"He's at home."

"I want to see him."

Alison thought this woman sounded nice. "He has an unlisted landline," she said. "His phone went down with the ship. I'd say he's in fairly decent shape right now, just very tired." Alison de Groot was certain that Mick would want to hear from "the dolly", as she put it. "But hang on, I'll call him and make sure it's all wonderful for you to call."

Momentarily she came back on the line. "He doesn't have a cell phone yet. Here's his landline. He said of course, he'd be delighted for your call."

When Grace arrived at Mick's apartment building, she found him on a chaise in the sun by the pool covered in a beach towel that looked like a Waikiki souvenir. She scooted over to him, set a brown paper bag on the concrete, and kissed him on top of his head. She was relieved to see that he had the energy to get up and give her a hug.

"I'm fine. It was a couple hours of not great. But back to normal.

Except I'm beat to shit," he said. "I'm so sorry I didn't call. I was going to any minute, honest."

"You did call. You just didn't leave your number."

"I did?" He didn't remember. "Spaced, I guess. Maybe drugs."

She had a face that radiated a smile that was half joy and half sympathy. She hugged him again. He let the hug linger.

She pulled away and looked at him closely. "I still want to know about the black eyes."

Mick nodded okay. "I hate to tell you that's another story. Started with you giving me a copy of that speeding ticket."

"Oh, gawd. I'm so sorry." She ran her soft fingers over the bruising under his eyes. "Do I want to hear it?"

"Maybe," Mick said. "Probably not." He glanced down at her feet. "What's in the bag?"

Grace looked down. "A few things. I'm making you dinner. Come. Show me this bachelor rathole you're living in."

The Equestrian Arms Apartments was in fact a bit ratty at first glance. The white stucco was stained, and the flight of stairs to the second floor featured rusting railings and spalls in the concrete steps.

But she was pleasantly surprised at the apartment itself. "Oh, cute," she said, glancing around at the spacious studio.

Opposite the bed, which Mick hadn't had time to mess up, was an L-shaped couch around an oak coffee table in front of a television. There was a small dining table for two, and a kitchen with the appliances one would need, which appeared to be both clean and in working order. A large window looked out on the traffic moving along Riverside Boulevard. The walls were in green wallpaper, giving the room the feel of an English country equestrian estate, complete with prints of famous horses. The entrance to the Los Angeles Equestrian Center was only a hundred yards down Riverside.

Grace was in jeans, running shoes, and a red scoop-neck short-sleeve shirt. She had her hair in a ponytail that bounced when she walked. If she was wearing makeup, it was so light as to be invisible; but her skin glowed, and her lips glistened. Her hazel eyes fairly sparkled at Mick. "I'm so glad you didn't die," she said, hugging him again.

Blushing, Mick hugged her back. Her breasts, straining at the fabric of that red top, pressed against his chest like an invitation.

She put the groceries in the kitchen, some in the fridge, some on the countertop. Mick couldn't quite tell what she planned to cook.

Mick felt tired again. He plopped down on the couch, put his feet up on the coffee table. Grace hurried back over. Her arm over his shoulder, she sat on the couch so close that the side of her body was pressed up against him from her ankle to her shoulder. Mick felt himself melting into her.

"Helluva third date, wouldn't you say?" she asked impishly. "Can you tell me what happened?"

"What did the news say? I missed it."

"Not much. They said you were pulled from the water after your boat burned. I didn't know you had a boat."

"Wasn't mine. I don't have a boat."

"Good. I was hoping you weren't keeping things from me."

"What else they say?"

"Another man drowned. They found his body floating a few hours after they found you."

"They say how the boat burned?"

"No. Not a word."

"Anything about the other guys left on Catalina?" Tony, Bill, Willis, Decker—it was a crowd.

"No. Just an unexplained boat fire. Two men had to abandon ship. One drowned. You survived. That was about it."

Mick laughed. "NBC knows exactly what happened."

"Well, tell me."

He was about to begin his story when he was interrupted by a knock at the door. "I'll get it," she said. "Just sit."

"Don't let anybody in," Mick said.

Grace called through the door, "Who is it?"

"LAPD," the voice said.

She looked through the peephole. A full view of an LAPD shield in a man's hand.

"It's the LAPD," she said to Mick in a soft voice.

"Shit," Mick mumbled. "Bet I know what this is about."

He got up slowly and went to the door. Grace retreated to the kitchen and started to busy herself with the groceries for her dinner. There wasn't another room to hide in.

The man on the other side of the door was in his early sixties. His face was fleshy, a large nose, a chin that disappeared into the wattles of his neck. He had a bad rug in middle-age gray. He wore a light blue sport coat, gray slacks, and a dark blue shirt with a white tie. Typical cop bad taste, Mick thought.

"I'm detective Van Atter," he said. "I need to ask you a few questions. May I come in?"

"Who told you where I live?" Mick asked, immediately suspicious. Had somebody at the Bureau ratted him out?

The detective grimaced. "We're the LAPD. We find people."

"Oh, right," Mick said, embarrassed. "Sure. Come on in."

They went to the couch, Mick extending a hand to offer Van Atter a seat. Mick didn't notice, but Grace's eyes flared wide, and she turned her back while she continued the dinner prep. The detective noticed her. Surprised, he kept his eye on her until he sat.

"Your name is Phil Van Atter, right?" Mick asked, sitting.

"That's right. And you are Mickey Judge?"

Mick nodded. "What's this about?"

"First thing. We found your car. Chevy Blazer, right?"

"Yeah. Fantastic."

"Not so much. It was torched. Nothing left but a hulk."

Mick grimaced. That fucker Jamal. "Bad luck, I guess."

"You think you know who did it?"

"Some guy named Jamal. Worked for Jumbo."

Van Atter scribbled a note, moved on. "We're trying to track down the people on the boat who attacked you and Mr. Blake." He paused. "I'm looking at your Coast Guard interview. There was an attack, right?"

"Yes. Certainly was."

"Can you describe the boat?"

"White, maybe a light blue stripe just above the waterline."

"How long?"

"I'd guess about twenty-five feet."

"Open deck, or covered?"

"Covered. The wheelhouse, anyway. Behind that, open deck."

Scribbling, Van Atter sighed. "You know that describes a lot of boats."

Mick agreed with a nod. "I know. But that's what it was."

"How about the men? Can you describe them?"

"White. Clean-shaven. Medium builds, I guess. Wearing dark windbreakers, knit caps."

"That's a lot of people."

Mick grimaced like he was sorry to not be more helpful. "I know."

Van Atter stopped, consulting his notes. After a few moments, he spoke again. "Frankly, we're getting nowhere on that. Two men on a white boat with a blue stripe, a covered wheelhouse and an open deck describes about half the vessels between Santa Barbara and San Diego." He paused. "That includes rentals. I'm exaggerating, but not by much."

"Look, I'd love to be more specific, but it was very fast and I was focused more on what they were shooting at us."

Van Atter met Mick's eyes. "With that very general description, we may never find that boat or those people. Just so you know."

Mick sat back. He didn't know what to think about that. "That's a bummer."

Van Atter continued. "I have something else."

"Okay. What?"

"The knife. We understand you had a lead on a knife we're interested in."

Mick knew the police had probably already seen Bill Prettyman's tapes. Probably the Lummie interview too.

"I figure you already know. I was chasing a lead," Mick said. "It didn't pan out."

"Didn't pan out how?"

"I thought I had it in sight. But the boat accident. . . ."

"Yeah, we know about the boat. . . ."

"Well, the knife—the supposed knife—was lost in the accident."

"Are you sure the knife you were looking for was on that boat?"

"No," Mick shook his head. "I shouldn't say I knew anything about a knife. Not for sure. I just know that a box, reportedly containing a backpack, which supposedly contained a knife, was on that boat. Last I saw, it was sinking."

"Let's go back. Did you ever see the actual knife?"

"No."

"Why did you think there was a knife?"

"I was told by a man who claims to have seen it that there was a knife in the backpack."

"Who else saw it?"

"Another man who is now dead. Two men who claimed to have seen it are dead. There is one guy who may have seen it who may still be alive."

"Who's that?"

"A man named Harry Sarkissian."

The detective was watching Mick closely, but occasionally pausing to write in his notebook. "How did he come by it?"

Mick was starting to get a headache. He'd been over this story so many times. "A guy named Armen Shabaglian had it. Gave it to Sarkissian."

"How did Shabaglian get it?"

"He got it at Gordon Grove's house in Inglewood."

"What was Sarkissian going to do with it?"

"He sold it to Jumbo Blake. I saw the transaction. Well, to be precise, I saw Sarkissian and Blake exchange the box for a satchel. I presume there was money in the satchel."

"Do you know what Jumbo Blake was going to do with it?"

"I guessed he was going to turn it over to you guys. A trade to get the DA to drop a drug case, I'm guessing."

Van Atter nodded again, still scribbling notes.

"But you know all this, don't you?" Mick asked.

"We do," he acknowledged. "We know what happened in your investigation. I'm just confirming what we've learned."

Mick didn't want to directly ask if the detective had seen all the tapes in NBC's possession. He had the feeling that someone had shown them to him. Probably Wimple. Maybe Danny Bowls. Hard to tell. At this point, Mick didn't really care.

"Have you talked to Sarkissian?"

Van Atter frowned. "I shouldn't say so, but yes."

"Are you going to charge him? He sold the box to Blake."

Van Atter shook his head no. "He confirmed that. He sold the box for two mil. Said he'd seen a knife. Aware someone thought it was OJ's knife, but had no way to say for sure it was. No crime. No arrest."

"It's okay to sell evidence?"

"Nobody can prove it was evidence at this point."

Mick took a deep breath. Sarkissian getting away with it was galling. "Sarkissian has the money. And Jumbo is dead."

Van Atter nodded vigorously. "Yup. Very dead."

The two men looked at each other as if the other was going to offer something else. Van Atter finally broke the silence. "The last remaining question. What happened to the box, the alleged backpack, and the alleged knife? You're the last one to see it."

"You just want to confirm that it's gone forever?"

Van Atter's penetrating blue eyes gave Mick a hard stare. "Is that what happened?"

Mick saw no reason to not tell. "Yes. I saw it sink. It's a mile down in the Channel, I expect."

"You're certain?"

"I watched the box soaking up water. I saw the Styrofoam peanuts floating out. Saw the backpack slide out of the box and into the water. Gone. Believe me, broke my heart."

The detective closed his notebook, slipped it into an inside pocket of his jacket. He stood up, extended his hand to Mick. "The knife angle is officially dead. Sorry about your ordeal. Thank you for your cooperation, Mr. Judge."

Mick shook his hand. "You're welcome."

Van Atter then turned to the kitchen. "Miss Russell?" he asked.

Standing, about to escort the cop to the door, Mick let out an involuntary "What?"

In the kitchen, Grace turned around, facing Mick and the detective. "Yes, Detective Van Atter?"

"Generally it's frowned upon for an employee of the Criminal Courts to be co-habitating with a reporter."

She gave him a grim smile. "I'm not co-habitating. I'm not even sleeping with Mr. Judge. Not yet, anyway. I'm making Mr. Judge dinner. As you noted, he's been through a terrible ordeal."

Van Atter gave her a hard eye, then turned to Mick. "We've noticed you made some great strides in your investigation. You found at least one person who was hard to find. You got key information at key moments. Most reporters can't do those things without help."

"Hold on," Mick said. "Nobody gave me any help. I hustled that story like a reporter is supposed to."

The detective didn't believe Mick. "Sure you did." He turned back to Grace. "I hope we don't discover you've been passing along information to a reporter. That's against the spirit of our rules, if not an outright violation."

Grace stood her ground. She struck a defiant pose with her hand on her hip. "Is it against the rules to show Mr. Judge how to prepare pasta pomodoro?"

Van Atter shook his head. "No, it's not. You're right about that. But your supervisor should be informed of your culinary instructions."

"I'm sure you'll take care of that," she replied, giving him a hard eye Mick hadn't seen before.

Van Atter turned to go. *"Bon appétit,"* he said.

But the detective stopped at the door. "One more thing, Miss

Russell," he said, turning back to her. "There are things called digital footprints now. We can see who looks things up."

Grace Russell tensed, but said nothing.

"I was able to see you accessed the filing of Mr. Judge's wife. The divorce papers. But you only looked at LA County. There's another in San Diego County. Before your access is shut down, you might want to look that one up too. The custody decree is especially interesting."

Mick's heart sank. He should have told her already. "You fucker," he hissed at Van Atter.

The detective grinned at Mick. "Keeping secrets? So sorry, then."

He opened the door and was gone.

Grace Russell stood in the kitchen staring straight ahead, but seeing nothing. She was stunned.

"Grace, I was getting to that, really."

She shook her head, blinking back tears. "You have a child?"

"A daughter. Yes."

"And you didn't tell me when I asked if you had kids?"

"We were talking about kids in this divorce."

She shook her head. "Why wouldn't you say there was a marriage before?"

"Honest, I was getting to it. That one is messy. Anybody would wonder how I could have married her. I didn't want you to run off. The time was now. I was—"

"I don't think you were honest," she interrupted him, genuine sorrow in her voice. "I think I have to go."

"Gracie—"

But she was past him and at the door like a gust of wind. "Make yourself dinner," she said, and she was gone in a half trot.

"Shit," Mick said to himself. "Shit, shit, shit."

That first ex-wife never stopped being a problem.

51

"So you left Diane? What took you so long?" He also hadn't told his daughter yet that he'd left his second wife, Diane Gormley. This one had never taken his name.

Kelly was hurt. The snark said it all.

Mick had himself another jolt of guilt. He should have told his daughter. She'd never liked the second wife anyway. But he'd had a hard time talking about it with anybody, much less his sixteen-year-old daughter.

"How'd you know?"

"She called Mom to commiserate about what a son of a bitch you are."

"I'm sure your mom was pleased."

"You have no idea. She was practically beaming. But pretending to be sympathetic. Where are you living? On somebody's couch?"

"No. I got a studio apartment near the Bureau."

"Room for me to come stay?"

"A couch. If you don't mind seeing Dad in his underwear."

"I'll bring you a robe. I want to come. I can bake you cookies."

"I'd like that."

"So, when?"

"When will your mom say it's okay?"

"Who cares?"

"She can make trouble. You're not eighteen yet."

"I swear she'd hardly notice. Might even like me gone for a few days. Give her a chance for time with her boyfriends."

"She has boyfriends?"

"In her dreams. Hardly anyone stupid enough."

"Ouch. I was stupid enough once."

"You were young. These guys are old enough to know better."

Okay, Mick thought, so this is how it is to have a sixteen-year-old daughter who's already thirty-five.

"I have someone I'd like you to meet."

"Oh, god. Not another one."

"I already pissed her off. I have some fence-mending to do first. But she's nice."

"You finally learned your lessons?"

"Finally."

They made plans for her to take the train. He'd pick her up at Union Station.

Mick felt his welcome back to the office was tentative at best. Tony Salt was his smartass self. "Owwwie, back from the dead!" Bill Prettyman and Willis Gillis gave him big hugs and high-fives. A few of the other producers who'd experienced life-threatening situations were both sympathetic and enthusiastic to see him back.

But not everybody. Wimple gave him a curt hello, and David Moody was, well, moody. Maybe somebody told him how close he'd come to getting completely shown up.

Alison de Groot was great. A big smile and a warm hug. "How's the dolly, sweetheart?"

Mick grimaced. "That took a bad turn. I didn't tell her about the first wife or the daughter quite quick enough. She got blindsided. She's pissed."

Alison's eyes got wide. "Oh, my. You need to be quicker with the résumé. Ladies don't like to be ambushed with the secret ex-wife."

"It's not a secret," Mick said. "Just a part of my life I try hard to forget."

She laughed in his face. "You can forget it after you tell your new dolly."

"I should have," he admitted.

It was a problem. He really hated blowing up Grace Russell. He'd spent a couple of days trying to get her to call him back. Flowers. Calls. Messages. So far, silence.

And then there was his friend Danny. Mick was still unsure whether Danny Bowls would be glad to see him.

He knew he had some making-up to do with Danny, but there was a little business he needed to take care of.

Since he'd been off for a few days and out of it, he'd let an important call slip. He needed to call David Green in New York and ask the big question: Was NBC going to let the day they could drop him—decline to renew his contract—come and go?

He got Green's office on the phone. "It's Mickey Judge. Can I speak to David?"

"Oh, sorry. He's on a plane to the West Coast. Can I take a message?"

Mick knew immediately that Green was flying to LA to tell Mick face to face. Only one reason to do that. The network was dropping him.

Another clue came later in the day. Alison told him he needn't bother with the weekend *Today Show*. "We're borrowing Shuman from downstairs," she said, sincere regret in her voice.

"I get it," Mick assured her.

"I'm so sorry, Mickey. I always pulled for you."

Mick knew that was true. She'd brought him in, and was suffering for it. New York didn't like bureau chiefs picking correspondents. They made her pay for her support for him. They turned him into a failure, which reflected back on her. The New York way. The network way.

The next morning, July 8, 1994, Mick made sure to be in his office at 7:30 a.m. It was a day he'd want to mark on his calendar.

Promptly at 8 a.m., David Green poked his head in the door. "Can we talk?"

What followed went about as Mick had expected.

At the end of the day at the Criminal Courts Building downtown, the Honorable Kathleen Kennedy-Powell brought the OJ Simpson preliminary hearing to a close. She declared: "*It appearing to me from the evidence presented that the following offenses have been committed and there is sufficient cause to believe this defendant guilty . . . the court holds the defendant be held to answer.*" Those "following offenses" were varieties of Penal Code 187, murder.

She ruled that there would be no bail, and OJ Simpson was bound over for trial, arraignment set for July 22, 1994.

After local's six o'clock show, Mick wandered down to the Channel 4 assignment desk. "Come on, man, lemme buy you a drink."

"Good idea," Danny said.

A short walk later, Mick and Danny slid into a booth at Chadney's. The *Nightly News* crew from the Bureau had already sloshed down their daily buckets and staggered away. The evening dinner-and-jazz crowd was drifting in.

Mick slipped a piece of paper across the table to Danny.

"What's this?"

"It's the address of a place just outside Selma up near Fresno. Big chop shop. Chances are, the goon has cleared it out by now; but who knows, maybe you can track him down. But don't let your crew go without cops. The guy is dangerous."

Danny looked over the paper. "How you pronounce this name?"

"Pa-boo-jan," Mick said. "Armenian."

"No shit." Danny looked up at Mick. "He wouldn't be the one who gave you the black eyes, would he?"

"The very same," Mick said. "Appreciate it if you'd cause him some trouble on my behalf."

They clinked their drinks.

"So, how many weeks you still get Peacock paychecks?" Danny asked.

Mick sipped his Absolut and soda. "Ninety days."

Danny thought it could be worse. "In local, it's two weeks."

"Yeah, it's not the worst possible," Mick said. "Gives me time to find a place to land. And if something comes up right away, I can bail."

Danny pursed his lips and agreed with a nod, moving on. "Look, I was pissed, but you were right. You did work the story like you were supposed to, frankly like nobody I've ever seen. And you got close. So fucking close." He held his thumb and index finger half an inch apart. "You almost had it. May be the greatest one-that-got-away story ever. It really was an awesome job. I'm proud of you."

It meant a lot to Mick that Danny Bowls would say something like that. "Coming from a real pro, I appreciate it, I really do."

With that, each man had enough stroking each other.

"So, what are you going to do?"

"Just trying to get that girl to call me back."

Danny laughed. "No. I meant about work."

"Oh, sorry. I kind of fucked things up with this really nice girl. Been on my mind. Far as work goes, the agent is on it. Supposedly."

"Would you go back to local?"

Mick shrugged. "Depends. Think I'd need a special unit or something. I'm past the live shot on the nothing story."

Danny snorted a laugh. "Most days, nothing stories is what local news is." He shook his head ruefully. Sometimes the truth hurt. "And forget those special units," he quickly added. "They're bullshit too. Nothing but phony investigations for sweeps."

Mick knew that drill. Ratings period three times a year. Crap flooding the airwaves.

"Ever thought of doing something else?"

Mick grimaced. "I've thought about it a few times. But you know what? You do this job for a while, you're unfit for any other job. This is one of those jobs that's new every day. Your desk is a mess. Your attitude is bad. You sass the boss, and it doesn't matter as long as you bring in the story."

"Maybe you're right," Danny said. "Hard to imagine anything else."

Mick leaned across the table to his friend. "You know what? It's all about the story. A big story comes along, it's worth all the bullshit to get that adrenalin rush."

"Of course," Danny agreed. "But you know we wait a long time between big ones."

Mick grinned. He reminded his friend of his personal motto for the news business. "There's a fuse burning somewhere."

Danny clinked his glass again. "And the devil provides."

Mick's pager buzzed. "Oh, shit. It's Gracie."

He flipped open his phone immediately and called her back.

"Are you still pissed at me?" he asked when she picked up.

Her voice wasn't ice-cold, but it was chilly, like early spring, maybe a hint that warmth is coming. "Yes, but I want you to come take me to dinner."

"I'll be right there." He gave Danny a thumbs-up.

"Let me just warn you."

"Okay, what?"

"I want to meet your daughter."

Mick took that as a very hopeful sign.

"Tomorrow's good," he said.

THE END

Over four decades **John Gibson** was a television news reporter, a network news correspondent, a cable news anchor and a radio talk show host. He lives in Texas. *OJ's Knife* is his first novel. He previously published non fiction titles *The War On Christmas*, *Hating America*, and *How the Left Swiftboated America*.

And for more in contemporary crime fiction, try these Stark House authors…

TIMOTHY J. LOCKHART

Smith
"There are sequences of edgy suspense and artfully done violence. And generous helpings of sex… a chilling story that knows what lurks beneath those superspy romances."—Don Crinklaw, *Booklist*

Pirates
"A high-seas adventure with modern-day pirates of the Caribbean. The story charts an unpredictable course with action as unrelenting as the tropical winds." —Brian Boland, author of *Caribbean's Keeper*

A Certain Man's Daughter
"…we get an inside look at Washington politics and the dirty way it is often played, complete with lobbyists, mob-connections, and hardball-playing politicians."—Ted Hertel, *Deadly Pleasures*

WILSON TONEY

Alibi for a Dead Man
"…delivers a lean, humorous, fast-moving crime story with a nod and a wink to pulp fiction… the first in what promises to be an entertaining series featuring Bug and Roche, two sharp though weary private dicks." —Nicholas Litchfield

Not Worth That Much
"These are fast paced and witty stories, an homage to golden age of hardboiled but with a touch of original flair… There's a lot of fun to be had here."—Paul Burke, *Crime Time*

STARK HOUSE

Stark House Press, 1315 H Street, Eureka, CA 95501
greg@starkhousepress.com / www.StarkHousePress.com
Available from your local bookstore, or order direct via our website.

CPSIA information can be obtained
at www.ICGtesting.com
Printed in the USA
LVHW021932060921
697132LV00013B/227